Joss Wood loves books  to the wild places of Sou anywhere! She's a wife, slave to two cats. After a development she now writes full-time. Joss is a member of Romance Writers of America and Romance Writers of South Africa.

Lorraine Hall is a part-time hermit and full-time writer. She was born with an old soul and her head in the clouds—which, it turns out, is the perfect combination for spending her days creating thunderous alpha heroes and the fierce, determined heroines who win their hearts. She lives in a potentially haunted house with her soulmate and a rumbustious band of hermits in training. When she's not writing romance, she's reading it.

HIRED FOR THE BILLIONAIRE'S SECRET SON

JOSS WOOD

THE FORBIDDEN PRINCESS HE CRAVES

LORRAINE HALL

MILLS & BOON

First published in Great Britain 2023
by Mills & Boon, an imprint of HarperCollins*Publishers* Ltd,
1 London Bridge Street, London, SE1 9GF

www.harpercollins.co.uk

HarperCollins*Publishers*, Macken House, 39/40 Mayor Street Upper,
Dublin 1, D01 C9W8, Ireland

Hired for the Billionaire's Secret Son © 2023 Joss Wood

The Forbidden Princess He Craves © 2023 Lorraine Hall

ISBN: 978-0-263-30699-6

10/23

HIRED FOR THE BILLIONAIRE'S SECRET SON

JOSS WOOD

MILLS & BOON

CHAPTER ONE

I'm sorry, but I am currently out of the office on my summer vacation and will only be checking my emails on a limited basis.

BO SØRENSON SCOWLED at his monitor and wondered whether the whole of Denmark was on vacation and whether he was the only sap working. He looked through the glass walls of his office and scowled at the free seats—his staff didn't have dedicated desks but picked their work station depending on their mood and task—and the lack of activity. Normally, he had people walking in and out of his office, asking questions, looking for guidance on a technical question, bouncing an idea off him or needing his approval for a staff hire or out-of-the-norm expenditure.

Here, on the third floor of the building he owned situated on Copenhagen's North Harbour, was his favourite place to be. He and the rest of the office staff employed by Sørenson Yachts, designs and builders, occupied the third floor of the modern building—the vessels were constructed at their boatyard in Skagen. The lines of the building were inspired by a cruise ship, and the floor-to-ceiling windows let in as much natural light as possible.

While his office might resemble a graveyard in summer, on the plus side, it was a great time for him to knuckle down and catch up with his design work. He had a long waiting list of exceptionally wealthy clients and corporations waiting for a Bo Sørenson-designed vessel. Sometimes that was a kick-ass yacht suitable for an oligarch, sometimes it was a racing yacht, sometimes it was a simple but incredibly luxurious wooden sailing boat. Regardless of the type of vessel, every design would reflect his love of clean lines, modern and unfussy but exceptionally detailed.

And the owner would have the bragging rights of saying it was a Bo Sørenson design. He'd worked all hours of the day for the past fifteen years to distinguish himself from his father and grandfather, both of whom were world-famous designers, and he finally felt that the yachting world no longer believed he was riding their coattails. It wasn't easy to distinguish yourself when you were the son of a genius who'd died far too young and who, they said, had never reached his full potential—and who had been the bad boy virtuoso of the maritime world.

Bo spun round in his ergonomic chair and looked at the framed photograph of his father standing on the *Miss Bea*, the first racing yacht Malte had designed, the wind blowing his thick blond hair. As everyone told him, Bo was the spitting image of his father and, if he never had to hear the expression 'two peas in a pod' again, it would be too soon. Yes, they were both tall, blond and fit, and he had his father's green eyes and rugged face, but that was where the similarities ended.

Unlike his father, Bo was a workaholic and didn't spend the year hopping from one glamorous yachting spot to another—from Monaco to Costa Smeralda to

Dubai—redeeming himself by occasionally producing ground-breaking, innovative designs.

Yes, the patents from those designs had allowed him to be the *enfant terrible* of the yachting world, and brought kudos and opportunity to Sørenson Yachts. But, in Bo's eyes, he'd wasted his talent and spent far too much time being frivolous. And maybe, if he'd partied less and stayed home more, Bo would have more memories of him than him sweeping in, ruffling his hair, handing him a present and sweeping out again, desperate to leave them behind, desperate for the next adventure—and the next woman.

As the years passed, Malte's visits diminished to once or twice a year and Bo watched his mother become more bitter, more emotionally distant, colder and harder. By the time he was a teenager, Bridget had morphed into a brittle, robotic creature who'd been more his bank manager and boss than his mother.

Bridget, who'd been determined that he did not follow in Malte's footsteps, had pushed him hard. If she'd had her way, she would've kept him from his paternal grandfather but neither Bo, nor Asger, would've tolerated her coming between them. He'd loved his stoic and silent grandfather, the one adult who seemed to enjoy his company. Bridget had been bitterly disappointed when he'd taken an engineering degree, specialised in yacht design and joined the family business under his grandfather as owner and CEO.

Within the first year of joining the company that had been in his family for seventy-five years, Bo realised that his grandfather's grip on the company, and reality, was slipping. As he'd taken over many of Asger's responsibilities, Bo discovered that his father's contribution to the company did not justify his enormous salary.

At the age of twenty-four, Bo had realised that Sørenson Yachts was on the verge of collapsing and knew that he had to do something or the company started by his grandfather—the man he respected and who was, mentally, fading away—would go bankrupt. It was up to him to save it. Bo's mum had the emotional range of a puppet, but she was a highly successful businesswoman who'd made a fortune in import and export. With her, Bo had wooed investors and, in the nick of time, put together a deal that had not only given him managerial control of Sørenson Yachts—Asger had given him his power of attorney—but had also injected a healthy amount of cash into the then-failing company.

It had also made him his father's boss. His father hadn't been happy about the board appointing him as his grandfather's successor, and had been furious when his son cut his exorbitant salary and cancelled his company credit cards. He'd been livid when Bo demanded his presence in the office and gave him deadlines for projects he needed to complete.

Malte had lasted six months and, on the day his dad resigned, the anvil resting on Bo's chest lifted. The company was his to do with once he took control, and was in the driver's seat.

But life, as it had the habit to do, wiped away his self-congratulations. His grandfather had died from a massive stroke and, just a few weeks later, his father slammed his newly purchased McLaren into a concrete barrier and died on impact.

Bo had been named as both their heirs, and he had sole ownership of Sørenson Yachts—something he'd dreamed of, but it had come at a cost. In what seemed to be the blink of an eye, more than half his family had been wiped out— a man he'd adored and a man he hadn't—and Bo understood, on a fundamental level, his mother's desire to keep her emotional distance. When feelings were invited to the party, they caused havoc—grief and loss when you loved someone, regret, anger and frustration when you didn't.

No, it was far easier to live his life solo, having bed-based relationships and keeping all relationships superficial. He had sporting friends, guys whose company he enjoyed, but he knew far more about their lives than they did his. He had lovers, not girlfriends or partners, and his sexual partners knew not to expect anything more from him than a good time in bed.

He had lunch with his mother once a month, and they spent ninety minutes discussing their mutual businesses. Her business was her favourite child, giving her everything she needed. She'd never been able to juggle being a businesswoman and a mother, and he'd suffered for it. One of the reasons why he eschewed having a wife and a family was because he never again wanted to feel like he or his children were less important than his or his partner's career.

He was sure that there were people out there who had the work-life balance figured out, but he preferred not to take the chance of being left behind emotionally. He knew what loneliness and parental lack of interest felt like, how busy and uninterested parents could scar a child. Having a partner and child would force him to redesign his working life, something he wasn't interested in doing. And, because he was only ever attracted to smart, ambitious women, he knew that a relationship with a career-orientated woman would mean putting him, or any child they had, in the position of begging for her time, interest and affection. A person only had so much to give and, as he knew, a business demanded a large portion of one's energy.

He preferred not to fight to be seen, heard or paid attention to.

Bo stood up and stretched, annoyed at his uncharacteristic bout of introspection. He had work to do, designs to start and designs to complete. He would spend the summer working, but that wasn't anything new; he got anxious and irritable when he was doing, and achieving. He only had a certain amount of time on this earth, and he intended to leave a legacy behind. Legacies weren't made by sitting on beaches sipping cocktails or lounging around reading. Legacies took work and work was what he did best.

An hour later, Bo was working at his drafting board, deep in the zone, his entire focus on the design of a high-tech racing yacht to compete in the Sydney Cup in 2026. It was a new concept, something that would hopefully revolutionise competitive sailing. He'd been concentrating so deeply that it took him ages to hear the knock on his door and, when he looked up, his junior receptionist stood on the other side of the door, a worried-looking, middle-aged woman standing behind her.

He walked across his expansive office and opened the door, wondering why he was being disturbed when he'd left strict instructions that he wasn't to be.

'Mr Sørenson, this is Mrs Daniels. She urgently needs to speak to you.'

'Make an appointment,' he told the woman, his voice sharp. 'I'm designing and I can't be distracted.'

Mrs Daniels, with sharp blue eyes, was not impressed by his curt statement. 'What I have to say can't wait, Mr Sørenson. And, unless you want me to discuss your private matters in front of your staff member, you'd best let me come in.'

He didn't have private matters to discuss. His last one-night stand had been a few weeks ago and he lived alone. He didn't have any brothers or sisters and his mother was as self-reliant and -contained as he was. He saw the curiosity on his receptionist's face and instructed Agnes to return to her work. He jerked his head, gesturing for the older woman to follow him into his office. He closed the door behind her and lifted his eyebrows. He had an intimidating face; people said that he could look scary, but it was his face, so what could he do? And, if it made her get to the point quicker, all the better. He had work to do.

'I work for Social Services, Mr Sørenson,' Mrs Daniels said, lowering her tote bag to the floor and clutching a brown, official-looking file to her chest.

So? What on earth could she want with him?

Mrs Daniels opened the file and looked down, her eyes scanning the documentation. 'Miss Christianson... Daniella Christianson...do you know her?'

Dani? Sure. He nodded. 'We had a brief relationship about eighteen months ago.' Though calling their three-week affair a relationship was stretching it—they'd had a couple of dinners and a lot of sex.

'I regret to tell you that Ms Christianson died a few days ago.'

Bo rubbed his lower jaw, shock running through his system. He'd met Daniella at a cocktail party and she'd been fun and vibrant, a tall Brazilian bombshell. Just a few years younger than himself, she'd been taking a six-month sabbatical in Copenhagen and had been both smart and sexy. 'I hadn't heard—I am sorry to hear that.' He was, but he didn't understand why a social worker was delivering the news.

'What happened?' Bo asked, unable to believe that someone so vibrant was no more.

'It was a car accident outside Rio de Janeiro.'

Mrs Daniels nailed him with a direct look. 'Were you aware that Ms Christianson was recently married, and that her husband was planning on adopting her son?'

'Why would I be? As I said, I haven't spoken to her for well over a year,' Bo replied.

'So she didn't tell you that you are the father of her son?'

Wait! What?

Bo felt his knees dissolve just a little and quickly decided that he hadn't heard her correctly. He didn't have a son.

Mrs Daniels grabbed a visitor's chair, shoved it behind his knees and Bo gratefully sank into it. Gripping the arms of the chair, he looked up, seeing a little sympathy in her blue eyes. 'I have a son?'

'Judging by your stunned reaction, I'm assuming you didn't know?'

'No, I had no idea. I haven't had any contact with Daniella since I called it done,' he told her. 'She left to go back to Brazil a month later and, no, she didn't tell me she was pregnant!'

But that could be because he'd made it very clear to her—as he made it clear to all his lovers—that he wasn't interested in long-term commitment or children.

'From what I gathered from her grandmother, her husband was her boyfriend from college and they reconnected when she was pregnant. They married and he wanted to raise the boy as his own.'

Okay. 'But he also died?'

Mrs Daniels nodded. 'The baby was also in the crash, but he came away unharmed.'

Dear Lord. Bo rested his forearms on his thighs, idly noticing that his hands were trembling. 'The baby's birth was registered in Brazil, but he has been returned to Denmark. She put you as his father and you are now responsible for him.'

'I am?'

'Mrs Christianson's husband's family has no legal claim to the child—the adoption papers weren't filed yet and, frankly, none of them is in a position to look after a nine-month-old child. Mrs Christianson is survived by her grandmother, who cannot look after the child either. He's yours to raise.'

But…

What was happening here? How had he gone from living his life solo, from eschewing relationships, to having a son? And how was it that Daniella had fallen pregnant by him? He was obsessively careful about using condoms.

He needed to ask. 'How can you be sure he's mine?' Bo asked. 'I'm a pretty careful guy.'

'Even though she never told you, you are named on his birth certificate as his father. And, even though he is very young, the resemblance between you is quite startling,' Mrs Daniels replied. 'But, if you require a DNA test for your peace of mind, that's your right. It will mean that he will stay with his foster family until the matter is settled.'

'He's with a foster family?' Bo asked. What he knew about babies was minimal, and he knew even less about the Social Services system, but he'd watched enough movies to be sceptical that the baby was being well cared for. He was probably wrong, but he didn't like the idea of the baby—his son?—being in a tumultuous environment.

'Since he arrived in Copenhagen last week, yes. The foster family is very nice, one of our best, but they are not a long-term solution,' Mrs Daniels stated. 'Living with you is.'

Bo swallowed and ran his hands over his face. 'Do I have any choice about raising him?'

Mrs Daniels's eyes cooled, and he caught the disappointment in them and felt three feet tall. 'We could arrange to have him adopted, if having a child would be such an imposition on your life, Mr Sørenson. That's an option.'

She wasn't impressed by him, and she didn't need to explain why. He came from one of the best and most well-known families in the country and he had money. He sounded like a self-centred idiot, someone who was more concerned about how this child would affect his life than about the welfare of his son.

He sounded like his own father and that was unacceptable.

Bo stood up and slid his hands into the pockets of his casual grey trousers, bunching his fists. 'And you say that he looks like me?' he asked, hoping she heard the apology and embarrassment in his voice. He rarely apologised, and he also didn't want this woman thinking badly of him, but he suspected that ship had sailed.

'What is his name, by the way?' Bo added, thinking that he couldn't keep calling his son 'him'.

'His name is Matheo, spelt in the Danish way. And he looks exactly like you,' she told him. 'Same eyes, same, nose, same chin. He's a big boy so I suspect he'll also have your height.'

Bo blew air over his lips and tried to find some moisture in his mouth. 'I genuinely don't know what to think or say.'

For the first time, Mrs Daniels smiled. 'I've just

handed you life-changing news—it's a lot to take in. But, unfortunately, we do need to move forward as quickly as possible. Matheo needs to get settled in a permanent environment. His needs are the only ones that matter.'

Yes, he got that. But he was rocked to his core. This stranger was telling him he had a child, something he'd never planned. He was the product of a horrible marriage between two wholly unsuited people. He'd vowed that he'd never risk putting a child through the trauma of being caught between a cold mother and a volatile father. The only way to guarantee that never happened—accepting that anyone could change their minds about having children at any point—was to stay single, unmarried and unattached.

But now he was a father, something he'd never considered. He'd discovered the delights of a female body in his mid-teens but, even as a young man, he'd understood that babies were a consequence of sex and he'd been ultra-careful about using protection. He'd never trusted any of his sexual partners enough to leave the issue of contraception in their hands, so he made sure to protect them both. Damn, how *had* this happened? Well, he understood the mechanics, he just didn't understand why his life had gone off-piste like this. Though, to be fair, so had little Matheo's.

'I have a photograph of him, if you'd like to see it,' Mrs Daniels offered.

He nodded, unable to speak past the lump in his throat. Bo waited, the fire ants of impatience crawling under his skin as he watched her look in her bag for her phone. She pulled it out, took another few minutes to find her glasses and then it took her ten years for her to find the picture she was looking for. Mrs Daniels thrust the phone at him, and he took it gingerly, hauling air into his lungs as he looked down.

Bo's world stopped as he looked down into that all too familiar face. He didn't need the DNA test; Matheo looked exactly as he had at the same age. As the social worker had said, his son looked a lot like him, and he could see little of Dani in his face. He was a Sørenson through and through, with eyes as deep a green as his.

'If you put our baby photographs together, I would be hard-pressed to tell you which one was of him and which one was of me,' Bo admitted, shoving a shaky hand into his hair.

'Do you need to sit down again?'

He managed a small smile. 'No, I'm fine. What's the next step?' He needed to focus on the practicalities, what happened next. He could panic later.

'So you want to do the DNA testing?'

'No, it's not necessary. The dates are right, and he looks exactly like I did as a child. I'll take him.'

Bo winced, knowing he'd made Matheo sound like a puppy left out in the rain. He hadn't meant to; it was just so difficult to think, to wrap his head around this stunning news. He was a father—he had a baby son. He didn't know anything about babies or being a dad. His dad hadn't been much of a father, and he did not doubt that Malte would say that he hadn't been much of a son either...

Now wasn't the time to dig into his complicated history with his father; he needed to focus on the here and now.

'Do you know how to look after a baby, Mr Sørenson?'

He didn't have the first clue. 'No,' he admitted.

'Do you have any family members who could help you?'

Bo thought about his mother trying to change Matheo's

nappy, dressed in Chanel or Balenciaga, her blonde hair perfect and her nails freshly painted. Nope, that wasn't going to happen. Bridget would be horrified by the latest addition to their family. Well, 'horrified' was a strong word—uninterested or unaffected would be a better choice.

'No.'

'Then I suggest you hire a nanny; there are several reputable agencies who can send you some help.'

Right, that was a good suggestion. He would need someone not only to look after Matheo but to teach him how to look after Matheo. How to make bottles and bath a toddler, how to put on a nappy. It couldn't be that hard, but having someone show him the ropes would make life so much easier. 'I have money—I could hire the best in the world,' he told Mrs Daniels, not caring if he sounded like an over-confident git. 'Where do I find the best nanny I can?'

'Sabine du Foy runs a very good agency out of Paris,' she replied. 'Expensive but, so I've heard, worth every cent.'

Bo walked over to his draft board and scribbled the name onto his drawing. He'd just ruined his work, but that was the least of his problems. 'Would they be able to get someone here quickly?'

The social worker shrugged. 'Call her and find out. When you have a nanny in place, I'll arrange to bring Matheo to you.'

Right—bring Matheo. To him…to live…for ever.

Bo felt the need to sit down again.

CHAPTER TWO

IN BERLIN, OLLIE COOPER removed a handful of lingerie from her dresser drawer and dumped it on her bed, thinking that, with so much practice, her packing process should be a lot more streamlined than it was.

Ollie was moving on, unexpectedly and two months sooner than she'd thought. After just four weeks of a three-month contract working as a nanny to a ten-and twelve-year-old—the sons of a dotcom millionaire and his ex-model American wife—she was no longer needed. They loved her, she was told, but an unexpected opportunity had arisen in the US, quite close to family, and they wouldn't require as much help over there as they did here. She'd be paid for the full three months, and they were sorry.

Ollie was sorry too; she now had an empty eight weeks before she had to return to London and she had no idea how to fill them. This was her last nanny assignment, and she felt both sad and glad, anxious and relieved. She didn't want to work as a nanny any more, but she didn't want to leave the role entirely.

She loved kids, she really did, but it was hard not to get attached, to keep her emotional distance. Not becoming too involved was why she'd swapped from long-term contracts to short-term assignments. She couldn't allow herself to become overly entangled in her charges' lives.

She'd done that with Becca and it'd nearly killed her. Watching the life fade from that bright, magical, stunning little soul had pushed her to the limits of her mental endurance and, after she'd passed, she'd realised that she needed to cultivate distance, to keep a barrier, for her mental health. The easiest way to do that was to limit the time she spent with her charges. The down side of the arrangement was that, just as she started to get to know the children, to understand their quirks and foibles, she left their lives. It was sad, and sometimes there were tears, but she walked away with her heart intact.

Normally she knew exactly where she was going, and would have a dossier on her next family from Sabine's agency, and familiarise herself with her charges. Not knowing where to go was a strange experience for her. For the first time in five years, she didn't have a job lined up or a family to help out.

You knew this time was coming, Cooper. It might be two months earlier than you envisioned but it shouldn't be a shock. You've had your five years of freedom and it's time for you to honour the deal you made.

But, technically, not until the first day of September, which was still a little way off.

The fact was, she was running out of time, and Ollie felt as though she was facing the guillotine. A bit dramatic, but she couldn't think of anything worse than going back to London and sitting behind a desk every day. She would rather watch paint dry.

But she'd made a deal, and her parents set a lot of store by their children keeping their word—as they should.

Ollie looked around the gorgeous apartment she'd been

using for the past few weeks and sighed at the mess she'd made. There were clothes on the bed, make-up scattered on the dresser and books she needed to box. Her family had left for the States yesterday and she needed to be out of here in two days—that was when the estate agents would hand over the keys to the new owner. She needed to make a decision: should she go back to London, take a long holiday that would make a dent in her savings, or should she take another quick assignment if she could find one?

Bored with packing and feeling anxious, Ollie picked up her mobile and walked onto the balcony overlooking the mansion's tiny garden, and beyond the tall hedge a small park. She'd spent a lot of time in that park, kicking a football around with the boys, or jogging round it before the boys woke up and the craziness of the day had begun. Ollie dialled the number of the agency she worked for and, on request, was immediately put through to Sabine, the agency's owner.

Switching to French—Ollie spoke four languages fluently—she greeted her boss and spent the next few minutes catching up with the woman, who was not only her boss but her friend and mentor. Sabine had suggested on more than one occasion that she buy into the agency as a junior partner, as Ollie was the only other person she could imagine running her precious business. There was nothing Ollie wanted more—she could see herself in the role of matching nannies and au pairs with families, ironing out issues and expanding the business—but first she had to fulfil her promise to her parents.

She filled Sabine in on her client's abrupt departure, to find that Sabine had already been informed. 'They've already paid me, and I paid you, for the full three months, although you've only worked for them for four weeks.'

'So what's your plan for the immediate future?' Sabine asked with her usual dose of French pragmatism.

'I've got to be back in London at the end of August,' Ollie told her. 'I don't know what I should do between now and then.'

'You could take a holiday,' Sabine suggested.

Ollie wrinkled her nose. Doing nothing for a few days would be nice but she'd soon get bored.

While she wasn't a workaholic, being productive was important to her. She'd seen how hard her father and mother had had to work to build their accountancy practice into the behemoth it was today and, like her brothers, she'd inherited their work ethic. She didn't like being idle and doing nothing—though sometimes 'nothing' was what her family thought she did.

Maybe that wasn't fair. They loved her; they just wished she did something a little more conventional. Her mum, especially, found it exceptionally difficult to reconcile the idea of her smart, *educated* daughter supervising homework, changing nappies or wiping snotty noses. No one in her family realised that she was one of the best rewarded nannies in the business and that she had a list of influential families, ranging from nobility to celebrities to sports icons, who wanted her to look after their little darlings. She had a reputation for excellence and the families who could afford her services wanted her. '*My daughter, the nanny* didn't have the same cachet as '*my daughter, the accountant*'.

'Maybe I should do another two-month stint,' Ollie suggested to Sabine, rubbing her fingertips across her forehead.

'You mean you'd rather find another short-term assignment than return to London early in case your family figures out, from your morbid face and droopy lips, that you would rather pull out your toenails with pliers than work as one of their accountants?'

That was it, in a nutshell.

A natural student, Ollie had won a place to study accountancy, following her parents and brothers into the field. But, two years into her degree, she'd come to realise that she'd made a mistake and that she was wholly unsuited to becoming an accountant. But she was too far in to switch courses, according to her family, and she needed to stick it out. So she'd gritted her teeth and ploughed through; luckily she hadn't found the work overly onerous and it had made her family happy.

They'd been less happy—as in, furious—when she'd told them that she had no intention of joining the family firm and that she wanted to travel. After many arguments, they'd worked out a deal: she could travel and do her own thing for five years but then she'd have to return to London or Johannesburg and work in one of the Cooper & Co branches for five years so that they could get some benefit, and a return on, the very expensive investment they'd made in her education.

If she didn't, then they'd all have to accept what she already suspected: that she'd wasted her education. Her parents would find that very hard to forgive.

Her degree was from the London School of Economics and, as a non-UK resident, it had cost them a bundle to send her to one of the most prestigious universities in the UK. In their eyes, she'd been playing at being a nanny for the past five years—it was time for her to settle down into a career and use her degree.

Her parents put the highest possible value on education and she and her brothers had been raised to believe that a university degree was not a right, but a privilege, and never to be taken for granted. She already felt guilty for not using her degree for the past five years and loathed the idea of wasting her time and efforts. But mostly, Ollie couldn't stand the fact that she might've wasted her parent's money.

No, she had to fulfil the terms of their deal and go back. She would white-knuckle her way through the next five years. Unfortunately, Ollie knew that, within a year of working for them, her family would also start pressurising her to get married and have babies. They wanted it all for her—a stunning career, a successful husband and for her to be a mother.

Ollie wasn't that interested in any of the above. She wasn't an accountant; the thought made her break out in hives. Her parents had a super-strong, amazing marriage, the type of marriage everyone aspired to. She wanted what they had but modern life, modern people, didn't manage marriages like that any more. That had been proved to her by her ex-fiancé, who'd had the emotional depth of a dirty puddle and the inability to keep his fly zipped, and she refused to settle for less than her parents had. As for having children, well, she'd had Becca, and she knew what it was like to love and then lose a kid.

No, she wasn't interested in being dismissed, ignored and cheated on again and she never wanted to be as emotionally involved with a child as she'd been with Becca. It hurt too much. She'd rather live alone, be alone, loving from a distance.

'You're right; I don't particularly want to go back to London early. I'd have to live with them while I look for a flat and I'd be pressurised to start work early. A vacation will take a chunk out of my savings. Do you have a couple of teenagers who need looking after for the summer?'

'Most parents with any sense have made their arrangements already, Ollie,' Sabine told her.

Yes, she knew that it was a bit late in the day to pick up last-minute work. 'I know; I just didn't expect my assignment to finish early.'

Now that she was faced with going home, she wasn't ready and really didn't want to do it. Spending two months in Goa doing nothing was rapidly becoming an attractive option.

Ollie heard the tap of Sabine's nails against her keyboard. 'A request did come in yesterday afternoon. A single father in Denmark needs a nanny for a nine-month-old baby. I told him that finding a permanent nanny will take some time, but he's so desperate he'll take anyone. I didn't think of you because, a, you were heading home, b, you were already committed in Berlin and, c, you prefer to work with older children.'

She didn't dislike babies—they were cute enough— but older kids, toddlers and up, were so much more fun. 'Tell me more about him,' Ollie said, sitting on the edge of her bed. She preferred to work for a couple or single mums. The one single dad she'd worked for at the start of her career had seemed to think that she'd provide additional services as well as looking after his two very precocious children. She'd reported him to Sabine, and he was no longer able to access nannies from Sabine's agency. That kind of behaviour was not tolerated by her.

'He's a yacht designer and builder and, unexpectedly, has gained custody of his nine-month-old son,' Sabine explained. 'He wants someone to help teach him how to care for a baby—he has zero experience—and we've also been tasked with finding him a long-term nanny.'

Most parents prepared themselves for the arrival of a baby, but this father hadn't. Why not? Colour her intrigued.

'And you say he's in Copenhagen?' Copenhagen in summer was supposedly gorgeous and she'd never spent any length of time in the city. It might be…interesting.

'He's offering above the normal rate, as he needs someone to help with the baby and show him what to do. He readily admits to not having a clue,' Sabine stated.

'I'm interested in the job, Sabine. I'm not crazy that it's a single dad, but I'm not twenty-two any more, and I could shut down any unwanted attention a lot quicker, and with more confidence, if it occurred.'

'Are you sure?' Sabine asked.

She was very sure that she wasn't ready to go back to London yet. 'Sure-ish,' she said. 'Send him my CV and see if he's interested.'

If he was, then they could do a video-conference call. 'But he'd have to make up his mind fairly quickly because I have to be out of this place the day after tomorrow.'

'You could always come to Paris and stay with me for a bit,' Sabine offered.

She could. But she knew that, if this job didn't pan out, then it was the universe's way of telling her that she needed to go home and face the music.

'I will call him and see what he says,' Sabine told her. 'I'll send you his file too.'

'That sounds like a plan,' Ollie agreed. 'Speak soon, yeah?'

Forty-five minutes later, before she'd had time to read the man's file, Ollie heard back from Sabine. She had an interview in Copenhagen the day after next, and she was to come prepared to start work immediately. If she wasn't successful in securing the position—and that wasn't likely, because this Bo Sørenson was desperate—he'd pay for her flight to any European destination. He was impressed by her references, he needed her and had offered to pay double her usual rate to secure her services to look after his son.

For Ollie, it was an offer she couldn't refuse. And a way to delay the inevitable.

Copenhagen in summer was a city filled with sunshine, busy with tourists and everyone seemed to be on a bike. As she made her way through the city, Ollie took in the juxtaposition between the grand old buildings and the sleek lines of modern architecture, the old and new co-habiting happily together.

It was bursting with cafés, shops, great-looking people and some of the best restaurants in the world. Honestly, there were worst places to be, and unless her new boss turned out to be a total prat this would be where she would stay for the next two months. How exciting!

She had plans to discover what made this city tick on her off days, which were written into her contract. She wanted to take a boat tour and see the city from the water, hire a bicycle, meander down the side streets or take a walking tour, sampling Danish pastries and *smør-rebrød*—an apparently delicious open sandwich—along the way. She'd heard about Reffen, an organic street-food market and urban area that had a reputation for innovation and sustainability and she wanted to explore that part of the city.

Oh, she wanted to explore it all—the sights, sounds, smells and food. So far, the city was looking good.

She hoped her new boss would be good too.

Ollie glanced down at her phone and re-read the message she'd received from Sabine fifteen minutes ago. She'd spoken with Mr Sørenson this morning and, despite him having met Matheo, the Danish Social Services were saying that Matheo would only be moved from his foster family into his father's care when she was in situ. Her eyebrows had raised when she'd realised that this was at Mr Sørenson's request. Was he so inexperienced that he couldn't look after a baby for a night, or did he only have his son's best interests at heart? Or both?

Time would tell.

Ollie watched as her taxi driver negotiated the streets of the city, her eyebrows raising when he whistled his appreciation as the car crawled down what he told her was one of the most expensive streets in the city. He parked at the end of the street, in front of a low concrete wall. A ladder was attached to the concrete wall, similar to ones used in public swimming pools, and Ollie realised that it was an easy way to get to the beach below the wall. In front of her was what she thought was the Øresund Strait, also known as The Sound, separating the city from the Swedish town of Malmo. It looked like a bolt of crushed, aqua velvet, embellished with Swarovski crystals. It was completely amazing.

Her new boss lived on the water... *Awesome.*

Ollie left the car and turned to look at the house on the right. The extensive property was clad in pale-pink-tinged timber, and sported multiple pitched roofs at different heights angled in different directions. It looked huge, which wasn't unexpected. Any man who could afford to pay her double her normal rate had deep pockets, so she'd expected a large, expensive house. But she hadn't expected such an interesting one and she couldn't wait to get inside.

Spending the summer here was not going to be a hardship in any way. The trees seemed greener, the flowers brighter and the air softer, as if nature was saying thank you for the break from the cold winter. She was looking forward to exploring this city, and hopefully she'd get a chance to see a bit more of the country while she was here. Because, frankly, anything was better than being in London and arguing with her family about her future with Cooper & Co.

Ollie, wearing her uniform of practical beige-coloured trousers and a white, men's-style button-down shirt, knocked on the black front door. She wore trendy trainers on her feet—high heels and little kids did not work well—and her corkscrew curls were pulled back by a plain black headband.

She was here for a job interview, not to compete in a 'model of the year' contest. Ollie felt a little nervous at hearing the sound of heavy footsteps behind the front door. She pulled a smile onto her face—just a small one; there was no need to look like an over-enthusiastic clown—and rubbed a suddenly damp hand on the seat of her trousers.

The door opened and Ollie's heart wasn't quite sure what to do with itself. On one hand, it wanted to do an over-excited backflip—if this was Bo Sørenson, then he was hot! But if it *was* her new boss, the one she would be sharing a house with, then it wanted to do a failed bungee jump and splatter on the floor. Because, it meant he was her new boss and he was, well, hot.

Argh!

Ollie's heart thump-thumped as she took him in. He was a classic Nordic blond, tall and built, but not as pretty as some of the handsome Danish men she'd passed on her brief tour through the city. He was more rugged, a great deal more masculine. And his eyes weren't blue, they were a deep, mysterious green, the green of ancient woods and rain-splattered moss. She approved of the strong jawline under three-day stubble, his straight nose and what could be a sensual mouth. He was also bigger and taller than a lot of the other Danish men she'd seen, with wide shoulders and muscled legs. The bottom line was that he was panty-melting hot and wholly alpha, from his nicely shaped head to his rather big feet. Oh, he was alpha...so alpha.

And, damn it, Bo Sørenson had one of the best bodies she'd ever seen. And she very much wanted to see it naked.

Oh...oh, not good. So not good. Bad—as in, terrible. Sleeping with her boss would be not only supremely unprofessional, but also misconduct for which she could be fired. It was shocking to realise that it was a risk she would be willing to take. And this was, after all, her last job as a nanny...

Really—she was going there, five minutes after first laying eyes on him?

'Olivia Cooper?'

Ollie gave herself a mental slap and lifted her hand to shake the huge paw he held out. He gripped it, scowled at her and told her she was late. Ollie looked at her watch. It was only a couple of minutes past eleven, the time she said she would arrive at his house. Right, he was picky—sexy but rude.

Wonderful.

'I'm barely late, Mr Sørenson, so let's not start this interview by you splitting hairs,' Ollie told him coolly, brushing past him to step into his light-filled hall. She looked into the living area and sighed at the cool white-and-pale-blue walls, the sleek lines of designer furniture and the abundance of natural light. The lounge area, with huge windows that looked out onto the sea, had extra-high ceilings and, under the next ceiling with its lower and differently angled roof, was the kitchen and dining area. The two areas were separated by a glass-covered courtyard. It was very different, very lovely and very Scandinavian.

Ollie placed her bag on a chair in the hallway and folded her hands, tipping her head up, and up, to look into Bo Sørenson's scowling face. If he lost the fierceness, he would be an exceptional-looking man. Right now, he simply looked like an annoyed Viking.

Wonderful; she was being interviewed by Erik the Grouch.

'I'm pedantic about punctuality, Ms Cooper,' he stated.

But she hadn't been late!

'How was your trip, Ms Cooper? Did the driver find the house all right?' she returned, lifting her eyebrows. He needed her more than she needed him, she reminded herself. She'd been paid by her last family: this would be a bonus job. And, if she didn't get it, Goa was always an option if she couldn't bring herself to return to London before she was due—and she couldn't.

'Would you like a cup of coffee, now that you are *finally* here?'

Bo shoved his hands into the pockets of his casual trousers and pulled in a deep breath, then another. He had dark circles under his eyes, from lack of sleep or stress, and a muscle jumped in his jaw. Maybe her sarcasm was out of line, but she wasn't a fan of a lack of manners, and being snapped at before she'd had the chance to say hello. Nor was she a fan of feeling sexually sideswiped, desperate to slap her mouth on his, needing to discover whether he tasted as fine as he looked.

Bo shoved a hand into his short curls. His hair was the perfect shade of light caramel and the thick stubble on his face was several shades lighter. His nose was long and straight but that strong chin suggested stubbornness and pugnaciousness.

When he said nothing, and simply stood there taking her in, his face utterly expressionless, Ollie sighed. Right, it would be up to her to restart this conversation. 'Shall we start again? I'm Ollie Cooper and I've come to interview about the live-in nanny position.'

If he said something sarcastic, she would be out of there. 'Bo Sørenson,' he muttered, in a water-over-gravel voice. His English was almost perfect, with barely a trace of an accent. 'How was your trip? Would you like some coffee?'

Oh, she *knew* he was being sarcastic, but he'd asked the questions in such a bland voice that she couldn't call him out. Ollie pulled up a fake smile and thanked him. 'Fine. And, yes—black, two sugars.'

Bo nodded toward the living room and Ollie took that to mean that she should wait for him there while he made their coffee. She went through and walked to the left side of the room, where she knew she would be out of his sight, and gently bashed her head on the pale grey wall. Why oh, why, did her potential boss have to look like he was a chieftain in *Vikings*? Oh, he didn't have the long hair or the tattoos—not that she could see, anyway—but he had that Ragnar vibe that men listened to and made women melt. His energy filled a room; he was the type of guy people noticed...and women lusted over.

No, no, no!

Ollie rested her forehead against the cool wall and told herself to pull herself together immediately! Yes, he was a good-looking man—fantastically hot—but she was here to do a job, not drool over the man who was going to pay her a vast amount of money to look after his son. She was a professional—she prided herself on her detachment, her ability to be a part of the family but not intrude—but she'd never felt so overwhelmed by a man before. It made her jumpy, scatty and sarcastic, none of which were good traits when she was trying to land a job.

You either get this job or you go back to London. You either control your raging hormones or you move back into your childhood bedroom, still decorated with butterflies. You pull yourself together or you will find yourself in an office in Cooper & Co a lot sooner than you'd like. What are you going to choose, Olivia?

CHAPTER THREE

IN HIS KITCHEN, Bo carefully closed the door and rubbed his hands up and down his face, wondering if he'd stepped into a vortex that had tossed him arse-over-elbow and scrambled his brain.

On hearing the car pull up, he'd stood up and walked to the front door, expecting to see a middle-aged, slightly frumpy, stocky woman standing on his porch, a not-quite-so-terrifying version of Nanny McPhee—not an upgraded, sexy and updated version of Mary Poppins.

All the blood had rushed from his head as he'd taken in her fine-featured face, luminous brown eyes that turned upward at the corners, high cheekbones and her luscious, unblemished and creamy light-brown skin. Her corkscrew curls fell down her back and were held back from that far too gorgeous face by a plain black headband. She wore no make-up, from what he could see—she didn't need any—and was dressed in casual and contemporary trousers and a shirt. The body under that shirt had a small waist and long legs…and, yes, he'd noticed her breasts, round and high. He hadn't lingered on them—he wasn't a Neanderthal—but he was also a guy who liked women and he hadn't been able to help but notice.

She looked amazing.

This couldn't be happening to him—where was the

stodgy, solid nanny he'd been expecting? The woman standing in his living room, probably wondering how long it took to make coffee, was reputedly one of the most sought-after nannies on the continent, spoken of in glowing terms by everyone who'd employed her. He'd read through her references carefully and recognised the names of some of the people she'd worked for, people of consequence and power. According to her references, she was punctual, honest, warm, kind and fantastic with children. Her former employers couldn't praise her enough and many stated they'd have her back in a heartbeat and that she would be a part of their lives for ever.

Well, he had told the owner of the agency he wanted the best, and it looked as though she'd delivered. But did the best have to come in such a drop-him-to-his-knees package? Olivia crackled with energy, and he loved her posh English accent and the unmistakable intelligence he saw in her eyes. Why was an accounting graduate working as a nanny? Where was her family? Did she have a lover?

Why was he so curious? He generally never asked these sorts of questions; he didn't have the time, energy or interest in small talk. But he wanted to know everything about Olivia—and immediately.

Bo sighed and wished he could put her on a plane and send her away, but he knew that finding another nanny so late in the day would be difficult—people would have made plans long before this, and finding someone as good as Olivia Cooper would be impossible. He would simply have to deal with his raging attraction to her and that would mean being even more imperturbable than he normally was. It was a good thing that he had so much practice hiding and dismissing his feelings. He'd need it today and over the next few months.

Right, get on with it, then, Sørenson.

Bo finished preparing the coffee. When he carried the tray into the room, he saw Olivia sitting on the edge of his couch, and noticed her looking as if she was about to jump out of her skin. So, he wasn't the only one feeling unbalanced. Good to know.

But there was no ignoring the fact that working and living with her was going to be a royal pain if they both couldn't relax. And that meant that he had to make an effort to make her feel welcome, to take the wariness out of her eyes.

The best way to do that was to address the elephant in the room and kick it out. 'I wasn't expecting an attractive young woman to be my new nanny.'

'Don't tell me, you were hoping for someone dressed like a bag lady with warts on her nose?' Olivia replied. 'Sorry to disappoint.'

The last thing Olivia could be called was disappointing. 'I reacted badly, and I was rude—I apologise. It's been a rough few days. But, before we go any further with this interview, we need to address the issue of me being a single father and you coming to live with a stranger.'

She hadn't expected him to be so upfront and surprise jumped into her very expressive eyes. She crossed her legs, leaned her forearm on her knee and held his gaze. 'Can I expect any trouble from you?'

Judging by her wary expression, she'd encountered that sort of trouble before. Men could be such morons.

'If by "trouble" you mean am I going to hit on you, then no. I have a very strict hands-off policy when it comes to my staff. I do not believe in making my life more complicated than it needs to be. You will be completely safe with me, Ms Cooper.'

Was that a flash of disappointment he caught in her eyes? No, it couldn't possibly be. He knew his imagination was playing tricks on him when her shoulders dropped and she leaned back slightly. Her actions told him that she wasn't attracted to him, and that she believed his reassurances. She should. Now that his words were out there, they couldn't be taken back. Unlike his father, Bo lived and died by his word. Once something was said, it was cast in stone.

Pity because, in any other situation, he would not have minded getting to know Olivia Cooper better. A lot better—naked better.

Yeah, not helpful, Sørenson.

'Thank you for that,' Olivia quietly stated. 'I appreciate you saying it.'

'But do you believe it?' It was important to Bo that if she took the job she felt safe here with him. He couldn't bear the thought of her tiptoeing around him on eggshells.

She held his eyes for a minute, as if looking for signs of deceit, and when she finally nodded he had to stop himself from sagging with relief. 'Yes, I do.'

Olivia nodded to the coffee on the table between them. 'Would you mind if I poured myself a cup? I'm gasping.'

'Absolutely.' Bo pushed the tray towards her and watched as her elegant fingers depressed the plunger, and then lifted the cafetière. Her nails were short and unvarnished, a pearly white against her skin. When she was done, he poured himself a cup, sat back and placed an ankle on the opposite knee. 'I've never interviewed a nanny before and, knowing nothing about children, I don't know what to ask you.'

She grinned and it was as if the sun had come out from behind a dark cloud. 'That's honest. So, why don't you tell me about your son and how he came to live with you? I understand it was...*unexpected*.'

'He's not here yet,' Bo informed her. He thought about how much to tell her and decided to give her the unvarnished truth.

Matheo's arrival in his life unexpected... 'Unexpected' was one word—'stunning' and 'world-changing' were others. 'I have never been shy about making my feelings about being in a committed relationship and having children known—I've never been interested in either and all my lovers knew where I stood. Somehow, despite my using condoms, Matheo's mother fell pregnant but she decided not to tell me. She returned to Brazil and she wanted to raise my son with the man she married after he was born. I am told he was going to adopt Matheo, but they both died in a car accident before that happened. Dani had put my name on the birth certificate and the authorities tracked me down and he's coming to live with me.'

He sipped at his coffee and tried and failed to smile. When he explained it out loud, it sounded even more outlandish than it did in his head. 'You're all up to date now, Olivia.'

'Call me Ollie,' she told him. 'That's an incredible story. So, where is Matheo now? Have you met him?'

Bo nodded, unable to explain his tumultuous day yesterday. He'd travelled to the house of Matheo's foster parents and, in their over-crowded living room, a homely woman had held a wide-eyed Matheo, his eyes big in his face. He'd been awake and had looked a little shellshocked. Bo had wondered whether, on a visceral level,

Matheo understood that his mum was gone. Their eyes had connected and a wave of love he'd never anticipated, hadn't expected or prepared for, had nearly dropped him to the floor.

This was his kid—*his*. His to raise, guide, protect and love. Look, he did not doubt that he could do the first three, but he was genuinely worried he couldn't give Matheo the love he needed. He'd never been shown how to love, how to nurture; he'd never been nurtured himself. But all he could do was his best, and he'd try.

Matheo had lunged forward and fallen into his arms, and he'd stood there for the longest time, feeling awkward as he held his son, trying to wrap his head around the fact that he was no longer alone and that he now had his own family. That, for the first time in his life, he'd fallen in love.

Bo looked at Ollie and tried to speak but found the words catching in his throat. Swallowing, he tried again. 'I met him yesterday. He's still at the foster mother's house; I am expecting him in an hour or so. The social worker wasn't convinced that I could look after him overnight without any help. I think she was worried that I'd lose him or forget about him or something. She wanted to wait until I had a nanny on the premises.'

Ollie tipped her head to the side. 'I think she was being overly protective. While you might be inexperienced, you would've muddled through, and Matheo would've been fine.'

He was surprised at the faith she showed in him. 'Why do you say that? I don't know anything about babies. Like, I know they cry and sleep, but that's about it.'

'You're not the first parent who would've had to learn on the job,' Ollie stated. She placed her cup on the tray and wrapped her hands around her knee. 'So, there are a few details we need to discuss. Can we do that?'

He liked her direct way of speaking, the way she looked him in the eye. He knew he could be intimidating but this woman, half his size, wasn't in the least bit afraid of him. That was a novelty, and he liked it. 'Sure.'

'You do realise that if I get the job I am only here for two months? I never take assignments that are longer than three months and the only reason I am here is because my other assignment was abruptly curtailed.'

He knew her sudden availability was due to her employer's change in plans, but he suspected there was a story behind that, and he wanted to know what it was.

No! He couldn't allow himself to become curious about his nanny, about what made her tick. At Sørenson Yachts, he kept his distance from his staff, but he might find that difficult to do with Ollie. Sure, his house was big—it had five bedrooms, each with its own *en suite*—but they were going to have to share the snug where he watched TV, this lounge and the kitchen and dining areas. If he hired her she would be employed to show him how to care for his son and that would mean they'd have to spend many hours together as he forged a bond with Matheo.

'The boss at the agency—Ms...' He frowned, not able to recall her name.

'Sabine du Foy,' Ollie interjected.

'Right, her—she made that clear. Apparently, you need to be back in London by the first of September.'

He saw her nose wrinkle just a little and wondered why she wasn't keen on that. That she was English was obvious, but why wouldn't she want to go back to her home country?

Too many questions, Sørenson. Wrap your head

*around the concept of emotional distance, please. This
has never been a problem for you before.*

'I'll need a long-term nanny to take over from you.
However, I'm not clear whether she will be looking for
one for me, or whether you will take on that task.'

Ollie tapped her finger against her knee. 'We both will.
Sabine will send me potential candidates and, if you are
willing, I can pre-interview them for you. By that time, I
will have a better understanding of your personality and
needs, and I will make a short list for you. You can then
interview the final candidates either by flying them to
Copenhagen, as you've done for me, or via video call. I
would suggest meeting them face to face.'

He did a lot of business over video but he far preferred
to meet with someone one on one. With something as
important as Matheo's safety, wellbeing and happiness
at stake, he needed to look into someone's eyes, breathe
the air they did and get a feel for them. He didn't want
the barrier of a screen between them.

Ollie went on. 'I get a sense of someone's energy when
I meet them face to face and I listen to my gut instincts.'

'What was your gut instinct reaction to me?' Bo asked,
and nearly cursed aloud when the words left his mouth.
What type of question was that, and how could he be so
foolish to ask it?

Ollie tipped her head to the side, her gaze frank. 'I
think you are take-no-prisoners direct, occasionally
grumpy, ridiculously punctual—' he deserved that sarcastic aside '—and I suspect that you can, on occasion,
be a considerable pain in the butt.'

Ollie smiled so sweetly that Bo couldn't help a small
grin hitting his lips. 'Accurate.'

'I know.' Bo expected her to ask him what his first

impressions of her had been—*sexy, gorgeous, confident and super smart*—but she didn't, and he liked that about her. She didn't seem to need his approval; she was immensely comfortable in her skin and in her abilities to do the job she'd applied for. Confidence was such a turn-on.

'So, are we going to do this, Mr Sørenson? Are you going to let me look after your son for the next eight weeks?'

Of course he was. He was sure she was the best there was. He nodded.

Ollie leaned back in her chair, a contented smile on her face. 'It's good to know that the flight wasn't wasted,' she said. 'Now, why don't you tell me about your working day, so that I know your routine?'

He rose early, hit the gym and was in his office before seven. He frequently didn't come home until after nine or ten. He seldom broke for lunch, drank pre-made smoothies for breakfast and picked up prepared meals for supper. If he kept up that schedule, he'd never see Matheo. But if he didn't work this summer, he'd never manage to hit his clients' deadlines. *Damn it.*

'Can I get back to you on that?' he asked Ollie. 'And, if I get to call you Ollie, then you must call me Bo.'

'Bo. So, get back to me on your schedule and we'll work something out.' She turned and cocked her head; Bo also heard the car pulling into his driveway. He shot to his feet and pushed a hand into his hair.

'Uh, that will be Matheo...'

Ollie was also on her feet but, in contrast to him, she looked completely calm. How could she be so calm? His life was taking a one-eighty spin; everyone should be as freaked out as he was. Ollie placed a hand on his bare forearm and her touch calmed his racing heart, allowing him to pull some air into his lungs. 'I'm here, Bo, and I'm here to help. Just take a couple of deep breaths, okay?'

She made it sound as if he was panicking and he never panicked. He'd sailed catamarans in the Bering Sea, had done the occasional free climb and had base-jumped before. He was the calmest person he knew. He knew how to regulate his breathing, to calm his nerves. He didn't let emotion affect him. He could, more often than not, be a robot in human form.

But, at this moment, his brain wanted to jump out of his skull and his heart was squeezing through a gap in his ribs. He was taking on a child, another human being. He was going to be *responsible* for a baby human—from this moment, Matheo's growth, mental, emotional and physical, would all be on him. He'd never wanted this and at that moment, consumed by terror, he hated Dani for dying and leaving him to raise a child he'd never wanted.

He dropped to his haunches and rested his fingertips on the floor to balance himself. Then he felt a small hand on his shoulder, a gentle *'you've got this'* squeeze, and a little air slid into his lungs. He wasn't alone, he wasn't doing this by himself. For the next two months or so, he'd have Ollie's help, her experienced, knowledgeable, studied help. She was his two-month back-up plan, a way to get him up to speed.

This situation was not Matheo's fault, and neither was it his—it just was what it was. And he could either sit here, imitating a rather wobbly jelly, or he could stand up, square his shoulders, open that door and face the future.

He could do this. Because he had no damn choice.

Bo stood up, walked to the hallway and placed his hand on the door, closing his eyes as he gathered his courage to open it. He was stepping out of his solo world and becoming a family... Man, he was terrified. But courage, as they said, was doing something whether you were scared or not.

He yanked the door open so hard that it bounced back and he had to step away so it didn't smack him in the face. Catching the frame, he eased the door out of his way and looked at Mrs Daniels with Matheo perched on her hip. His son was awake but Bo could see the streaks of dried tears on his face. And maybe he was projecting here, but in his green eyes he saw all his fear.

Matheo shoved a thumb into his mouth. Bo didn't pull his eyes off him and ran his knuckle down his smooth cheek. 'Have you had a rough day, little man?'

Surprising him, Matheo, leaned towards him and Mrs Daniels handed him over. Matheo immediately curled himself into Bo's chest, resting his head against it. Through his thin shirt, Bo could feel the rhythmic beat of his little heart. Bo covered Matheo's head with his big hand and, ignoring Mrs Daniels, dropped a kiss in his hair. 'It's okay, Mat, you're home. I've got you.'

Matheo looked up at him, blinked once and sent Bo the sweetest smile, revealing one little tooth. And Bo, hard and short-tempered, realised that his heart—that misshapen, mangled organ that's sole purpose was to pump blood around his body—no longer belonged to him.

CHAPTER FOUR

THE SOCIAL WORKER arrived with not much more than a few clothes, a couple of nappies and a yellow, ratty dog that Matheo couldn't seem to live without. On doing a quick inspection of Bo's house, Ollie realised he didn't have anything they'd need for the child. They wouldn't last the night.

What had he been thinking—that Matheo would move in and eat adult food and drink whiskey? Where was the baby going to sleep; what was he going to eat, wear? Ollie understood that acquiring a baby had been a shock but Bo—obviously intelligent—was either clueless, still in shock or maybe a little of both.

To be fair, she wasn't at her best either. Not only was she dreading the future, but this job would go by super-quickly, and she was also feeling way off-balance. Her new, single boss was the sexual equivalent of an asteroid strike and she felt as if she was a tiny star he'd bumped off course and was now spinning around in space.

She'd never had such an intense reaction to a man before: she was far too sensible and practical to be blown out of her sexual boots. Her ex had been a good choice, a sensible choice and, had he not cheated on her and been so unsympathetic about Becca—she'd been more upset by the second than the first—she'd still be with him. He'd been a reasonable and safe option, someone her family had liked: good-looking enough, with a good job and a good conversationalist. A steady, not too shiny star.

Bo was a meteorite, a shooting star and a black hole—mysterious, foreign, unexplained, interesting and utterly fascinating.

And, as he'd taken care to explain earlier, very off-limits. She had to stop thinking about him as a sexy man she'd like to kiss and get it into her head that he was her boss. And that meant sorting out this rag-tag, thrown-together family.

Because it was her job, Ollie immediately sprang into action. When Matheo—henceforth to be known as the cutest kid in the world and a Bo mini-me—fell asleep in the middle of Bo's huge California King bed, surrounded by cushions higher than the Great Wall of China, Ollie sat down at the rustic table in Bo's gourmet kitchen and started making a list.

She looked up as Bo entered the kitchen, having changed into a smarter shirt and pulled a pair of loafers over his sockless feet. He held his car keys in his hand and his hair was brushed. Ollie leaned back in her chair and gave him a long up-and-down look.

'I'm going to go to work for a few hours—I need to get some things done.'

Nope. Not going to happen. Ollie draped her arm over the back of the chair and shook her head. 'No, you're not.'

His deep-green gaze turned cold. 'I'm sorry, I thought I heard you trying to tell me what to do. In case this arrangement wasn't clear, I tell you what to do.'

Ollie didn't have time to deal with his lord of the manor routine right now. 'So tell me, *Mr Sørenson*—' she put extra emphasis on the word '—where is Mat going to sleep tonight? In your bed with you? I don't recommend that. How is he going to eat—off a lap or in a chair? You can't bathe him with your expensive, top-of-the-range products, he needs toiletries suitable for a baby. You're running low on nappies and there is no baby formula, so what do you intend to feed him? I'm not going to run out at midnight in a city I don't know looking for emergency supplies.'

His eyes bounced from her face to the list on the table in front of her. His shoulders slumped. 'I...eh...didn't think.'

Well, that much was obvious.

'What did you think? That he was just going to fall asleep and then wake up when you were done with your work?' Ollie asked, trying not to roll her eyes. When Bo frowned, she knew she hadn't been successful in hiding her impatience.

'Okay, clever clogs, I get your point.'

'We need supplies, and we need them fast.'

He gestured to a closed laptop sitting on the dining table. 'You can use that. It runs everything in the house. You can order whatever you need and they'll deliver.'

Ollie shook her head. 'I think I need to go myself. I saw a speciality baby shop not far from here. It will have everything I need.' She saw the confusion in his eyes and knew that he'd never noticed the impressive-looking baby shop just a few blocks away. Why should he? Babies hadn't been his thing up until the day before yesterday.

The man was going to have a big wake-up call.

'If you can stay here and look after Mat, I'll drive down to the store and get everything I need. Also, walking around the store will jolt my memory—there will be things we'll need that I've forgotten. It's been a while since I looked after a baby.'

Bo ran a hand through his hair in frustration. 'I've just got him and you want to leave me alone with him?' he demanded, fear jumping into his eyes.

'He's probably going to sleep for a couple of hours and I should be back by then,' Ollie told him.

Bo shook his head, dug into his back pocket and pulled out a slim-line wallet. He flipped it open, removed a black credit card, handed it over and told her the pin. 'Buy whatever you need but be quick about it. I'll go to work when you get back.'

Seriously? Again, no.

Ollie felt another spurt of annoyance but it died when she saw the confusion and fear in his eyes. He was very out of his depth and floundering. He needed to feel in control and he could do that at work, the place where everything made complete sense and there were few surprises. But running off would just delay the inevitable and, the sooner he and Matheo settled into their new reality, the better they'd all be.

'I'm going to have to order a load of stuff to be delivered here. When I get back, I will need help assembling it—Mat's cot, putting his feeding chair together and maybe even assembling his changing station. I cannot do all of that and look after a baby. And I thought you wanted to learn how to look after him?'

'I do, but—'

'But?'

He glanced away. 'But I also need to work.'

The quicker he learned that he had to fit into Matheo's timetable, and not the demands of the company, the easier this process would be. At least until they established some routine and found some long-term help.

'I think you should consider putting work onto the back burner for the next little while—or, if you must work, do it when Mat goes down for the night. He needs to get used to you and to start recognising you as his primary care-giver, the one stable person in his life. He's not going to be able to do that if you keep flitting off to work.'

Bo opened his mouth to argue and Ollie lifted her eye-brows, waiting for his response. He was looking for an out clause, a way to make this work for him, but in the end couldn't come up with one. This was his new reality and it was smacking him in the face.

Ollie picked up the list and tucked it in the back pocket of her trousers with his credit card. 'I need a car.'

Bo nodded to a lovely pottery bowl on the dining table, in swirls of rich blues and green, within which lay a key-less fob. 'I suppose you'll have to take my car. Can you drive a manual? Are you used to power? Maybe I should go grab what's needed and you should stay here.'

He was grabbing at the last straw, still trying to run, but she wouldn't let him. She shook her head. 'Bo, I have driven a variety of expensive cars and, yes, I can drive a manual car. What is it?'

'It's a two-seater Mercedes GLS,' Bo told her. Right, it was only a rare, pricey car—she'd better not ding it. It was also hugely impractical for a man with a baby.

'Where are you going to put a baby seat in that?' Ollie asked him. 'On the roof? Maybe, while I'm gone, you could consider doing some car shopping, unless you never intend to take Mat anywhere.'

Ollie scooped up the fob and walked out of the kitchen and down the passage. Matheo hadn't moved from his position within the pillows. She returned to the kitchen where Bo still stood, looking a little shell-shocked. She placed her hand on his muscled, warm forearm and looked up into his hunky face. 'Bo, you need to keep checking on Mat—like, every ten minutes. You do not want him falling off the bed.'

He nodded. 'I'll take my laptop into the bedroom and work from there.'

Right, he hadn't got the message. He rolled his eyes at her disbelief. 'I was going to research which cars are the safest children-carriers and then I was going to call my car guy.'

Ah. Right. She'd made an assumption and it was way off the mark. It wouldn't pay to underestimate Bo Sørenson. He might not say a lot but he heard a great deal.

It was past nine when Bo finally sat down with a glass of wine. He slumped down onto his white couch and propped his bare feet up onto the coffee table. He was categorically exhausted. His first Mat-centric day had wiped him out. For a guy who regularly ran half-marathons, who spent hours in the gym and who was known for being able to work sixteen-hour days without breaking a sweat, he could not believe that a twenty-pound child had made him want to sleep for a week.

And it wasn't as if he'd had to do that much. A few minutes after Ollie had swung back into his driveway and parked his precious car, a delivery van had pulled up and started unloading what looked to be half a house. The men were dressed in smart overalls bearing the logo of the shop where she'd spent the equivalent of a small country's health budget—he'd got a notification from the bank when she'd swiped his card, convinced the comma was in the wrong place. The men hauled the furniture out of the van and carried it into the room they'd designated should be Mat's. They'd then hauled out screwdrivers and Allen keys and had swiftly built the furniture she'd bought, including a wooden feeding chair and a cabinet for the pile of clothes she'd purchased.

A cot with sides that dropped down was pushed into the corner of the room and a colourful mobile was attached to the side. Toiletries were placed in the *en suite* bathroom and Ollie, who'd turned into a whirling dervish of activity, tossed his new clothes into the washer/dryer. She had also purchased a range of organic baby food, telling him that it would do for now, but she'd teach him how to make Mat's food herself.

He didn't even cook for himself and she expected him to cook for his son?

While all this was going on, Ollie taught him how to change a nappy, how to bathe a wriggling Mat and made him hold and walk him while he yelled his head off for who knew what. Ollie had told him that he was just feeling unsettled and a little scared, and that he had to remain calm, that babies were amazingly good at picking up on emotions. Bo had tried but, judging by how long it had taken Mat to stop crying, he knew he needed better relaxation techniques.

He took a huge sip of wine and looked at the baby monitor on the coffee table. He could hear Mat's soft breathing and he closed his eyes and inhaled. He had a child…in his house. And would be sharing his space for at least the next eighteen to twenty years…

A couple of days ago he'd been responsible for no one but himself, and today he was raising a child. Bo sat up, placed his forearms on his knees and tried to keep the ribbons of terror threatening to wrap him up in knots. He couldn't do this, he didn't know how to...

'Are you okay there? You're looking a little green.'

Bo looked up to see Ollie standing in the doorway to the living room, her face still looking as fresh as it had when she'd first arrived this morning. Her white shirt looked a little wilted, her trousers had a streak of something on her thigh and she'd lost her hairband, so her curls fell in disarray down the sides of her heart-shaped face, but he could feel waves of energy rolling off her. He had all the energy of a wet noodle but he suspected she could carry on for a few more hours. All he wanted was his bed—and, preferably, Ollie in it.

Was he just reacting to her like this because his life had been turned inside out and because, at times like these, it was natural to look for help, for someone to share the load of what was honestly an overwhelming experience? Was he just experiencing a millennia-old biological urge?

There's a woman, she knows what she's doing, I'll have her.

He was too honest with himself, about himself, to use that handy excuse for his prickly skin, the movement in his trousers or the hitch of his breath. The inconvenient truth was that Ollie would have caught his eye and interest no matter where or when he'd met her. There was something about her that made him look, look again and wonder.

She wasn't cover-girl pretty—he'd had lovers who'd strutted the catwalks of Milan and Paris—but his eyes were constantly drawn back to her face. He liked eyes upturned at the corners, her wide smile and the hint of a dimple in her left cheek. She was a combination of sexy and sensible, practical and pretty. Ollie was efficient and unflappable and he wouldn't have coped today—*had he coped?*—without her calm attitude, flashes of sly humour and pragmatism.

Bo ran his hand down his face; an employee living with him was not a good idea. He gestured to his wine glass. 'Would you like a glass?'

Ollie wrinkled her nose. 'I shouldn't.'

Bo knew she was thinking about whether it was professional or not to have a glass of wine with her employer. 'Ollie, you've had a long, long day. Mat is asleep. Have a glass of wine and wind down.'

She stepped into the room and nodded her thanks. Bo headed for the kitchen, found another glass, poured her some wine and handed it over. Ollie immediately kicked off her shoes and curled up in his favourite chair, her feet tucked under her bottom and her head resting against the soft leather. She sipped and sighed. Bo resumed his seat on the leather couch and stretched out his long legs, placing his hand over his mouth to cover a yawn. 'How can I be so tired?' he asked.

'It's been a life-changing day for you, and emotional tiredness is a lot more sapping than physical tiredness,' Ollie told him, and there was a depth of authenticity in her voice that made Bo suspect that she knew of what she spoke. She met his eyes, lifted her glass in a toast and handed him a soft smile. 'Congratulations on your new kid, Bo. He's a cracker.'

A wave of pride washed over him and he smiled. 'He really is,' he admitted. 'But, man, I didn't realise how much work babies involved.'

'Today was an extraordinary day. Once you are in a routine and know what you're doing, it'll get easier and will come more naturally to you.'

He so didn't know what he was doing. He hoped she

was right. If not, he was going to spend the next twenty years running around like a headless chicken. For someone who loved control and order, a man who enjoyed being successful and knowledgeable, it was a terrifying thought. He looked over to Ollie and took in her shocking-pink toenails, the ring on her middle toe, and her soft-looking, elegant feet. He had a hot, smart woman sitting in his living room and he was not only exhausted but they'd only discussed babies. A day or two ago, he'd been an in-demand yacht designer, melded to his work. Today he was a dad.

He rested the foot of his glass on one knee. 'I never really interviewed you this morning,' he said, thinking back on the day.

Ollie raised her eyebrows. 'Are you telling me you are still deciding whether to hire me?'

Bo thought he heard a hint of tease in her voice but he was so out of the practice with being teased—if he ever had been—that he couldn't be sure. 'No, of course not—you're hired.'

He caught the twitch of her lips and knew that he'd been had. It was so strange that this pint-sized person wasn't in the least bit wary of his bark—compared to his six-four height and big build, she was a feather. 'Does anyone intimidate you?'

She considered his question, her hair dropping way past her shoulder as she tipped her head to the side. 'Honestly? My mum.'

Ollie waved her hand in the general direction of the bedrooms. 'Take my organisational skills today and multiply them by a thousand and you'll get my mum. She worked full-time as a chartered accountant, raised four boys and a girl and still managed to be a very hands-on mum. God help the world if my mum decides to ever take it in hand.'

That Ollie loved her mum was obvious, but there was a note of wistful defiance in her voice, something that suggested that she and her mum bumped heads on occasion. Choosing not to pry, as he hated it when people dug into his family situation, he asked another question. 'You have *four* brothers?'

Ollie took another sip of her wine and nodded. 'Four older, very bossy, very protective brothers. I'm the youngest.'

Ah. With four brothers and a strong mum, it was no wonder that he didn't intimidate her. Actually, it was quite nice. Having people tiptoe around him was sometimes annoying, mostly unnecessary and always frustrating. Yeah, he was big, and he had a serious face, but he didn't routinely bite people's heads off. He demanded a certain standard from his employees, and made it known if he wasn't happy with their performance, but he didn't play games and he never held grudges.

'I'm starving,' Bo realised, looking towards the kitchen and then at his watch. It was past nine, he didn't have the energy to cook and the last thing he wanted to do was go out to eat. *Oh, wait, I can't do that any more.*

Ollie looked at her watch and smiled. 'I ordered two pizzas—one fully loaded, one a plain Margherita. They should be here in about ten minutes.'

Ah...what? Ollie smiled at his confusion. 'When you were trying to dry and dress Mat—not very successfully—I realised that neither of us would have the time to cook tonight. I was starving, and I presumed you would be too, so I ordered pizza. I thought it was the easiest option because everyone eats pizza.'

He was impressed by her ability to think ahead but couldn't resist trying his hand at teasing. 'I could be gluten-intolerant.'

Ollie started to roll her eyes and then seemed to remember that he was her boss and stopped. Yep, his new nanny was not going to be deferential or demure. He genuinely couldn't be more thrilled about that. 'I saw you stuffing a biscuit into your mouth earlier, so I figured you weren't.'

'Smart arse,' he grumbled, but his small smile told her that he was amused. And she did amuse him. When had a woman last done that? He couldn't remember.

Hoping that the pizza would arrive soon, he walked over to the kitchen area and picked up the bottle of wine standing on the marble island. He nodded to her half-empty glass. 'Can I give you more?'

Ollie clutched the glass to her chest and shook her head, causing her curls to bounce. 'I'm a lightweight with alcohol. One glass is my limit, and I probably won't even finish that.'

Bo topped up his own glass, walked over to the window and looked out onto the fantastic view of the Øresund Strait. He opened the bi-fold doors and sucked up in a dose of fresh, warm air. He watched the lights of a boat, maybe a trawling vessel, making its way up the straight and asked Ollie another question. 'How did you become a nanny? I think I remember seeing something about you having an accounting degree. Quite a good one, if I recall correctly.'

He turned round just in time to see a flash of distaste cross her face. 'Not a fan of figures?' he asked.

'I left university and, instead of joining the family's accounting business, I wanted to travel. I needed a way to support myself so I applied to an agency—Sabine du Foy's—and I looked after Sabine's sister's kids for a year or two. Sabine, as you can imagine, has connections all over Europe and I went to look after the children of another influential family. I've been doing this for five years, and have worked for a lot of families.'

'And were they all good?'

Ollie rocked her right hand. 'Mostly. Mostly they were fabulous, one or two were less than. It happens.'

He wondered which side of the scale he'd tip when she left. And that reminded him of something else. 'Ms du Foy said that I was lucky to get you and that you only work three-month contracts. Why? Why don't you stay longer?'

Those long legs unfurled and her feet hit the floor. Ollie stood up, her expression shuttered. Right, whatever ease they'd developed he'd blown up with his last question. It hadn't been highly personal, and one he should've asked earlier when interviewing her for the position. But, seeing her reaction, he could see it was a hot button for her. And he wanted to know why.

Ollie drained the last of her wine and, when her brown eyes met his, he couldn't see any of the flecks of gold he'd caught in them earlier. 'I don't stay longer because I won't allow myself to get attached.' She managed to smile but it was tight. 'I'm just going to wash my hands; by the time I get back the pizza should be here. If you don't mind, I'm going to have a quick slice and then go to bed. It's been a very long day.'

Bo watched her walk away, her spine straight and her rounded hips swaying. If he hadn't asked that last question, they would've shared the pizza, sitting on either side of the island, chatting amicably, getting to know each other.

But his curiosity had blown that possibility out of the water. And maybe that wasn't a bad thing. She was his nanny, an employee, and he shouldn't be getting friendly with her.

Employee.

Hired to look after his son.

Then why couldn't he stop thinking about how her body must look under her clothes, whether her hair was as soft as it looked and whether her mouth was sexy or spicy?

Good job on making a complicated situation way more intricate than it needed to be, Sørenson.

CHAPTER FIVE

OLLIE, IN THE small garden outside the kitchen door, moved her body into a downward dog pose and turned her head to the right to look at Mat, who sat on a blanket she'd laid out on the grass, gnawing on a plastic teething toy she'd picked up yesterday. She'd heard him wake just before six. He'd slept through the night, the amazing child, and she'd gone to him, changing his nappy and giving him a 'good morning' cuddle. She'd warmed a bottle for him and he'd happily sucked the milk down. Since he'd looked happy enough, she plopped him down next to her and decided to try and get in a quick yoga routine.

Yoga and running kept her centred and supple, and calmed her constantly whirring mind. But this morning she was finding it difficult to clear her mind. She pulled in a deep breath and wished she'd handled Bo's question about why she only worked for three months at a time with more sangfroid. She'd answered the question many times before, blithely telling people that she was the bridge between their old nanny and their new. Bo was the first person whom she'd told, openly and honesty, that she didn't stick around because she was afraid of getting attached. She'd never voiced those words aloud before.

Memories, both sweet and sour, tumbled through her. She'd loved working for the De Freidmans. They'd been a perfect family—three kids under the age of ten, the mother a human rights lawyer, and the father a heart surgeon. The older boys had been mischievous but lovely, but it was four-year-old Rebecca who'd captured Ollie's heart. Serious and a little geeky, the little girl had asked profound questions, was a frequent hugger and was simply the nicest child she'd ever come across. Becca had loved everyone and everyone had loved her. Their house in Bruges had been lovely, and Ollie had been so happy with her converted attic apartment, the city and the friends she'd made there.

Then everything had changed when Ollie had suggested a check-up because she thought Becca was low on energy. The doctors had done myriad tests on her tiny body and Rebecca had been diagnosed with brain cancer. There had been no cure: if they were lucky, Becca had a year to live.

Although Ollie had been close to the family up until that point, she'd been accepted as part of it then, and she'd become Johannes's and Petra's strength and support. To them, she'd been the one person who understood, like no one else could, what the world would lose when Becca passed on. As Becca's illness progressed, Ollie's connection to the little girl, and the family, had grown stronger. Every day she'd fallen a little more in love as she'd stored up memories of the precious child she'd have so little time with.

For eight months the De Friedmans had become her world and their house was the only place she'd wanted to be. Calls to Fred, her fiancé, had stopped, his calls to her had gone unanswered and she'd rarely connected with her family. Fred, her family and Sabine had all warned her she was getting in too deep and that she was losing perspective but all she'd been able to think about that was that Becca was dying. She'd needed to spend as much time with her as she could, and had been driven to support the family through what was the worst situation any parents could find themselves in.

In hindsight, she'd lost herself for those eight months. Sabine had even flown to Bruges to talk to her, and she'd tried to get Ollie to take some time off, but Ollie had refused.

And then Rebecca had died and a little piece of Ollie died with her too. Just a week after the funeral, a conversation with Johannes and Petra had ripped her apart...

'Miss?'

Ollie looked up from her downward dog pose into a round, homely face dominated by the most amazing pair of blue eyes. She stood up, putting herself between Mat and this stranger. While she did not doubt that this lady was harmless, as she was in Bo's garden, she was still a stranger to Ollie.

'I was wondering if you'd like some breakfast, miss.'

Ollie folded her arms across her bare stomach—she wore only a cropped exercise top and a brief pair of cycling shorts. 'I'm sorry but who are you?'

'I'm Greta Jensen, Bo's housekeeper.' She dropped to her haunches in front of Mat and smiled at the baby boy. Mat's reciprocal smile was a great deal more gummy and drooly. 'And this is little Mat. Oh, he looks just like Bo.'

Right, so Bo had told his housekeeper that he had a son, but he'd failed to inform Ollie that he had a housekeeper. They were going to have to work on their communication skills. And where was the man? It was after seven; shouldn't he be up by now?

'I'm Ollie, Mat's nanny,' Ollie said, looking at her yoga

mat. She was only halfway through her routine and she needed another twenty minutes to unwind and work the knots out of her body.

Because she'd been thinking about Rebecca, Fred and her family—focusing on past grief, hurt and her current confusion—her mind would take a great deal more time to unknot. She needed hours of stretching, possibly days of meditation. It was time she didn't have and, frankly, didn't want to spend.

It was easier to stay unattached and remaining distant than work through emotional quagmires, another good reason to live her life solo. Why would she want the insecurity associated with a boyfriend or a lover? Who needed the 'does he love me?', 'is this just about sex?', and 'will he still want me if I pick up five kilograms and get a spot on my chin?' questions? She was already dealing with one situation she wasn't keen on—the thought of working as an accountant—why would she want to deal with more than she needed to?

'Shall I take him inside with me?' Greta asked. 'I will put him in his new feeding chair. I see you put some porridge out for his breakfast. I can make that for him, if you'd like. He can keep me company while I make Bo's breakfast. I can make you some too.'

She'd been a nanny long enough to know that it was in her best interests to take any help when it was offered. And she could see Mat's high chair from here and would know within seconds if he got fretful or weepy. 'That sounds amazing, thank you.'

Greta scooped Mat up and placed him on her slim hip. It was obvious that she had experience with children. 'I raised four children and have six grandchildren,' Greta told her when Ollie asked.

Right. Why on earth had Bo employed her as a nanny when he had such an experienced woman working for him already? 'You should be Mat's nanny,' Ollie told her, keeping her tone light.

'I only work half-days for Bo a few times a week,' Greta explained. She sent Ollie a naughty smile. 'And, while I adore children, I very much like being able to give them back when I've had enough.'

Fair enough. Greta walked Mat into the kitchen and Ollie dropped back down to her mat, pushing her body into a cat cow. She'd continue with some basic moves for a few minutes before attempting the more complicated poses she'd spent a long time mastering.

Ollie was just getting into the zone, her mind reasonably still, when she heard the side gate open and slam close and rough breathing behind her. Dropping her foot, she whirled around to see Bo standing next to the gate, his attention on the smart watch on his wrist. He pushed buttons and nodded his satisfaction as Ollie stood there, staring at him.

That he was a big guy was obvious but, with him dressed in casual clothes yesterday, she hadn't quite realised how big he was, or how muscled. In his athletic shorts and low-hanging vest, she noticed that his arms were huge, his legs muscled and that big muscles covered the balls of his shoulders and above his collarbone. She knew, without a shadow of a doubt, that he'd have a washboard stomach and could see that his chest, sprinkled with a fine layer of blond-brown hair, was as defined. He was gorgeous. Hot, ripped...

So very off-limits.

'Morning,' she said, shocked to hear her voice sounding deeper than normal and a little sultry.

His eyes darted between her, the blanket on the grass and the teething ring Greta had left behind. 'Where's Mat?'

'Greta has him.'

Bo nodded. His eyes met hers and she was pulled into a glinting green fire as he took in what she was wearing. His eyes meandered down her body and over her breasts. Annoyingly, her nipples puckered, and his lips quirked. His gaze moved down her flat stomach and she felt the heat of his gaze on her legs, between her legs. She saw him swallow and watched as he pushed back his hair with one forearm.

His erection tented his shorts, and Ollie knew he liked what he saw. He was as attracted to her as she was to him. She'd been hoping that he'd be the one to keep the situation professional, their interactions on an even keel. She was wrong.

Damn this was not good. She really, really wanted to kiss him, to lay her hands on that big, masculine, oh-so-strong body. It had been a while, so she desperately wanted his arms around her, his mouth covering hers...

And the desire burning in his eyes told her he wanted that too.

'We shouldn't act on our mutual attraction...that would complicate matters.'

Ollie appreciated the fact that he could be honest about their attraction, that he didn't pussy-foot around and pretend it wasn't happening. She appreciated people being candid and preferred to look at situations as they were, not how she wanted them to be.

'I know,' she agreed, rubbing the back of her neck. 'I don't sleep with my employers.'

'And I don't sleep with my employees,' he countered.

Ollie nodded and folded her arms across her chest, locking them in tight so that she didn't throw herself at him. She didn't recognise herself: she'd never reacted so intensely, so quickly, to a man. She felt as if she was a piece of kindle soaked in petrol and he was an unexpected spark...

Together she was certain they could burn down Copenhagen.

Ollie watched as Bo pulled in some deep breaths, and she did the same. The crackle of electricity that arced between them faded to a low buzz and, now that she wasn't feeling overwhelmed by lust, Ollie could hear the sound of Greta talking to Mat, the sound of the washing machine churning and the little boy laughing.

She should be looking after Mat right now, making his breakfast and planning a new routine to make the baby feel more settled. She should not be out here, waiting and hoping to be kissed by her boss. Bo was paying her an extraordinary amount of money to give his son the best care she could, and she was doing yoga and dreaming of snogging his father.

She might be leaving the industry but she could leave with her head held high, knowing that she'd done the best she could. She shuffled down the wall and stepped away from Bo. 'If you'll excuse me, Mr Sørenson...'

'Look, Ollie, we don't need to be so formal.'

She gave him a tight smile. 'I really think we do. It might...' she hesitated, looking for the right word '... help.'

Ollie walked away from him, knowing that she did need to keep the formalities, and a considerable amount of personal space, between her and her employer. She didn't allow herself to have affairs with her employers and Bo would be no different.

Neither would she get attached. She'd look after Mat for two months and move on. Not staying still, not allowing roots to find any soil, was what she did best.

Two nights later, Bo walked Mat up and down the living room, jiggling his sobbing son in his arms. It was Ollie's night off, he was on Mat duty and he couldn't get his son to stop crying. He'd changed his nappy, given him a bottle and rocked him incessantly but Mat had yet to stop howling. Bo thought that there was a good possibility that he would cave and start crying soon too. It was three-forty in the morning and he'd had about an hour's sleep. He had a client meeting in the morning to talk over the changes he'd made to his racing yacht and, thanks to Mat falling into his life, he hadn't done enough preparation. It was going to be a disaster but, right now, Bo was too tired to care.

He'd heard that having a kid was hard, but this was beyond ridiculous. How did parents do this day in and day out without going off their heads? He missed his life, he missed his sleep, he missed work and he missed making decisions without having to think about how they affected anyone else.

Bo looked down into his little boy's miserable face and guilt rushed through him, as cold as a melting glacier. His parents had resented him; they'd never admitted it but, even with the help of au pairs and nannies, he'd seriously cramped their style. He'd felt as if he was a burden, a hanger-on, standing outside the circle of their lives.

He'd never make his child feel anything but loved. And if that meant sacrificing some sleep, not being at his best at a client meeting or delegating some responsibility at work, that was what he'd do. He could be a dad. He *was* a dad. This was his life now.

His life had flipped over and inside out, but becoming a single father was as far as he would go. Despite coming close to kissing Ollie the other day, nothing would, or could, happen between them. She wasn't going to morph from being a nanny to being Mat's mummy: she was a short-term solution, not a long-term fixture. He'd paid for her help but he couldn't allow any woman into his life on a long-term basis; he couldn't trust anyone with that much of himself. He couldn't allow his feelings to take over, to crack open his hard carapace.

He'd wanted to be loved once and, when that love had never come, he'd vowed he'd never seek it again. Rejection hurt, and not being loved enough, or at all, would rip his soul apart. He'd avoid that, thank you very much.

'Please stop crying, Mat,' Bo whispered, his lips on Mat's blond hair. 'I beg of you, just please stop.'

Bo moved Mat up onto his shoulder and held him under his butt, his big hand almost covering Mat's back, which he gently patted. Mat snuffled, yawned and Bo held his breath. Was this it? Was he finally going to go to sleep? He'd do anything...

'Waah...!'

Bo walked over to the nearest wall and banged his forehead against it.

'No luck, huh?'

Bo turned to see Ollie standing in the doorway to the hall, her light cotton dressing-gown open over a vest top and a small pair of sleeping shorts. She was barefoot and he caught the shimmer of the fine silver ankle chain she wore around her left ankle. Her hair was all over the place and there was a pillow crease on her left cheek.

'Sorry, I thought this house was big enough that his crying wouldn't wake you up,' Bo said as she walked across the room to where he stood. Bo caught a whiff of citrus, wondered whether it was her soap or shampoo and told himself to concentrate.

Ollie placed the back of her hand on Bo's forehead and shook her head. 'He doesn't have a temperature,' she observed, her hand on Mat's back. 'I don't think he's sick.'

'Then why won't he stop crying?' Bo demanded, feeling as though he was hanging onto the last strand of a very frayed rope.

'He's teething,' Ollie told him. She slipped her finger into Mat's mouth and, surprisingly, Mat let her. When she removed it, she nodded. 'Yep, his gum is swollen.'

Right. Teething was the last thing he would've checked for.

'We can give him a spoonful of a mild, perfectly harmless painkiller, if you feel comfortable doing that,' Ollie suggested.

'You bought him medicine?' Bo asked, following Ollie as she walked back to Mat's nursery.

In the shadows of the dark nursery, he saw the flash of white teeth and the gleam in her eye. 'I bought him *everything.* Didn't you see how much I spent?' Ollie asked as they moved further into the room.

He had and he didn't much care. He had money and, right now, if it meant Mat getting some sleep, and him getting some too, he'd pay anything he needed to. Ollie walked into the bathroom attached to Mat's room and Bo heard the cabinet opening and closing. She returned with a tiny syringe filled with liquid and placed it in Mat's mouth, depressing the plunger.

'It should work fairly quickly,' Ollie told him. Bo felt Mat's body getting heavier, and he'd sunk a little more into him. Dared he hope?

When Ollie placed her small, warm hand on his bare forearm, he looked down into her lovely, sympathetic face. 'I didn't know what to do. What if you weren't here?'

'You would've figured it out. You would've done an Internet check, called a doctor or taken him to an all-night clinic. You would've made a plan,' Ollie reassured him. 'You've got this, Bo. I have faith in you.'

I have faith in you…

Five little words but ones he hadn't heard since his grandfather, the only person who'd believed in him, had passed. They filled Bo with strength and peace. And, as he watched Ollie walk away, he was terrified of how much he'd liked hearing those words on her lips—how much her good opinion of him had come to mean to him in such a short time.

What he felt for her was sexual, not emotional: he didn't do emotions. Yes, he wanted her—under him, over him, up against the wall. But that was just lust—and nothing else but lust. He needed to remind her of that.

Bo followed her into the hallway and his fingers locked around her wrist. She spun around to face him and he saw everything he was feeling in her rich brown eyes. Desire, need, want and confusion Ollie looked up into his face, raw with need, and she waited for him to speak. He was an articulate guy; why was he struggling to find words? And, when they did arrive, they weren't what he'd intended to say.

'I know that nothing can happen between us, and I would never presume that something could. But…but if I do not taste you soon, kiss you senseless just once, I might lose my mind.'

Ollie knew Bo was waiting for her to say something, to permit him to kiss her. She also knew that if she said no then he would step away and they'd never mention this encounter again. The thing was…she couldn't say no. It wasn't a word her tongue could wrap itself around. Yes… She could manage yes.

She was normally so clear-thinking. How could he confuse her like this? She could figure that out later. Right now there was only one thing she wanted from him and that was for him to push his body into hers and kiss her as fiercely as he could. Ollie lifted her hand and placed it on the back of Bo's neck, surprised at how hot he was. Standing on her tiptoes, she placed her other hand on his chest and placed her lips on his. For a few seconds, she wondered if she'd made a huge mistake, because he stood statue-still.

Then his lips softened under hers, they nibbled and explored, and his hands came up to hold her face, his thumbs gently brushing her cheekbones. But, if this was the only kiss she was going to get from him, she wanted more than her face to be touched, her lips to be explored. She wanted to be so close to him that a sheet of paper couldn't slide between them. She wanted his tongue in her mouth, his hand on her breast and her stomach pushing into his erection.

As if he heard her unspoken demands, Bo changed tempo and Ollie knew the exact moment that the fuse inside him detonated. His hands dropped, one to her breast the other to cup her left butt cheek, and he pulled her up and into him, pushing his shaft into her stomach. His tongue slid into her mouth, hot and demanding, and lust and heat skittered through her. Her nipple bloomed under the swiping motion of his thumb and she groaned when he pushed aside the fabric of her sleeping vest. Sliding her hands under his shirt, she explored his back, running her fingers down the deep valley of her spine, allowing them to drift over his hard, well-shaped and truly spectacular butt. Under her hands, he felt perfect.

'You are so very gorgeous,' Bo muttered, yanking his mouth off hers to mutter the words.

Frustrated because he'd stopped kissing her, she gripped his shirt in her hands and twisted the fabric, lifting her chin and mouth in a silent plea for him to kiss her again. The world stopped and faded away when he kissed her and she rather liked it.

'Bo, kiss me again…' She murmured the words against his lips.

He rested his forehead on hers, his knees bending to make allowance for their difference in height. 'I can't,' he told her, his breath ragged. 'If I start kissing you again, I swear I'll take you up against this wall.'

She simply looked at him, unable to find a flaw in that plan.

'Olivia!' he said, his hands tightening on her biceps. 'This is crazy. We can't—you *know* we can't.'

Why not? There was no one in the house but Mat and he wouldn't care.

Wow, she really was losing her mind. One kiss and she was ready to fall into bed with him, forgetting that he was paying her salary and that she was there to look after his child. Ollie released his shirt and she placed her hands on the wall behind her, her palms flat against the surface. Bo pulled away from her and he gripped her hips with white-tipped fingers. He didn't look embarrassed about his tented bottoms so she figured she shouldn't be either. She closed her eyes and pulled in a few deep breaths until her blood came off the boil and her brain started working again.

Ollie looked away and pulled her bottom lip between her teeth. She'd been unprofessional in the extreme, and if Sabine got wind of this—friend or not, mentor or not—she'd be fired. Thank goodness that this would be her last professional gig: if she messed up and slept with an employer, it wouldn't affect her ability to get any more work. She had work, just not the kind she wanted.

Anyway, you are not going to sleep with your client, Olivia.

Well, she was going to try not to. As hard as she could.

The thing was, nobody had ever made her feel so jittery before, so alive, as if she'd been plugged into a source of universal energy. She just needed to look into Bo's craggy face and the space between her legs heated and her body wanted.

It craved.

Stupid thing. What on earth was wrong with her?

'We can't do this, Ollie,' Bo told her, his voice sounding gruff. 'It was a mistake.'

A mistake. Of all the words he could've chosen to use, that was the one that hurt her the most. It was the word that her parents had used when she'd told them she wanted to go travelling; what Fred had used when he'd called off their engagement; the word Sabine had used when she'd told Ollie she was getting in too deep with

Rebecca, as if loving that little girl and giving her all that attention could be a mistake.

Mistake, mistake, mistake.

She'd made so many of them, including trusting Fred and making that deal with her parents to return to work after five years.

No, she couldn't think about the past now. She wouldn't add tears to this already embarrassing interlude. Ollie looked down so that he couldn't see her eyes, silently cursing. She blinked rapidly and, when she was sure they were clear, she looked up again. In the morning, she'd resume her search for a permanent nanny for him, someone to take her place. She needed something to take her mind off what had just happened, and it would also be a good reminder that her position here was temporary and that she was just passing through his life.

Straightening her shoulders, she forced herself to smile. 'That should never have happened, but it did. But maybe we could forget it?'

There wasn't a snowball's chance in a volcano, but it sounded like something she should say.

Bo sent her a *'who are you kidding?'* look. 'We can try.'

CHAPTER SIX

A FEW DAYS LATER, Bo looked out of his study window and watched Ollie move her supple body from one yoga pose to another. Mat sat on the blanket next to her, and Ollie occasionally stopped to hand him a toy or to talk to him. She was incredibly patient and didn't seem to mind that he was interrupting her yoga routine.

Bo was grateful she wore a T-shirt over her brief exercise shorts, ones that hit her mid-thigh, although the shirt didn't cover much when she had her butt in the air. Bo told himself to walk away; he shouldn't be ogling his nanny and thinking about how her amazing body would feel under his hands. If he didn't, he'd walk out there and kiss her senseless again. And this time, he wasn't sure he could stop himself from going past the point of no return. Ollie, inexplicably, seemed to want him as much as he wanted her, so she wouldn't be the one to put the brakes on...

He had the hots for his nanny. It was so tacky, so Hollywood.

Forcing himself to turn away, Bo walked over to the drafting board in the corner of his study, knowing he needed to get some work done. He'd managed a little, not very much at all, and he was so far behind it was ridiculous. But it was still only the second week since Mat's arrival and he was taking the time for his son to get used to him. And for him to get used to Mat.

On his desk, his phone vibrated and Bo scooped it up, grimacing when he saw his mother's name on the screen. At some point, he'd have to tell her that she was a grandmother and it was news that wouldn't excite her. It was hard enough for her to see and spend time with Bo, and she wouldn't be prepared to give Mat any attention. There was no play in her emotional rope.

He greeted Bridget—he'd started calling her Bridget in his late teens to goad her, but had been quickly informed that she preferred it to 'Mum'. He rubbed the back of his neck as his mother launched into a description of the latest deal she'd concluded and how much money she made. Honestly, he didn't care.

'And you?' Bridget demanded. 'Are you on track to make your third-quarter projections?'

He had no idea. He presumed so. His accountant hadn't told him otherwise.

'Business is good, Bridget.' He grimaced at the design on his easel. It would be a lot better if he could finish his designs.

'You sound distracted, Boland,' she retorted. 'That's not like you. What's happened?'

Bo was not about to tell her about Mat over the phone. No, he'd need to ply her with a couple of martinis first before telling her she was a grandmother.

'I'm fine, just busy.'

She didn't speak for a few beats, and Bo knew it was her way to get him to fill the silence. Nope, that wasn't going to happen. He hadn't fallen for that trick since he'd been eight. Bridget eventually huffed and he easily imagined her blue eyes narrowed with frustration. Bridget didn't love him—he didn't think she even liked him—but she enjoyed the cachet of being his mother. And, like all self-centred people, she hated being out of the loop.

Tough. He hated the fact that she'd never tried to connect with him emotionally.

'So I presume I will see you at the ball tonight?' Bridget said, her voice taking on an extra edge of crispness.

Ball? What ball? 'Sorry, what are you talking about?'

'Darling...' Bo didn't react to the endearment; she called everyone darling. 'It's the social event of the season, and the last before everyone scatters to take their summer holiday. You RSVP'd months ago. I know you did, because I saw Freja's guest list, and you said you would attend with a guest.'

Bridget and Freja, along with a couple of their cronies, were the doyennes of the country's A-list social scene and were not to be crossed. Not if he wanted to keep getting invitations to the events his clients—the rich and famous, the people who were in the market to buy yachts—attended. The balls and cocktail parties were endlessly tedious but his attendance was expected and it was where many a deal was initiated.

'Henry Foo will be there,' Bridget stated, more than a little smugly.

Henry Foo? Really? He was a Hong Kong banker who'd recently purchased the famous Spirit of the East racing team. Bo had heard that Henry Foo was looking to upgrade. The Sørensons had a long history with the Spirit of the East team: his grandfather had designed one of their first winning yachts, and his father another. It would make history if he could design a third, incorporating the newest technology.

'Who are you bringing to the ball, darling? Do I know her?'

Bo closed his eyes and tipped his head back, his hand tightening around his phone. He'd meant to find a date, but he'd forgotten. And he could not rock up at the ball solo: that would a social faux pas, especially at such late notice.

Bo ended the call, swore and rubbed his hand over his face. He was in a world of hurt here, and he mentally ran through his long list of potential dates. It was time to start phoning around...

'Problem?' Ollie asked, walking into the room with Mat on her hip. Before he could answer, his housekeeper called Ollie's name and she turned round. Greta bustled into his study—it was like Copenhagen Central Station at rush hour this morning—and cooed at Mat before taking him from Ollie. His housekeeper was enamoured by his son and Mat spent a great deal of time with her on the mornings she cleaned his house—somehow she managed to get everything done with Mat on her hip.

Bo looked at the folder in Ollie's hands and knew she wanted him to look at the CVs for a nanny to replace her. The idea made his head, and heart, hurt.

'Well?' Ollie demanded after Greta had left the room. 'What's wrong?'

Bo looked down at his phone and sighed, frustrated. 'I need a date for a function tonight—one I forgot about, and that's very unlike me.'

Ollie rested the water bottle against her flushed cheek and he thought that she looked stunning with her skin flushed pink from exercise. 'It's no wonder you forgot.

Mat's arrival was bound to push other less important things out of your head.'

He pushed an agitated hand through his hair. 'Normally I'd send my apologies and blow it off, but I've just heard the hostess has arranged for me to meet a man I want to impress.'

Ollie sat on the arm of the nearest chair and crossed one slim leg over the other. 'You don't strike me as being someone who needs validation. Why this guy? And why do you need to impress him?'

She was so direct, so honest in her questions and pointed in her remarks. He liked her ability to cut through the nonsense and hone in on what was important.

'He's just bought a sailing operation that my family has a long association with. He wants to upgrade with some new yachts and I want to design them. Whenever they've needed a new direction and technology in the past, a Sørenson has provided it. First, my grandfather, then my father. I want to carry on the tradition.'

'Ah, the weight of family expectation,' Ollie murmured. He heard the irritation in her voice and wanted to know how her family annoyed her, wanted to find out more. But, before he could, Ollie spoke again. 'It sounds like an awesome opportunity. You should go.'

That was the plan. 'I need a date.'

Ollie raised her eyebrows. 'Surely you're big enough and old enough and sophisticated enough to attend a function on your own, Sørenson?'

He narrowed his eyes at her jibe. 'I said I'd take a date and that's what I have to do.'

Ollie shrugged, looking unconcerned 'Then you'd better find one.' She shoved her tongue into her cheek. 'If you tell me where to find it, I'll fetch your little black book for you. That's what you older folk use, isn't it?'

Older folk?

'I'm thirty-eight years old,' Bo retorted.

'You are nearly ten years older than me—that's practically a generation.'

He caught the amusement in her eyes and knew she was trying to wind him up. He felt laughter bubbling up inside him and shook his head. He'd laughed more, and felt more, since she'd arrived in his life than he had in the past ten years. Somehow she made his house seem lighter, his responsibilities to Mat not quite so petrifying and she made him think he could be a good dad to Mat.

And she was also the solution to his current predicament. Why should he go out of his way to find a date when a gorgeous woman was standing in front of him? 'Because you made that crack about me being old, you can be my date tonight.'

Ollie held up her hand, her curls shimmying as she shook her head. 'At a ball? Uh…no.'

'Uh…yes.'

Yep, he could easily imagine walking into Freja's incredible Carrera marble hallway with Ollie on his arm, standing at the double-volume doors, waiting for her butler to announce their entrance into the room. She was nothing like the women who normally accompanied him to social events, those cool, haughty blondes who expected the world to stop when they walked into a room. And, if Ollie agreed to go with him, then he wouldn't have to spend the next hour looking for a date, apologising for the late request and stroking some egos. He was an extremely eligible bachelor, and he'd quickly find someone who'd say yes, but he might have to do a small amount of grovelling first.

He really couldn't be bothered. Not when the woman he most wanted to take to the ball was standing right in front of him. Yes, he knew it wasn't a good idea—he was blurring the lines between work and play—but he was tired of downplaying his attraction to Ollie. His hands itched to touch her stunning body and desperately wanted her wide, full mouth under his again. He wanted to hear the hitch in her breath as he pulled her into his body... He didn't know how he'd found the willpower to stop kissing her the other day. The lower portions of his body were still unimpressed.

But getting involved with Ollie—Mat's nanny—would be flirting with danger. Or...would it? Maybe she was the perfect person to have a fling with because her time in Copenhagen was limited. She'd told him that she needed to be back in London at the end of the summer. By then, he'd not only feel far more confident in his abilities to take care of Mat, but the initial excitement of a new rela-tionship—fling, affair—would be starting to fade. They wouldn't have to call it quits because there would always be an end date, a time to stop.

Why hadn't he thought about this before? 'So? What do you say?' he asked Ollie.

Ollie folded her arms across her chest and frowned at him. 'I'm here to look after Mat, Sørenson, not be your last-minute date. And, even if I wanted to go, who would look after Mat while we were out?'

That was easy. He looked past her to see Greta, who was vacuuming the passage with Mat on her hip. His boy looked as if he was having the time of his life. 'Hey, Greta?' he called.

Greta turned and poked her head round the frame of his study door. 'Is there any chance you could babysit Mat tonight if I can persuade Ollie to come with me to the Møller ball?'

Greta's eyes widened in surprise, as he'd known they would. The ball raised millions of euros for good causes and the next day the residents of Copenhagen, and the rest of the country, discussed who wore what, and who went with whom. Greta nodded enthusiastically. 'Of course I will. Ollie, you must go!'

'I don't think so,' Ollie told her.

'But they have fireworks and entertainment, and the food is cooked by one of the country's greatest chefs! You will see one of the oldest and grandest houses in the country.'

Ollie, damn her, still didn't look impressed. 'Even if I wanted to go, which I'm not sure I do, I don't have a dress or shoes or anything like that.'

There were some perks to being a billionaire and one of them was having a personal stylist on a retainer. Carla purchased his clothes, put his outfits together and made sure he never made a fashion mistake. Clothes weren't something he spent a lot of time thinking about. 'If that wasn't a problem, would you say yes?'

Ollie looked like a deer caught in the headlights, a little excited and even more terrified. 'Oh, come on, Bo! There has to be someone else you could ask.'

There were several someones but he didn't want to take any of them; he wanted Ollie to accompany him to the Møller Ball. He wanted to see the house through her eyes, watch her as she marvelled over the firework display, the fire eaters and the trapeze artists. He was a little blasé and a lot cynical—he'd seen and done it all—but maybe, through her, he'd see things a little differently. He held her eyes and waited for her answer. As he expected, she tried another way to wriggle her way out of it.

'I can't ask you to pay for a dress and shoes I will never wear again.'

She hadn't asked him to pay, but he would. He couldn't expect her to fund an outfit suitable for the very lavish function. And, if he never worked again, he had enough money to last several lifetimes. He wouldn't notice the cost of her designer dress or shoes. 'That's not an issue. If you give me your sizes, I will arrange for my stylist to bring over several outfits for your consideration.'

'You have a stylist?' Ollie asked before sighing. 'Of course you do.'

She bit her bottom lip and Bo had to stop himself from crossing the room to her and soothing the bite mark with his tongue. She was as sexy as sin in her skimpy exercise clothes, and he knew she'd look stunning in a ball gown and high heels. Resisting her was a losing battle. It was a good thing that he'd decided to surrender.

'Of course she's going to go,' Greta told him. He'd forgotten that she'd been listening in, that she was still holding Mat. What was it about Ollie? She made the world around him fade away until she was all that remained. Bo rubbed his lower jaw with his hand. He'd thought that Mat dropping into his life had been a life-changing event, and it was, but Ollie's arrival was also causing waves in his previously still-as-a-pond life. He felt as if he were standing in an unsteady bucket in the middle of the Bering Sea.

It was terrifying, exciting and, weirdly, thrilling.

Greta looked at Ollie, pursing her lips. 'She's an eight, foot size UK seven.'

Bo looked at Ollie, waiting for her confirmation. 'She's not wrong,' she reluctantly admitted. Throwing her hands up into the air, she nodded. 'If you can arrange a suitable dress and shoes, Cinderella will accompany you to the ball.'

Eight and seven, clothes and shoes. Do not mix them up or you'll never hear the end of it. 'I think it would be pushing it to call me Prince Charming,' he told Ollie.

She handed him an impertinent smile. 'I didn't,' she pointed out. 'You're more of a *nisse*—or do you call him a *tomte*?'

A *nisse* or *tomte* was a short-tempered troll common in Danish folklore. Bo didn't know whether to be amused at her quick wit, impressed that she'd been reading up on Denmark or offended by the reference.

Unable to decide, he shook his head and picked up his phone to call the stylist and make her very happy indeed.

The stylist brought ten dresses for Ollie to try and in the end she settled for a fluid, sleeveless, blindingly white evening gown with a low neckline and a far too high ruffled slit that exposed her right thigh. A bright-red silk rose rested on her hip and it gave the gown a hint of fun and colour.

Ollie looked at her reflection in the freestanding mirror. The make-up-artist-slash-hairdresser who'd accompanied the stylist had pulled her hair back into a complicated twist and she found it hard to recognise her reflection. She looked sophisticated and stunning, nothing like the down-to-earth nanny she prided herself on being. Her skin glowed and her make-up was light but her lips were the exact colour of the rose on her hip. She looked like someone who would be at home attending a ball hosted by an influential family at one of Denmark's oldest houses, on the arm of the country's most eligible bachelor.

She didn't feel as if she belonged anywhere—not at the ball, not as a nanny and definitely not in London as an accountant. She felt like a fish out of water and had no idea where to find her pond. And what was she thinking, accepting the invitation to accompany Bo to this ball? It was highly unprofessional and she was breaking the cardinal rule of being a good nanny: do not blur the line between the professional and the personal. The problem was that she wanted to get very personal with Bo, as soon as possible.

Ollie glared at her reflection, upset with herself. Yes, Bo was a very good-looking guy—male magazine-cover sexy—and he was smart and successful. But he was her boss...

Normally she wasn't a slave to her libido, and she wasn't someone who galloped into relationships. She took her time and made clever decisions. It took her a while to open up and allow someone behind her walls. It had taken her three months to agree to date Fred, and another two months before she'd slept with him. Agreeing to marry him had required a lot of thought. After a few weeks and many sleepless nights, Ollie had eventually decided they could make their marriage work.

After loving and losing Becca, and realising that Fred was not only an unsympathetic jerk but also a cheat, she'd built her barriers higher and retreated further into herself. She rarely dated and she hadn't had a lover since Fred.

But Bo made her feel things she shouldn't. He made her want, he made her burn and, yes, he made her yearn. He made her feel unsettled and off-balance and she knew she should put more space between them. Because she was fantasising about her boss, because thoughts of him naked bombarded her—him sliding into her and making her sigh and scream—she knew she should be even more professional than she normally was.

So what was she doing, accompanying Bo to this function, allowing him to pay for her dress, her make-up, her hair and the silver three-inch heels on her feet? Why couldn't she stop thinking about how good they'd be in bed? Why couldn't she stop wishing for a repeat, and more, of their fire-hot kiss? She wasn't a woman who lost her head, but he could make hers spin.

If she was clever, she'd pull off this dress, wash her face and tell him that he was going alone, that she was pretty sure the world wouldn't stop turning if he didn't arrive with a woman on his arm. But tonight she didn't want to be Ollie the nanny, she wanted to be Ollie his date, the woman he looked at with masculine appreciation. For the first time in years, she wanted to be an object of desire.

Yes, it was a very bad idea, but she was going to the ball. She hoped she wouldn't end up regretting it.

CHAPTER SEVEN

IN THE SOPHISTICATED, double-height hallway of the Møllers' wonderful house, Bo placed his hand low on Ollie's bare back and thanked the waiter for their champagne. Ollie took hers and lifted the glass to her lovely red lips, and he noticed the fine tremble in her hand.

Around them, elegantly dressed couples mingled in the enormous hallway, caught up in conversation before entering the massive reception room on the right of the hallway. He smiled at an acquaintance and looked down at Ollie's lovely face. Despite her heels, he still had a few inches on her, and he could see the trepidation in her eyes and knew she was feeling out of her depth.

She shouldn't—she looked utterly ravishing. He'd expected his stylist to come up with something nice for her to wear but the ice-white dress against her light-brown skin was stunning and showed off her slim but strong body to perfection. Occasionally the ruffles of her dress would part, drawing attention to a long and shapely leg. She looked ravishing and, yes, ravishing her was something he couldn't wait to do.

Man, he was in a world of trouble here.

Ollie looked at her champagne glass and a smile curved her lips. 'This is great champagne,' she told him.

He grinned. It should be: it was a one of the best champagnes in the world. 'You do look lovely, Olivia.'

Ollie tipped her head to the side and lifted her thin, arched eyebrows. 'Olivia?'

He shrugged. Her full name was strong and lovely, gracious even. 'Ollie' didn't suit her, not tonight. 'How did you come to be called Ollie?' he asked, steering her towards the reception area.

'I have four brothers, so I got lumped with a boy's name,' she explained. 'My ex-fiancé called me Olivia sometimes.'

She'd been engaged? Bo tugged her to the side of the room and they stood in front of eight-feet-high windows decorated with pure silk, fuchsia-coloured curtains. Pieces of incredible art dotted the walls but he only had eyes for Ollie. Nothing painted by Reuben or Vermeer could compete with the lovely woman standing next to him. 'How long have you been unengaged?' he asked, trying to sound casual and missing by a mile.

'Ah, for a few years now,' Ollie replied, her eyes not meeting his.

He caught the flash of hurt in her eyes, the twist of her lips. 'What happened?' he asked, confused by his curiosity. He'd never cared about his lovers' pasts before; it had never been a factor, mostly because they'd never lasted long enough for it to be an issue. He was also in his late thirties and knew what had happened before his arrival was none of his business. But, with Ollie, he couldn't help feeling annoyed and a little jealous.

Ollie took her time replying. 'When I needed his support the most, when I needed him to step up and be there for me, to listen and not try to fix the situation, he couldn't give me the support and empathy I needed.'

The sadness in her voice couldn't be missed and Bo knew it had been caused by something other than their break-up. She'd been hurt deeply and her ex's behaviour had compounded that hurt.

'How long were you together?' Bo asked, wondering why he was still asking questions, the conversational equivalent of jabbing a sore tooth with his tongue.

'We met in our first year of university. He dropped out, joined the army and is now a captain in the Grenadiers. We had a very long-distance relationship for most of our time together and maybe that's why it lasted longer than it should've. In hindsight, I don't think we knew each other very well,' she admitted.

'There's nothing like living together to get to the heart of a person very quickly,' Bo said. 'Take us, for instance—you've only been in my life and house a short time, but I know that you need three cups of coffee to wake up, that you are more patient with children than you are with adults and that you are struggling to make a decision.'

Her eyes widened and her mouth dropped open in surprise. 'Why would you think that?' she asked.

She had the worst poker face in the world. 'Eh, it might be the fact that you spend a lot of time staring off into space and you bite the inside of your cheek when you do it.'

A hit of pink flooded her face and she looked younger than her twenty-eight years. 'Well, I've learned some things about you too,' Ollie told him, lifting her chin. Oh, he enjoyed her fighting spirit, and liked that she gave as good as she got.

He leaned a shoulder into the wall, his tuxedo brushing the gilt frame of a Monet. 'Really? Like what?'

'That you are completely in love with Matheo and your emotions scare you. You never expected to love him this much. You thought he would slide into your life and you'd be able to keep your emotional distance.'

Well, yes. It was his turn to feel shocked, but he hoped he hid it better than Ollie did. He considered denying her words but didn't see the point. 'You're right, I didn't expect to feel so emotionally connected to him so quickly.'

'He is your son, Bo, that's what happens between parents and children,' she pointed out.

Not always, he wanted to tell her. Sometimes parents had children and didn't feel much for them. His mother didn't love him. Then again, as the spoiled only child of a media mogul, she'd never been taught to love anybody. His father had never spent any time with him; partying and being seen had been far more important than spending time with his son.

And, at that moment, Bo made a conscious decision, a silent promise that he would never neglect his son the way his father had him. He'd never put himself, or his work, first. But wasn't that what he was doing tonight— leaving Mat with Greta to land a client? Had he already failed his first test?

'Good grief, you look like you've sucked on an ultra-bitter lemon,' Ollie commented. 'Whatever is the matter?'

'I left my son to attend a ball so that I could land a client,' Bo told her, his voice sounding a little strangled.

She nodded. 'Yes, you did. And why is that suddenly a huge problem?'

'I don't want to neglect him, Olivia. I *won't* neglect him. He has to know that he's not second best, or an afterthought, or way down on my list of priorities.'

Ollie placed a hand on his arm, and through his tuxedo

and his cotton dress shirt he felt the heat of her hand. 'Bo, when we left Mat was asleep; he doesn't even know that you aren't there. And, while I firmly believe that you as his primary caregiver should spend most of your nights at home, you are still allowed a life. Kids are smart—they know when they are wanted or not—and you spending a night out of the house now and then isn't a big deal. In fact, it's important that you do.'

He kept his eyes on hers, his panic receding at her soothing voice. 'Why?'

'Because, if you don't, you will go off your head. You're a new dad—you were Bo before and, like any single parent, it's not healthy to have your life completely consumed by your child.'

He took her hand and squeezed her fingers, keeping his fingers linked in hers. 'This would be so much harder if you weren't around, Olivia.'

'Well, don't get too used to me—I'll be leaving soon-ish,' she told him. He thought she'd aimed to sound crisp, but he heard a hint of sadness. Or maybe he was projecting his feelings onto her. He couldn't imagine her leaving, and didn't want to. She'd slid into his life and Mat's without so much as causing a ripple and, in some ways, it felt as though she'd always been there, a part of the furniture and the fabric of the house, in the nicest way possible.

It seemed right to look up from working at his desk in the mornings to see her stumbling to the kitchen, some-times with Mat on her hip, sometimes without, yawn-ing as she made herself a cup of coffee and working his complicated coffee machine with practised ease even though she was still half-asleep. Watching her do yoga in the garden was a pleasure—she was hot. He often found himself laughing at the silly things she said to Mat, at her dry commentary on her yoga skills.

He'd spent a few mornings at work, at meetings he couldn't miss, but for the first time in his life his entire focus wasn't on his business, it was on his house and what was happening within it. He frequently wondered what Ollie and Mat were up to and resented time spent away from his son.

And his son's nanny.

No woman had ever intrigued him as Ollie did. No one had ever made him want to scrape that superficial layer and see what lay beneath her smooth skin and within those deep-brown eyes. He wanted to know her history, what made her tick, what twists and turns she'd taken to bring her to his son and him. Why he'd lucked out on having one of the Europe's best nannies looking after his son; the owner of the agency she worked for had been deeply serious when she'd made that claim.

That she was great for Mat was no surprise, and his little boy was calmer when she was around, less anxious. There was something about her energy that soothed, and it didn't only work on his little boy. Sometimes, while working on a design, he'd find himself getting frustrated and he'd lift his head and hear Ollie singing to Mat, or tickling him, their laughter mingling. He'd immediately feel calmer, more focused. When she was around, he felt both energised and relaxed, turned on and laid back. It was as if he existed in two states at one time, something that had never happened to him before.

And he liked her, more than any woman he'd met before. She was funny and smart, and he loved the fact that he didn't intimidate her, that she called a spade a spade and wasn't afraid to point out the mistakes he made with

Mat. But, instead of making him feel like he was incapable or clumsy, she gently guided him in all Mat-related tasks, pleased when he got things right or remembered something, and patient when he took a little longer to recall what he needed to do.

He was learning so much from her: not only how to look after Mat's physical needs but how to connect with his son on an emotional level. He'd scoffed when she'd suggested that he spend fifteen minutes reading to Mat before he put him in his cot to sleep—he'd protested, saying he was too young and wouldn't understand. But after two nights Bo had realised it wasn't about the words, or Mat's understanding, but about connecting with his son.

Unfortunately, she still had to remind him to cuddle Mat, something that didn't come naturally to him. He did love him, and understood that he should hug his son, but didn't know how to do it or how often. And that was a huge source of embarrassment. He was a grown man, but he had no idea how to express affection. So he copied Ollie, watching how she wrapped her arms around Matheo's little body and held him tight; how she kissed his cheek, ran her hand over his head and down his arm.

Initially, he'd felt weird, but he was getting better. He had to have this nailed before Ollie left. Mat's next nanny might not be as patient or, almost certainly, he might not have the same connection to her as he did to Ollie. If he didn't learn everything he could from Ollie now, he might be in big trouble down the line.

And why was she so attached to that end-of-summer date? Why couldn't she stay longer; why wasn't she flexible? There was so much he wanted to know about Olivia Cooper, far more than he needed to know about the woman who was looking after his son. Much more than he'd wanted to know about any woman before her.

And that terrified him.

The sound of a gong reverberated through the house and the guests started walking towards the dining room. Ollie, looking nervous again, slipped her hand into his, her fingers interlocking with his.

It was second nature to snatch his hand away, to detach his fingers from hers. His actions were partly because he wasn't affectionate, but mostly because he was in the habit of keeping a certain distance between himself and his female companions in public. There had been so many women in the past who'd tried to give the impression that they were more than friends, that he was their significant other, and hand-holding was something they'd all seemed to have in common. It was a way to silently shout, 'Look, I have him, he's mine'. Shutting down the hand-holding, not allowing them to rest their heads on his shoulder as they talked in a group and keeping his physical distance had been his way of showing the world that she was his date for the evening, not a potential love interest.

Bo looked down at Ollie and saw the hurt in her eyes, her flushed pink cheeks. He'd embarrassed her, and he hadn't meant to, but he couldn't let her or anyone think that she was anyone special, that she would be the one to snare him, to become the first Mrs Bo Sørenson.

That wasn't going to happen. Marriage and love weren't for him—they couldn't be. Not even with this woman who made him feel so much.

In the ladies' bathroom, Ollie cursed her burning eyes and blinked back her very unwelcome tears. Bo had treated her as if she had a contagious disease, and his jerking his hand away from hers had hurt more than it should have. She'd just wanted some reassurance that she was doing okay, to know that he wouldn't abandon her, but he'd made her feel like Typhoid Mary.

Yes, he was her boss, and maybe she'd stepped over the line, but hadn't this entire evening been one huge experiment in over-stepping? From the moment she'd agreed to accompany him to this ball, she'd jumped over the barrier between professionalism and personal, and now she was paying the price for being an idiot.

She was just the nanny doing the boss a favour.

Ollie looked at her reflection in the huge, framed mirror and thought that the bathroom was more suited to a hotel than someone's house. There were two stalls, two basins, a huge mirror and enough lotions and potions stocked by an exclusive cosmetic supplier to keep the hands of dozens of socialites soft and smooth.

Ollie washed her hands, checked that no mascara had landed on her cheeks and pulled her lipstick out of her clutch bag. She didn't need it but reapplying it would give her a minute, maybe two, before she had to pull up her big girl panties and walk back into that room where she felt she didn't belong.

For the first time in ages, she longed to be home, sitting at the battered table in her parents' kitchen, listening to her *gogo*, her mother's mother, when she'd been visiting from South Africa—recounting yet again how she'd met Nelson Mandela when he'd still been a young lawyer in Soweto.

Her eldest brother had studied in London, eventually become a UK citizen and had opened a branch of his family's business there. Before they'd established their business in the UK, her parents had both been staunch anti-apartheid activists, and people assumed her white dad was the privileged one, the one who'd gone to university. Actually, it was the other way round—it was her mum who came from a wealthy family and had studied at the top university in the country. Her dad's parents hadn't been able to afford to send him to university to further his studies. It was her dad who'd worked a ten-hours-a-day blue-collar job and who'd studied after hours for his accounting degree. As a result, both her parents felt a university education was a privilege and that it was never to be wasted.

Ollie understood where they were coming from but she wished they'd accept that she'd found something she loved better—okay, she'd never loved accountancy, she was just good at it—and that being a nanny was a good, steady job.

She'd been given five years of freedom, and in return she'd agreed that she would return to the UK and work for their accounting business for five years. It was time to pay the piper.

So, instead of getting herself in a state about the fact that her boss wouldn't hold her hand—*how old was she, thirteen?*—she should give up her dream of buying into Sabine's business and start planning her return to join the London branch of her parents' firm and a life filled with figures. And boredom.

As for Bo, well, even if she wasn't leaving and she was interested in a relationship with him—*she wasn't!*—he didn't do relationships and he wasn't into making any sort of commitments to anybody. According to the many articles about him she'd read online, he only ever engaged in brief affairs. So expecting him to hold her hand, expecting anything from him, was simply stupid.

And she was not a stupid girl. She was a girl who was leaving the country in less than two months and, in time, he'd be just another boss she'd worked for.

But as Ollie walked into that huge dining room, one of the last to sit down at the extra-long table, she saw Bo stand up to pull her chair out, his hot eyes on her face, a small, apologetic smile on his lips. Ollie reluctantly admitted he wasn't someone she'd easily forget.

Or forget at all. Worse than that, he was the one man she'd probably have a lot of trouble walking away from.

Maybe she was a stupid girl after all.

CHAPTER EIGHT

AFTER STANDING BACK to let Ollie into his house, Bo waved goodbye to Greta and closed the front door behind them. Conscious of her aching feet, as she wasn't used to wearing heels, Ollie kicked off her shoes and placed her clutch bag on the hallway table.

She bent over to massage one foot, then the other, thinking that it was his fault her feet were on fire. Despite his refusing to hold her hand, she'd spent half the evening in his arms, being expertly whirled around the dance floor. She silently thanked her *gogo*, who'd ferried her to ballet, tap, modern and ballroom dance lessons for most of her childhood and into her teens. She'd felt many eyes on them, and was grateful that the great and good of Danish society wouldn't judge her for having two left feet.

Picking up the hem of her dress from the floor, Ollie swallowed a yawn. She was in that weird state of feeling both energised and exhausted, and in a few hours she'd be waking up to look after Matheo. Nine-month-old little boys didn't care if you'd spent the night in a fancy dress, drinking lovely champagne: they wanted a fresh nappy, breakfast and attention. And not necessarily in that order.

Ollie walked from the hallway into the living room, Bo beside her. His hand came to rest on her bare lower back, his thumb swiping rhythmically against her skin, sending flickers of heat and sparks dancing across her skin. Right, so he couldn't hold her hand in public, but he could touch her in private.

She knew she should call him out on his actions and move away from him, but she loved that small connection, the heat he managed to generate with so little contact. She pulled in a hit of his aftershave, an understated scent reminding her of Italian lemons and fresh sea air. He looked gorgeous in his tuxedo. He had that clothes-horse body that was required for male models—wide shoulders, long legs, slim hips—and she could easily understand why so many eyes followed him around the room.

He was a stunning-looking specimen of a male in his prime...

And, man, she wanted him.

She shouldn't—it was such a bad idea—but she couldn't imagine padding down the hallway to her bedroom, shutting her door and going to bed alone.

Ollie hesitated, not sure what to do, and opted to walk over to the floor-to-ceiling window that looked onto the sound. Bo headed down the hallway to where Mat slept in his nursery. She heard his door open and then close a few minutes later.

Mat was asleep and they were alone.

'Would you like a drink?' Bo asked, his deep voice sounding rougher than normal.

She shouldn't, but a drink would give her an excuse to prolong this evening, to spend more non-nanny time with him. She nodded and she heard the sound of liquid being sloshed into a glass. When he approached her, coming to stand next to her at the window, she noticed that he'd shed his jacket, pulled off his tie and undone the top buttons of his shirt. Handing her a glass of cognac, he slowly, oh, so slowly, rolled up the cuffs of his shirt to reveal his muscled forearms. The low light of the single lamp turned the hair on his arms a light golden colour and glinted off the face of his expensive watch.

Ollie sipped, grateful for the burn of expensive liquor as it slid down her throat. She knew she should speak, but the words were stuck in her throat. There were words that she could say—*I want you* and *please take me to bed*—but she knew that if they walked down that road they'd make this situation far more complicated than it needed to be.

She was his employee, he was her boss.

It was unprofessional...

This would be her last nanny job...

All the above was true but she knew she would regret not kissing him, not sharing his bed, for the rest of her life... Being with him was a gift she could give herself.

Ollie watched as he picked up his glass and raised it to his lips. Her eyes met his and he watched her, his eyes hooded and glinting with...was that need? Want? Flat-out desire? A mixture of all three?

She pulled her bottom lip between her teeth, unable to break the eye contact. Needing fortification, she lifted her glass again but Bo snatched it out of her hand and banged it down on the closest table, causing the glass to tip over onto its side. Ollie watched the expensive liquid drip over the edge of the expensive table and hit the hardwood floor. They should clean it up, but neither of them made a move.

Her head felt extra-heavy when she lifted her eyes to look at Bo again, and this time she had no doubt what he wanted. It was in his eyes, blazing across his face, expressed in the tenting of his tuxedo trousers.

He wanted her...

They were about to cross a line, a pretty big one. He caught her hesitation and frowned. 'It's a big step, Ollie,' he stated, echoing her thoughts.

'I know,' she replied. 'But it's one I want to take. Do you?'

His 'oh, yeah' came quickly and those two words, and the relieved sigh he released, were all the reassurance she needed. His hands gripped her hips, pulling her into him. Ollie felt her breasts pushing into his hard chest, the hardness of his erection against her stomach. She wasn't a novice when it came to sex. She and Fred—when they'd seen each other—had had what she'd thought was a very healthy sex life. But she'd never felt this shaky and off-balance with her ex. With Bo's green eyes on hers, she felt as if he was striding into her soul, looking around and taking stock.

His sexy mouth, with its thinner top lip, headed for hers and Ollie realised that this was what she'd been waiting for—more of the heat they'd shared a few days ago. But, while she thought they might've left scorch marks on the wall in the hallway when they'd kissed, it was nothing to being on the receiving end of Bo's unleashed passion now.

This was a grown-up kiss, a '*take everything I have*' kiss, a kiss for the ages, a kiss to measure against for the rest of her life. He pushed his fingers into her hair and held her head to his, and his other hand rested low on her back, keeping the lower half of her body tight against his. She felt captured and enveloped, but she didn't care, and she had no wish to escape.

As his tongue slid into her mouth, she tasted cognac and the faint hint of the cigar he'd smoked before they'd left the ball. But her overwhelming sensation was his need to take her, claim her and make her his.

She'd never been a fan of being possessed, of cleaving herself to a man—she was far too independent and modern-thinking for that. But something in Bo's kiss made her think of plundering Vikings and dominant men who scooped up maidens and threw them over their shoulders.

Right now, she got the appeal. He was elementally male, primordially alpha, and she loved it. She loved the way he was making her feel: sexy, desired and oh, so female.

There was power in being desired so fiercely by a man like this, to feel his impatience in his kiss, to know that you were the one he wanted. Ollie felt like a princess, a goddess, someone who had a great deal more power and allure than she usually did.

Unable to help herself, her hands skated up and down his muscled back, and she pushed her body into his, needing to get closer. She explored his neck with her fingers, allowing his soft hair to slide over her fingers, running her hand over his muscled shoulders. Needing more, needing to feel his skin, she pulled his shirt from the band of his trousers and made a muffled noise when she encountered hot male skin. She enjoyed the sizzle, the way his kiss deepened when she pushed her finger between the band of his trousers and under his briefs. She couldn't get very far, and her hands moved to the front of his trousers, seeking the snap that kept them together.

His hands left her hips to hold hers against his stomach and he wrenched his mouth away to look down at her with glittering eyes. 'Are we doing this, Ollie?'

She knew that if she backed away she would regret it for the rest of her life. For one night she wanted to be the object of his attention, the reason his world turned. She needed to feel him shatter beneath her hands, to know she'd made him gasp and groan.

'I want you,' she told him, deciding to be honest. What was the point of lying when he could see her pointed nipples and her skin flushed from need?

'You work for me,' he reminded her, resting his forehead against hers, his hands still holding hers so that she couldn't touch him. And she wanted to, very much. But she hadn't had sex since she and Fred had broken up three years ago and she never had one-night stands. This was totally out of the ordinary for her and she was winging it here. The only thing she knew was that she couldn't walk away from him, not now, not tonight.

'We are adults,' she told him. 'We can separate work from pleasure. This has nothing to do with my job, with Mat, with why I came to Copenhagen,' she continued. Then she remembered how Bo must normally deal with situations like this. 'This is only about sex, about some bed-based fun. I don't do commitment; I won't do commitment. And I'm leaving anyway...'

She sounded so much more confident than she felt. And why wasn't he jumping all over this? Why wasn't he leading her to his bed? Why was he even hesitating? He was the king of no commitment, so what was his problem?

Deciding that there was nothing else she could say to persuade him, she cupped her hand around his strong neck, lifted her thigh, the ruffled split giving her room to move, and draped it over his hip. Dragging her mouth across his, she whispered against it, 'I need you to take me to bed, Bo. Can you do that?'

She knew he wanted her, and she wanted him—more than she'd ever wanted anybody or anything in her life— so she decided to stack the odds in her favour. Moving her hand down his chest, she skimmed her fingers over his stomach…yep, there was a six-pack under the fabric waiting to be explored. She cupped him, sighing when her hands couldn't cover the length of him, realising how big he was.

When his eyes deepened, flaring with lust, she knew that there would be no more talk, only action.

This might be a mistake, but it was hers to make and one she would never regret. She needed this experience. She needed to know him in the most intimate way a woman could know a man.

Ollie had used words he normally would—no expectations, no commitments, *blah-blah-blah*—but he was tired of doing the right thing, the clever thing, the sensible thing.

Right now, and for the rest of the night, he just wanted to feel.

All reservations about what they were doing, about this journey of discovery they were embarking on, gone, Bo released the air he'd been holding and stopped fighting temptation, currently wearing a long white dress. All night, he'd imagined, hoped and dreamed of watching the garment pool around her feet, exposing her to his hungry, needy gaze. He was going to get to love her and Bo felt like the luckiest man in the world. But he wasn't about to make love to her in front of this window or on a couch. No, he needed his massive bed, the space to stretch out, to move and to love her properly. They might only ever have this one night, a few hours until morning broke and reality intruded, and he was determined to make them count.

Scooping Ollie off her feet—was that a sigh of relief he'd heard?—he walked her down the hallway to the massive suite of rooms under another high, angled roof. He had a small sitting room and a big bathroom attached to either side of his room but to his mind, most importantly, dominating the centre of the room was his California king. The doors leading onto his private balcony and hot tub were open and in the darkness of the Norwegian summer he could see stars hanging low in the sky, close to the purple sea, and he enjoyed the warm, scented air blowing in from the sea. This was his space, his sanctuary, the place he came to relax. He never brought women back to his house, he always went to theirs—it was so much easier to leave! But it felt right that Ollie was the first woman to share his bed, his space.

When her feet hit the floor, he cupped her face and lowered his lips to hers, keeping his touch gentle. He wanted to savour and sip, to take his time exploring her curves and dips, the secret wonderland that was her body—this undiscovered and wonderful land he'd been given access to. He kissed her again, but her lips were a little hesitant, so he pulled away to look down at her. The difference in their height was exacerbated by the fact that she'd kicked off her sexy heels. He bent his knees so that their eyes were level.

'Are you okay?' he asked. 'Do you want to stop?'

If she said she did, he might just howl. But he'd take her back to her room and leave her there. No was no, no matter how far they'd travelled down this road.

She shook her head, then nodded. She looked as confused as he felt. 'Being in your bedroom sort of broke the crazy spell.'

The crazy spell—that was a good way to describe the wave of lust they'd surfed back in the living room. What they were doing was very real and a little scary, similar to the anticipation he felt when standing on the edge of a steep, untested ski slope, or diving off a boat into the blue ocean. But he also felt so, so alive...

Then Ollie looked up at him with her gorgeous, deep-brown, almost black eyes. 'Maybe we can...you know... just kiss again?'

Yes, they could do that—absolutely. Bo led her to the bed. 'Let's get comfortable while we do that, okay?'

Ollie, unembarrassed, hiked her dress up her thighs and climbed onto the bed, watching as he toed off his shoes and bent down to remove his socks. When he lay down next to her, she rolled into him, half-draping herself across his chest. He dragged his thumb over her cheekbone and explored the pretty shell of her ear. 'You are so beautiful,' he told her, his voice sounding as rough as sandpaper.

'You're pretty hot yourself,' Ollie told him, her fingers sliding inside his shirt to find bare skin. He ran his hand down the bumps of her spine and felt her shiver. Yeah, the heat was building. He pulled the grips from her hair, tossed them to the floor and watched, fascinated, as her hair fell to her shoulders and down her back. He picked one curl up and wound it around his finger, thinking it was so soft.

Wanting her to set the pace, his eyes caught hers again and she smiled, a feminine, secret smile that he recognised as being girl code for *'I'm going to blow your mind'*.

He had no problem with that. He really didn't.

Ollie scooted up onto her knees and held back her hair so that she could kiss him without him getting a mouthful of curls, but he pulled her hand away so that her hair hung like a wavy curtain on either side of their faces. Her curls tickled his cheek and his neck as he plundered her mouth, wanting to get them back to feeling wild and inhibited again. While still trying to kiss him, Ollie fumbled with the buttons of his shirt and, impatient to have her hands on him, he gripped the fabric at his collar and ripped the shirt apart, exposing his chest to her roving hands.

Ollie murmured her approval and her mouth moved across his jaw, down his neck and across his collarbone, tracing the lines of the geometric tattoo that flowed from his right pec across his shoulder.

'So sexy,' she murmured.

'Not as sexy as you,' he countered, meaning every word. And if she didn't get out of that dress, if he didn't get his tongue on her nipples or his hands between her legs some time soon, her dress was going the same way as his shirt. 'How attached are you to this dress?' he asked. He'd paid for it, but that meant nothing; she'd worn it, so it was hers.

Ollie's head snapped up. 'I rather like it. Why?'

He narrowed his eyes at her. 'Then get it off before I tear it off you.'

Yes, he sounded bossy, like the CEO barking orders his staff knew him to be. Ollie just grinned. 'You're bossy,' she told him, amused.

No, he was desperate. 'When I need to be,' he agreed. 'But that dress needs to come off.'

Ollie surprised him by flashing a heart-stopping grin, and Bo put his hand on his chest just to make sure that the organ responsible for pumping blood around his body was still working.

Ollie reached for the zipper under her left arm and, as she pulled it down, the fabric of her dress loosened and he forgot how to breathe. Ollie was almost naked and nothing else was important. Her dress fell to her waist and revealed her perky breasts, and her dark-cherry-coloured nipples. Her waist was tiny and Bo needed to see all of her immediately. Using his core muscles, he placed his hands on her bare hips and lifted her up, out of her dress and onto him, her legs straddling him leaving a frothy puddle of white fabric on his deep-brown comforter.

Ollie, naked except for the smallest and most pointless pair of panties he'd ever seen in his life—they covered nothing but a small strip of her mound—started playing with the snap of his trousers again. Pulling her down, Bo dragged his tongue over her nipple before sucking it against the roof of his mouth. Despite the fabric of his trousers and his underwear separating them, he felt the heat between Ollie's legs burning against his shaft.

He needed to be inside her—now, immediately. He couldn't wait any longer.

He ignored the voice of caution telling him he was feeling too much, that he was too emotionally connected and that this felt like more than sex, more than a one-night stand. He pushed his underwear and trousers over his hips and down his legs. He tossed the garments to the floor and, when Ollie repositioned herself on his shaft, he groaned.

Protection... He needed to find a condom.

'Get those panties off while I track down a condom,' he told her, sounding gruff. He didn't keep condoms in the drawer of his bedside table because he always conducted his liaisons elsewhere. There might be a box in his bathroom cabinet, and there was one tucked into his wallet. But leaving Ollie was proving more difficult than he expected.

She leaned down, gently biting down on his bottom lip, and soothed the tiny sting with the tip of her tongue. 'I'm clean and on the pill,' she told him, her eyes begging him not to leave her, to wait any longer.

He shouldn't; he didn't trust anyone to take care of protection but himself, but he couldn't find the will to move out from under her. He was a father because he'd somehow slipped up with Dani but, strangely, even that terrifying thought couldn't make him shift.

Tired of his thoughts, the constant merry-go-round in his head, Bo used his strength to flip Ollie so that she lay under him. He slid his hand between her legs to check that she was ready for him—she so was. Without hesitation he pushed into her, rocked by the exquisite feeling of skin on skin, being condom-free. She felt amazing, hot, wet and like...

She felt like home.

CHAPTER NINE

IT WAS EARLY the next morning when Bo walked into his bedroom holding two cups of coffee. When he sat down next to Ollie, his big shoulder pressing into hers, she lifted his wrist to look at his Rolex watch. It was shortly after six, and they hopefully had at least an hour together before Mat woke up. An hour when she could be Ollie the woman, not Ollie the nanny.

Ollie wrapped her hands around her mug and stared into the rich, dark liquid, thinking that making love to Bo had been far better than she'd expected, far more intense than she'd imagined. He'd pulled emotions to the surface she'd thought she'd buried three years ago, soft emotions, emotions that dealt with connection, intimacy and like. She was scared to the soles of her feet and beyond. He'd pushed her out of her emotional comfort zone and she felt a little disconnected.

Bo dropped a kiss on her head and picked up his mug from the bedside table. He'd pulled on a pair of pyjama bottoms and a white T-shirt and Ollie thought that nobody had the right to look so hot this early in the morning. Dressed in Bo's T-shirt, the open neck of his shirt falling off one shoulder, she felt she didn't measure up.

Silly, because Bo had told her frequently that she was delicious, gorgeous and that she was heaven in his arms.

Get over yourself, Cooper.

Pushing her curls off her forehead, she sipped her coffee and, when he sat down next to her, she hooked her bare leg over Bo's.

'What are your plans for today?' she asked Bo, turning her head to kiss the ball of his shoulder. When she left this room, nobody would suspect her of having an affair with her boss but here, right now, she could be affectionate.

'I have a meeting with the Hong Kong businessman I met last night at the ball,' Bo told her. He sighed. 'It'll be one of those highly technical and long meetings where we work through all the design elements he wants and needs. He'll expect too much and, as diplomatically as possible, I'll have to explain to him what can be achieved and what can't.'

'And at the end of it you'll get a fat contract to design his new racing yachts.' Ollie had no doubt that was exactly what would happen. Bo didn't fail; he always achieved what he set out to do.

'And you? What are you planning?'

'I might take Mat to the beach,' she told him. 'It's going to be a hot day.'

'I wish I could join you,' Bo replied, sounding regretful. 'I hate the idea of being cooped up in an office on such a gorgeous day.'

'A few weeks back, you planned on spending most of the summer in your office,' Ollie teased.

His slow smile caused her stomach to do barrel rolls. 'Well, now I've found a better way to spend my time, and wasting the sunlight doesn't seem the wisest course of action.'

Ollie looked away, thinking that she would be leaving as summer drew to an end, when the days grew shorter and the nights cooler.

Talking of...

'Did you manage to go through the CVs of the candidates to take over from me as Matheo's nanny?' she asked him, desperate to get back to reality. And the reality was that in five or six weeks—she'd lost count—she'd be in the UK and Bo and Mat would be here. And they'd have a new nanny in their lives. Because she wanted the best for them—how could she not? They were amazing!—she needed to find the best, most qualified, nicest nanny she could. And good nannies didn't grow on trees.

'No,' Bo told her.

'Good nannies are hard to come by, Bo, and they often secure their next appointments months in advance.'

'I got you at the last minute,' Bo pointed out.

Yes, but she wasn't staying in the game. 'As I told you, you are my last nannying job,' she told him.

He pulled away to look at her, his expression quizzical. 'Have we been that much of a trial that you are chucking it all in?' he asked, and Ollie wasn't sure whether he was being serious or not.

'No, of course not. My last assignment in Berlin was supposed to be my last one, but then Sabine asked whether I'd be interested in spending the summer in Copenhagen. The city, and the lure of a little more cash, was too difficult to resist.'

Bo's eyebrows shot up. 'A little more cash? Damn, woman, your fees are extortionate!'

She shrugged, then grinned. 'But I am amazing,' she retorted.

He slung an arm around her shoulders. 'You are,' he admitted. 'You are brilliant with Mat. But why are you giving it up?'

Needing to put some physical as well as emotional

distance between them, Ollie threw back the covers and walked over to the window, sitting down in the window seat. She lifted her feet onto the cushion, bent her knees and rested her coffee cup on one of them. She couldn't think when she was so close to Bo. He turned her brain to soup.

'I'm going back because I promised my parents I would join their company five years after I graduated from university. I am supposed to walk into my new office and start my new career at the beginning of September.'

Bo walked over to where she was and sat down opposite her in the U-shaped window. 'I don't understand,' he said, pushing his hand through his wavy hair. It needed a cut, Ollie noticed, but the longer length made him look young, soft. 'What are you supposed to start work as?'

'An accountant.'

'Right, I remember that you have a degree in accountancy,' Bo commented. 'From which university?'

Oh, just a little one called... 'The London School of Economics.'

He released a sound that was part-laughter, part-snort. 'Of course you did.' He leaned back and placed his ankle on his knee, amused. 'So I take it your parents were less than happy when you decided to become a nanny?'

'If by "less than happy" you mean they went ballistic. They told me that they didn't fund my studies at one of the most prestigious universities in the world—at a huge cost to them, as I still wasn't a UK resident at that time—for me to waste it wiping runny noses and ferrying kids around.'

Bo winced.

'After much screaming and yelling, and me digging my heels in, we negotiated a five-year deal. I could be a nanny for that period but I had to work for the company for five years so that they could realise some return on the investment they made in my education.'

'Mmm.' There was a long pause before he spoke again. 'If you didn't have to return home, would you stay on as a nanny?'

She couldn't with him, not now they'd made love. She shook her head. 'No, I'd buy into Sabine's nanny agency. She's offered me a junior partnership and I'd love to do that.'

'But you can't take the opportunity because your parents are holding you to this deal you made?' Bo asked. 'Have you told them about her offer?'

She hadn't because it wouldn't make a difference. They wanted her in London, working for them. That was what had been decided years ago and Coopers didn't change their minds.

And there was a back story that Bo didn't understand. 'My dad didn't get the opportunity to go to university; it simply wasn't possible,' Ollie explained. 'To him, education is an absolute privilege, not something that should be taken for granted. The fact that I am not using the education they paid for is a slap in the face. They love me, but they don't understand how I can love this more. Looking after children does not have the same cachet as being an accountant. It's a blue-collar job and, working in this field when I have a superlative degree offends them.

'And I feel guilty because my degree cost them so much money, and I haven't used it, nor have I followed the path they expected me to. I feel like I need to pay them back.'

Bo stared out onto the harbour, his brow furrowed in thought. 'I can understand that, to an extent, but you are also allowed to change your mind—to do something you love doing.'

It wasn't that easy. She wished it was.

'Can you not talk to your parents again, have another conversation?' Bo asked. 'Can you not find another solution?'

The issues went so much deeper than the cost of her tuition. It was difficult for people who'd been raised outside of South Africa to understand all the discriminations and humiliations of the apartheid system. As a biracial woman born after the country had become a democracy, Ollie didn't fully understand all the nuances either. How could she? She hadn't lived through the trauma of institutionalised racism, of *apartheid,* as her mother and her mother's family had for generations.

Her mum had been part of the first wave of black students who'd joined formerly white-only universities in the eighties when those institutions, reading the signs of change in the country, had opened the doors to start the mammoth task of educational equality—yet to be completed. In her parents' eyes, education was something that could never be taken from you. Ollie suspected that they thought she'd taken her opportunities for granted—opportunities they'd fought so hard for—and that she wasn't appreciative of the sacrifices they and her grandparents had made for the generations that had followed—there'd been frequent stints in jail and near-constant harassment.

Talking to her parents wouldn't take the guilt away. 'I don't know if it would help, Bo.'

He winced. Then he stood up and bent down so that his eyes were level with hers. 'It's not something you can solve now, so come back to bed.' He pulled her to her feet, slid his hand around her waist and dropped it to cup her butt cheek, to pull her into him. He was erect and Ollie sucked in an excited breath.

'I need to have you again but we're running out of time because another, younger Sørenson is going to start demanding your attention soon.'

Ollie glanced at his watch and realised that he wasn't wrong. They had maybe half an hour before Mat woke up. Since Bo could take her far away from reality to a world where only pleasure existed, she was happy to follow him back to bed.

A week later, in his office, Bo scowled at his phone and released a series of hot curses. His mother, damn her, was demanding that they get together. In her words, she wanted to hear about the woman who'd accompanied him to the Møller ball. Bridget had missed the social event of the season because a potential client had demanded a last-minute dinner meeting. His mother wasn't one to let a ball—or a family or her son—get in the way of a potential deal.

Since his mother never concerned herself with his love life, Bo surmised that the gossips in her circle had noticed the amount of time, and the amount of attention, he'd given Ollie at the ball. His mother wasn't particularly interested in his life but she hated not being in the know...

She didn't suspect that he was keeping bigger news from her...

Bo tossed his phone onto the desk. A month had passed since Mat had arrived in his life and he'd yet to tell his mother about his son.

And he knew why... Because, while he might be head over feet in love with Mat, he knew Bridget wouldn't be, and he didn't want to see the lack of interest in his son that he'd experienced his whole life.

It was only when he'd hit his late teens that his mother had started to show him any sort of attention, and had made space for him in her busy calendar. When he'd asked her why, she'd told him, with her usual forthrightness, that he'd finally arrived at a point of being interesting. Babies were ridiculously annoying, children even more so, and teenagers were tedious. It was only when he'd became an adult that she'd found him worthy of expending her energy to have a conversation with him.

He couldn't explain Ollie without explaining Mat, not that he needed to. And he wasn't ready for her to meet Mat, not yet. He wasn't prepared to share him with anyone but Ollie. He was too new, too precious, and he wanted to keep him to himself for now.

He would postpone having lunch with his mother for as long as he could and he'd use work as an excuse. After all, it had been her favourite excuse to get out of spending time with him for most of his life.

Bo looked at the designs on his drawing board and pulled a face. Between spending his nights with Ollie and Mat—they'd agreed that they would continue to sleep together until she left to return to the UK—he wasn't getting much work done. This summer was turning out to be less than productive but, in his defence, it was the first summer he'd had a baby.

And a lover who'd lasted more than a week.

And, to be honest, his feelings, if he could believe he was even using the word, were causing him more grief and loss of sleep than his many concerns about being a brand-new father. The line between Ollie as nanny and Ollie as his lover had been obliterated and his house was no longer the same quiet and controlled space it had been before. It was now filled with the sounds of his son laughing, his lover singing—off key—and the smell of her subtle scent perfuming the rooms. In his bed he found an innovative and sexy lover; her enthusiasm for him and how he loved her was such a turn-on. Out of bed, he found a stunningly bright and well-read companion, someone whose mind he enjoyed as much as he did her body.

He was, in a nutshell, temporarily domesticated and the idea scared him to his core.

He felt so at ease with her, calm and in control. Oh, they bickered—Ollie tried anything she could to get out of making coffee in the morning and he'd never met anyone who shed hair as she did. But they argued lightly and he found an excellent way to get her to be quiet was to kiss her.

Ollie, bless her, loved to be kissed.

Damn, he was in a world of trouble here. She was leaving in four weeks, stepping out of his and Mat's lives. There were ten CVs on his laptop, ten potential nannies for Mat who needed to be interviewed. He wasn't interested in any of them. He only wanted Ollie and couldn't see how he and Mat would go on without her.

But they had to; they would. He wasn't a guy who did commitment. What they had was new, bright and shiny, and his feelings for Ollie were probably more intense because they were mixed up in his feelings for Mat. But he wasn't prepared to expose his son to a relationship that mightn't work. He'd watched his parents' relationship as it had moved through its various stages of decay: they'd started with barbs, moved onto arguments and had then ended in outright hatred.

Then they'd stopped talking and acknowledging each other at all. Bo thought that stage had been the worst of all. Arguing and fighting had meant that there was

some emotion involved; dismissing and ignoring someone meant they couldn't even summon the energy to do
that. He'd watched and hated the process. He'd never put
Mat in the position of having to do the same.

A small part of him wished that Ollie had never
dropped into his life, but another part of him was grateful
she had. He was a mess of conflicting emotions, something he was very unaccustomed to. He needed her to
go, but he wanted her to stay. He didn't want to feel any
more for her than he already did, but he wanted to know
every last thing about her.

He wanted to make love to her for the rest of his life,
but he couldn't keep her in his life...

It was official: he was a mess. And he might just be
losing his mind.

Bo turned at the quick rap on his door and turned to
see Ollie standing there, dressed in a short navy-and-
white summer dress. She wore white trainers on her feet,
and she'd piled her hair up into a messy knot on the top
of her head. She looked fresh, lovely and, at that moment,
far too young for him. Mat sat on her hip, the ear of his
stuffed giraffe in his mouth.

'Hey,' she said, resting one hand on the empty pram.
'We're going to Torvehallerne for lunch and to look at
the food stalls. I thought that you might like to join us.'

He should stay, should try and catch up on all his work,
but he knew he wouldn't be able to concentrate. Wherever
Ollie and Mat were was where he wanted to be. And it
had been ages since he'd visited the beautiful glass hall
with its many food vendors selling local produce, arti-
sanal products and delicious food.

After putting Mat in his pram, Ollie walked towards
him, placed her hand on his chest, and stood up on her

tiptoe to brush her mouth across his. She pulled away, but he lifted his hand to grip the back of her head to keep her lips in place. One small kiss wasn't enough, he needed more. If he could have laid her down on his couch and stripped her naked, he would have done that too. In Ollie's arms, when her mouth was under his, he forgot everything else. He forgot he had a difficult mother, that he was a single father, that she was leaving...

She made that sexy sound in the back of her throat as his tongue tangled with hers, and her hand curled around his neck as she pushed her slim body into his. He ran his hand up the back of her thigh and, when she lifted her leg, he slid his hand under the dress to cup her butt.

She made him feel powerful, more masculine than he ever had before. How could he be expected to give her, *this*, up?

He deepened the kiss, allowing them to roll away on a wave of passion, to forget they had a baby in a pram, that he should be working and that Greta was somewhere in the house. Nothing mattered but the fact that he was kissing this gorgeous woman...

Ollie pulled back and looked up at him with sparkling eyes. Her breathing was faster than it had been before, and a delicate flush painted the skin of her chest, face and throat blush-pink. 'Wow. If I haven't told you before, you truly are an excellent kisser, Sørenson,' she told him, her smile wide.

Kissing had never been a big thing for him until she'd come along. An orgasm had always been the end goal but, if kissing was all he could get from Ollie right now, he'd take it. He was toast, burned beyond belief.

Ollie tipped her head to the side, her brown eyes narrowing a little in concern. 'What's the matter?' she asked him.

Nothing. And, because his life seemed practically perfect at that exact moment, he knew that everything was out of sync and definitely out of control. Perfect wasn't—couldn't be!—a gorgeous woman, and his chortling son babbling away to his soft giraffe.

He plucked Mat from his pram and carried him to the window, turning his back to her. He didn't need her to see any emotion in his eyes. He was having a hard time dealing with it; he didn't need to burden her with his feelings. He'd sort himself out without anyone else's input.

Mat threw his giraffe against the glass and it dropped to the floor. Bo picked up the giraffe from the floor and handed it back to him. Mat, who thought this was a great game, tossed it again. 'I'm good,' he told Ollie, tossing the words over his shoulder.

She walked over to him and placed her hand on his shoulder and, through the fabric of his cotton shirt, he felt the gentle heat of her palm. 'Why don't I believe you?' she asked softly.

He couldn't tell her that he felt as though he was too big for his skin, as though any room that had her in it was the perfect place to be. It was too much and too soon, and he had to regain a measure of control.

He needed his old life back—he felt in control there.

And, thinking about his old life, he stumbled across a subject that would blow all his warm and fuzzy feelings away. 'My mother wants to meet me for lunch or dinner,' he said, standing up.

'Could you sound more unenthusiastic if you tried?' Ollie asked him.

Fair point.

'Does she want to see Mat?' Ollie asked.

Bo pulled a face and Ollie placed a hand on his arm.

When his eyes met hers, he saw the astonishment on her face. 'You haven't told her yet?'

He shrugged.

'Bo, you need to tell her she has a grandson!' Ollie chided him. 'And the longer you leave it, the harder it will be to tell her. What's the problem, anyway?'

Oh, only that if she ignored Mat as she had him his heart would break all over again. 'He's not someone my mother will be excited about,' Bo told her, walking out of his office and towards the front door, Ollie following him out.

'Well, you can't keep him a secret,' Ollie pressed, still looking confused. 'Why don't you invite her to supper tomorrow night?'

No, he wouldn't have wrapped his head around her meeting Mat by then. 'I think the queen of Sørenson Media needs more than a day's notice,' he told Ollie. 'Her calendar is booked up months in advance.'

'She said she wanted to meet you for a meal,' Ollie pointed out, sounding ridiculously reasonable. 'Choose the venue, here or somewhere else, and introduce your son to his grandmother, Bo.'

He heard the order in her voice, the note of *don't mess with me*, and wondered why it didn't annoy him. He was usually too alpha to listen to anyone, and he hated taking orders. That she thought she could order him about was too funny for words; she was tiny and he out-weighed her by a hundred pounds. What wasn't funny was the fact that he was going to do exactly as she said.

He was in a huge amount of trouble here...

CHAPTER TEN

OLLIE MADE IT a habit to give everyone a fair chance, and she tried not to dislike people without getting to know them, but Bo's mum, Bridget, was the exception to that rule.

She did not like her—at all.

In Mat's nursery, she walked the length of his too-small room, holding the sleeping baby in her arms. It had taken her a long time to get him to settle, and she'd yet to place him in his cot. Mostly because she thought that, if she did, she might use her free hands to wrap them around Bo's mum's throat and squeeze it.

Ollie glared at the mobile hanging over Mat's bed. She'd encountered many rich people in her line of work, her employees and their friends, and she'd dealt with more snobs than most people should. She'd encountered the snooty and the disdainful, the bossy and the belligerent, but Bridget took the cake.

She was truly awful.

Dear Lord, she felt sorry for whomever got her in the mother-in-law lottery draw. Warm and engaging she was not...

She'd given Bo some space to talk to his mum about Mat, to explain how he'd come to have a son. She'd taken Mat out into the garden but their raised voices had drifted out through the open windows, and Ollie could tell that Bo had been doing his best to keep his temper. Bridget had demanded to know how he could be sure Mat was his kid—even though he was his spitting image!—whether he'd done a DNA test and whether there was anyone else who could take Mat.

He was a little boy, Ollie wanted to howl, not an unwanted box of family keepsakes! How would having a child affect his business? What would Bo be sacrificing by taking on the challenge of raising him? It had taken all of Ollie's willpower not to storm into the house and strip sixteen layers of skin off her boss's—and lover's—mother.

When Bridget had deigned to be introduced to Mat, she hadn't taken him in her arms, neither had she touched his cheek or his hand. She'd admitted that, as far she could remember, he looked a little like Bo when he'd been a baby—but Bo's nanny would know better—and she supposed she would have to add him to her birthday calendar. But Bo shouldn't expect her to babysit, or for her to have much to do with him. As she'd told him on more than one occasion, children only became interesting when they became adults and were no longer a drain on her finances.

She'd heard of tall, cool blondes but Bridget was a solid block of ice.

'You're still frowning,' Bo said, stepping into the nursery.

Ollie looked past his broad shoulder to the open door. 'Is she gone?' she whispered.

'Yep. Her driver collected her,' he replied in a normal tone of voice. 'Fun, isn't she?'

Ollie grimaced. She knew he was trying to make light

of his mother's rudeness, and her lack of interest in Mat, but she'd picked up the hurt in his eyes, on his face. 'How did she manage to raise you?' Ollie demanded as Bo took the sleeping Mat from her to cuddle him.

'I mean, you aren't extroverted—you're much too implacable to be that—but you do have a sense of humour and know how to laugh.'

Bo kissed Mat's forehead. 'She didn't raise me. A series of nannies did. And I spent a lot of time with my grandfather, my father's father, the man who started our boat-building business. He was awesome.'

Bo sat down in the rocking chair next to the cot and Ollie perched on an ottoman in front of him. She watched as he leaned his head back and closed his eyes. Ollie thought that the mental snapshot she took of Mat and him could be a perfect advert for something baby-related. A hot guy and his gorgeous son: they'd move a ton of product.

'I guess she's the reason I decided not to have kids,' Bo said, his voice softer than before. 'She and my father are the reason I decided to live my life solo.'

Ollie leaned forward and clasped her hands together. 'They weren't good together?' she asked.

Bo shrugged. 'I don't know if my father made her cold, or her coldness made him stay away, but they were horrible together. They were one of those couples who brought out the worst in each other.'

Ollie wrinkled her nose. 'How?'

'My mum was demanding and ambitious and she thought, probably correctly, that my father should work harder, do more, make more of a splash and be more ambitious. But he liked to work a little and party more. He thought she should relax a little, take some time off and be a wife and mother, and not a robot. He had a point. But neither would compromise, so Bridget worked even longer hours so that she didn't have to come home to an empty house.'

'A house you were in,' Ollie pointed out.

'But I wasn't *interesting*, Ollie, I didn't get to be interesting until I hit my late teens and twenties and became—in her words—less needy. And my father didn't come home because there was fun to be had, and warm and willing women who were prepared to share that fun with him.'

'And you were caught in the middle,' Ollie observed.

Desolation hit his eyes. 'I was never in the middle. I was relegated to the outskirts of their lives. Neither of them could be bothered with me, and each thought I was the other's responsibility. I never wanted to be in the position of wanting love, looking for love and not getting it again. So I made up my mind to devote my attention to my business and my work, and to live my life by myself.'

Sure, Ollie had had her disagreements with her parents about her career, but she'd always felt part of a family, and she felt loved. A few couples she'd worked for had had marital issues but nothing so bad that the kids had been affected. Or at least, she didn't think so.

But she knew that children picked up on emotion, and they could read a room better than any adult. Having met Bridget, she now understood on a fundamental level why Bo had so many reservations about falling in love, marriage and commitment. He'd only ever seen the very worst of what people who said they loved each other could do. Love, to him, meant pulling people down, not building them up.

How horrible.

'I don't want to mess Mat up the same way I was

messed up, Ol. I want him to grow up feeling secure in my love—I want him to know that he *is* loved.'

Ollie heard the break in his voice and could see the emotion bubbling through the cracks in his facade. If he lowered some of his shields and broke a hole in his castle-thick wall, people would see the sensitive, loving and thoughtful side behind the alpha man he presented to the world. The man worried about how good a father he'd be, who worried whether he'd do right by his son.

She leaned forward and placed a hand on his knees, her thumb digging into the hollows of his knees. 'There are no perfect parents, Bo, of this I am sure. But the smart parents, well, they take the lessons they've learned from their parents—or identify the way they were messed up—and try not to inflict the same pain on their kids. That's not to say they won't make mistakes, but hopefully they won't make the *same* mistakes.'

She, for instance, wouldn't put provisos on her kids' education. Her job would be to have her kids educated—their job would be to use or not use what she'd give them.

'I just figure that, whatever my parents did, I'll just do the opposite. I figure I can't go far wrong,' Bo stated, sounding infinitely weary.

That was a good place to start and Ollie told him so. She stood up and bent down to place a kiss on his cheek. 'Just love your son, Bo. Honestly, that's all he needs. I'll see you in bed.'

She walked out of the room to give him some time alone with the bundle of wonderfulness that had dropped into his life.

Later that evening, and after a few hours of losing and finding herself in Bo's arms, Ollie rolled away from him, immediately missing his warmth and the length of his strong body against hers. She'd never had such good sex, had never felt so intimately connected with a man, before. His eyes were closed. Picking up a T-shirt of Bo's, she slid it over her head and walked out of his bedroom.

She needed to rehydrate.

After checking on Mat and dropping a kiss on his head, she padded to the kitchen and pulled a bottle of water from the fridge. Cracking the top, she swallowed half the bottle and stared out into the night. The last few hours—and weeks!—with Bo and Mat had been sublime, a step out of time and completely wonderful.

But it wasn't real life.

Ollie rested the water bottle against her forehead and pulled in a deep breath. She was grateful she'd only met him on her last nanny job and sleeping with him wouldn't affect her professional life. Oh, she doubted Bo would tell anyone they'd slept together, but she knew she'd stepped so far over the line that it was out of sight.

Professionally, that was. Personally, her body was singing. She felt both relaxed and energised, sleepy and excited. But, more than anything, she wanted to stay in his bed for as long as she could and keep loving him.

She felt so comfortable with him, so at ease in her body, happy to tell him what she liked or didn't. There was a freedom with him that she'd never felt with Fred—she'd been so worried about disappointing him. With Bo, she felt as if she couldn't let him down, that everything she did, liked or responded to was fine. Maybe it was because he had a whole bunch of tricks up his sleeve, and Fred had been a bit of a one-trick pony.

Either way, she felt sexually emancipated, as if she'd

been given the freedom to explore. It was liberating and rather lovely.

But she had to be careful that she kept her emotions in check, that she didn't allow like to bleed into love, that she guarded her foolish and impetuous heart. As lovely as this was, whatever it was, Bo wasn't a long-term prospect. Even if she hadn't been returning to the UK in a few weeks, he'd made it very clear that he didn't do commitment and that he wasn't looking for a long-term lover.

She'd been warned and if she fell for him, if she allowed her heart to come to the party, she'd have no one to blame but herself.

Ollie swallowed some more water.

Be wise, Olivia, be strong and do not do anything stupid. Sleeping with him was a choice. If you get hurt, you can only blame yourself. Sex is sex, love is love...do not muddle the two!

'Can I get one of those?'

Ollie jerked her head up and blinked. Bo stood in front of her, dressed in a pair of black cotton sleeping shorts, his chest bare and his hair mussed. Why hadn't she heard him approaching? Really, the man should wear a bell around his neck to warn her of his approach. Nobody should move that quietly; it was against the law of nature...

'Okay, she's spaced out,' Bo said. He stepped towards her, banded his arm around her waist and lifted her off her feet, swivelling her so that he could open the door to the fridge. Still holding her feet off the ground, he used his free hand to pull another bottle of water out of the fridge and kicked the door closed with his foot. Then he put Ollie down in the exact position in which she was standing before.

'You can't just move me around like I'm a piece of furniture,' Ollie complained, but there was no heat in her voice. Honestly, she rather liked it.

And, judging by his small smirk, Bo knew it. 'You're as light as a feather so it's easy to do,' he told her, opening his bottle of water. He drank deeply before sitting on a stool next to the granite-topped island. 'Are you okay? You were miles away.'

Ollie nodded and sat down next to him, placing her bare feet on the rungs of his chair. The inside of Bo's knees touched the outside of hers and she instantly felt anchored and safe. She ran her finger up and down the side of her bottle, collecting condensation on her finger.

They sat in silence for a while and Ollie was surprised by how comfortable it felt. There was no need to rush in with chatter, to make inane comments or to issue platitudes. There was freedom in saying nothing, in being comfortable in silence, and she revelled in it. In most of the homes she'd lived in, ad in her childhood home, people had spoken all the time, and a lack of noise had meant an argument or that there'd been an issue.

With Bo, it just felt peaceful.

Maybe if she and the De Freidmans had sat with their grief a little more, allowed it to have its space and time, instead of filling their days with people and being busy, they might've handled Becca's death better. There was such power in sitting with your emotions, not having to explain them or validate them or, more importantly, push them away. Whether it was a new sexual experience or the loss of a young life, feelings and people shouldn't be contained by boxes, have time frames or be squashed into what society demanded.

Bo ran his hand down her arm and linked his fingers with hers. 'You have very loud thoughts, Olivia.'

She smiled at him, knowing that he wasn't demanding to know where she was mentally but that he'd listen if she needed to talk. 'I was just thinking how wonderful it is to sit in silence.'

Ollie placed her chin in her hand, grateful he hadn't turned on any lights when he'd entered the kitchen. In the semi-darkness, she felt as if she and Bo were in a cocoon, a bubble, a place where they temporarily couldn't be reached by anyone outside of this house by the sea.

'Maybe if I'd taken a little more time to sit with my thoughts and my grief I would've coped better,' Ollie stated. She turned her head to look at him. 'Do you remember me telling you that there's a reason I only stay three months with a family?'

'Yeah,' Bo replied, his voice sounding deep and rich in the semi-darkness. It sounded like dark, rich chocolate tasted…

I would kill for chocolate right now.

Bo left his seat and she frowned when he headed into the pantry. When he returned, holding a bar of chocolate, she realised she'd spoken aloud. Bo ripped off the packaging and handed her the bar so she could snap off a square…or six.

She saw that it was white chocolate and not dark, her preference. She shook her head. 'I don't think we can be friends any more, Sørenson,' she told him, shaking her head. 'White chocolate—really?'

'I gather you are a dark chocolate girl?'

'The higher the cocoa content, the better,' she replied, squinting down at the bar. 'Is there any cocoa in white chocolate? This is mostly sugar.'

He tried to pull the bar out of her hand but she held on tight. 'You don't have to have any if you are going to lift your nose at my chocolate choices,' he told her, trying, and failing to sound sniffy.

'Now, let's not get carried away,' Ollie told him. It wasn't Belgian chocolate, but she'd deal. She snapped off two blocks and popped one in her mouth. It was sweet, too sweet, but that wouldn't stop her from eating the second piece.

Bo grinned at her before breaking off his own piece. 'You were about to tell me why you only take on three-month contracts.'

Ollie wrinkled her nose. Right, they were back to that. But she didn't mind: she wanted Bo to know. And that felt strange because it had taken all her courage to tell Fred that Becca had died: she'd been so worried about his reaction and hadn't wanted to fight when she'd barely been holding it together.

'I was with a family, two older boys and a four-year-old girl, for about six months when the little girl—her name was Becca—was diagnosed with a fast-spreading, virulent brain tumour.'

Bo placed his hand on her knee and squeezed. He didn't need to express his sympathy. It was there on his face.

'There are some families where you are simply the nanny, another staff member, and then there are families where you become another member of that family. I loved them all so much, and they loved me. And I adored Becca. We had this instant, crazy bond.'

Ollie went on to explain that she'd often taken Becca to her chemo treatments due to her parents' demanding, high-powered careers. She had walked the passageways of the hospital when she'd had exploratory surgery, and then again when she'd been admitted with pneumonia because her little body had been so immune-compromised. She explained that she'd played with her, held her, slept in her bed and that Becca had become like a daughter. And she tried to explain how her soul had crumbled when she'd passed away.

'Her parents had each other and, strangely, they coped with her passing better than I did,' Ollie explained. 'I'm not saying they didn't suffer—they were eviscerated—but I felt pretty alone after her death. They took comfort in each other, their sons and their work, but Becca had been my work. And my fun. I felt like I'd been picked up in a tornado and didn't know where to go or how to land.'

'Did your family support you? Your fiancé?'

Ollie shook her head. 'I don't talk to my family about my work because we always end up fighting about what I do. As for my fiancé, well, he couldn't understand why I'd let myself become so involved, and he thought I should just get over it.'

Bo's expression told her what he thought about Fred's response.

'About a month after Becca's funeral, the De Freid- mans asked me to leave. They said that my being there was too difficult and that they needed a clean break. They'd decided to move to the States to start a new life and I wasn't invited to accompany them.' She recalled every minute of that excruciatingly hard conversation, how incredibly sad they'd looked but how determined; how they'd all cried. 'I knew, intellectually, that it was the best thing for all of us, but emotionally I felt like they'd ripped the rug out from under my feet. I was devastated on top of being devastated.'

'Sweetheart,' Bo murmured, the endearment rumbling over her. Ollie was so grateful he didn't spout any clichés. She just needed him to listen and not try to fix the situation, or her, as Fred had.

'They left and I told Sabine that I couldn't do another long-term placement. I knew I couldn't put myself in that situation where I could get so attached again. I knew it wasn't healthy for me. I've been offered many long-term assignments, but I've turned them all down, because I simply couldn't take the risk of falling in love again.'

She saw an emotion she didn't recognise flicker in his eyes and, assuming that he disagreed with her, as Fred had time and time again, she lifted her chin. 'It's not only men and women who fall in love,' she told him, her voice taking on a hint of bitterness.

'I'm not judging you, Olivia,' Bo told her, keeping his voice even. 'Actually, for the first time in my life, I now understand how it's possible to walk around with your heart in someone else's body. That's how I feel about Mat. I didn't know about him, then I did, then he came to live with me and boom! I was head-over-heels crazy about him.'

She nodded. 'I know that I wasn't Becca's mum, but that's how I felt about her.'

'Tell me about her,' Bo said, gripping the sides of her bar stool and pulling her closer to him so that she was enveloped by his long legs, sharing his breath. He ran his fingers down her cheekbone and tucked a long curl behind her ear. His touch was pure comfort, and Ollie sighed. She wanted to tell him about Becca, probably because she'd never spoken to anyone else about her.

So she told Bo about the red-headed little girl with a face full of freckles and eyes the colour of a summer sky. How she'd loved owls, Willy Wonka and the colour purple. How brave she'd been when she'd been prodded and poked, how stoic she'd been about facing death. She'd known and she'd been so accepting, so gracious...

Light and love... Becca had been an old soul in a new, broken body.

When she finally stopped talking, maybe an hour later, Ollie realised that her face was wet with tears. When her words petered out, he reached for a dish towel left in a crumpled heap on the island and gently, oh so gently, wiped her tears away. Then he picked her up, held her against his chest and took her back to his bed, where he loved the hurt away.

By allowing her to speak, to cry, he'd washed away her grief. Oh, it was still there—it always would be—but it was cleaner, lighter, brighter. And it was the best and biggest gift she'd received in a long, long time.

CHAPTER ELEVEN

OLLIE, WITH MAT on her lap, sat at an outside table in the Tivoli Gardens, watching crowds of people as they walked by. She and Mat were enjoying the sights and sounds of the amazing garden. Mat seemed fascinated by the bright colours and the happy faces, and many people smiled at the cheerful little boy dressed in his red-and-white-striped T-shirt and a pair of denim shorts.

Ollie was also fizzing with excitement.

On social media this morning she'd seen that one of her favourite colleagues, an older woman she'd met during her first job in France, was in Copenhagen on holiday with the family she worked for.

Taking a chance, she'd messaged Helen and had been thrilled when she'd told Ollie she had the morning free and would love to meet anywhere Ollie suggested. They'd settled on meeting at one of the many coffee shops in the Tivoli Gardens, and Ollie couldn't wait to see her.

A few minutes later, Helen's short and round figure stepped out from behind a group of teenagers and Ollie jumped up, squealed and placed Mat on her hip. With her free hand, she wrapped her arm around her old friend and breathed in her familiar scent. At nearly twenty years her senior, Helen had married young and, when her husband had died suddenly, she'd become a nanny, and she'd been with only two families since she'd started her new career.

Because she adored babies, Helen immediately took Mat from Ollie and, after sitting down, sat him on the edge of the table, her hands on his stout waist as she cooed at Bo's baby boy.

'He's gorgeous, Ol,' she told her, smiling. Ollie noticed Helen had more grey in her hair but her eyes were the same steady blue, sharply intelligent and full of fun. 'He's going to be a looker when he grows up.'

'You should see his dad,' Ollie told her.

Helen's gaze narrowed and she immediately understood Ollie's subtext. 'You're attracted to him?'

How could she not be? Not wanting to tell Helen that she was sleeping with her boss five minutes into their conversation—though Helen would winkle it out of her at some point, she was sure—she asked Helen about her family and how she was.

After Helen's explanations were over, they placed an order for coffee and *brunsviger*, a cake-like dough covered with a thick drizzle of melted brown sugar and butter. It was one of Denmark's speciality pastries. Taking over as she always did, Helen placed a sleepy Mat in his pram, found his bottle of milk, handed it to him and nodded her approval when the little boy sucked it down while he watched the world out from under the shady roof of the pram. Ollie noticed his heavy eyelids and knew he'd be asleep before he finished his bottle. Mat was a heavy sleeper and could sleep anywhere and through anything. Once he was asleep, she and Helen would have some time to talk.

Their coffees were delivered and they ate most of their pastry; Ollie knew she'd have to go for a run later to work off all those extra calories. Afterwards, Helen leaned back and folded her arms across her ample chest. 'So, what's worrying you, darling?'

So much. Bo, leaving Mat—she was far more attached to him than she wanted to be—going back to the UK, her parents and their insistence that she join the firm.

Ollie sighed, picked up her phone and flipped it over then over again. 'I wasn't supposed to take this job, did you know that?'

'Sabine said something about you giving up the nanny's life and going home to become a career girl.' She wrinkled her nose. 'A lawyer?'

Ollie sighed. 'Accountant.' She picked up her water glass and took a sip. 'My parents are expecting me to join the family firm in September.'

'And I can see you are brimming over with enthusiasm to do that,' Helen replied, sounding sarcastic. 'Just tell your family that you don't want to work for them. Sabine mentioned the possibility of you becoming a junior partner in the agency.' She should be cross about Sabine and Helen discussing her but they were her best friends, her mentors, and they both thought of her as a younger sister. 'She said something about you buying a small share and then working with her for a couple of years until she retires. Then you could buy out the rest of her shares or she could stay a silent partner.'

'That's the dream,' Ollie said and released a heavy sigh.

'I want to hear why you're not jumping at this opportunity, but first a question—wouldn't you need to live in Paris to run the agency?'

Ollie shook her head. 'Not necessarily. I can be based anywhere in Europe. With video calling, we can run the business virtually to a large extent. I mean, I would have to go to Paris occasionally, but I wouldn't have to relocate there.'

'So, what's the problem, Ol?'

Ollie looked at her. 'I know that Sabine offered the same opportunity to you a while back. Why did you turn it down?'

She smiled. 'Because I want to be involved with the kids, I don't want to run a business. You know I don't do this for the money—' Helen had inherited a bundle from her late husband, a stockbroker '—and I like being a part of a family. But also separate.'

Ollie nodded, preparing to explain why joining the agency wasn't possible.

'When I graduated, I promised my parents I would return to the business and work for them. I struck that deal.'

Helen wrinkled her nose. 'And can that deal not be renegotiated?'

Ollie explained her parents' deeply held beliefs that education was a privilege, not a right. And that they had the right to demand a return on the investment they'd made by paying for her education.

'But you are not an investment.'

Ollie touched her hand, not wanting her to think badly of her parents. 'They love me, they do. It's just one thing we disagree on. And it'd be more than saying I don't want to do this: it's about sticking to my word and not trying to move the goalposts because they don't suit me any more.'

'The weight of parental expectation can be a heavy load to carry,' Helen said, her expression serious. 'Have you told them that you don't want to be an accountant?'

'Not in so many words. I guess I don't want to disappoint them more than I already have.'

'I'd talk to them if I were you, Ol.'

That was so much easier said than done.

Helen snagged her uneaten quarter of *brunsviger* and popped a piece into her mouth. 'So delicious,' she murmured. 'So, you are only in Copenhagen for another month or so?'

Ollie was grateful for the change of subject. Thinking about her parents and leaving gave her a headache. 'Roughly, yes. It's a stunning place and I've loved every minute.'

Helen leaned back and crossed one leg over the other. 'I watched you for a while before joining you. You seem besotted by Mat.'

Ollie's eyes snapped up to her face and Helen just lifted her eyebrows, as if waiting for an answer. When Ollie didn't reply, she spoke again. 'I've been quite worried about you since Becca died, Olivia.'

She didn't want to talk about her parents, and she definitely didn't want to talk about Becca. But, judging by the stubborn look on Helen's face, they were going to have this conversation whether she liked it or not. Since Helen had taken many late-night calls and listened to her sob before and after Bec's death, Ollie couldn't cut her off at the knees. 'You've become attached to Mat,' she stated in her no-nonsense way.

And to his father. Ollie wanted to disagree, but she couldn't. 'I'll still be able to leave,' she told Helen. 'It's not a big deal.'

She was simply looking after Mat, and she was simply fiercely attracted to Bo. It was nothing she couldn't handle.

She hoped.

'Good grief, Olivia, please tell me that you haven't

fallen for his father?' Helen demanded, reading the truth in her eyes and on her face.

She couldn't, so she stared down into her cup and closed her eyes. Helen whispered a curse, a word she wouldn't have thought that Helen knew, and she opened one eye to see her friend frowning at her. She lifted her hands and shrugged. 'He's gorgeous and nice and, as soon as I saw him, the room shrunk and the air disappeared and I got shivery.'

Helen placed her hand on her forehead and groaned. 'That bad, huh?'

'That bad,' Ollie confirmed. 'Look, please don't give me the "*it's so unprofessional*" lecture. There's nothing you can say that I haven't told myself. It is stupid, irrational, crazy but, given the circumstances, I'd do it all over again.'

Helen nodded, pulled in some air and caught the waiter's eye. She ordered two glasses of wine and an espresso. Ollie pointed to the sleeping Mat. 'I can't drink wine, I'm on duty.'

'Who said they are for you?' Helen demanded. 'It's my day off and I'm drinking your share.'

Fair enough, Ollie conceded.

'Please tell me that you aren't thinking of making this a long-term arrangement, Olivia?'

She wouldn't dare. Partly because Helen would rip her head off but mostly because she knew that she couldn't stay with Bo, working as his nanny and being his lover. The balance of power was out, and she couldn't live like that on an ongoing basis. 'If I stayed with him, I'd expect a commitment, some promises, all the things that Bo can't give me,' she told Helen.

Helen released a sigh. 'At least you aren't looking at this with stars in your eyes.'

As if! She was smarter than that. 'No, I'm leaving and he knows it. I think that's why he's with me, because there is a finite end to our relationship. But I do need to find Bo another nanny, someone to replace me. I keep shoving CVs in front of Bo's face but he won't look at them.'

'Have you explained that finding a good nanny on short notice is practically impossible?' Helen asked.

'I have, but I think he thinks that, because he found me at the last minute, he'll be able to do that again.'

'Not going to happen,' Helen stated. She thanked the waiter, who placed the wine in front of her, and lifted her first glass to toast Ollie. 'So what are you going to do, Olivia? Are you going back to London and are you going to talk to your parents?'

Nobody seemed to understand that there wasn't a way out for her, that going back to the UK was what she *had* to do. 'I made my parents a promise, so it's back to London to accountancy for five years. Maybe after that, I'll open up an agency.'

'But by then you'd have been out of the game for a while.'

Ollie rolled her eyes. 'You are such a ball of optimism, Helen. Thank you.'

'Mmm,' Helen replied. Then she slapped her hand on the table and nodded decisively. 'I have faith that you'll work something out, that something will change.'

'At least one of us does,' Ollie told her, looking longingly at Helen's glasses of wine.

The island of Bornholm was possibly the most beautiful place she'd ever seen, Ollie decided as Bo pulled into a lookout point on the east side of the island. Below them was a red-roofed town and she could see a harbour blasted into a rocky outcrop. The town, like so many others they'd seen, looked quaint, quirky and utterly lovely.

It was too beautiful a day to spend another minute in Bo's luxurious SUV, so Ollie left the car and spun round, taking in the green forests and the blue water in front of her.

'Where are we?' she asked Bo, who was walking round the bonnet of the car to join her. Mat was fast asleep in his car seat and Ollie sighed when Bo stood behind her and wrapped his arms around her waist.

'That is the town of Gundjem,' Bo told her. 'My holiday house is a ten-minute drive from here but I wanted you to see this view.'

On the drive, she'd done a quick Internet search about the island of Bornholm. It was called 'the sunshine island' and Ollie could see why. The light was incredible, bright and pure. 'The island looks laid back.'

'It is,' Bo told her. 'I like to think that God was in a particularly good mood when he created this place. It's exceptionally pretty with its rocky cliffs, mountains and dense forests. It also has really friendly locals and great food.'

Ollie couldn't wait to see more of the island and was so grateful that she'd get to do it with Bo. She was making memories she'd never forget. 'Do you come here often?'

'Not as often as I should, but I did spend a lot of time here when I was a child,' Bo replied. 'The house was my grandfather's and I spent every summer here. I inherited it when he died.'

She was so lucky to get to spend time here, Ollie thought. When Bo had suggested that they drive to Bornholm, she'd immediately agreed, as she always took every opportunity she could to see more of the region in which she was working.

With little Mat in his pram, she had explored Copenhagen's many tourist attractions. She'd visited its stunning museums, ambled its streets and taken a harbour tour, and Bo had also taken the time to show her the hidden-away gems of the city he called his home. They'd also made trips to Dragor. She'd adored its narrow streets and low houses built in the eighteenth and nineteenth centuries, and had been entranced by its old port. They'd also visited the cultural harbour city of Helsingør and Ollie had explored Kronberg Castle. There was so much of the country to see but she was out of time.

She had just ten days left in Denmark and, every time she thought about getting on a plane and returning home, her stomach filled with acid-covered concrete. But she had to leave, she couldn't stay.

Stupidly, she'd been living in a fool's paradise since she'd started sleeping with Bo, pretending that the idyll they'd created would last—her looking after Mat and him going off to work, coming home at night to spend time with his son before turning his attention to loving her. Nothing lasted and Ollie tried to remind herself that she preferred it that way.

She wasn't convinced.

The truth was that she was a hair's breadth away from falling in love with Bo, with Mat, with Copenhagen and with this amazing country. Their holiday in Bornholm would be the last bit of concentrated time they'd spend with each other, and three days after they returned to the city she would catch a flight to London.

Staying with Bo was not an option.

Ollie looked down when her phone vibrated. She'd taken a photo of Gundjem shortly after leaving the car and posted it on the Cooper family's group. Her mum's reply was a picture of Ollie's empty but decorated office at Cooper & Co complete with its state-of-the-art computer and a framed copy of her degree on the wall.

Standing there, overlooking Gundjem and watching the fishing boats coming into the harbour, with Bo's arms around her, Ollie knew with absolute certainty that she didn't want to join the family firm or to go back to London. She'd thought she could do the job for five years, that it was something she could do with some gritting of her teeth. She now knew she couldn't. Not now and not at any time in the future.

It wasn't an office job she was allergic to—if she joined Sabine it would mean she could mostly work remotely. But working with figures and company law in a fast-paced, corporate environment would sap her and make her miserable.

She wanted to be here, with Bo and Mat, living with them, loving them. But, even if they weren't part of her future, given Bo had made it clear that she couldn't expect a long-term commitment from him, she still wanted to buy a share in Sabine's business. She wanted to learn from her as she supplied au pairs and nannies to good families who needed their help and input.

She'd made a promise to her parents, and that was important to her. At the very, very least, she needed to have a sensible, reasonable discussion about how she could fulfil her obligations without selling her soul and drowning in misery.

She knew, standing here on Denmark's sunshine island, that she couldn't be a part of Cooper & Co and somehow she and her family would have to come to terms with that. She was going to be without the man she loved—she knew that Bo would not change his mind and ask her to stay—but five years was far too long to spend time not doing what she loved. It was too long to be without the people she loved, but she didn't have a choice in that. She did with her career.

'You're a million miles away,' Bo said, his mouth close to her ear. She jumped a little and squeezed his forearm. She turned in his arms and tipped her head back to look at him, trying to burn all the details of this moment into her brain. Bo was dressed in a button-down navy-and-white-striped shirt with the sleeves rolled up, blue shorts and boat shoes, his hair blowing in the warm wind. His eyes crinkled at the corners as he smiled down at her, and she loved the fact that he hadn't shaved for a day or two. His stubble made him look a little more devil-may-care, a lot more disreputable. More like a sailor than the owner of one of the continent's premier boat-building yards and an amazing yacht designer.

Over the past few weeks, she'd come to know the man behind the reserved facade he showed the world. He had a dry sense of humour and a fondness for the ridiculous and, now that he was used to it, enjoyed her gentle teasing. He was considerate, occasionally affectionate and, if he sometimes spent far too much time on his drawing boards or on his laptop in a world of his own, she let him be, understanding that he was in his happy place, zoned out on water displacement, bows, masts and drag.

But sometimes he'd look up from working on his laptop, see her sitting on the couch reading or watching a movie and hand her a warm smile, as if to say 'hey, you're still here and that's pretty damn marvellous'. He'd started singing folk songs to Mat after reading to him and, when she'd asked him what he was singing, he'd told her they were songs his grandmother had sung to him when he was a young boy. She was glad that he'd reconnected with music and enjoyed his baritone. It was an improvement on the out-of-tune eighties rock tunes she belted out that caused the neighbourhood cats to flee and Mat to slap his hands over his ears.

Bo lifted his hand and dragged his thumb over her bottom lip. 'You are so very beautiful, Olivia,' he murmured, and Ollie saw the sincerity in his eyes. He'd told her she was lovely before, but she couldn't wrap her head around the fact that such a gorgeous guy thought she was hot.

She just wished he could think of her as something more than a blip on his radar, someone who was worth more than an eight-week affair. But while she could speak to her parents, rearrange her work priorities, change her career and flip things around in her own life, she could not influence his.

She couldn't make him love her, she couldn't make him commit. She didn't have the power to grant him the ability to trust or to take a risk. She was just a girl who was lucky to have shared his life for as long as she had.

But, damn, saying goodbye, leaving, was going to be the mental equivalent of being flayed with a whip.

CHAPTER TWELVE

IN FRONT OF the floor-to-ceiling window that overlooked the bleach-white beach and glistening sea, Bo looked down into Ollie's lovely eyes and lifted his hands to cradle her face. She looked ethereal in the pale light flowing in from the yet-to-set sun. From the moment he'd first seen her just shy of two months ago, he'd visualised making love to her here, in the bedroom of his island home. He'd wanted to see the evening light on her skin, watch her eyes fog over as the water smacked the beach below the house, breathing in the air coming off the sea as he painted his desire on her glorious skin.

Ever so slowly, wanting to take his time, desperate to make a memory, Bo undid the neck-to-hem buttons of her pretty, short sundress, eventually spreading it open to reveal her lacy, mint-green bra and high-cut matching panties. He dragged his finger down the centre of her chest and watched her nipples pebble, hardening in anticipation of how he would make her feel.

Oh, he intended to make her feel...*everything*.

Lifting his hand, he gripped the clip that held her soft curls against the back of her head and let the heavy mass fall down her back, over her slim shoulders. Ollie lifted her chin and parted her lips, and he knew she wanted him to kiss her. But if he lost himself in her mouth this would be over far too soon. Avoiding her mouth, he dragged his lips over her jaw, before tugging her ear lobe into his mouth. She reached for him, but he shook his head, tipping her head back so that he could look into her deep-brown, glowing eyes.

'I need to explore you softly, slowly, intensely.'

He saw the tremble in her fingers, the way her skin pebbled in response to his words. He knew he turned her on—he was old enough and experienced enough to have worked that out weeks ago—but he doubted she knew how she affected him. She walked into the room and a barrage of images hit him: how he'd like to take her by that window, on that table. Time after time, his knees weakened and the air in the room seemed to evaporate. The urge to cover her mouth with his, whether they were in company or alone, was always present.

There had never been anyone in his life who made him lose his head so thoroughly; who could, with one look or one word, penetrate his carefully constructed armour. Ollie *got* him in a way that no one ever had. She knew more of him, of who he was and what he stood for, than anyone ever had before.

And, in just over a week, she would be leaving his life for ever. What would he do with Mat? Could he cope on his own? He didn't want her to go, but he knew she couldn't stay. She had promises to keep, a life to establish elsewhere.

Bo pushed those thoughts aside; they were for later. Right now, his only job was to love Ollie as thoroughly as he could. Pushing her dress off her shoulders, he led her over to the bed and sat down on the edge, pulling her between his legs. He rested his forehead on her sternum, inhaling her fresh air and jasmine scent, his lips resting on her lovely skin, his hands on her shapely hips.

Hooking one finger under the cup of her bra, he pulled it down and blew on her puckered nipple. Above his head, Ollie sighed and rested her hands on his shoulders, moving them to his hair and down his neck. He knew she wanted to touch him but also seemed to understand that something else was happening this evening, something bigger, bolder and brighter than their previous couplings.

Something important...

He didn't know if he loved her. Bo didn't know, with his family history, whether he was capable of loving anyone. But he couldn't deny that with Ollie he was close, as near to that elusive emotion they called love as he thought he could get. But it wasn't enough. He couldn't give Ollie all that she needed, everything she deserved.

But he could love her with his body, worship her with his lips, tongue and hands.

Bo reached behind her, undid the clasp holding her bra together and gently pulled the sexy garment from her body. When it landed on the floor, he covered her breast with his hands, his thumbs dragging across her nipples, making them tighter and harder. Knowing what she needed, he pulled one nipple into his mouth, sucking hard before pulling away to love the other. She was beautiful and tonight, for the next week, she was his. He'd take these long summer days, the few they'd been gifted, and he'd love her as best as he could, as much as he could.

At the end of it, he'd face his and Mat's Ollie-free future.

The thought made him want to howl, and then break things.

Bo gave himself a mental kick and told himself to

concentrate. He had a gorgeous woman in his arms; he should give her, and her body, all the attention it deserved. And that meant running his lips over her ribs, dipping his tongue into her cute, ring-studded belly button. She had a tattoo of a swallow on her hip, pretty and perfect.

Bo dragged her panties down her hips and, when she stepped out of them, he stood up and told her to sit on the edge of the bed. Feeling hot, he stripped off to his briefs and sank to his knees between Ollie's thighs, smiling a little when her mouth dropped into a perfect 'O'.

He'd kissed her intimately a few times before, but he'd never made her orgasm with his fingers and tongue— he'd always been so desperate to be inside her.

Not being inside her when she came might kill him but certain things were worth losing his life for...

Bo lay next to Ollie and watched the aftermath of her intense orgasm, feeling as if he'd conquered Everest and rowed across the Southern Ocean. He was an experienced lover, but nothing was more important than her being fully satisfied. Bo watched as she opened her intensely dark eyes, smiled and reached for him.

'That was a very one-sided couple of minutes, Sørenson,' she whispered as his hand encircled her, her thumb moving slowly across his tip. 'How do you want it? How do you want me?'

He mentally flipped through a couple of positions, discounted them all and settled for covering her slim body with his, hooking her legs over his hips. There was nothing exotic about the missionary position but it allowed them to be face to face, eye to eye, and he could watch her lovely face as passion spun him away.

Bo pushed inside her and sighed. She felt like home,

the person he didn't think he'd been looking for. He didn't know how he was going to let her go but neither could he ask her to stay.

Ollie sat on the beach below Bo's house and watched Bo walk along the shoreline with Mat on his hip. He wore a pair of low-slung swimming shorts and a navy chambray shirt half-buttoned up. His big feet left an impression in the wet sand and he was chatting to Mat, who seemed to find his father extraordinarily funny.

Mat and Bo had bonded, and Bo was now confident in his ability to look after his son. For Ollie, time was running out and she was deeply concerned that Bo didn't have someone to take her place as a nanny when she left. Greta had agreed to help Bo out temporarily but Bo using his housekeeper as Mat's nanny, as wonderful as Greta was, was not a long-term solution.

This afternoon, while Mat took his nap, she intended to make Bo read the CVs of the five nannies she and Sabine had decided were good enough for Bo to interview. Despite Bo's lack of interest in the process, she couldn't, *wouldn't*, leave them without a solid back-up plan. It was going to be hard enough to leave but leaving Bo without a nanny to back him up would be an additional stress. Oh, she knew that Bo would cope—he could deal with anything and everything life tossed him—but she knew that being a single parent was taxing. He couldn't run a successful company and give Mat the time and attention he needed without some help. If she couldn't stay, then she wanted him to have a sensible, strong, loving person to look after Mat when Bo had to work.

She so wanted to stay. Ollie placed her hand on her heart, cursing herself for becoming so involved in this little family. She'd promised herself that she wouldn't become attached, but here she was, the human equivalent of a barnacle. She loved Mat and she was probably, *definitely*, in love with Bo.

And she had to leave.

Last night, after lying awake in Bo's arms, she'd considered her options, one of which was taking out a business loan to buy shares in Sabine's business. If she managed to secure a loan, then she could split her savings between paying back her parents some of the money they'd spent on her education—it was all she could think to do or offer—servicing the loan repayments and putting a little towards establishing a new life in Paris. But was Paris where she wanted to live? Was London?

If she couldn't have Copenhagen—and she couldn't— where could she see herself living?

She could live in any European city: most of her work would be online. She'd run through a dozen cities last night, finding something, or a few things, wrong with all of them. After getting into a total tizz, she'd reminded herself that she had a couple of hurdles to negotiate—she needed to talk to her parents, secure the loan and make Sabine a formal offer—before she needed to make such a big decision.

She knew that Copenhagen would always be top of her list. But having her around full-time wasn't something Bo wanted. She was a temporary fling, on her way out. That made Bo sound callous and selfish, when he wasn't. He enjoyed her company, was a kind, considerate and thoughtful house mate, a clear-headed and calm boss and a blow-her-socks-off lover—but he'd never hinted, not once, that he wanted her to stay.

And if he did, she couldn't, not the way things were now.

She needed a lot, *lot* more from Bo before she could consider staying in Copenhagen: love, trust, some sort of commitment. She needed everything that Bo couldn't give her.

Her phone jangled in her back pocket and Ollie pulled it out, grateful for the reprieve. She saw Helen's name on the screen and pushed the green button, happy to hear from her good friend.

'Hey, you. Where are you?'

Helen's face appeared on the screen. It looked as though she was sitting at a dining-room table, with a painting behind her by Degas, depicting his beloved ballerinas. Knowing how wealthy Helen's employers were, it was probably an original.

Helen placed her chin in her hand. 'So, I have news. I think you know that my boys are getting big now—one is already at boarding school, and another is going to be starting soon. The youngest is only ten, but Adele wants to cut back at work, and she's planning on working from home more.'

Ollie wrinkled her nose. 'Are they letting you go?'

Helen nodded and Ollie winced. It was never easy to leave a family, especially when she'd been with them for such a long time. 'And how are you feeling about that?' she asked her friend.

Helen smiled. 'Better than they are, frankly! We had a long conversation last night and they were in tears. They don't want me to go but there won't be much for me to do. And they don't want me to think I've done anything wrong, because they adore me...'

Ollie smiled, happy for her friend and proud of the excellent relationship she had with her employers. 'The truth is, I need a change,' Helen admitted. 'That's why I'm calling...'

Ollie frowned, not understanding the expectant look on Helen's face. 'I fell in love with Copenhagen when I was there, and I wouldn't mind going back.'

'I'd love to have you, but I'm leaving in a week.' Ollie placed her hand on her heart, trying to rub the stabbing pain away.

'I'm hinting when I should just come out and say this. I want to interview for the position of little Mat's nanny, if it hasn't already been filled.'

It took a little time for Helen's words to make sense and, when they did, Ollie released a squeal of delight. 'Are you serious?'

If it were up to her, she'd employ Helen in a heartbeat. She was warm, funny, organised and had an affinity for children of all ages. She'd studied to be a teacher, but she was an exceptional nanny, the best Ollie had come across. There was no one she wanted to look after Mat more.

'Has the position been filled?' Helen asked, looking worried. 'Please tell me it's not been filled.'

Ollie looked to where Bo was and saw that he was walking back to her. 'No, it hasn't, mostly because my boss won't look at applications. Send me your CV and I will campaign hard to get him to employ you. I couldn't leave Mat in better hands, Helen.'

Helen tipped her head to the side. 'Then why do I sense a note of un-enthusiasm in your voice? An "*I don't want to leave*"?'

Because she didn't. But she couldn't stay, and she couldn't let this situation continue as it was. She had decisions to make, conversations to have and hurdles to overcome. But Helen as Mat's nanny would be a weight off her mind.

'Send me your CV immediately and I'll put it in front

of his nose,' Ollie told her, rushing her words. 'I was planning on pinning him down this afternoon anyway.'

'Sounds like fun.'

Ollie looked up and saw Bo standing a few feet from her, a naughty *"can't wait to have you"* look in his eyes. Yeah, that would be fun, but their conversation wouldn't be.

But it was time to face the music...

'I'll speak to you soon, Helen. Just send me that email quickly, yeah?'

Ollie disconnected the call and stood up, brushing sand off the seat of her denim shorts. Mat leaned towards her and Ollie took him from Bo, smiling when he wrapped his chubby legs around her and buried his face in her neck. The combination of sun, sand and sea had tired him out and she knew he'd be asleep before they reached the house. She turned her head to kiss Mat's head and watched Bo gather their towels, their beach basket and the cooler they'd brought down earlier that morning.

Bo looked at her, a slight smile on his face. 'Time to go home?'

Ollie nodded. Yes, it was time to go home. She just wished she didn't think that home was wherever he and Mat were.

After a quick shower, Ollie walked from the master suite into the study that adjoined the magnificent master study. Opening up Bo's computer, she logged into her email account and printed off the five CVs she wanted to show him, happy to add in Helen's.

They were going to have this conversation now, today. She wanted Bo and Mat to have the best nanny there was and that meant Helen needed to replace her when she left. She was even more highly in demand than Ollie and would be snapped up in a heartbeat if Bo didn't hire her immediately. He could not dilly-dally on this, he needed to act, and act immediately.

Having Helen looking after Mat would be a huge relief, and she wouldn't have to worry about whether Bo was coping, or how he was juggling being a full-time dad with being a busy CEO and yacht designer. Thank goodness that Mat was still so young while all these changes were happening in his life. If he'd been older, she'd have been a great deal more concerned about the number of caregivers he'd had in his life. But Helen was a stayer, and she would be there for five years, possibly a lot longer, a loving and stable influence in Mat's life. Between Bo and her, Mat would have all the love, support, discipline and care he needed.

The sad thing was that he'd never remember Ollie.

Would Bo, in time, forget about her too? Would she be relegated to the outskirts of the mind, to that place where memories gradually faded? The reality was that, in a few months, she'd be a nice memory; in a few years, he wouldn't be able to recall her features.

Ollie sucked in a deep breath and cursed her burning eyes.

It is what it is, Olivia, you can't change it because you don't like it.

This was the price she was paying because, once again, despite knowing it wasn't a clever option or idea, she'd become attached.

She had no one to blame but herself.

Ollie walked down the long hallway of Bo's magnificent summer house, knowing that she would find Bo on the outside deck, the one that overlooked the private beach nestled between two rocky outcrops. He stood by the tempered-glass railing, a beer in his hand and the light wind lifting the strands of his hair. For as long as she lived, she'd remember him standing there, bare feet and looking relaxed, with the seascape behind him.

He sent her a slow smile and lifted his beer. 'Would you like one?'

She shook her head. A look of confusion crossed his face when, instead of walking over to him and curling herself into him as she normally did, she pulled out a dining chair at the handcrafted wooden table and gestured for him to join her. When he took a seat opposite her, he noticed the pile of papers on the table and groaned. 'It's too beautiful a day to be serious, Ol. Let's just enjoy our time together while Mat is asleep.'

Ollie wavered. She loved his little boy, but she'd come to crave those hours when she could lie in Bo's arms, discussing everything and nothing. They also spent a lot of their alone time making love but, while she was tempted—she was always tempted; Bo just did it for her!—she knew that they had to talk about the future. *Right now.* Helen wouldn't hang around waiting for Mr Picky to make up his mind.

Ollie put her hand on the CVs and sent Bo a serious look. 'You've been ignoring my and Sabine's requests to discuss my replacement for weeks now, and we can't put it off any longer.'

Bo lifted his beer bottle to his mouth and she saw the irritation in those green depths. He liked calling the shots and controlling the conversation but she wasn't going to allow him to do that today. This was too important to leave until the very last minute.

'Do you remember that I told you that I met my friend

Helen in Copenhagen a couple of weeks back?' Ollie
began. 'We met at a cafe in Tivoli Gardens.'

He lifted one shoulder. 'Vaguely.'

Of course he remembered; the man had a mind like a
steel trap. He was just punishing her for pushing ahead
with this conversation, for spoiling their time together
by inviting reality to the party. Ollie narrowed her eyes
in a warning he couldn't miss. He shrugged and rolled
his finger in a gesture for her to continue.

'Helen is a hugely experienced nanny and a lovely,
lovely person. She's been with the same family for a
long time, nearly ten years, and it's time for her to move
on. She's expressed an interest in being Mat's nanny and
I think you'd be a fool if you didn't snap her up. Now.
Today.'

'I'm not ready to decide on a new nanny for Mat,' Bo
said, looking obstinate.

'Bo, I am leaving soon. If you employ Helen today, she
could give her family two weeks' notice—they love her
and would allow her to go, knowing that she's needed—
and you'll have somebody to help you out a lot sooner
than I thought. You can't look after Mat and run your
business.'

'I'll have Greta to help me.'

'Greta has her own life; she is not a long-term solution. Why are you burying your head in the sand?' she
demanded. 'It's not like you, Bo.'

Bo pushed his chair back from the table so hard that
it toppled over as he stood up. He stomped back over to
the railing and gripped the edge, straightened his arms
and looked down.

Ollie followed him to where he stood and placed a
hand on his back. 'What's going on, Bo?'

'I need you to stay here, Ol.'

Damn. 'You know I can't do that, Bo. It's not possible.'

He stood up straight and folded his arms, looking like an annoyed Viking chief. 'You can. Just tell your parents you don't want to be an accountant and tell Sabine that you aren't interested in buying a share in her business. Stay in Copenhagen with me and Mat.'

She could not possibly be hearing him correctly. Had he just dismissed her concerns about her family, brushed off her ambitions and demanded that she give up everything important to her to stay in her position as Mat's nanny?

Ollie frowned at him, unable to believe he could be so glib and dismissive. This wasn't the Bo she'd come to know and adore.

Ollie hauled in a deep breath and tried to hold onto her slipping temper. 'From the beginning, I told you I could only give you two months, Bo. You knew that. Look, I'm going to tell my parents I won't be joining their firm, and I'm going to offer to compensate them for the cost of my studies.'

'I'll pay them. How much is it? I can do the bank transfer today.'

He did not just say that! Ollie blinked and waited for him to apologise or to take back his words. He did neither. What was going on here?

'And how do I pay you back?' Ollie asked, increasingly annoyed by his high-handedness and arrogance. He was being a typical, bolshie alpha male, demanding and commanding.

'You can work it off,' he shot back.

By looking after Mat or by sleeping with him? Maybe her anger was clouding her judgement, but she was furious at his blithe dismissal of her feelings and her predicament. He simply wanted to throw his money at her to get the result he wanted. He had an excellent nanny to look after Mat and a willing bed partner and he didn't want to be inconvenienced. The arrogant jerk!

'I will never let you pay off my debts for me,' Ollie told him, ice coating her words. 'And as great as you are in bed, and as much as I love Mat, I have my own life to lead and goals to meet. I need more than this, Bo.'

And at that moment she did. Oh, she'd been happy being a nanny, but Ollie knew that it wasn't something she could do for the next five or ten years. While she didn't want to be an accountant, she did want to go into business. And, on the plus side, her accountancy degree would come in handy when it came to tax season.

Bo shoved the fingers of both hands into his hair. 'What's wrong with what we are doing now?'

How could he even ask her that? 'What's wrong with it is that it's all about me working for you, Bo! I can't spend the next few months or years looking after your kid during the day and warming your bed at night! Do you not see that?'

'You love being with Mat and me!'

She did, of course she did, but it wasn't enough, not long term. Even if Bo told her he loved her, she still didn't think being his partner and Mat's mum would be enough. She had a good brain, and she wanted to do more and be more. She wanted to be able to test her wings and try to fly.

She couldn't sacrifice her goals and ambitions because Bo wasn't a fan of change and because having her around made life easy for him. She loved him...but she loved herself too.

'I need to be more, do more, have more.'

His eyes sharpened and he slid his hands into the pockets of his shorts. 'I suppose you are going to tell me that you want more from me, from *us*. That you aren't going to stay here without a ring on your finger and without me telling you that I love you and that I can't live without you?'

His words were so scathing, and his eyes were so cold that Ollie felt her bottom lip wobble. She would not cry, damn it! She lifted her chin and pushed steel into her spine. She was a Cooper, and they did not buckle.

'My contract is ending,' she told him, trying to hold onto her temper. 'You need a nanny. I have found someone brilliant for you. I hope you employ her because, if you don't, you'll regret it.

'I am doing what I always said I would and that's moving on,' Ollie continued. 'You might not like it—'

'And you do? Like it?' he interrupted. 'Then why do you look like you are about to cry?'

He knew why—he knew that she loved him, that she wanted more—but she refused to utter any words she couldn't take back. She wouldn't admit that she'd allowed herself to become attached to Mat and him. Telling him that she loved him and not hearing the words back would emotionally eviscerate her.

She was hurting enough as it was. Before today, she'd harboured a small hope that he might love her, that he might come out and admit there might be a future for them, but his cold speech had destroyed any lingering dreams she still had.

He didn't love her, was never going to love her, and probably *couldn't* love her.

And damn him for noticing the tears she refused to let fall.

She wasn't going to explain herself and it was time to walk away. She still had several days left in his company, and she needed to be professional, so saying anything else that would raise the temperature between them wasn't an option. As it was, they were surface-of-the-sun hot.

Ollie stomped back over to the table, picked up the thin stack of papers and slapped the pile against his chest. Because he was stubborn, the CVs fluttered to the deck and Ollie was damned if she was going to pick them up. 'Hire a nanny, Sørenson.'

Spinning round, she walked away from Bo, her tears creating pools of acid in her eyes and her throat.

CHAPTER THIRTEEN

BO LOOKED AT Ollie's straight, taut back and silently cursed. He'd suspected for a while now that Ollie had feelings for him that went beyond the bedroom, and that he meant more to her than a quick fling with her boss.

It was in her warm eyes, in the way she looked at him and sighed. He could see it when her face softened and in her many, sometimes subconscious, gestures of affection: a head on his shoulder here, a hand on his knee there. Despite her vow not to become attached again, she had—with Mat and with him.

She loved Mat, of that he had no doubt. She might even be in love with him…

And he was halfway to being in love with her…but it wasn't enough. Love never was.

Honestly, it would be easy to tell her that he had feelings for her—it was the truth—and to ask her to stay. He could see them living together, being together, raising Mat and any other kids they had together. Her staying in Copenhagen with him would be an elegant solution to some of his current problems.

But…

But she wanted more than to be a wife and mother, she wanted her own business, to make her mark on the world. Deep down inside, he knew she wasn't being unreasonable, and could admit he was being ridiculously unfair by asking her to make Mat and him her entire focus, but he felt the need to push the envelope. He wanted to test whether she'd make the sacrifices for him his parents never had. He wanted her to prove that she wasn't anything like his mother, to show him over and over again that his heart, and Mat's, would be in super-safe hands.

But, in doing that, wasn't he emulating his father, placing what he needed and wanted above what his wife and son needed? He was a product of two dysfunctional people and today he was showing Ollie exactly how messed up he truly was.

But he couldn't stop. If he did, he would have to slice himself open emotionally and allow her to take full possession of his heart, to trust that she wouldn't hurt him.

He couldn't do it. It was too much of a risk, and he knew that any hope and optimism—love—were being obliterated by fear, old hurts and the reopening of ancient wounds.

'You can't have it all, Ollie,' he said, halting her progress off the deck.

He watched as she turned round and walked back to him, her back ramrod-straight and her eyes narrowed.

'What do you mean by that?'

'You can't be a wife and a mother and a lover. Not with me, at least.'

He knew that his words would be a death blow, killing whatever they'd had. He also knew that Ollie would never stand for the ultimatum he was laying down, but wasn't killing this quickly better than death by degrees? In the long run, wouldn't this hurt less?

'What are you trying to say, Bo?' she asked, genuinely confused.

'You've been imagining us being together, that we could commit to each other and raise Mat together,' he said, pushing the words out. Man, this was more painful than he'd thought it would be. When she didn't issue a denial, he sighed and pushed on. 'If you stayed, you would have to choose between me and having a business, and we'd have to be your only priority.'

She looked at him for a long time before speaking again. 'So, you are asking me to stay here with you as your lover? And nanny to Mat?'

Ollie blinked, waiting for him to say something else. He frowned, wondering what was going on in her sharp brain and behind her now cool eyes.

'For interest's sake, what do I get if I agree to that, Bo?'

Because he'd never imagined that this conversation would get this far, he had to think quickly. He shrugged and gestured to his house. 'You'd get to live in one of the most beautiful countries in the world, in one of the most exciting capitals on the planet and stay in spectacular houses. You and Mat would travel with me, five star all the way. I'd give you a generous allowance and...'

Her instruction to stop talking wasn't loud but he heard it. He searched her face for what she was feeling but, for the first time, he couldn't read her and knew he'd gone too far. She was a blank canvas, remote and impenetrable. 'No.'

Right, well, there it was—finally. Although he'd expected her to refuse his offer, he still felt wildly disappointed.

She looked past his shoulder to the sea beyond him and he watched her shoulders rise and fall. When she looked back at him, he saw the disappointment in her eyes. 'You made that offer knowing that I would never agree to it and it was beneath you.'

Maybe.

'The sad thing is, you have no idea what I want and need from you—even less than my ex-fiancé, and that's saying something. Or any man.'

'And what's that?'

'Your unquestionable support. I'd need you to hand me a set of wings and tell me to fly, to tell me that'll you'll catch me if I fall. I'd need you to love me enough to allow me to reach my full potential as a person.

'I'm worth that, Bo. And, if you can't see that, if you can't give that to me, then it's right that I walk away... just as you intended me to.'

Anger, pain and disappointment chased each other across her face and a cold hand squeezed his heart. He'd hurt her and he hadn't wanted to do that. But he knew that, if someone tried to be everything, they ended up failing somewhere down the line and people got hurt.

Ollie tipped her head and narrowed her eyes at him. 'Here's a counter-offer for you: why don't you stay at home full-time and look after Mat? You have lots of money and I doubt you'd need to work again if you didn't have to. Why don't you give up work and look after Mat full-time? Then I'll run my business.'

Give up designing? Walk away from Sørenson Yachts? Was she mad? Before he could tell her how ludicrous her suggestion was, she lifted her eyebrows. 'I can see the "no" all over your face. So, tell me, why is there a set of rules for you but they don't apply to me? Why is your professional fulfilment so much more important than mine?'

Bo rubbed the back of his neck. Of course it wasn't and he had no defence. So he dug his hole a little deeper when he spoke again. 'I design yachts and you look after kids for a living—it's not the same!'

'Of course it is!' Ollie whipped back. 'That is such a weak argument, Sørenson!'

Ollie held up her hand. 'Look, we're going around in circles. I want it all, Bo, and you can't give me that. You know it and I know it. So I am going to make this easy on both of us and walk away from you and Mat as you very obviously want me to do. I survived Becca's death, and I'll survive losing you and Mat too. It'll hurt, but I will be okay.'

She pushed her curls off her face and tried to smile. 'Was I an idiot for becoming attached to you? Sure. I knew that it would end like this. But I'd rather be an idiot who had two wonderful months with you than be careful and miss out. I'd rather be an idiot who's prepared to take a chance on love and being hurt than living in the past and being too scared to step outside his comfort zone.'

Right, it was obvious he was the idiot.

Ollie looked down at the papers lying at their feet before allowing her eyes to connect with his. 'Hire Helen, Bo. You won't regret it, I promise you.'

'Love.'

It was such a small word, just four letters, but it had the power to make or break a person's spirit, to buoy them up or to make them plummet down into the depths of hell.

Bo felt plenty of other 'L' words for her—like and lust came to mind. Love was not one of them. If he did, he would want what was best for her, he'd want her to be everything she could be with no restrictions. If he loved her, he would trust her to make good decisions, for herself and them, the family she so desperately wanted with him. He'd want her to be more, do more and achieve more than just being his nanny-cum-lover.

Ollie loved her job—it was an honour and a responsibility looking after someone else's child—but, damn it, she was allowed to want more, to be more. She was allowed to have a career, as well as be a parent and a lover. To love and be loved. As her parents' marriage had shown her, two strong, successful people could have it all.

She understood why Bo thought it wasn't possible. He had a terrible relationship with Bridget, and had not had much of a relationship with his father. His mother's primary focus had been, and still was, on her work. She'd never given her husband or son any emotional support or showed any interest in them as people, in their lives or in their interests.

But, man, it hurt that Bo was confusing her with his fridge-for-a-heart mother. Ollie knew about boundaries and was emotionally aware enough to lead a balanced life—she'd watched her mum do it all her life. Her mum worked full-time but neither she nor her brothers had felt as if they were emotionally neglected. Her parents had always made sure that they were home at a reasonable hour, they'd eaten dinner together as a family and weekends had been declared work-free zones. They'd been present, interested and involved. Apart from their disagreement about her choice of career, they'd been pretty awesome parents.

But it was her career, her life, and she wouldn't let Bo or her parents tell her how to live it. Becca's death had taught her that she didn't know how much time she had on this rock called Earth and she wasn't going to waste any of it.

She'd find a way around her parents' expectations; it

required her to have a tough conversation with them but she was up for that. She should've addressed this issue a long time ago but, feeling numb from Becca's death, she'd simply pushed it away and shoved her head into the sand. After her hard conversation with Bo two days ago, she felt she was strong enough to tackle her parents. After all, her heart was broken already.

Standing on the beach, Ollie looked up at the house above her, thinking of the man inside who would be waking up around now. She'd slipped out of the house much earlier, unable to sleep in the guest bedroom alone.

Their relationship had shifted seismically and the words they'd said couldn't be pulled back. She'd been too hurt and angry to sleep with, or even talk to him, so she'd removed her clothes from Bo's closet and her toiletries from his bathroom and decamped to the luxurious guest bedroom, the one furthest from his.

She was now his son's nanny, nothing more and nothing less. The baby monitor in her hand vibrated and she turned up the volume. Through the state-of-the-art speaker, she heard Mat's snuffle and knew it was time to head back to the house. She was exhausted, emotionally wiped out, and was operating on minimal sleep. She didn't know how she was going to get through the day.

But she would. She had a job to do and money to earn.

'Hello, my beautiful boy.'

Ollie heard Bo's voice on the baby monitor and placed her hand on her heart. She sank to the sand and placed her head on her knees as she listened to her lover tell his son how amazing he was and how much he loved him.

She heard the sound of Mat's baby grow being unsnapped, the crackle of a nappy being laid out and Mat's gurgling laughter as Bo blew raspberries on his fat tummy. It was what Bo did every time he changed Mat's nappy.

Bo was madly, crazy, head-over-heels in love with Mat. She just wished he felt the same way about her.

But if wishes were horses and all that... He didn't love her, he couldn't commit to her and she should get used to the fact.

'So, this morning I spoke to a lovely lady who wants to meet you again,' Bo told Mat. 'I interviewed her, and she sounds amazing, and I think you'll like her. And, best of all, she'll be a nanny and only a nanny. I won't be distracted again.'

Helen? It had to be...

'I told her that I needed her urgently and she's agreed to be here by the end of the week.'

Mat released another stream of babble and Ollie imagined he was telling his dad that nobody was as wonderful as Ollie and that he'd miss her. It was far more likely that the little boy was probably just asking for his breakfast.

'I'm going to miss her too, but we can't find a middle ground.'

Ollie frowned at the baby monitor. What? He hadn't offered her a middle ground! It had been his way or no way—'stay here and don't do or be anything else'.

Ollie resisted the urge to storm up to the house and set him straight. But she didn't have the energy and her heart had been kicked around enough as it was. Bo had drawn his line in the sand and that was as far and as deep as he wanted to go.

It wasn't deep enough and far enough for her. Knowing she couldn't listen any more, Ollie switched off the baby monitor and allowed the tears to trickle down her face.

Bo was with Mat, and she could take a few more minutes to sit on the private beach on this special island. It was, Ollie admitted, a spectacularly pretty place to get heartbroken.

Well done, Ollie.

In the end, their parting was terribly civil and very mature. It was everything Ollie didn't feel. Helen had arrived in Copenhagen when they returned from Bornholm, and Ollie had helped Helen move into the second of Bo's very luxurious guest bedrooms and and had taken her through Mat's routine.

Mat, being the sunny character he was, had gurgled and laughed his way through the transition, happy to spend the majority of his time in Helen's arms. With Bo avoiding her, or only talking to her when he absolutely had to, Ollie had felt as if he'd pushed her to the side, a spare part for a well-tuned car.

But her immense sadness at leaving Bo and Mat had been tempered by relief as she couldn't live with the implacable and reticent Bo any longer. She hardly recognised the man she'd loved and laughed with, the one who'd loved her so thoroughly, who'd looked at her with affection and who'd bestowed his sweet, slow smiles on her.

On the morning she was due to fly out, Ollie promised herself she wouldn't cry. But tears burned her eyes when she hugged Mat for the last time, and her heart cracked when Helen kissed her cheek, hugged her and walked Mat back into Bo's house, leaving Bo and her alone outside. Bo placed her luggage in the taxi and, when he came back to stand in front of her, she couldn't meet his eyes, choosing to stare at the walnut-brown sweater covering his wide chest.

'I'm sorry I can't give you what you need, Olivia,' Bo said as he opened the door to the taxi for her.

She tipped her head back to look at him, taking in the two-day-old stubble on his hard jaw, the furrow between his eyebrows and his taut mouth. 'Do you even know what I need, Bo?'

Confusion jumped into his eyes, and she knew that he didn't get it. Or, if he did, he didn't want to acknowledge the truth. She considered getting into the taxi and leaving, but she didn't want to leave with misunderstandings between them.

Gathering her courage, she looked into those eyes she loved so much and forced her tongue to form the words she needed to say and he needed to hear. 'I love you and I want to be with you. I want to help you raise Mat. But I also want to work, to do something worthwhile and important. I wish you could trust me when I tell you that I wouldn't hurt you or Mat, Bo.'

He looked as though an invisible pair of hands was around his neck and squeezing tight. 'You're asking me to take too big a chance, Olivia, a massive risk. And I can't.'

She nodded, blinking back her tears. 'I guess I knew that but I had to try.' Knowing that there was nothing more to say, she stood on her tiptoes and kissed his cheek, inhaling his fresh, clean, citrusy aftershave for the last time. 'Goodbye, Bo. Hug your boy every day for me.'

Ollie slipped into the back seat, shut the door, rested her head on the headrest and closed her eyes.

It was done. Her Copenhagen caper was over. Now she just had to find a way to live her life without Bo and Mat in it.

CHAPTER FOURTEEN

OLLIE'S PARENTS HAD a strict dress code for all their employees—suit and tie for the men, corporate boring for the women—and Ollie knew that arriving in tight, skinny jeans, an off-the-shoulder top and high-top trainers was not suitable corporate attire. She saw eyebrows rising as she walked down the long hallway of Cooper & Co, trying to ignore the pointed glances of her parents' employees behind the glass-walled offices.

Taking a deep breath, she walked to the end of the hallway where her parents and two of her brothers had their offices, and looked to the left at the empty office she knew had been designated for her use. She shook her head. Nope, not happening. Her office was next to her oldest brother's and, feeling her eyes on him, Michael lifted his head and grinned. Then his grin faded, and he grimaced as he looked to the conference room behind her.

A talk with their parents in the conference room was never a good thing. He mouthed, 'Are you okay?' and Ollie responded by rocking her hand up and down.

She would be; she just had to get through the next half hour. It wasn't going to be fun in any way.

Through the glass walls of the swish conference room, Ollie watched her parents walk out of the massive office they shared. They'd managed to live and work together for so many years and it amazed her. Her father was tall and dignified. Her mum was shorter and rounder but, as always, was immaculately dressed. Energy crackled off her. Her mum could work, raise kids, be the chair of the PTA and bake bread. She was a master at multitasking and, because of her, Ollie knew that she could be a wife, a lover, a mother and a businesswoman.

But it didn't matter what she *knew* she could do. Bo had needed to be convinced and that hadn't happened. That wouldn't happen.

She missed him. Since leaving Copenhagen three days ago, she hadn't heard from him. Helen had sent her a couple of messages and photos of Mat, and he seemed fine, as happy and wonderful as always. Helen hadn't mentioned Bo and Ollie hadn't asked.

Her phone remained stupidly, stubbornly silent and Ollie cursed herself for thinking that he would message or call, or that he would follow her to London. She was spinning impossible dreams and she pushed those thoughts away. He'd made his position clear—he couldn't, wouldn't, commit to her. He wouldn't commit to anyone, ever. She would never hear from him again and it was time to start accepting that reality.

But it hurt so much. She felt as if she were walking around with a heart punctured by porcupine quills. And that the quills were still lodged in her barely functioning organ.

The door to the conference room opened and her father stepped back to let her mum precede him. Her dad had beautiful manners and, despite being a force of nature herself and a feminist to the core, her mum loved her dad's courtly gestures.

Ollie crossed the room to him, allowing his strong

arms to come around her, resting her head on his strong chest. Her dad gave the best hugs and she wished that she didn't have to disappoint him.

But she couldn't live a lie. Nor could she spend the next five years hating every minute of her job and life.

Her mum looked at her watch and cleared her throat. 'We have a busy day and need to get on,' she told Ollie, and then raised her eyebrows at her super-casual outfit. 'That's not how I expect you to dress at work, Olivia.'

'But I'm not one of your employees, Mum,' Ollie said, pulling out a chair and sitting down. And she never would be. Her parents just didn't know it yet.

After her parents were seated, her mum directly opposite her and her dad one chair to the right, Ollie gathered her courage. She just needed to spit it out and be done.

Expect fireworks, expect recriminations, and maybe some raised voices, but you can't let that put you off.

She was convinced that they could find a solution that wouldn't involve her sacrificing the next five years of her life.

'I came here to talk to you about the fact that I am supposed to start work here in ten days,' Ollie said.

Jasmine leaned forward and tapped her bright-pink nails on the glass table. 'Olivia, please don't tell me you are taking another nannying position. We made a deal that you would return to work.'

Ollie shook her head. 'I can't do it, Mum, please don't ask me to.' Ollie hauled in a deep breath before continuing. 'I understand that you spent an enormous amount of money on my education, and I am prepared to pay you back. I can do a transfer this afternoon, and maybe we could work out a payment plan, with interest, for me to repay you the rest over a couple of years.'

Her mum looked as though she'd been hit with a thick branch of a tree. Her father, strangely, didn't look that surprised. He simply leaned back, folded his arms across his chest and sent her an easy smile.

'We never expected you to repay us the money, Olivia, and I'm sorry if you felt like there were conditions attached to us educating you. That was our choice and our pleasure. We know that you love what you do, but you can be more than a nanny. It's a fine job, I'm not knocking it, but you have a first-class brain and we'd like to see you use it in a more—' he hesitated '—business-like setting. But, if being a nanny is what you have your heart set on, then we will support you.'

He frowned at her mum, who was staring down at her nails. Paul cleared his throat, and her mum finally lifted her head and nodded.

It was a huge concession and Ollie knew how lucky she was to have parents who loved her beyond reason.

'I'm still not happy about you not joining our firm,' Jasmine told her, lifting her chin. 'You'd earn a huge salary and all the perks that come with a corporate job.'

'What makes you think I don't have that now?' Ollie asked. 'I earn a very good salary, Mum!'

'You earn a good wage, darling—professionals earn salaries,' her mum snapped back.

Sighing, Ollie tapped her phone, pulled up her latest wage slip and pushed her phone across the table. Her father grinned when he saw her take-home pay and a touch of pink touched her cheeks. Right, that should shut her mum up for a minute—maybe two.

'So what's the plan, Olivia?' her dad asked her.

'Why do you think I have a plan?' Ollie asked him,

surprised at his perspicacity. If still waters ran deep, then her dad was a mile-deep aquifer.

'Because we didn't raise a fool. You've always had a plan—you've always thought ahead. So, what is it?'

She shrugged. She might as well tell them. 'I want to buy into Sabine's nanny business. If you are being serious about me not needing to repay you for the cost of my education—'

'We are,' her dad assured her.

She sent him a grateful, tremulous smile. 'Then I can buy a quarter-share of her business. It will take me a while but I will eventually, hopefully, buy her out.'

Paul nodded and scratched his chin. 'Right. And how much would you need to buy this business?' he asked.

Ollie told him the figure and waited for him to flinch. When he didn't, she was reminded that her father dealt with huge figures and numbers all the time. 'Ask her to send me her financials: I want to do a deep-dive into her books. I'm not letting my daughter buy into a company if I haven't inspected the company financials.'

It took all of Ollie's willpower not to fling herself across the table and hug her dad. Instead, she sent him another tremulous smile and blinked away her tears. He *got* her. He sent her a small wink and spoke again.

'And you won't be buying a small share. With what you have to spend, you could buy half her business,' Paul added.

Ollie stared at her dad, wondering if this was the moment when he'd lost the plot. She spread her hands out. She didn't have that sort of money. 'Dad, what are you talking about?'

He smiled at her. 'I received an email from a Bo Sørenson earlier this week.'

Bo? Her Bo? What was happening here?

'He transferred a hundred thousand pounds into our trust account, with explicit instructions that the money was to be used any way you wanted to. He explained the money as being an additional bonus for looking after his son. You weren't joking when you said that your clients were wealthy, sweetheart. That's a huge bonus...'

'But why did he send it to you?'

'He wanted to bypass the agency—he wanted this to be between you and him—and he didn't think you would send him your bank details if he asked.'

No, she wouldn't have, because he'd already paid her a bonus via Sabine, the standard amount Sabine had suggested as per the contract he'd signed. He'd paid her more—and for what, exactly?

She was going to kill him. She really was.

What?
Are You?
Playing at?

Bo grimaced at the three messages that had dropped into his phone a few minutes ago and felt the heat of Ollie's anger across the miles that separated them. Right, talking her round was going to take more effort than he'd thought.

Sitting in a taxi on his way to her parents' accounting firm in Wimbledon, Bo ran a hand over his jaw, wincing at the scruff beneath his fingers. He hadn't had the energy to do much over the past week, and shaving hadn't been high on his list of priorities. Neither had been eating. Sleeping had been impossible.

He'd spent time with Mat, and his little boy had kept him from climbing into bed, pulling the covers over his head and pretending the world didn't exist. But he had a company to run, an example to set and a son to be responsible for.

But work, once his whole world and his solace, meant nothing when his thoughts constantly went to Ollie, wondering what she was doing and how she was, whether she missed him at all.

Helen was wonderful with Mat, but she wasn't Ollie. Nobody was and nobody could be. Nobody made his house smell of roses. He missed hearing her laughter and her very off-key singing. He missed waking up with her, loving her at night—and in the morning, the afternoon and every minute in between. His life without her was miserable and bleak. When she left, she'd drained all the colour from his world.

He missed her. The guy who never missed anyone, who'd never allowed himself to feel, was pining for a woman.

It was no less than he deserved.

But, over the past few days, he'd realised that his current state of existence wasn't any way to live. Being apart from Ollie had made him realise that he wasn't his mother, cold and emotionless, that he couldn't view life the way she did and that not everything was a transaction. Neither was he his father: Bo had tried to flit from woman to woman and keep his relationships shallow and that had worked until Ollie had dropped into his life with her sparkling eyes and bouncing curls, bringing happiness to his cold, barren life.

It was as though someone had switched the light on in his life and when she'd left—when he'd sent her away—the power to his world had been turned off.

He was tired of moping around, of being sad, hurt

and lonely. If having her in his life meant marrying her, fully throwing himself into those waters, then that was what he would do.

Nothing was worse than being a walking, talking, flesh-and muscle-covered broken heart.

My girl's not happy with you.

Bo pulled a face at Paul's incoming text and knew he hadn't made a great impression on the man he hoped would be his future father-in-law. He hadn't even met the guy yet but he'd asked him via a video call—because he wasn't a complete moron—whether he could marry his daughter. Paul, dignified and quietly spoken, had made it very clear that, if he hurt his daughter again, he would bury his body so deep that not even Satan would be able to find it.

Bo believed him.

Paul had also told him where Ollie was and for that he'd be in his debt for ever. As long as he had Ollie, he didn't care.

The car approached the Cooper & Co building and Bo directed his driver to pull up before he reached it. As he did so, he saw Ollie flounce out of the building, irritation radiating from her face.

Right, she was mad. Well, she'd just have to get over it.

He got out of the car, slammed the door shut and leaned his butt on the closed door, folding his arms as he watched her fumble in her bag for her phone. He shoved his hand into the back pocket of his trousers and waited for his own phone to vibrate. Yep, there she was.

'Olivia.'

'Don't you Olivia me,' she yelled, spinning away from

a man who gave her a dirty look for her loud voice. 'What do you think you were doing, contacting my father and paying me an additional bonus through him? My parents aren't expecting me to repay my education costs and I can buy my way into Sabine's business on my own.'

'Call it a wedding gift,' he murmured but she was too angry to hear his heartfelt words. But, honestly, he couldn't wait to call her his wife... If he managed to get to the point of proposing without her ripping his head off.

'What do you think you were doing? How dare you contact my father? What do you mean it's a wedding gift?' she shouted so loudly that he could hear her from where he stood. Right, so much for the English sense of decorum. Olivia was missing that today.

Frankly, he didn't care. He could work with anger. It scared him far less than a studied non-reaction. Ignoring him would have meant that she didn't care enough to feel anything.

Heat was fine, cold was a problem.

'Argh! I cannot believe I am fighting with you over the phone!' she yelled.

'Well, you can fight with me in person, if you prefer.'

'I want to fight with you now and not have to catch a flight, Sørenson!'

'Your wish is my command,' he told her, lifting his hand to wave. He saw her look over at him, her eyes bouncing over the car before snapping back to look at him. She slapped her free hand on a slim hip and pushed her sunglasses up into her hair. Even from a slight distance, he could see that her eyes were narrowed. If anyone held a lit match to her, she'd explode like a Catherine wheel.

'Are you coming to me or am I coming to you?' Bo asked, keeping his tone reasonable.

Ollie looked around, her shoulders hunched up around her ears. 'I'll meet you at the entrance to the Italian garden in Cannizaro Park in twenty minutes.'

'Why don't you just get in the car and the driver can take us there?' Bo suggested, frustrated at being separated from her for one minute more.

'Twenty minutes, Sørenson,' she snapped. 'And, hopefully, that's enough time for my temper to cool.'

Right, okay then. He knew better than to push his luck.

Ollie stomped up to the low brick wall of the Italian garden, thinking that no man should look so good wearing a plain white polo-shirt, walnut-brown chinos and white trainers worn without socks. He looked as though he'd just stepped out of a cool, air-conditioned car—which he had—while she was hot and a little sticky from her mile-and-a-half stomp through Wimbledon. On leaving Cooper & Co, she'd pulled her hair up into a messy bun, but a few curls stuck to her neck and forehead.

She did not doubt that the little make-up she'd worn this morning was long gone and that she looked as frazzled and freaked out as she felt. Crossing her arms across her torso, she slowed her pace as she approached Bo, unable to believe he was in London. And, if he was here, where was Mat?

He answered her unspoken question. 'Helen, Mat and I booked into Brown's Hotel this morning,' Bo told her, handing her a cold bottle of water. She looked down at it and saw that he'd cracked open the lid for her. Hot and grumpy, and feeling as if she was a taut wire about to snap, she swallowed half the water in the bottle.

'Is he okay?' she demanded. 'Mat?'

'Mat is fine,' Bo replied, sitting on the edge of the wall

and stretching out his long legs. 'I, on the other hand, am a wreck.'

Sure he was, Ollie silently scoffed. With his smart clothing and fancy watch, and expensive sunglasses over his eyes, he looked like the rich, urbane success story he was. Then Bo lifted his glasses off his forehead and pushed them into his hair and Ollie realised he was anything *but* fine.

The circles under his eyes were even darker than hers and he looked a shade paler than when she'd left him in Copenhagen. And a few years older. Right, so maybe her leaving had affected him.

She was not going to think about his comment about her additional bonus being a wedding gift. He was being sarcastic, making a joke...he couldn't possibly have meant it.

Ollie rested the cool bottle against her hot cheek. 'What are you doing in London, Bo? And why did you give me such a huge bonus? It was totally over the top. You gave me a bonus when I left Copenhagen.'

'You know why, Olivia. Although your father is squawking that he will repay the money if you decide you don't want me, Ol.'

Want him? Of course she wanted him. The problem was that she wanted him all in, not just him dipping a toe or foot...

So he'd been talking to her dad—when? And for how long had that been going on? Bo stood up and came to stand in front of her, so close that the hand holding the water bottle pushed the fabric of his shirt into his hard chest. How was she supposed to think when he was so close and he smelled so good?

She looked up into his deep-green eyes. 'Can you give

me some breathing room, please?' He had to move because there was no way she could make her feet step away from him.

He smiled. 'It's a big park, Ollie, with lots of space. All you have to do is take a step back.'

Argh! She tried, she really did, but her brain sent the wrong signal and, instead of moving away, she placed her palm on his chest, stood on her tiptoes and placed her mouth on his. He was here: how was she supposed not to kiss him? Given the chance, she always would. Kissing Bo was what she was put on this earth to do.

Bo lifted his hands to hold her face as his mouth took a lovely and leisurely exploration of hers, taking his time to reacquaint himself with her. It was a kiss that said 'I missed you' and 'so glad you are here', gentle but with a hint of heat. Ollie knew that it wouldn't take much to make them spark and then burn. They were that combustible.

After a few minutes, Bo pulled back, wrapped his arms around her back and pulled her into his chest, wrapping her up in his embrace. He placed his mouth by her ear and his words were soft but powerful. 'Please don't leave me again, Ol.'

She had to be strong; she couldn't allow the wonderfulness of being back in Bo's arms strip her of her sensibility. She pushed herself back and his arms fell to his sides, disappointment on his face. Ollie lifted her hands to her face, mortified to feel hot tears on her skin. 'I can't do this, Bo.'

Bo gently peeled his hands off her face and, with the pads of his thumbs, wiped her tears away. 'Olivia, why do you think I am here?'

She stared at a spot below his size-thirteen trainer.

'Because you feel sorry for me? Because you want me to come back to Copenhagen to look after Mat, because you can kill two birds with one stone? So that you can have a lover and a nanny'?

He dropped a kiss on her forehead and his mouth curved into a smile. 'Sorry, but I'm not firing Helen for you. She's awesome.'

'She is?' Of course she was, she'd recommended her, and there was no one better to look after Mat. No one could do a better job...except her. Didn't Bo think she was as good as Helen?

'I have no idea what you are trying to say,' Ollie complained.

'And I'm making a hash of it because I've never done this before. I don't know how to tell a woman I love her, that she's my world, that I can't live without her. I don't know the words to tell her I'm a miserable, grumpy shell without her.'

With every word, Ollie felt herself lightening and brightening. 'You tell her like that, Bo.'

He looked surprised to find that his words had made an impression. Curling a hand around her neck, he looked down at her, his eyes warm with affection, desire and, yes, love—*woohoo*!

'I'm so in love with you, Olivia. Loving someone so much scares me but I'd rather live my life scared than live it without you.'

Ollie reached up to kiss him, smiling against his mouth. 'I love you too, Bo.'

Bo released a shuddery sigh. 'Thank goodness for that.' He banded an arm around her waist and hauled her into him. 'Now kiss me properly, Olivia. I've missed you so damn much.'

She would, she told him, but if they started to kiss they wouldn't talk, and they needed to. 'Let's just get it all said and done so that we can move on, Bo.'

Bo nodded and looked around. Spotting an empty bench, he took her hand and tugged her over to it. Thankfully, it was in the shade. When Bo sat down, Ollie put her hand on his thigh and turned to face him. She pulled her bottom lip between her teeth. 'Did you mean what you said earlier, about wanting to marry me? That the bonus money you sent my dad was a wedding gift?'

He lifted her hand and kissed the tips of her fingers. 'I did. I even asked your dad if I could marry you.'

Ollie's mouth dropped open. 'But you don't believe in marriage!'

'I do with *you*,' Bo told her. 'With you, I want the white wedding and the matching gold rings, the wedding contracts and the licence. I want more kids and to renew those vows on our tenth, twentieth and fiftieth wedding anniversaries. I want it all, Olivia, and you know how determined I can be when I want something.'

She did and every nerve ending was on fire thinking that *she* was what he wanted. But there was still one hurdle she needed to jump over. 'I can't be a stay-at-home wife and mother, Bo. I can't be someone who dedicates every last breath she has to her family. I mean, I will be the best partner I can be, but I want to work as well.'

Ollie held her breath, waiting for the anvil to drop. He took his time answering and, when he did, his words were accompanied by an understanding smile. 'Of course you do, Olivia, that's why I said I wasn't going to let Helen go.' He ran his fingers up and down her arm, his expression thoughtful. 'When you were gone, I realised how wrong it was of me to expect that from you. I wouldn't want to give up my work, not even for you.

'You being a working mum wasn't an unreasonable request, Olivia, I just let my fear run away with me. I got the past, my parents' neglect and you tangled up and I was terrified of getting hurt again, of needing love and not getting it. I was being unfair and was more than a little ridiculous. I'm so sorry I made light of your dreams and aspirations. They are no less important than mine.'

His smile was soft and tender. 'I want you to have everything, experience everything, be and do everything that makes you happy. And, if owning an au pair agency is what you want, then you have my full support.'

He was telling her everything she'd so desperately needed to hear and nothing she'd expected him to say. He'd handed her the world.

And then he gave her a little more.

'And, if I need to pull back from my company, then that's what I will do. I can hand over some of my responsibilities to my managers and spend more time at home if you need to be in Paris,' he told her, sounding determined. 'You living there isn't ideal, but Mat and I can fly to you one weekend, and you can fly to us the next. We'll make it work,' he added. 'I'll do whatever I can to have you in my life, Ol.'

Her heart caught at the determination in his voice, the love in his eyes. 'Bo, I might need to be in Paris occasionally, especially at the beginning, but not on an ongoing basis. Most of what I need to do can be done online. The pandemic showed us that.'

'So all you'd need is a place to work?'

She grinned at his excitement. 'Do you think you can find a spare corner for me in your little house? You know, the one with the four guest rooms and the apartment above the garage in one of the most sought-after suburbs in Copenhagen?'

'Yeah, I'm not sure about that,' Bo teased back. 'Maybe you can work out of my closet off the master bedroom. Preferably naked.'

'Not going to happen, Sørenson!' Ollie hooked her arm around his neck and placed her cheek against his. 'Are we doing this, Bo? Are we going to get married?'

'We are.' He tucked a curl behind her ear and dragged his mouth across hers. 'I'm sorry I don't have a ring, but I wasn't that confident I could pull this off.'

Ollie laughed. 'Your standards are slipping, Sørenson,' she teased him. 'You only gave me the means to buy into a business I love and, far more importantly, your heart and your love.'

'And my son,' he reminded her. 'Will you be his mum, Ol? Will you be mine? Be ours?'

'Always,' she promised him. But always might not be long enough…

* * * * *

THE FORBIDDEN
PRINCESS
HE CRAVES

LORRAINE HALL

MILLS & BOON

For Soraya.

Thank you for your boundless enthusiasm.

CHAPTER ONE

PRINCESS ELSEBET THORE knew she was a princess, and as such her role in life was very simple. She was nothing more than a pawn to be used by her father, King of Mathav, to keep their tiny nation from being absorbed by the larger ones that surrounded it.

As such, Elsebet had been secluded on her father's private, secret island in the North Sea since she'd become *of* age. To protect her, he insisted.

Elsebet hadn't always been cognizant of *what* she was being protected from, considering her father had kept her under lock and key back at home, but at least on the island she had some sense of freedom. The staff was small, though devoted and more like family than staff. Because the island was so isolated, so unknown and so inaccessible because of its craggy peaks and inhospitable shoreline, she had some measures of liberty she'd never enjoyed back in Mathav.

She could walk the beaches alone, as she did this windy, stormy morning. She could nap in the library unchaperoned. She helped with chores, felt *useful* here, and sometimes, she could even make her own meals if she so wished. These were all things that never would have happened back at her father's castle in Mathav. She would have *always* had a chaperone, and never been allowed to do anything that might be viewed as beneath a princess.

It had taken her a while to appreciate this, but now she did. Unfortunately, regardless of what freedom she'd found here, she was twenty-two years old now and her entire adolescence had been spent on this island. Her only company the staff of three and her father when he visited.

She was lonely. She was bored. As she took her usual morning walk along the little alcove of sandy beach, searching for the seashells she had taken to making art murals out of just to have something to do, she looked out at the sea and wished for something other than what she had.

She had tried to express her restlessness to her father as a child. She knew he cared for her. He had, in fact, doted on her for most of her childhood. But the older she'd gotten, the more she'd looked like her late mother, the more she'd *expressed* her frustration, and the less she'd seen him. The more she'd demanded or cried or begged, the more certain and determined he'd become to keep her on this tiny island to await the political marriage that would help Mathav.

These days, she didn't even try to express her negative feelings, and he seemed content to believe that once he had chosen a husband for her, she would be too busy starting a family to want anything more.

Elsebet wished she could believe that. But marriage seemed, much like her current life, rather confining. Though she supposed a husband and children would make her less lonely.

She hoped.

Regardless of how she felt about any of it, she would do her duty to Mathav. Her mother had died in childbirth, trying to give the King a son who would rule. Instead, her father had been left with a girl he hadn't known what to do with, and without the heart to remarry and produce more heirs. A girl who had become an *emotional* outburst of an adolescent and needed to be sent away.

Elsebet tried not to dwell on that now. She had her island, her small measure of freedom, and the promise she would do her duty to her family name and to her country someday. She would certainly never let his devotion to the mother she'd never known be punished by not being exactly what he needed. Now that she was grown, she fully understood this.

It would be a failure and betrayal to entertain any other ideas.

She just wished her duty didn't include being *stuck* here, waiting to marry a stranger her father hadn't even chosen yet. All politics and power and no *love*.

You have indulged in far too many fairy tales, Elsebet," her father had admonished her when she'd still been naive enough to express her desire for *more* to him. *"Love threatens duty. Love is more pain than it's worth."*

She knew her father spoke from his own experience, having lost his wife and feeling incapable of putting duty before her memory. But if Elsebet's life was destined to be nothing more than isolation and duty, why not find enjoyment where she could?

On a sigh, she kicked another rock. The ocean was angry today, the wind was cold. She looked at the castle with its rustic, ancient stones, built to weather just this…and it had, for centuries. Here on this tiny island—the castle towers taking up most of the land—the stones had survived everything the ocean could throw at it.

She was part of that, and she would remain. Her father told her this should fill her with pride, with purpose. She tried to feel all those things. Sometimes, when the castle withstood particularly violent storms, she did. Proud that she was from a long line of Thores who had survived these harsh lands and led their people with strength and courage.

Today, she could not find that sense of pride. Restlessness was the only thing inside of her, no matter how she tried to force it away. She wished she could be the ocean, angry and dramatic. Beating against the boundaries the land tried to keep it in.

On a frown, Elsebet turned toward the sea. The lashing waves. The gray, angry skies. Sometimes she dreamed of wading out there, to see what was beyond the dangerous, rocky cove. Was there a calm sea? More islands? Something like adventure?

It was certain death, so she didn't *actually* consider doing it, but sometimes she daydreamed she was brave enough to find out for certain.

Today, she was only brave enough to walk out onto the rocks and sand of shore, but still out of the reach of the angry surf, in search of something that might have washed ashore that she could collect to turn into art. It was her only outlet here on this tiny island. Turning ocean wreckage into something beautiful. Dramatic or dreary. Angry or sad.

But only for her.

While dreaming of where each piece of debris or shell might have come from. What a world beyond this small slice of it might look like, feel like.

As she walked, she heard something strange. Not just the howling wind, not the usual crashing surf, but a kind of… *squelch*. A *thud* that spoke of great movement.

Surely she was hearing things on this loud, lonely morning. But still she moved toward the direction she thought she heard the sound. There was an odd little pile of wreckage behind one large boulder. Some wood, a few twisted pieces of shiny metal and then a hint of fabric.

As she got closer she realized the fabric wasn't just debris. It was a man's clothes. *On* a man. Not just a human who happened to be *male*, but a large and muscled figure, curled in a kind of heap. His clothes were torn, and his head and arm were bloody. But he was most definitely a *man*.

He moved, and just the twitch of his arm produced an odd, sucking sound in the sand. Elsebet jumped back, startled, but then quickly rushed forward. She had no idea how this man had washed up on her isolated beach, where no one dared sail. Perhaps she should have been more cautious approaching him, but it was clear he was hurt.

She knelt next to him, the damp from the cold sand seeping into her dress. Gingerly, she reached out and touched a cheek that wasn't bloody but was far too cold. "Come. Wake up."

Dark eyelashes fluttered, then she was pinned by nearly black eyes that met hers. She could see pain. And confusion. But he breathed. He lived. Her heart thundered in her chest, but she smiled.

"There, there. I've found you," she soothed. "We'll take care of you just fine."

Danil Laurentius never allowed himself to be caught off guard. He was not his king's most trusted guard simply because King Aras of Gintaras was his half brother. Danil was trusted because he was the best. Because he would give his life for his half brother, and the small nation Aras ruled. Danil was strong, ruthless, cunning and *never* at a disadvantage.

He had built himself into a legend, and had never once faltered. Because this was what Aras required, and Danil owed his brother *everything*.

These were all things he remembered, with some clarity.

How he got to be on this beach, aching and confused…this he was not clear about. Particularly when dark blue eyes the color of an angry ocean looked at him with a sweetness incongruous with anything angry.

He half believed her to be a siren. He *had* been sailing, hadn't he? He cast back in his memory for some answer. He had been sailing one of his smaller boats, but…why? Where? Had she lured him to the rocks? Would she drown him now?

He was just addled enough to wonder if it was even worth trying to escape someone so beautiful.

Foolish thought, that. He stared at the woman—blonde, slight and dressed in a plain frock that nipped in at the waist. Her long hair was pulled back, but many tendrils had escaped in the harsh wind and blew around her face. She wore sturdy boots that looked like they might keep out the wet and cold.

She had a fragile air about her, but she knelt next to him as if she didn't feel the cold at all. Something about her was oddly familiar and this gave him the errant thought to reach out and touch her wind-whipped cheek.

It would be warm, and he was very, *very* cold.

Her mouth curved, and she said something, but he didn't quite catch it in the rushing wind.

This all felt like little more than a dream. He blinked, wondering if he could dislodge her. Maybe she was a hallucination.

He tried to say something, but at the attempt everything inside of him erupted in a fire of pain. He moved, but that too started a cascade of new agony through him. So much so he could not clarify the jumble of his thoughts. If this was a dream, it was a nightmare.

Except for her.

"Stay here and I will get help," she said, louder now. Her

voice was oddly accented, and she did not speak his native tongue, but it was still a language he knew.

But could not think of the name of it.

Well, this was not good.

She stood as if to leave him here. And though he'd *heard* her mention help, the thought of being left alone filled him with a dread he did not understand.

He was *often* alone. It was how he lived his life. How he *preferred* things. All the better to turn himself into the invincible machine that would protect his brother at all costs. The legend of Danil Laurentius, King's Guard, fierce and fearsome warrior and commander of a navy he'd built up himself and a troop of Aras's soldiers, whom he'd spent his adult life training.

The Weapon.

But the thought of losing this little bright spot in the midst of a howling wind had him reaching out, in spite of the pain that shot through him. His hand curled around her forearm before she could stand and move away.

She was so warm. He needed…something.

Her eyes widened at his grip, but she did not wrench her arm away as he'd half expected. Her eyes softened even more and she knelt again. "Oh, you poor thing." She swept a hand over his brow, but it came away bloody. She tsked. "I can't possibly move you to the castle myself. You must let me go get you some help. I promise, it will be quick. And we will take good care of you, sir. You need help, and quickly."

He knew he must have a head injury, because his instinct was to believe her when he knew better than to trust random strangers on an empty beach. No matter how pretty she was or how sweet her voice.

Ignoring all the pain in his body, he moved, forcing himself into a sitting position. All the while she tutted at him and told him not to. He ignored her and fought off her attempts to keep him still.

His head throbbed. It was like excruciating fire to breathe, to swallow. And still he did not let himself rest. He used a rock to leverage himself onto his feet. He fought off the dizziness with every last shred of strength he could manage.

"You shouldn't be doing this," the woman continued to scold, as if he'd ever listened to a scold in his life outside of his grandmother's kitchen, and even that had been lifetimes ago.

The siren moved to his side at once, pressing her insubstantial frame to him as if he should lean on her, when his size and weight would no doubt crush her.

Though he didn't dare lean too heavily, the warmth of her and the way she stood upright while the world around him spun helped him find his footing. And not pitch back to the sand. He felt something thick and wet slide down his forehead, then his cheek.

It landed with a *plop* on the tip of his frayed boot. Blood.

"Well. You're up. So we'll get you inside and warm at once. Nielson will take a look at you. He's a doctor, so you needn't worry. We'll stitch up what needs stitching. Get you warm and fed and then figure out how to get you home. Are you alone?"

He opened his mouth to tell her he'd never had use for a doctor in his entire life. He cleaned up his own scrapes and broken bones, *thank you*. But it hurt, and no sound would come from his mouth.

As for being alone…he couldn't remember just yet. He looked out at the sea. Angry and stormy. Yes, he'd been alone, hadn't he? On the small boat he'd built years back. But why would he have sailed that small boat into such a place as this?

He shook his head.

"Your throat looks very bruised," she said, those soft eyes of hers looking anguished as she encouraged him to step forward with her. "It would likely be best if you didn't try to speak until Nielson has checked you over."

Danil pressed his lips together. He had no desire for someone to check him over, but it seemed *impossible* to speak. Not just because of the pain. He had pushed through all manner of physical pain and torture. Something was *wrong*.

Well, he was half-naked, frozen and injured. So *many* things were wrong. But the woman was leading him away from the rocks and sea and toward a building.

No, not anything as simple as a building.

It was a castle. Narrow though it was, it reached up in brooding, looming towers. Despite its small size when compared with his brother's castle, it took up almost the entire island—because the island was very small. He could see the ocean on every side.

Not just a tiny island, but minuscule. Taken up mostly by castle. With a surrounding rocky beach dangerous and precarious to any sailor who would be stupid enough to try and outsmart them.

Add the pretty, kind blonde currently leading him to the castle, away from the ocean and what likely had been meant to be his death.

Castle. Island. Rocks. *Princess*.

He wasn't sure everything came together then, but he remembered how he'd gotten here. And why.

His gaze moved to the woman at his side. Beautiful. *Royal*. No matter how simply she was dressed, how kind her eyes were. She was not just any random woman.

She was Princess Elsebet Thore. Who was meant to

marry his brother. Her father had broken his agreement with Danil's brother, but King Aras of Gintaras would not be denied by a change of heart.

So Aras had sent Danil to this no-name island, this isolated castle protected by only its rocky shores and dangerous coast, with one simple goal: kidnap the Princess and bring her home to Gintaras.

CHAPTER TWO

ELSEBET KNEW THIS was not right. The man should have remained sitting and allowed her to bring Nielson to him. He dripped blood as they walked, but she supposed the fact he walked at all was promising.

She had a million questions to ask him, but there was significant bruising and swelling all over his face, neck and chest—where clearly at some point whatever coat or shirt he'd been wearing had been ripped clean of him. His pants were torn and frayed but remained mostly intact, but his boots were falling apart as they walked.

Blood continued to trickle from gashes to his head and side. It made her heart hurt that anyone could be so injured.

She walked next to him, trying to be some kind of support though he seemed determined not to lean his weight on her. There were a million things she wanted to say, but she pressed her mouth shut. Clearly he needed medical attention before she peppered him with questions.

Though there were so many.

What is your name?

Where are you from?

How did you end up here?

How does one become quite so...muscular?

It was wrong to notice his muscles, the sheer *breadth* of him, when he was in such obvious distress.

Well, no, that wasn't fair. Despite the bruises and the blood and the slow, pained walk, the man did not radiate *distress*. He seemed quite contained for someone who had to be frozen through and injured beyond anything she'd ever seen. Each step had to be excruciating, but he never faltered or made a sound.

All the while, his bare chest kept drawing her attention.

Because he had to be so *cold*. Not because she was fascinated by the ridges of muscles and marks of old scars mixed with new injuries.

They made it to the castle door and Elsebet hesitated. The door was heavy and she was afraid to stop being the anchor he led himself by. But he reached out and, though he made no sound, she knew he was in pain so she stepped away from him and took the heavy door before he could, pulling it open and ushering him inside.

"Nielson?" she called out, knowing he was likely in the kitchen and her voice would carry in the narrow, tall towers even if he was somewhere else.

"Is something amiss, Prin—?" He stepped out and stopped short, his mouth falling open. "What...?"

"This poor man was on the beach. He needs medical attention."

"Win, bring my medical bag. Inga? Bring us some sheets. Old sheets." Nielson shouted, calling for the remaining staff.

"What's happened?" Win asked, rushing out of the kitchen as well. Just like Nielson, she stopped short, though her eyes took a tour of the impressive form of the man standing next to Elsebet. "Oh, my."

"My bag, Win," Nielson said disapprovingly, already stepping forward, his stern doctor-face in place.

When he'd sent her here, her father had been insistent the "head of the castle" be a man who could take care of things, so he'd chosen Nielson. Nielson had been the King's doctor in Mathav, and since coming to the island had taken on the added roles of main communicator with the King and Elsebet's advisor, along with a million other small jobs that kept the castle running—and Elsebet safe and healthy.

But not happy.

She shoved that thought away as Nielson instructed her to lead the man into the cozy living area, where a fire snapped and crackled in the hearth and warmed the room. Inga hurried in with sheets and Nielson instructed her to put them on the couch.

After a few bustling minutes, they got the injured man to lie down on the covered couch while Elsebet and Win washed out his injuries and Inga threaded a needle per Nielson's directions.

Elsebet had never dealt with much blood or injury before, so she assisted Nielson with a kind of gruesome fascination. He stitched up the deep cuts on the man's body, instructed the rest of them to bandage others after they'd been cleaned. He tutted over the bruises and told Win to get some painkillers and ice.

The stranger winced as he swallowed the pills down but was otherwise perfectly stoic as Nielson ran competent hands over the rest of him, checking for other injuries.

The man did not speak, but he'd nod or shake his head as he answered the Nielson's questions.

Elsebet knew she *shouldn't*, but she couldn't help but wonder what it might feel like if *she* was the one running her hands over this man's body.

"We have stitched you up and bandaged you, sir," Nielson said. "You have some severe bruising and swelling at your throat. I would recommend not trying to speak for a few days to allow the swelling to subside, and some of the bruises to heal. We will do what we can to make arrangements to have you transported to a hospital, but this will take some time as we are quite isolated."

The man shook his head. A clear refusal of the hospital.

Nielson's eyebrows drew together. "You'll need more help than I can offer."

The man's dark eyes moved from Nielson and met Elsebet's gaze. He shook his head once again. He clearly wanted her to refuse *for* him.

Elsebet did not know why she felt honor bound to do so, only that she did. She turned to Nielson, who often capitulated to what she wanted.

Except when it came to her safety.

"Nielson, surely we don't need to worry about hospitals if the man could walk himself into the castle?"

"It is not for you to say," Nielson said firmly.

But Elsebet knew how to get around his firmness. While Inga and Win fluttered around the injured man, putting a blanket over him and whatnot, Elsebet drew Nielson aside, far away enough the man wouldn't be able to hear their conversation.

"He's conscious and able to understand what's happening. He just needs some rest," she suggested.

"I can only examine him from the outside. He could have internal injuries. It is a danger to the man to keep him here."

Elsebet looked over at the large, uncompromising form on the couch. It was hard to believe anything about him was *in* danger.

"The idea of a hospital seems to distress him. If he takes a turn for the worse, we can worry about transporting him to the mainland then."

Nielson's frown was stern and disapproving. "This is quite irregular, Princess."

Elsebet nodded. "It is, but he walked in here of his own accord. He doesn't want a hospital. Let's give him a few days to recover, then reevaluate." Nielson was always a fan of waiting and reevaluating when it came to *her*.

Nielson frowned deeper. "The King would not approve."

"Father doesn't need to know."

"Elsebet."

He only used her first name when he was *deeply* disapproving. But Elsebet knew what would happen if they told her father about any of this. And so did Nielson.

Elsebet tried not to let emotion seep into her voice. She did not wish to hurt Nielson's feelings or have him withdrawing. So she kept her gentle smile in careful place. "He would not allow me to leave the castle. I would be under lock and key once again. Nielson." Her voice threatened to waver, but she could not let it. "I cannot go back to that."

Nielson sighed heavily, a sure sign he would give in to her. In some ways, he was more a father to her than her own, no matter how unfair it was. But Nielson was always here. She only saw her father in person a handful of times a year. Less if she was particularly *emotional* during his visits.

This man had nursed her through illnesses, eaten breakfasts with her, tutored her in math and science. He'd continued her lessons on her responsibility and duties as a royal. He'd taught her how to identify the shells on the beach and dried her tears when she faltered and he saw her sadness.

She loved him as a father, and she was quite sure that he loved her as a daughter, though they never said those words. She smiled brightly at him, knowing she could get what she wanted because he *did* care for her. Her freedom. "It will only be our secret until we can decide how to get him home. He's simply a wayward sailor. There is no threat here."

Nielson's face hardened at that. "That man is not *simply* anything."

Elsebet looked over her shoulder at the man currently dwarfing the couch. Even with the bandages, his bruises were visible. Even under the blanket Win had settled over him, it was clear he was...

Dangerous.

No, not that, of course. Just very...big and strong.

And what was wrong with that?

"Only until he gets his voice back, Elsebet," Nielson said, clearly trying very hard to sound fierce. "Then he must go."

After some time spent whispering and eyeing Danil warily, the small group found him clothes that apparently belonged to this Nielson person, and made quick alterations to let out seams and hems to fit his much larger body.

Danil was fed some flavorful broth that he could not enjoy due to the pain in his throat—even after the painkillers. Then Nielson and one of the maids, Win, informed him that he would stay on the couch through the night as there were no bedrooms on the main level and he was clearly not well enough to climb stairs.

Danil was fine with the arrangements, as it left him close enough to the door should he require escape. The Princess was kind—too kind—but her staff was far more mistrustful of him.

He respected them for it.

His two biggest challenges at the moment were his injuries and the fact he'd lost his ship in the storm he now remembered. Fierce, sudden and inexorable.

When he'd been *so* close. But he did not count this as a failure. He was here and alive, wasn't he?

He would need his voice to make arrangements to get another ship though, as he could not risk any communication that could be found or traced. There could be no evidence of what he needed to do prior to him doing it.

He would need to get a little stronger to accomplish what he'd come for anyway. He wouldn't call himself *weak* by any means, but the injuries had definitely slowed him down, and likely would for a few more days.

The Princess would be easy enough to kidnap. Her dedicated and suspicious staff of one old man and two women were certainly no match for Danil, even weakened by his injuries.

All that soft kindness in Elsebet made her the perfect mark, if not a perfect queen. But that was his brother's problem. Not Danil's.

The true challenge would be getting another ship into and out of the dangerous cove. He had been the only one brave enough to sail it in the first place. Finding someone in his brother's employ who could bring him a ship safely, without meeting the same fate or worse, would be a problem. And even if they could do it, Danil would need his strength at a hundred percent to make certain he could get Elsebet out.

He pushed the blanket off now that he'd been left alone. Lying about would not help him any. He would only get stiff and find himself in more pain. He needed to stay mobile. Stay *ready*.

A weapon was always prepared.

But before he could get to his feet, the Princess swept in. She had changed, though her new dress was as bland and serviceable as the last. It showed off an hourglass figure that would no doubt look beautiful in silks and jewels. She might be too soft to be a good queen for Gintaras, but she would certainly *look* the part.

She'd refastened her hair so few tendrils spilled out, but

the wavy golden mass of it fell down her back. No doubt as soft and silky as it looked. And those dark blue eyes, all warmth and liveliness. Yes, she could be a siren, no doubt.

But she was not dressed like a princess, nor did she fully act like one. She fit in well with the servants and had no qualms about seeing to him. Something that should be far beneath her notice.

Perhaps they did things quite differently in Mathav.

"You must rest, sir," she greeted with just the hint of admonition in her warm tone.

She was a princess and yet she called him *sir*. It was quite strange. Danil was not royal himself—a king's bastard who had been raised in poverty, then found out and saved from his sadistic biological father by his brother, the true heir, who had not concerned himself with legitimacy but given Danil a place in his guard.

So, no, Danil was nothing royal, but he was *around* royalty all the time as his brother's guard. He knew the way they acted and thought.

Except Princess Elsebet did not act like any of the royals he knew. Aras would not be caught dead in drab attire. The women of Aras's court would *never* lower themselves to take care of an injured man on the beach. Danil could not help but think Elsebet would have quite a struggle ahead of her when she became the Queen of Gintaras.

But, again, that was not his problem.

Elsebet held a notebook under her arm and dragged a chair over to where he sat on the couch. She settled herself on the chair, only a few inches away from him. They were alone in this cozy little room, a fire crackling in the middle of it while the wind lashed the small, recessed windows that dotted the stone walls.

This would have never been acceptable back home. A princess and a commoner alone in a room? Insanity.

"Nielson is quite adamant you should not try to speak," Elsebet said, holding out a notebook and pencil. "But that doesn't mean we shouldn't try to communicate. How lonely it would be for you to sit here in silence with no company."

Danil studied the outstretched items, then the Princess's delicate face. No one had ever been concerned about his *loneliness*, least of all him. He should be suspicious of it, but she only smiled, and he found himself…feeling something odd. Something he could not find a name for. A wanting…to speak to her.

Luckily, he could not.

"It would be much easier if there was a name I could call you by," she said, pushing the paper and writing utensil at him.

He slowly took the pad of paper in his lap, the pencil in his hand. She wanted his name.

The name Danil Laurentius would likely mean nothing to her, but it might mean something to her father. Then again, outside of his brother's kingdom, he was usually only referred to as *The Weapon*. The more faceless and nameless he was, the better for his missions, he had always believed.

But it was always good to leave a bit of a calling card. It was good that people knew all he was capable of. They would *fear* him and all he could do in service to his brother.

No one else could have survived the storm Danil had just come through. No one else could have gotten as close to the rocky cove as he had successfully—before the gale had swept up, angry and bitter and with no warning.

No *man* was match for him, but Danil had a healthy respect for the screaming, deadly pride of Mother Nature, a woman to the last. Once again, she had bested him.

But she had not won.

He was here. Where he'd meant to be. Bloodied and bruised, but alive. Once he recovered his voice, made arrangements to get a ship, he would take the Princess and return to Gintaras, only a few days later than planned.

Danil would not be thwarted. Such was his confidence that he scrawled his actual name on the paper.

Danil.

He left *Laurentius* out of it for now. Perhaps once he succeeded in taking the Princess to his brother, it would be a kind of clever calling card. Far, far too late for her meager staff to do anything about it.

"Danil," she said, and it was strange. Something about her accent, or the gentleness she spoke with, imbued his name with a softness that reminded him of a sunny, cramped kitchen in his grandparents' home—such an old memory he thought he'd erased.

So few people used his name these days, but even when they did, it was with the same ferocity they called him *The Weapon.*

Because that was what he was.

The Princess beamed at him and something inside of him shifted. Uneasy and foreign. A kind of warmth when he was from a cold, cruel country. *Proudly.*

"Where are you from, Danil?" she asked pleasantly. "Is there someone we can contact for you? Surely someone out there is worried for you? Family? Parents?" She looked down at her lap, then up at him through her golden lashes. "A wife, perhaps?"

Danil did not raise an eyebrow, though he wanted to. She had all the hallmarks of an innocent, and even if she had not, it was quite well known in the royal circles his brother frequented that Princess Elsebet had been isolated here in this tiny castle as a youth, hidden from the world while her father shopped her about. His virginal princess sacrifice meant to save his pitiful country.

Perhaps her father did not know everything if she was bold enough to be questioning Danil about his marital status. He *had* noticed her gaze on his body, more than once. And yes, she was meant for his brother, but Danil was no stranger to using a woman's reaction to him to get what was required.

So he smiled at her. Slowly. Darkly. Until a faint hint of pink crept up her elegant throat and into her cheeks.

If her reaction caused a stirring of his own, he ignored it. He took his pleasures in the appropriate places befitting his station. His lack of heart and soul. With women who understood.

Not soft virginal princesses who blushed and were meant for his brother.

But it was a surprise how hard he had to fight that reaction away. He focused on writing, though his arm throbbed with a dull pain, even after the pills he'd been given. He used the pain to control himself.

I am from nowhere and have no one.

It was a bit dramatic, but sometimes a flair for drama suited the situation.

And intrigued a woman.

Kidnapping was so much easier when a woman was intrigued. So he showed her his response with another silky smile and ignored his own leaping response to the way the flush on her cheeks deepened.

CHAPTER THREE

ELSEBET TRIED NOT to fidget, though strange sensations fluttered through her. Made her cheeks heat. Something deep and likely shameful throbbed within her.

But the way Danil smiled at her was like sin itself, all the adventure she craved promised in his dark brows, high cheekbones and sensuous mouth.

He looked no less dangerous covered in Nielson's altered sweater. The bruising, stitches and bandages on his face only added to the undercurrent of threat. And yet she was drawn to it like moth to the flame.

"I'm very sorry to hear that," she managed, though her voice did not sound like her own but instead a strangled kind of thing.

He shrugged as if it was no consequence to be from nowhere and have no one. When to her…well, it sounded worse than what little she had. Because perhaps she'd never had freedom or choice, but she had Nielson, Win and Inga. She had her father, sort of. She had this castle and this beach. Her birthright—even if it involved marrying a stranger.

She studied Danil once more. Because he too was a stranger. Obviously not one her father would ever allow her to marry, nor one that she would *want* to, since she knew next to nothing about him. Just that…actually coming into contact with a stranger put her father's plans for her in a new light.

She had always considered it a boring kind of duty. Say *I do*. Unite two kingdoms. Have children. Hopefully find a better balance with her father if he could see her as her own woman and not just the ghost of her mother. But she had never considered it in more than those sort of fuzzy, fairy-tale images.

Danil made *a stranger* seem...dangerous. Would her future husband be so big and strong and...*essential*? Would he make her stomach tie in knots with a simple, wordless stare? Would she *pulse* every time he smiled at her just like that?

Her father had long since bemoaned her obsession with *questions*, and she bemoaned herself in this moment. None of these questions were helpful—answers or no.

She cleared her throat, straightened in her chair and affixed the smile her tutors back on Mathav had insisted she learn. Kind but bland. Warm but not an *offer* of warmth. *"You must seem approachable but remote."*

That hadn't made much sense as a child, but it did now. Putting some kind of barrier between her and Danil seemed...necessary for her very survival. It helped her every day when her wayward emotions got to be "too much."

"How did you arrive here, Danil from nowhere and no one?"

He wrote once more, with short, sharp strokes.

I am a sailor. I suppose I got turned around.

He held the notebook toward her, and that same dangerous smile flashed on his face, but Elsebet was not quite *that* naive. She saw it for the lie it was, because she could not imagine this man had ever gotten *turned around* a day in his life.

"There isn't much this way to be heading for," she said, as if genuinely confused rather than suspicious. "You must have had some goal though? Some end destination in mind out there on the ocean?"

He looked down at the paper, paused, then wrote very carefully.

The details are a little...fuzzy.

He waved a hand around his face as if to demonstrate *fuzzy.*

Elsebet did not narrow her eyes at him, but she wanted to. Turned around and fuzzy? She didn't think so.

It was hard to believe a man this injured could wash up on her beach and be some kind of direct threat to her... but this *particular* man did not give off *accidental* vibes. She simply couldn't believe he'd ever landed somewhere he didn't want to, no more than she believed he didn't remember every last detail he wished to.

His eyes watched everything with an intensity that spoke of filing every detail away. The way he moved, even seated on a couch in borrowed clothes, was with confidence and a sense of ownership—even injured, even in a castle decidedly not his.

And there was simply *no* reason any sailor's ship should be close enough to this isolated island to be *turned around* and washed up to shore. So there had to be something he was hiding.

Elsebet could not decide if it was narcissistic or simply *smart* to wonder if his secret had something to do with *her.* After all, her father had ensconced her on this island for her "protection." Just because that safety had never been breached before didn't mean it couldn't be now.

No doubt Nielson was right, and letting this man stay

here while he recovered without telling her father was dangerous, but...

Letting her father in on her suspicions would result in her having even fewer freedoms than she did now. The thought made her entire body feel weighted with a heavy depression she could not fathom living through.

She had so little already. How could she give up more?

She would simply have to be careful. Watch Danil. Be smart about it. Because she would not give up her freedom.

Even if it put her in danger.

And what kind of danger might this man offer?

She should be afraid. Worried. Instead, all she could seem to think about was what an *adventure* that might be.

Win's voice rang out from the kitchen. "Dinner!"

Nielson had cautioned Danil against any difficult-to-swallow food while his throat healed, but no doubt Win had put together some more broth or something soft for him. So Elsebet smiled his way.

"Ah, dinner." She stood. She couldn't say she was hungry. The insides of her body were too busy doing acrobatics. But it was a good distraction. Besides, regardless of his injuries, he needed to eat and keep his impressive strength up.

But he did not stand or make any move. So she held out her hand. "Come. You must eat with us. You're our guest."

He studied her, then her hand. A silence stretched out that swept around them. She felt darkly compelled to close the distance between them, though she did not move. She just stood, a few feet away, her hand extended.

He took his time. Moving. Standing. She told herself it was because he was hurt, but the slow unfurling of his body seemed to make that *thing* throb deeper inside of her. As he towered above, so tall, so large. His eyes so dark and so intent on her.

His slid his hand into hers and her breath caught. It was rough, large, strong. It was a simple touch, casual even, but a thread of heat poured into her body, wound through her limbs, until it felt like everything around her was gone. And there was only him and her and where they touched.

She didn't breathe. He did not speak.

Because he cannot, Elsebet, she reminded herself harshly. And still she did not look away from the dark depths of his eyes.

Maybe she was drowning.

He nodded, a sign he was ready to move into the kitchen.

A sign you should stop being such a ridiculous ninny.

So she finally dragged her gaze away, though it felt as physically demanding as trying to move boulders at the beach. She didn't pull her hand away from his because that would appear like some kind of weakness.

And she knew what she looked like, sounded like. She knew there was great weakness in her, but she also knew she was a princess. A Thore.

She would not give in to her weaknesses quite so easily. She would *not* wear them on her sleeve any more than she had to.

She let out a shaky breath and tried to find some inner peace and strength. Held her head high as she led Danil into the kitchen for dinner.

Because he might be dangerous, but she was no shrinking violet. Not when it mattered.

Danil found himself beyond confused by the situation in this castle. The Princess ate with the staff. They all came together, shoving elbow to elbow around a small table filled with plates and bowls and food that looked and smelled delicious and hearty.

It reminded him, fondly, of eating in the mess on one of his larger ships with his crew when they were off on a mission for his brother. Certainly not of the stifling, formal dinners he was sometimes forced to attend with his brother at the royal court as personal guard.

But Elsebet was a *princess*, and none of this was befitting royalty. Maybe his brother had the wrong of it when it came to Elsebet and what she might offer Gintaras. Maybe the Kingdom of Mathav was very poor and would offer Aras next to nothing. After all, no princess of Gintaras would eat in such a humble setting.

And speaking of princesses, the one seated to his right was an interesting puzzle. She was clearly innocent, naive, not guarded when she should be. He had seen the reactions chase over her face—when he smiled at her, when he placed his hand over hers. These were not the blushes, shudders or breath catches of a sophisticated, worldly woman.

And yet there were little moments when they'd spoken before dinner, where she'd looked at him just a tad askance, and Danil had wondered if she saw through him.

Then her expression of distrust would be gone, and her warm smile or blushes would replace it.

Since *no one* saw through him, he supposed he was imagining it. It paid to be careful, after all. But she was a kind, soft little isolated princess and she could not know what he had in store for her. There was no need to worry.

Food was doled out family-style, though Danil had been cautioned by Nielson to stick with things that would not irritate his injured, swollen throat. And Danil noted there were quite a few options on the table that were soft, like Win had very kindly made things just for him.

He did not know what to do with this possibility, so he did not dwell on it. He took what food would not be pure agony on his throat and set about eating, because he would indeed need his strength.

Conversation around him was very casual. He was quite certain his brother would have termed it *gauche*. The staff spoke of what items the pantry was running low on, what damage the storm had done to the castle, and how they would repair it.

But it wasn't just the staff who spoke of such things. The Princess was also part of the conversation. As though she *worked*.

"I'll handle the tower window," she said, after they'd discussed a crack in one of the panes. And there were no gasps or horror, no looks of censure. Everyone nodded as if it was typical for the Princess to do menial repairs.

"Nielson is *terrified* of heights," Win supplied, giving Danil a kind of conspiratorial smile.

"Oh, come now. *Terrified* is an exaggeration," Elsebet corrected kindly. "The tower *is* quite high, and it can be a bit intimidating if you're afraid of falling."

"And our Elsebet isn't afraid at all," Inga said. "She even once tried to climb down the outside, Rapunzel-style, just to see if it was possible!"

Danil slid a glance at Elsebet, wondering what her reaction to this story would be. But she smiled into her cup as they continued on about this childish prank. That, if he was pressed, he supposed he could admit required *some* bravery.

Foolish though that bravery might have been. Usually all true courage started with foolish bravery.

Not his, of course. His had been born of having absolutely nothing to lose. Much like Win had said of Elsebet.
He was not afraid of falling at all.

He'd already seen life at its worst.

"Then there she was, hanging from the balcony," Win
continued. "Nielson practically a puddle of nerves on the
ground." Everyone laughed, even poor Nielson.

Danil would have joined them if it didn't cause such pain,
and he did not know the last time he had ever been prompted
to laugh at something quite so…tame. But he smiled kindly,
because it seemed there was little else to do with all of them
shoved together like poor commoners.

"I simply don't know what else Father expected me to
do, installing me in this fairy-tale castle, cut off from everything. It's truly a miracle I haven't tried to build my own
boat and sail away."

"Come now, Princess," Nielson said, his voice warm and
fond, further confusing Danil about how this country treated
its royalty. "Don't pretend you haven't attempted to build
a boat."

Elsebet laughed at that, clearly pleased to her toes, though
Danil couldn't understand why such impertinence would
make *anyone* at this table laugh.

No, he did not understand this little group of people or
the country they came from.

"Danil is a sailor," Elsebet said to the table. "I was asking
him questions and having him write down answers for me."

"Elsebet. The man was nearly killed," Inga said with
a tsk. "Your questions are enough to fell a fully healthy
man."

Again this censure did not cause anger or hurt or even
a hush to fall over the room—as any complaint about his

brother's behavior would have caused back in Gintaras—resulting in either angry outbursts or, worse, icy silences that would lead to punishments.

"I'm a curious woman," Elsebet replied, and her gaze slid to his. The curve of her smile had been warm and friendly, but when her midnight blue gaze met his, something changed. Sharpened.

He might have called it sultry if he thought she *meant* it to be. But he was quite convinced whatever changed in Elsebet's smile was completely unknown to her.

Still, it didn't matter. His body reacted. Much like when he'd put his hand over hers. Everything inside of him that he usually controlled to every last twitch had involuntarily leaped to life. He was very injured, and a dull, constant kind of pain gnawed at every cell of his body, and still his blood heated.

She looked away, that faint pink creeping into the apples of her cheeks, and still he stared at her. Not because he couldn't look away—he was *The Weapon* after all—but because he would force himself to look and *not* heat, harden or react in any way.

The goal was to make *her* weak. Not him.

Never him.

So he watched her take a sip from her cup. Her lips perched on the glass, full and pink. The way her throat moved when she swallowed. How she dropped one hand to her lap…and fisted it there, as if she felt his gaze. Deep within.

Underneath the hazy pain he was accustomed to beat a lust that took him off guard, and it could not win.

But maybe he needed another day of recovery yet. He looked away from her and took another spoonful of his broth, ignoring the heavily disapproving gaze of Nielson. And the highly *approving* gaze of Inga.

Neither served him well. It was best if no one thought very much of him at all.

Except Elsebet.

He glanced at her again. As if she *felt* his gaze, she stilled. Curled her fingers in her lap into a fist once more. Was she imagining his gaze as some kind of caress? Would she be as soft as she looked? Would she smell like the kitchens or the sea? Would she taste...

Well, he would be doing no tasting as she was meant for Aras. So.

At the end of the meal, inexplicably, Elsebet helped clear dishes. Like common staff. Maybe this was all a mistake and she wasn't a true princess at all.

He supposed it didn't matter. He would take her to his brother and let Aras determine how to move forward from there. By that time, Danil should have his voice back and would be able to express his concerns with his brother.

But first, he had to complete his mission. He stood, moving to help clear the table, but Win tsked at him. "It's very kind of you to want to chip in, but you are our guest and injured. You must rest."

He held out his hands as if to prove he didn't need rest, because look how strong and capable he was, but Win only shook her head.

"Elsebet? Why don't you take Danil back to the couch. Maybe find him something to read."

Danil frowned. He did not *do* rest, any more than the royals he knew did anything but. He opened his mouth to speak, but even that hurt and reminded him he should not. So he pressed his lips together.

"Come, Danil. We have many books to keep you company this evening." Elsebet gestured him to exit the kitchen.

He didn't want to. He wanted to prove he was strong enough. Well enough. But Elsebet's staff were looking at him as though they would fight him off from bringing even one dish to the sink.

So he sighed, then gave them all a polite bow and turned to leave the kitchen. Elsebet followed him, and when he glanced back at her, he watched the direction of her gaze. Down the length of his body.

"I'm a curious woman," she'd said at dinner. He wondered how deep she would allow that curiosity to go if she was willing to scale castles and build boats to escape this tiny place.

Which was not for him to know. Ever.

She walked over to a bookcase and dragged her fingertips over the spines. "There's much to choose from."

He frowned at her. He had no wish to read. What he really wanted to do was attempt to build himself a boat. To complete his mission. To speak so he could make a phone call to his brother, who no doubt thought him dead.

Which caught him sideways. If everyone thought he was dead, if he could slip away into a different life…

But of course that was foolish. He owed his brother everything. He could hardly repay Aras's generosity and loyalty with desertion.

So he put that thought away, the same place where he put any curiosity over what Elsebet might taste like.

"I'm a curious woman."

It was possible those words would haunt him.

"Here. Try this one," she said, pulling a book off the shelf and handing it to him. "Sit. Rest." She pointed at the couch.

He took the book but looked at the couch without sitting down. He did not wish to be confined. He needed to move this restless feeling out of him.

"Well. Good night," she said, somewhat stiffly and suddenly. She turned to leave, but…

A good sailor acted on instinct quickly. He moved without always knowing why or what he intended. He let that instinct guide him because he knew the ship, the ocean, and how to survive them.

Reaching out and taking her arm before she could leave was like hoisting the sail at exactly the right time. Some kind of innate knowing, the move accomplished before he'd even thought it through.

She looked down at where his fingers curled around her bicep. Then up at him. "Did you need something?" she asked, and he could hear how hard she tried to sound *royal* then. A kind of blandness mixed with just the very hint of disdain.

It made him smile. But he could not speak. Could not say anything as incendiary as he wanted to.

This was a blessing, in the moment.

He tossed the book on the couch and shook his head. A clear sign he did not want to read. He pointed at the door. Then mimed walking with two fingers.

"You wish to take a walk?"

He nodded. Then pointed at her.

"With me?"

He nodded once more, not letting go of her arm. It was all in a bid to soften her to him. So that when it came time to escape, it would be easy enough to do. He would not *seduce* her.

He would not need to.

"I do usually walk the beaches every evening after dinner, but…" She hesitated. "You should rest. Read or sleep or…rest."

He shook his head.

Elsebet looked back at the kitchen, no doubt wondering if her little staff would approve.

But no, he realized. She *knew* they wouldn't approve. She was wondering if she could get away with it.

Then she took his hand off her arm but did not take the moment to escape. Instead, she threaded her fingers with his and hurried them both toward the door.

CHAPTER FOUR

NIELSON WOULD NOT approve of her walking unchaperoned with Danil. She was risking him making a call to her father, she knew. Nielson was more on *her* side than her father's, but he had no desire to see her compromised or in danger.

Surely everyone saw the danger in Danil even if Elsebet wasn't totally certain what that danger was.

And yet the opportunity, even if it promised freedom for only a few minutes, was far too tempting to ignore. Like scaling the castle walls and building a boat that would never be seaworthy. Sometimes there was only so much suffocation she could take before she needed a gasp of fresh air.

She no longer threw tantrums. She didn't yell or cry in front of anyone. None of those things had ever been well received or fair, so she'd let them go. But there were certain...pressure valves that needed opening sometimes. And in this moment, Danil felt like one of those. Cold and wild and *necessary*, if only in this small moment before she was passed off to some stranger to be a wife.

"You will save Mathav, Elsebet," she heard in her father's stern voice. *"And you will not be burned by love."*

So she dropped Danil's hand and rushed ahead, away from her father's voice and her own duty.

She was very aware that Danil's injuries kept him in a kind of...cage. No doubt once he was healed one of his strides would make up two of hers, even if she ran. No doubt nothing would stop him then from whatever it was he sought.

A shiver ran through her. She knew it should be fear, but it wasn't.

Still, though he walked with a precision she did not think was natural to him, he did not fall behind. They made it to the beach and both simply stopped and stood there at the edge, between scrubby grass and rocks and sand, and watched the ocean beat angrily against the shore.

The weather had not calmed any since this morning, but instead of gray the skies were a wild kind of orange, glowing eerily from behind the thin clouds. It wasn't stormy weather—likely they'd wake up to a clear beach tomorrow—but it was as if the storm from last night was holding on to the sky by a thread, not quite ready to give up its grip on the cove.

Elsebet glanced at Danil. Something about the idea of storms and calm necessitated seeing his face, his expression, and what his dark eyes looked like when he beheld the sea.

She saw something in him, something she recognized on a soul level: that gasp of fresh air she'd needed. His eyes tracked a wave far out in the dusk, as though he'd held himself into a million tiny compartments inside the castle but here on the beach he could let go.

Expand.

If she were alone, she would climb to the top of a boulder, spread her arms wide and fling her head back, letting the icy wind move over her and through her—a reminder that no matter how tiny and inconsequential and isolated she felt, there was a wild world out there. Somewhere.

Even if she never got a slice of it.

But standing with Danil on this beach felt similar anyway, so there was no need to embarrass herself.

She eyed him as he studied the misty, narrow entrance to the cove. She did not think embarrassment would be what she felt with his eyes on her. Ever.

Oh, this was dangerous. She heard all the warnings she'd always been taught whisper in her mind. But here on the beach, she was free. She could do as she pleased.

Before she could decide what that was, Danil began to walk down the length of the beach. His stride was careful but certain as he made a beeline to where she'd found him, curled in a heap in the rocks.

How *had* he survived?

Occasionally he paused, toed something with the boots that Inga had attempted to mend since nothing they had would fit him. He seemed to have a destination in mind, so Elsebet trailed after him, watching the way his body moved. For a large man, an injured man, he was incredibly graceful. Like some sort of large, feline predator.

Another shiver ran through her that she *wished* was from the cold, but she had more self-awareness than that.

She hadn't paid much attention to his surroundings when she'd found him—she'd been too concerned with the blood. *And his chest.*

She shoved that thought away. When they reached the spot where she'd discovered him, she found little evidence he'd ever been here. The wind and surf had washed away any indentations, any trails of blood. It was just sand and debris once more. Broken boards and sticks and other flotsam and jetsam from the ocean.

But she paid more attention to the boards. They weren't what she would normally salvage for her art, because these were very big and straightforward. She preferred putting the small and delicate together to make something fearsome and pretend it was her.

Danil's brow furrowed as he stared at the spot. Perhaps the planks were the debris of his own ship? Because while she did not believe he'd been turned around or didn't remember, she did believe he had to have been a sailor to wash up here so injured. No matter *why*, surely he hadn't meant to do that.

He certainly hadn't inflicted those bruises and gashes on himself.

"Was it yours?" she asked gently as he stared.

He knelt carefully. No doubt the movement hurt, but he didn't stop. He picked up one of the broken planks and turned it over in his hand. Then he gave a simple, curt nod. She could not say she saw emotion cross over his face, but there was something about the way he held the single piece of splintered wood that made her heart twist.

She had often heard that sailors loved their ships like wives or children, and his had been splintered into pieces. While he had barely survived. There must be *some* kind of grief in that. She was too accustomed to grief not to want to offer some solace.

She stepped forward, placed her hand on his shoulder in some thought to comfort. Because she could not imagine what he'd seen. What fear must have swept through him. Surely he'd imagined he might die. He could have, if she had not found him. If he'd swept up on some deserted isle.

It weighed heavily on her. That anyone could simply be swept to sea and...be lost. That someone like Danil, so large and full of...mystery and wild *otherness* to her, might have simply been killed by the conscienceless whims of Mother Nature.

"I am sorry such a thing happened to you," she said solemnly.

For a moment, he crouched there, perfectly still. Then slowly, he turned his head to look up at her. Confusion knit his brows together, but he smoothed it out as he straightened, unfurling to that great height. She had to tilt her head back to hold his gaze.

She moved onto a rock, so she felt less like she was being intimidated by a giant, though she still had to incline her head back to meet his gaze. But this move also put her closer to him. So there were mere inches between her chest and his. The wind whipped around them like a vortex, but she felt warmth in the midst of all this cold.

He was wild and unknown, nothing she could ever really have. *Dangerous.*

But, oh, how she wanted something wild and unknown. Just a little slice. Just *once.* Something of her own that no one—not her father, Nielson, or the Kingdom of Mathav—had any say in. Something outside of the life that kept her in a very careful box.

She wanted to scale the castle walls, sail the ocean in a boat she'd built. She wanted to press her lips to this unknown man and see what it might be to taste danger.

So that was what she allowed herself to do. Reach to her toes on the rock, curl her hand around his neck and kiss him.

The kiss was timid. Danil could see the pulse scrambling in Elsebet's neck, feel the tremor in her hand on his neck before she even pressed that soft, innocent mouth to his.

He did not stop her, as that would not get him what he wanted. What he *needed,* actually, as his wants had nothing to do with this mission.

Danil watched her as she squeezed her eyes shut and

pressed herself to him with more enthusiasm than skill. It was clear she did not know what she was doing.

But he did.

And *knowing,* he should be careful. He'd certainly always been careful and calculated before in everything he did, but all that seemed to desert him for a moment. Because the warmth of Elsebet's slender body pressed to him felt like sunlight on his face after sailing through nothing but clouds for weeks on end.

Before he'd thought the motion through, he lifted a hand and tested his fingers against the soft skin of her cheek, her jaw, angling her head to soften her lips against his. To run his tongue across the seam of her mouth.

To taste.

He had a purpose here, a reason for doing things, or so he thought. Then her mouth parted on a little surprised inhale, granting him a deeper access he shouldn't take but in the moment craved more than his next breath.

Because she tasted like the *sea.* Crisp and promising. Deep and dark underneath the pretty, sparkling surface. It was meant to be a bit of a lark. See exactly what she might offer, how he could use this surprising turn of events to complete his mission.

But the water was closing in over his head. Her kiss was potent, surprising, not what he'd prepared himself for. His body throbbed with the pain he'd felt since waking on the beach, but desire twined through it, turning it into one formidable feeling he did not recognize. Her hands clutched his shirt as she pressed herself closer. And his arms came around her waist, holding her securely on that little rock she was perched on to give herself some height.

His fingers spread wide, spanning her waist. So slim, so delicate. But her mouth was eager, hot, willing. The pang she drew out of him was sharp and old, something he'd thought he'd eradicated as he'd turned himself into *The Weapon*.

A tool. Heartless and soulless. More machine than man, needing no one and nothing. A kiss was a kiss meant to lead to sex and nothing more.

But this was...not that. She was...

Innocent.

Meant for your brother.

It was this reminder that brought him back to who he was. *The Weapon.* He did not jerk away. He had to be smarter than that. He eased her instead, lingering another second or two at simply the gentle brush of lips. When he finally pulled his mouth free, he focused on the pain in his throat, in his arm, in his head rather than the sweet softness of Elsebet or the warm bubble she'd encased them in.

He stared down at her, trying to put his thoughts back into their proper order. Trying to ignore the demands of lust his own body seemed intent on satisfying while her blue eyes swirled like a tantalizing, tranquil sea...that no doubt hid dangerous reefs and icebergs.

Elsebet was not his to have. A few smiles, even some kisses—these could all be forgiven as a means to an end, but that was all his brother would forgive. Elsebet was meant to be Aras's, and Aras did not share.

Still, Danil stared down at her. Because she had been the one to initiate an act she clearly didn't know much about.

Why had she done such a thing?

She did not scramble away as he half expected, though her expression was arrested. Perhaps she was terrified frozen since she wasn't blinking.

"Did I hurt you?" she asked on a soft whisper, concern clouding her eyes. But her fingers were still clutched in his shirt, like she didn't know how to let him go.

He might have laughed if his throat did not scream at him. This little slip of a princess hurting him? He didn't think so.

He shook his head, brushing a hand over the wind in her hair, ignoring an old shift in his chest that ventured too close to a tenderness he no longer had nor believed in.

She *was* a siren, innocent though she was, but he would not be felled. He could not reject her out of hand. It would create an emotional response in her that would make his eventual kidnapping attempt more difficult. A woman scorned and all that.

But he needed to tread carefully.

"I am sorry such a thing happened to you." She had said this to him with such genuine empathy there in the wreckage of his ship.

As if she truly was sorry. As if it mattered to her. When that storm and shipwreck and *this* were some of the easiest challenges he'd ever faced. He'd lived, hadn't he? That was all that mattered. Survival.

He sucked in a deep breath of cold air, painful though it was. He needed to think more clearly, and no doubt being alone with her on this moody beach heading toward dark would not do much for *clarity*. Because dark creeping in only tempted him to think of the things they could do in the dark. Where no one could see.

Where no one needed to know.

And this could not be. She would soon be his queen. Never his lover. Though his hardened body demanded other eventualities. But he was the master of himself. Always.

He took her hand in his. Small but not soft. Not like a princess's hands should be. Because she washed dishes and baked bread and scaled castle walls, apparently.

He was going to have to recalculate. His initial plan had

been the element of surprise. Sweep in, take her, sweep out. But now he was beginning to see the story of her.

A woman locked away in isolation. Maybe not unhappy, but restless. Restless enough to kiss a stranger, clearly not knowing what she was getting herself into. Desperate for some freedom.

She would not get freedom in Gintaras, but she didn't know that. Nor did she need to. She only needed to want to escape *this* prison before she worried about the next.

So he could offer her that escape. Once the time was right. He helped her off the rock and then began walking them back toward the castle. She mounted no objections, but she kept her hand in his as they walked. As if they were innocent lovers taking a sunset stroll. He might have laughed to if he'd been able at such a ridiculous thought if he'd been able.

When they reached the castle, he felt her hesitation. He was leading her back to her prison. No matter how good that prison was, how nice her jailors were, Elsebet clearly wanted a taste of the unknown. Danger. *Freedom.*

He knew this desire well enough to recognize it on anyone. And he would use it for his own means.

She made a move to open the door, but he stopped her. He lifted her hand and brushed his mouth across her knuckles, gaze meeting hers in the faint glow the castle windows offered. He even smiled and tried to make it soft. Then he reached out himself, ignoring the stiffness and pain in his arm, and opened the door for her.

She looked up at him through her lashes before she moved inside, under his arm. She gave him one last look over her shoulder, then strode inside to where her staff was already speaking to her. And frowning at him suspiciously.

But Danil only smiled, attempting to make himself look

smaller than he was. He wasn't a threat. He was simply a shipwrecked sailor rendered dazzled by their beautiful princess. Who would not be?

He would turn himself into a fairy tale they *all* wanted to believe in. For Elsebet, the miracle that might help her escape her isolation. For her staff, simply a nice, innocent sailor in puppy love with her.

And alone, where the staff could not hear, he would make Elsebet promises of the world out there so when the time came, she would join him easily, willingly.

He would offer her all she clearly wanted—badly enough to inexpertly kiss a stranger on a beach. Adventure. Romance. He could be the castle she scaled, or at least thought she did. Perhaps she was more dangerous to his control than he had counted on, but he was *The Weapon*.

She wouldn't even realize it was a kidnapping until it was too late.

CHAPTER FIVE

ELSEBET'S MIND WAS a scramble, but she smiled and nodded and spoke with Nielson and Win as if everything was
just fine. Yes, she'd gone for her regular evening walk and
Danil had joined her. No, nothing was amiss.

She did not miss Nielson's disapproval, but she held on
to the hope that his concern would not outweigh his sympathy over her isolation.

And he could *never* ever know she'd kissed the man.
Kissed. She wanted to laugh. That word did *not* do what
had happened out on the beach justice.

Inga handled everything to help Danil get ready for bed,
and Elsebet was ushered away. Up and into her tower.

A prisoner.

She tried to push that thought away. It was unkind and
untrue. Everyone wanted what was best for her and Mathav.
She was hardly treated poorly. She had nothing to complain
about. Nothing to be upset over. That never did any good.

She tried very hard to convince herself of that, but all
she could think about was the way she'd felt when Danil's
arms had spanned her waist. Like an entire new world had
opened up for her. Wild and unknown. Something with no
plan, no walls, no *cage*. Just a soaring feeling of being *free*.

And no matter how she tried to convince herself she
might feel the same with *any* man, with the man her father

chose even, she had a hard time believing that feeling was *ordinary*. That it was generic to kissing, and not specific to Danil himself.

He'd kissed her and she'd felt like *his*, like they were two interlocking pieces that belonged together. Always.

Too many fairy tales, Elsebet.

"You should not be alone with him," Nielson said grimly as Elsebet swept into her room, hoping to leave Nielson and Win behind.

"A walk on the beach is hardly being alone." She crossed her room to her window seat, where her little turret window looked out over the cove. The one place she felt free.

And Danil had kissed her there, as if she was. She resisted the urge to touch her fingers to her lips that still tingled like a kiss could be magic.

"He could have hurt you or forced you into any number of terrible things out there!" Win cried, then looked over her shoulder, clearly worried Danil might have heard her shout all the way down the stairs.

"And then what?" Elsebet returned, very calmly. "There's nowhere for him to go. He can't even speak. I understand the desire to be cautious, I really do. But Danil isn't a threat." She knew this was a lie.

She did not care.

He'd kissed her. She was sure she was supposed to be… shamed somehow. But she had initiated it, she had *thoroughly* enjoyed it, and she wasn't so foolish to throw away her entire kingdom just because she had.

Sometimes, a taste could be enough.

She was going to try very hard to believe that.

"Elsebet. I am warning you. Even a hint of untoward behavior will *have* to be reported to your father. I know you crave more than this isolation, and I understand it. I feel as though I've been very lenient," Nielson said with a restrained kind of anger Elsebet knew spoke of fear. Of her father's disapproval. "Perhaps *too* lenient."

Elsebet looked away from the window and to Nielson, who had indeed always been lenient. She knew that he loved her like a daughter, that he gave her as much as he could. She never questioned it. And she didn't now.

She only questioned if his love for her was more important than her father's will. Which would win out? What she wanted, desired, perhaps even needed—or what her father did?

Still, she smiled at Nielson in an effort to soothe. They did not need to carry the weight of her feelings. "It was a walk. He can't even talk. It's simply me babbling on and him being forced to listen. Just like you lot. We found a bit of the wreckage of his boat, and I feel that might have been cathartic for him."

"We like listening to you, Princess," Win said loyally.

"And I appreciate you all. Along with your concern. But there is nothing to be concerned about here. I'm sure Danil will be eager to leave in a day or two, once he's recovered a bit more and can contact someone from his homeland. He does not seem like the kind of man content to haunt a castle on a tiny, isolated island. Does he?"

Nielson and Win exchanged a look. Elsebet knew they agreed with her on that point, but there was something more in that look that she couldn't read, and she could only blame it on her inexperience.

Which did not help with the frustrated feeling swirling through her. The desire to do something reckless and *more* that might free her from...

What? Your duty? The one thing you've promised to uphold?

"We only want what's best, Princess," Nielson said softly.

Elsebet nodded and smiled and did her best not to let her eyes fill with tears. Unfortunately, just because some people who cared about her did their best did not mean this felt tenable. How long could she go on, getting older and more alone? "I don't suppose Father has given any estimated time of when he might pick my husband?" Which she didn't want, but she didn't know how long she could keep *waiting*.

Nielson shook his head. "I could check with him again, Your Highness."

"No, there is no need. He will make the decision when it's best for Mathav, and that's what's important." She smiled brightly at them, or at least tried to. "Now, I'm very tired after the excitement of the day. I'll bid you both good-night."

Nielson bowed, Win curtseyed, and they left her with soft *Sleep wells*. For a moment, Elsebet only stood in her little room perfectly still. She had endured the loneliness this long, the heavy weight of it, the dark, spiraling frustration of it. She could keep surviving it.

After all, she'd done something today that she'd never done before. She'd kissed a man. He'd kissed her back. Her first kiss. And not just a *kiss*. His hands had been on her body. She had *tasted* his mouth.

It had been wild, like the waves crashing into the cove. It had been the promise of something bigger out in the world than she'd ever imagined, and oh, had she *imagined*.

The way his fingers had spread wide. The strength inside of him, the sound he'd made when his tongue had touched hers. A kind of *growl*, when she'd never heard him say anything due to his injuries.

Elsebet was very sheltered, this she knew. But knowing it meant she'd also endeavored to be slightly less sheltered. She read whatever she could that might give some glimpse into what happened between a man and woman. What might be expected of her on a personal level when she was married off to some stranger to uphold her duty, her family line.

She liked to think she'd been *somewhat* educated by her curiosity, and tonight had given a new glimpse into *all* of that.

She was very grateful for fiction. It allowed her to at least *understand* the pulse between her legs. She had read enough to fantasize about what it might be like, to have a man touch her in all the places she was meant to keep *pure* for her future husband.

But now the fantasy man had a face. Large hands. Scars. And dark, piercing eyes. A man who could never be her husband.

And was that really so terrible? She couldn't have real adventure, real danger, which Danil seemed to embody on a cellular level. Her duty would never allow it.

But maybe she could have the fantasy. A kiss. A daydream. It didn't have to be *real* danger. It was relatively safe, all in all.

But when she dreamed that night, nothing about Danil or his hands, or his mouth, was *safe*.

As the days passed, Danil tried to not think he was being imprisoned. He was a patient man, laying the groundwork and all that. He smiled. He helped with chores. He played the role of meek, humble sailor gone astray—a role he had long trotted out when it served him.

As a large man, as the King's bastard whom for years only Aras had trusted, Danil had learned how to make himself look smaller, kinder. While also learning how to use his size, his temper to intimidate and terrify when necessary.

If he was being honest with himself, intimidate and terrify was much easier. But as long as his injured throat kept him from speaking, there was no way out of this with intimidation.

No doubt everyone back home thought he was dead. There would be no ships waiting for him outside the cove— he'd been the only one brave enough to attempt it in the first place. So he needed a few more days to get his voice back, and then he could make contact with someone in Gintaras to get a ship sent to him. Give specific orders on how to make that happen, and whom he trusted enough to bring one of his ships here.

Danil could not let this opportunity slip out of his fingers. It would be a failure, and that was not tolerated. By Aras or Danil himself. Because Aras had once saved him, and Danil could not betray his brother with failure.

When his father had wanted him killed for being the blight he was—an unsanctioned bastard who dared be a son, older than Aras by two days—it was Aras who had interceded.

This would not have been needed, of course, if his mother's husband hadn't gotten wind of his true parentage and thought it some kind of get-out-of-poverty-free card. Trying to claim the crown for Danil had been foolish on every level. As if the King would have ever let him be heir. As if Danil *wanted* such a thing.

So the man who'd married his mother after his grandparents had died was sentenced right along with him. *This* at least was justice. Frick had died in prison. Danil had been saved by Aras, who had asked only fidelity in return.

Danil owed his brother so many things it did not do to count them all. So he would not. He would bring Aras Elsebet, his chosen bride. Failure would break all those old, dungeon promises.

It would be the end of their brotherhood.

And it was clear after a few days that Elsebet would be a fine enough queen for Aras. At first Danil had only seen her softness, but she had a kindness, a cunning way about her in how she dealt with people—him, her staff that she treated more like family—that Aras critically needed. To smooth out his rough edges, his impetuousness. That rage of temper that so often got Aras, and the Kingdom, into trouble. Trouble Danil often had to clean up.

If it settled uncomfortably that Elsebet would have to deal with such things, it did not signify. If it felt wrong to put that kind of responsibility on her shoulders, he needed to lose those feelings, the way Aras had endeavored to beat them out of him.

It was not *The Weapon*'s job to have opinions, thoughts, or feelings. It was his job to be his brother's tool.

A position that had come to him out of his brother's generosity. Of his own doing over time, because he liked being that machine that had no feelings to be betrayed by, the kind he had struggled with as a child.

His mother's broken promises after his grandparents had died. The man she'd married, who had "known better" than her. Who would make him into a "man." He had invaded their home, and his mother hadn't just let him, she'd *welcomed* him. Allowed him to parade Danil up to the vicious king, knowing full well what would happen. There'd been a reason she'd kept that secret all those years prior, hadn't there been?

The old anger swirled through him, bitter and ugly. And utterly useless. So he froze them out, as he had learned to do from his brother.

Better to be a weapon.

It didn't matter how blue Elsebet's eyes were, how her

smile unfurled inside of him like sunlight. That she asked him questions as if those thoughts, opinions and feelings *did* matter. That she had welcomed him into her family—as had all of them, no matter how suspicious—and made it easy to feel *belonging*.

When there was none to be had. He was *The Weapon*. She was Aras's prize.

Never his.

Every day that passed, Danil was grateful to her eagle-eyed staff that they never let Elsebet alone with him. He could have gotten around this of course, but he was biding his time. Letting Elsebet set the rules, test the limits. Being the perfect guest to her staff.

And not letting himself get too tied up in Elsebet. A minute-by-minute struggle he had never counted on.

Because despite the fact there were always eyes on them, Elsebet did not act all that differently. Oh, there were no kisses, but she talked to him as if it was just the two of them. Tales of her most favorite finds washed up on the beach. Why she enjoyed making bread. What she thought existed beyond the cove—a mix of practicality and fantasy he found himself drawn to.

Making her more and more real to him, when it was better to think of her as a prize to be won and handed over to his brother.

She talked about her art until he was curious enough to write out the words *May I see it?* Mostly because it seemed to be secret, and the more secrets he knew the better chance he had of kidnapping her without her knowing it.

Or so he told himself. He certainly couldn't allow it to be actual curiosity.

He had no curiosity left. He had seen everything. The bleak, the bad, the terrible. Freedom, all the blues of the ocean, and many beautiful women, who had been more than eager for a bit of rough.

And yet he could not recall ever feeling the way he had when Elsebet's lips had been on his. As if despite how little they knew about each other, their souls were made to connect.

He willed these thoughts away as Elsebet seemed to mull over whether she would show him her art.

"I have a little studio of sorts, but it requires many stairs as it's up in the tower."

He nodded, a signal he could handle it. Though much of his body still ached, most of his injuries had been sustained from the chest up. Not only was he capable of mounting many stairs, he *wanted* the exercise. He hated feeling so pent up and useless.

He hated even more the idea of putting that feeling to pen and paper. So he simply gestured at the stairs. She glanced at the kitchen, where they both knew Win was half listening to their conversation.

Then she stood. "Well, I shall take your leave for a bit. I'll be back for tea." But instead of leaving the room, she walked toward him. Leaning close so the sweet smell of vanilla enveloped him.

Her lips at his ear, sending sensations through him that should have warned him this was a very bad idea. "Wait until Win starts humming. Then quietly come up the stairs. Just keep going until you can't go any more. I'll be there."

She straightened and then walked away, and he watched her go. The braid down her back, the soft, unconscious sway of her hips. She didn't look back, not even once. But she would wait for him, he knew.

It was strange to feel as though he stood on the cusp of

danger. Like facing down a tidal wave in his tiny ship. His body hard and wanting.

I'll be there.

He shook his head. It was ridiculous to let his injuries affect him like this. To consider a little slip of a woman a danger when he had faced down monsters. He was stronger, savvier than some innocent. No matter what kind of siren she was.

He always had control in any situation. Desire, lust, yearning, these were no match for an iron will forged in honest-to-goodness dungeons, his life on the line. He would use this *attraction* between them to get what his brother wanted.

But only that.

So he sat where he was until he heard the soft strains of Win humming from the kitchen. Then he got to his feet, and though there was something beating at him to hurry, he took his time.

Just to prove he could.

The stairs seemed to go on forever, twisting in a constant spiral all the way up into the height of the tower. It was almost dizzying, and this too he blamed on his injuries.

But she waited for him at the top of the stairs, that soft smile on her lips. Mischief and excitement in her blue eyes.

Siren.

And you are The Weapon.

"Follow me," she whispered, as if there was anywhere else to go when he reached the top. They passed a closed door as they curved around the tower to the other side. She led him into a room with an open door. The walls were stone and it might have been dark and dingy, but there was a series of windows—ovals, squares, circles, diamonds—all around the rounded walls. They let in little shafts of light.

But most of the light came from the domed ceiling made of stained glass. He looked up, considering the marvel that all this glass could act as a ceiling.

Surely it wasn't very practical. But it was stunning. Two sides spiraling together—either in fight or embrace—sun on one side, moon and stars on the other.

"It's so high up, and the glass so thick and carefully arranged, we've never had any damage to it," Elsebet offered as if reading his thoughts.

He looked from the ceiling to her, and how she stood in the middle of the room, all that colored light settling over her like a mask. They stood there, silent and staring at one another, for too long.

She was the one to break his gaze, gesturing around the room at the tables that were set up at places where the light was best. Projects littered the tables, even clustered along the curved wall.

He might have considered it little more than the arts and crafts of a child, but the end result of her work was all over the room.

It was all...astonishingly beautiful. He was no art expert, but Aras had quite the collection of art—antique and modern—and these pieces would easily fit among those famous ones.

There was a little corner where the projects were more rudimentary, dark and angrier, and it said something about her—something he wished he didn't see—that she hadn't gotten rid of those early attempts.

She had it all. A clear progression from furious, clumsier adolescent to graceful, understanding woman. He did not look at her but perused her art instead. Most of them were mosaics of sorts, made up of beach flotsam and jetsam cobbled together in interesting ways. There were a few paintings, some driftwood carved into interesting shapes. Some of it was abstract. Like emotions swirling to life in vibrant colors and interesting shapes. He could not put to words what those made him feel.

"I've always wanted to sail out to sea where you can't see land," she said as he stared at one that was blues, grays and shocking bolts of yellow. "To be untethered. Free." She pointed at the mosaic. "I suppose that's my best guess."

He could not speak, but it was…not a guess. It was as if she'd been there before. Even though it was abstract, it reminded him of exactly what she described. Boat in the middle of the ocean. Just him and water and sky and sparking light. So beautiful it could make even *The Weapon* sigh.

He nodded at her, trying to make it clear that her best guess was correct. Her beaming smile in response was like the sun shining through the window. Warm and bright. He wanted to bask in it for eternity.

But he had a sailor's sense of danger and forced himself to look away. To not let himself be blinded by anything that might be too good to be true. Anything that was not *his*.

And she was not. No matter how that art piece settled inside of him like belonging. Understanding. Things he had not felt, warm and comforting, since he'd been a small boy, fishing from the pier on his grandfather's knee.

He shook these memories away. What was she doing to *him*? This was supposed to be about getting her to trust him. To want him. So she would come with him.

He moved away from the abstract pieces to the largest piece dominating the bigger portion of one wall. It depicted a sprawling castle, not unlike his brother's, though the world around this castle was sunny. There was a colorful village in the background, bright churches, villagers on the streets and beams of light in the blue sky. It was made out of bits of seashell and glass. It had to have taken an incredible amount of time and patience to put it together.

"That is Mathav," she said, standing a good few yards away from him. He half wondered if she was afraid of being close. "My home. Well, before I was sent here. Though I like here better. Mostly."

It was the *mostly* that poked at him. The tool he would use to get her away from her kind staff. Her family. That feeling of *mostly*.

Because anyone who was *mostly* happy was tugged at by something that made them unhappy. A thread they couldn't stop tugging at.

You should know.

He frowned a little. He had snipped all his threads. He was not unhappy, because he was nothing. He was a weapon, that was all. And this reprieve of recovery had no bearing on the choices he would make.

Once he had his voice, a ship, he would take her—willing or not—to his brother. She would be the Queen of Gintaras.

And Danil would need to somehow scrub from his memory all he had already filed away.

Like how her eyes changed color with the sun. Or what her laugh sounded like. Now he knew what she could create with that fascinating mind and her own two hands.

He knew what she tasted like, and this most of all haunted him every night.

Elsebet was getting to be a *problem* that wasn't so easy to shove away, no matter how strong he was.

"I guess you can't tell me what you think," she said, with a sweet little laugh that swirled around inside his chest as if he had a heart that beat there. "But you aren't frowning, so I'll take that as a good sign."

He nodded. Once. There was no way to express how

impressed he was with simple hand gestures, and that was likely for the best. As would getting out of here be.

"It has helped fill my time anyway," she said, her gaze traveling back to the mosaic castle. "Back home, there was not much more to do. My father has always been very protective. So it's not like I was out roaming the streets."

He looked at the streets in question. The pretty shops. The way the sun glistened on them in her artistic depiction. He could feel the yearning.

Knew all too well the yearning. Their prisons had been very different—hers protection, his an actual dungeon—but he knew what it was to look out a window and see a world you could not be part of.

Well, she would have...some freedom in Gintaras. Sort of. Aras could be somewhat...overbearing to the women in his life, but Elsebet would be different. She would be his wife. The Queen. She would have to be seen. She would have to have duties.

She laughed a little. "I was such a little hellion it's a wonder he kept me around as long as he did."

He frowned at this, shook his head. Though he could see the passionate side to her, *hellion* seemed incongruous to the sweet, kind woman who'd taken such good care of him.

"You don't believe me?" She shook her head, and he could see her try to laugh it off, smile about it like she'd left childish rebellion behind, but there was a sadness in everything she said. "The more he tried to protect me, the more I chafed. The more I yelled or cried or made myself a nuisance. Really, he had no quarter but to send me away. For my own good."

Again Danil shook his head. There was no *good* from being sent away. He knew this. Maybe he'd been more like taken away when his mother's husband had taken him to the

King, but still he knew what it felt like to be ripped from that which you loved.

Loved. He had loved his childhood home, and his mother, and then Frick had poisoned it. Because love was far too fragile a thing to survive *life*. He reached for Elsebet, without thinking the move through. Because he was driven by emotion. By feeling.

When he wasn't supposed to have any of that left inside of him. *Stop this at once*, he ordered himself. He smiled and gave her hand a kind squeeze, because he needed her to trust him.

Then he dropped her hand and stepped back.

"Is it what you expected?" she asked brightly, purposefully turning away from the mural. She was smiling at him, but he saw the sadness in her eyes. Like she was trying very hard to be *bright* when she felt anything but.

He nodded again, knowing it would be best to find another piece of art to focus on, or perhaps return downstairs. But his feet were planted, and the air around them glittered with colorful sunbeams.

She looked like a fairy tale brought to life, and if he believed in fairy tales, he was the villain. At *best*.

But she moved toward him, studying him just as she had on the beach. With curiosity. Interest. She even reached out, placed her small hand over his heart. She had nothing to stand on here, so there was only their height difference between them. And he realized that he'd bent his head, without ever meaning to.

When every moment since he'd been an adult had been purposeful.

"Danil," she whispered as her hands slid up his chest, burning through him like fire. Overtaking him like a wave. His name in her accent, her soft, sweet voice. It pierced him clean through and it was in that *feeling* he wasn't allowed to have, didn't *want*, that he found the strength to step back.

"I cannot." It was a rasp, barely audible, and it hurt like the devil. But there it was. His voice. His truth.

Another taste of her might ruin him.

But over the thrumming of his heart, the roar in his veins of wants thwarted, he dimly realized she had *also* said something in that moment when his traitorous voice had come back to him.

And it had sounded a lot like *I cannot*.

CHAPTER SIX

ELSEBET'S HEART BEAT so hard she thought she was vibrating. She'd wanted to kiss him again. Resisting had nothing to do with what she *actually* wanted. Which was his mouth on hers.

No, that was a lie, and she should not fool herself in this moment.

She'd wanted far more than a kiss. She wanted to know what his hands on her body would feel like, without any of her clothes on. She wanted to taste him. More than just his mouth. She wanted all those things she had never experienced, and she wanted them with Danil.

She had not been raised to believe in fairy tales, even if she had always found happiness inside their pages. Her father had always and only spoken of duty, responsibility, the Kingdom. Not of love or contentment or joy—he had so clearly cut those things off when her mother had died.

So she had always known she shouldn't believe the stories she read. That she should think of adventure and love and pleasure as nothing more than fiction. It had been easy to believe when she'd been virtually alone. When it was only her and the sea and her little surrogate family.

But it was harder to believe that there weren't a million experiences out there, just beyond her reach, now that Danil had arrived. It now felt like adventure must be just outside the cove if a man such as Danil stood before her.

She did not know this man. She might *feel* things because of him, but so much of *who* he was remained a mystery.

But whether she knew him or not didn't matter to this desperate, throbbing electricity that sparked between them. With a look, with a touch.

How could she believe duty was superior when she knew he tasted dark and rich and like a million mysteries?

It was physical, yes. Because he'd never spoken until this moment, and even how he'd only spoken two words. Still, these days he'd been here, he'd listened to her. Maybe he didn't have much of a choice, but he always made her feel as if he took every little detail on board, no matter how silly. No matter how she'd just been filling the silences with old stories and childish wishes to remind herself she could not kiss him again.

And always his eyes were on her. Always he nodded. *Always* he at least acted like he understood. She was not a fragile bloom to be protected, an emotional roller coaster to be hidden away. She was someone worthy of company, of *interest*.

She had three people in this castle who cared about her, this she knew. But she had never had the sense any of them *understood* her. Not her yearning or her curiosity or her desire for something beyond duty. They thought that was as childish as her father thought her tears were.

Still, they loved her and she loved them and that made Danil even more dangerous. Because it wasn't just *her* he listened to, spent time with, helped. Danil listened to them as well. He helped without being asked, even when he was told he should rest. He got things off high shelves for Win, carried heavy things for Inga, and even helped Nielson deal with some temperamental light fixtures in the library.

He fit into this little life she had learned to love for its sweetness, its little snatches of freedom. Its family and love. She wished he could stay long enough to speak, for her to get to know him, to make fairy tales a reality.

And now, here in this moment, he'd looked at her art with interest, and she had seen a matching…something in his eyes as she'd spoken of a protective father. She could not explain it. She only knew that he understood something of being held back.

It made no sense, a man of his size, his power. Surely he did and got whatever he wanted.

But he had to understand *yearning*, or that look would not have appeared in his eyes.

In that moment, so quick but so potent, she'd wanted something she yearned for to come true. For a split second, she'd been willing to risk everything for that. Just *once* getting exactly what she wished for. Just like the other night on the beach, pressing her mouth to his.

But it had been her father's castle behind Danil, in mosaic form, that had reminded her of who she was.

What she was.

What she'd promised.

And though she had touched Danil, she had also pulled back.

But so had he. And now Danil stared at her as if she'd spoken a foreign language. Like he couldn't understand *her* resistance, though he had some of his own.

Because *he'd* spoken, too. He'd sounded rough and pained, and whether it was because of how he felt or because of his injuries she could not begin to parse.

I cannot.

Cannot. That word meant something held him back, and the only thing she could think of was... "Oh, so you do have someone waiting for you." It crashed inside of her, dark and horrible. When it didn't matter or shouldn't. He had someone, a woman he'd likely pledged himself to. Kissed, touched, loved.

Why else could he not take what she'd *offered*, no matter how wrongly on her part.

But he shook his head. "I do not," he said, though his expression was one of pain. And the pain got through to her more than anything.

"No, don't speak. It hurts too much." She patted his chest, this time to soothe. "Just because you can doesn't mean you're fully healed. Rest."

He looked down at her, mouth in a grim line, but slowly he raised his hand and put it over hers on his chest. So warm, so large, so rough. The scratches on his hands were healing, but old scars marked his skin.

She should step away from this. It was too much, and her father had always warned her that her many *too much* vices would lead her down the same path he'd walked. Pain. Loss. A dereliction of his sacred duty as a Thore.

For the first time in her life, she thought she understood. That emotions could be dangerous, threatening, even when they *felt* good. For the first time, she was faced with a want that *threatened* something.

And now she knew why she'd been taught that a dutiful princess did not test herself. She kept herself above reproach. She thought of her duty, her promises.

Because she wanted Danil, not a future husband. She

wanted to share her body with him, chase these feelings, not save herself as she was meant to. *Danger*.

She knew why she could not, once more, press herself to him. Touch her mouth to his. Why she could not have what her body desired—a pounding need that had become something more than *needy*. There was weakness in *needy*, but she felt nothing weak about this.

It was as strong and vast as the ocean, this feeling swirling inside of her. As demanding as the storm that had brought Danil to her beach.

How could a man who'd spoken only a few words to her sweep inside of her like those things? How could her responsibilities be shaken by a man who'd only showed up and *listened*?

But no, it wasn't *all* him. Because she'd had questions before. Wondered why her duty mattered. But that had always felt vaguely self-pitying. Whiny. Or maybe her father had only made certain she felt that way when she'd complained. Cut her off more and more until there was little left. Of course, Nielson had told her once that the older she got the more she looked like a carbon copy of her mother, and that might explain some of her father's increasing distance as she'd gotten older.

But King Alfred hadn't been completely wrong about her early anger and frustration at being sent here. Her complaints *had* been childish then. Her thoughts had all been about her own feelings and not the Kingdom, because she had been *thirteen*, and she hadn't been able to care about the Kingdom.

But now, as the years had passed, her feelings had become adult. Why did she not get to make the choices? Why was it someone else's decision that she could not kiss this man, learn this man, give herself to this man who brought out so many sensations within her with just a *look*?

She cared for Mathav and her legacy, but why should her father's devotion to her long-gone mother be seen as a failure? Wasn't it *beautiful*? Why did she not get to chase that beauty?

Danil made all her dreams of something else seem real and vibrant and *possible*, instead of the foolish fantasies of a bored little girl reading too many fairy tales.

He represented what else there might be. Because surely whoever her father might pick out for her wouldn't affect her like *this*. Surely this thing that bloomed between them was unique.

Or was it? How would she know?

"I could save you from that which you do not want." His voice was little more than a rasped whisper, but it wound through her like a booming proclamation.

Save.

She should say no. She should adamantly shut this conversation down—she was not really a prisoner, not really in any situation that required *saving*. She had accepted her duty.

But for a moment, fleeting and irresponsible, she could picture a whole different future than she'd ever considered. Somewhere else. Free of kingdoms and duties. In the middle of the ocean, just the two of them. No need to hope for her father's approval, because it would not matter there.

"How?" she whispered, though there was no need to speak so softly.

He shook his head. "Think about what you want, Else-bet."

Elsebet of course could not *think* about it. There was no rescue from what she'd chosen. She had a duty to Mathav.

To her father. And maybe it wasn't fair, but it was what mattered.

More so than this man.

But the way he rasped her name lived inside of her now. On repeat, for the next few days, as she considered all that she could not do.

Danil spent the next two days testing the limits of his voice, but only when he was alone and no one could hear. He couldn't speak for long. His vocal cords seemed to stop working at all after a few words. So he waited. He did not want to find the opportunity to call his brother only to be rendered mute after a few words. It was frustrating to have been here over a week, and still not be well enough to set his plan into action.

He did not speak to Elsebet after that moment in the tower. He was not alone with her again.

Even when her gaze felt as heavy as any caress and his body acted in kind. He focused on being the perfect guest. So that when he left here, Elsebet in tow, everyone would be surprised the kind, shipwrecked sailor could do such a thing. He was determined it would be before the next week was out.

Maybe the staff would even create their own fairy tale around it. Nielson seemed too practical and devoted to his king, but the women might sigh over a love story for their princess.

He did not think they were so removed that they did not see the way Elsebet looked at him when she thought no one was paying attention.

Or the way you look at her. He scowled at that thought as he sat around the dinner table. Everyone was cheerfully discussing topics related to the keeping of the castle. Pantry stores, repairs that needed done.

Danil had the strangest thought sneak through. That he might…miss this. The conversation, the warmth, the *hominess*. It tried to remind him of bits and pieces of his childhood he'd long since shoved into the recesses of his mind.

His grandmother's shaky voice and warm breakfast biscuits—better than anything he'd ever eaten at the palace. Mornings on his grandfather's lap, the smell of strong coffee wrapped around them. His mother tucking him into bed before she'd married and soured everything.

How dare these strangers stir up these old memories best left behind? How dare they include him in their little conversations and warm dinners and *care*?

He had no use for this. He did not belong in the midst of *this*. He was *The Weapon*. Whom loss could not hurt. Who would not allow loss to change *everything*, as his grandparents' deaths had.

"Are you in pain, Danil?"

Danil raised his gaze to the concern in Inga's eyes. She blinked once, as if taken aback by the expression on his face.

Which no doubt had been dark and mean as he'd been thinking about Frick and all the spaces he'd swept into after he'd lost his grandparents. All the things he'd ruined simply because his mother had been blinded by grief and stress.

Danil tried to smooth out his expression, along with everything inside of him. The past didn't matter. He'd left it behind, so he shook his head.

He had not spoken to anyone except Elsebet back in her tower. He did not think she'd informed her staff of his returned voice, and he would also use this in his favor as long as it lasted. It helped him look far meeker than he could ever be and would ideally keep the trio from becoming too curious about him that they might actually look into him. Or tell their king about him.

"If everything is feeling okay," Win said, smiling at him with a mix of kindness and something far more canny in her expression. "A sailor has some knowledge of these repairs, does he not?"

Danil had not been paying attention to the conversation before Inga's question, but he nodded. He used the pen and paper he now always carried with him to write *I would be happy to help*.

"The materials should come in next week," Nielson said, looking Danil over skeptically. Danil did not know what the man was skeptical about, but he could not help but respect the man for his carefulness.

Danil did not plan to be here in a week's time. But he smiled and nodded, nonetheless.

But then Nielson skewered him with a hard look. "However, the ship that brings them could also take you back to Mathav once it drops its cargo, if you are up to the short voyage back. From there, you could return home. Wherever that may be."

There was clear censure in that last sentence. That he had never told them where that was. That he had let himself remain a mystery.

Danil did not let it poke at him. He took it for what it was. Growing suspicion. But his voice was back, his plans were in place. Suspicion didn't matter because he—and Elsebet—would be gone before Nielson grew the courage to do anything about it.

So Danil took his pen and wrote, before showing the paper to Nielson.

Whose frown only deepened.

I would be happy to take the ship back and return home. My imposition has gone on long enough.

"Oh, you're no imposition," Win said, giving Nielson a hard look. "I'm sure the Princess has enjoyed having someone besides us to keep her company."

Danil smiled at Win's kindness, then slid a look to Elsebet. She was looking down at her plate. She had been less... cheerful since their encounter in her art studio. She still smiled, spoke sweetly, of course. But she was not as chatty. She acted as though something weighed on her.

Which could only mean she was considering his proposition, no matter how vague it had been. No matter how she'd claimed she could not.

After a few moments, as if sensing his eyes on her, she looked up. Their gazes clashed. Like swords in battle. Sparks. Heat. Memory of that kiss on the beach with the cold wind whipping around them. Of the way her eyes had gotten soft as she'd spoken of her home country, with all that *yearning* for things she could not have. Heartbreak over being sent away, thinking it was her fault.

That echoed so deep in his soul he was afraid he would forget who he was.

The Weapon. He broke her gaze, trying to find some triumph in the pink stain on her cheeks. He had fooled her. She would go with him because she *wanted* him.

And he would hand her over to his brother.

The hand he held in his lap curled into a fist.

Inga sighed a little dreamily. Yes, they would weave stories. As long as Elsebet's father questioned *all* the staff, it was possible he would be confused enough by Inga and Win's reports that he wouldn't suspect Danil of working at Aras's behest and *immediately* go after Aras. Hopefully, he would think instead that Danil had taken Elsebet for himself.

The way that idea sang within him like a symphony was clearly a side effect of his head injury. So he focused on the next steps. Because he knew well enough that nothing would stop her father from coming for her, but Gintaras was a much stronger country militarily than Mathav. There was only so much King Alfred could do. And it was the King's own fault for breaking a deal with Aras anyway.

No one broke their promise to Aras and survived to tell the tale. As his enforcer, Danil should know.

But Danil also knew that timing was important. Because who knew how the ocean would treat him once he got Elsebet on a ship. It could take anywhere from three days to a week to sail back to Gintaras, depending on the weather, the type of ship and the number of men Aras sent as crew— likely not many, since everyone was afraid to sail to the cove and large ships could not handle the narrow strait.

So he would need time.

But first he needed a ship to *get* here. Tonight would be the night to arrange that. He would find a way to make a call to his brother.

He helped clean up after dinner, did not fully understand why he enjoyed making Win and Inga tut at him for doing too much. Or proving to Nielson that he was indeed a helpful member of the castle. Or looking at Elsebet until she blushed a deep red.

It was similar to sailing with his crew back in Gintaras when he was commanding the navy somewhere. You became a kind of...family unit.

The idea of *family* often had him withdrawing on his ship,

and it had the same effect here. It was just harder to remove himself from the warmth. There was nothing to do when he did. Only silence and the memories he did not wish to relive would plague him if he isolated himself.

But he had plans to make. So he excused himself—silently. He said nothing to Elsebet even when she bade him good-night in the living room while everyone else was in the kitchen. She even paused, and he knew she was giving him a chance to speak, to offer to save her once more, to explain himself in some way.

But he did not.

He had a feeling the more he pressed, the more she would resist. Because she had a duty too. It was what kept her hesitating, no matter how much she wanted freedom.

She would cave. She would give in to that desire, but only if he did not push until the right moment.

He waited until everyone was asleep, and the castle was dark and peaceful. Until he was absolutely certain there was no way for anyone to be near, to be listening. In the dead of night, with only the sounds of an old castle and the wind outside, he finally found his moment.

He crept through the castle. It hadn't taken much to find out from Win that there was a phone in the library that was rarely used, but always functioning so Nielson could call the King and vice versa.

Which meant Danil would be able to call his brother. And the only way to trace it would be for the King of Mathav to get his hands on the phone records. Which he could do, of course, but it would take time.

Time was all Danil needed.

Danil turned on no lights, having familiarized himself with every piece of furniture, every creak of the floorboard on the way to the library. Once he reached the door, he eased himself into the dark room without needing a light or making a sound.

He found the chair at the desk, sat himself in it, then lifted the phone receiver. It glowed in the dark and he carefully inputted the number to his brother's personal assistant.

It would be a few hours later in Gintaras, and the number would come in as unknown, but Danil hoped that since it was Olev's private mobile, he would be curious enough to answer.

"Hello?" a deep voice asked suspiciously.

Success. "Olev. It is Danil."

There was a pause. "You don't sound yourself," Olev said, all suspicion.

"Near death will do that to a person, but I managed to survive my shipwreck, and have been nursed back to health by the target. I need a ship." His throat burned as he talked, and it was difficult to enunciate while speaking softly enough he didn't wake anyone.

"But...you were the only one brave enough to sail out there in the first place."

Danil did not groan in frustration. It would only hurt and there was no point. "I need a ship. Before the week is out. On the island. Tell His Majesty."

"Do you have the Princess?"

Danil stared into the dark around him. He was not convinced she would come with him willingly. There was a sense of duty embedded in her that made him wonder if she would be brave enough to buck it.

Would you?

That question settled in him like a thorn wedged deep. The truth was, he did not know. He *had* known.

Before Elsebet.

Now he felt they were both living in a strange place where a duty they'd never questioned had been made tenuous simply by the existence of each other.

But tenuous mattered not. Succeeding in his mission was the only thing that would ever matter.

"Sir, do you have the Princess?" Olev repeated impatiently.

"I will," he growled, the pain a throbbing, aching thing that spread from throat to chest. Surely it was only his injuries causing that pain to settle on his heart. "Send Peet. He will know how to signal me from the cove entrance. By the end of the week." Then, orders given, Danil hung up.

And sat in the dark of the library, wondering what he'd done.

CHAPTER SEVEN

ELSEBET HAD MADE a concerted effort to stay away from Danil following the moment in the tower. Of course, this was difficult when he was at every meal, when he jumped to offer assistance in any of the chores she usually helped Win or Inga with.

Or when Win and Inga seemed *determined* to throw her and Danil together at every opportunity. Like this morning while making bread. Happily and peacefully by herself in the kitchen. Thinking about an upcoming spring rather than isolation and Danil. Or trying to anyway.

Then he'd entered.

For a moment, they'd simply stared at one another. Her hands deep in the large bowl of dough, his eyes tracking over her like they always seemed to. That had her cheeks heating and heart beating triple time.

"Inga said to help," he said, his voice still a rasp though it didn't seem to pain him as much. He didn't speak around Inga or Win or Nielson. He still always had his pad of paper and wrote answers to them.

She wondered why if he *could* speak now, he didn't, but couldn't bring herself to ask.

Getting to know or understand this man any more was a danger to everything she'd promised herself. And her father.

But she could hardly send him away. It didn't make sense.

Or you just want him near even if you know it's wrong. She frowned down at her dough but gave Danil a little nod. "I'm making bread for the week."

He walked over to the sink and washed his hands. He still studied her as he dried them off on a towel, so she looked down at the large bowl once more. "We have to shape them into loaves and put them in the pans so they can rise one more time. Watch me."

But his hand dipped into her bowl, taking a handful of dough. She frowned over at him, then watched as he expertly crafted a loaf shape and dropped it into one of the waiting pans.

Her mouth dropped open in wonder. Why, they looked better than hers! "Where did you learn to do this?" she demanded.

"My grandmother," he said, precisely taking another ball of dough to shape.

She tried to picture Danil as a young boy with a grandmother teaching him how to shape loaves. She simply couldn't manage it. He was such a *man*, so vital. How could he have ever been a vulnerable child?

It wasn't something she could bear to think about right now. So she focused on her work. They were nearly hip to hip, their elbows sometimes brushing. It was entirely too domestic. Which was...wonderful. Like he was part of her little family here. Like he could be.

But he was leaving. *He wants to save you.*

From her duty. From her family. From her country. These were not things she needed to be saved from, because she had chosen them.

For the right reasons?

"How is it a princess knows how to bake bread?" he asked. Conversationally.

It seemed a better topic of conversation than the round-about going on in her head. "I wouldn't have if I had not been sent here. But, if you haven't noticed, there isn't much to do and I was going stir-crazy. And driving Inga and Win to fits with it. So we agreed to let me do some chores around the castle."

"*Let* you," he said, something like a scoff in his tone. "Such a hardship, Princess. Begging to do work most of us are required to do to get by."

She frowned over at him, surprised at what felt like censure in his tone. But there was a smile on his face. Not censure. Teasing.

That Danil could tease was… Well, it was probably her fairy-tale-addled heart that made her think it meant something. Like he had to *care*, to use his voice to tease.

"And I suppose you were slaving over loaves of bread and chores aplenty?"

Stop asking questions, Elsebet.

"More or less. We lived with my grandparents, and as I got older, their health suffered. It was up to me to do much of the work around the house."

Her heart ached for him. Such responsibility for a little boy. "Do you have any siblings?"

There was a pause. "A brother."

"How different my life might have been with a brother." Her gaze slid to his. She should not let it linger, but it was such a painful thought. If her mother had lived, if she'd had a brother to inherit the throne…

You still would have been a princess. Likely not isolated on an island and therefore unlikely to have ever met this poor sailor your father would never approve of regardless.

This was why her father had warned her against fairy tales. Once you finally realized they were never possible, it only hurt almost as deeply as any actual loss. The next time she saw her father, she would apologize to him. He'd always done his best. Maybe warnings weren't what an eight-year-old needed, but she understood the *point* of them now.

Danil was closer now, but he didn't touch her, and she didn't dare look at him as she shaped her loaf in the pan.

"I never knew my father. Not really," he said. "He left my mother before I was born. I spent much of my life consumed by what-ifs. What would have been different if he'd been involved? If my mother had found a nice man to settle down with instead of the leech she finally did."

She couldn't keep her determination not to look at him when he said that. Couldn't stop the conversation, couldn't stop learning about him. "You didn't like your stepfather?"

Danil's expression was ice-cold. "He was never anything to me. And I was nothing to him." On the *him*, his voice cracked and he began to cough, pain etched over his face. Elsebet rushed to get him a glass of water.

She pushed him onto a stool and insisted he drink. "Don't talk anymore," she said, rubbing his back and watching the color in his face. He wasn't as pale as he had been, but still she worried about him. Nielson had been a doctor, but maybe Danil needed better attention. Better equipment to make certain everything inside was working and healing as it should.

He sipped the water, his cough subsiding. "I am all right," he rasped.

"No more talking," she said again. She set the now-empty glass aside but didn't stop rubbing his back. Until he took her free hand in his. Clasping her small one between his two large ones.

She looked down at him and her heart tripped over itself in all those ways she couldn't allow.

"You are the kindest woman I've known, Elsebet," he said, with such gravity she thought her knees might buckle. And he kissed her hand in a romantic, gallant gesture. The kind she'd dreamed about, knowing her father would never approve of love.

Danil looked down at her hand in his. She should pull it away.

But she did not. Because his dark eyes, grim and serious, were locked with hers.

"I will not ask again. I will not push or beg." His voice got more and more cracked as he spoke and she wanted to tell him to stop, but she knew he wouldn't.

"When it is time for me to leave, I do not wish to leave you behind. I want you to come with me, Elsebet."

He said it so earnestly. Like it was possible.

She began to shake her head, because giving in to her wants was not the duty of a princess. Of her father's daughter.

"Don't refuse," Danil insisted. "Simply...think on it. Don't give me an answer until the time comes."

She could not stand to be around him after that. It made her question everything. It hurt. And all those questions and all that hurt built inside of her like a tempest. She'd thrown herself out of the kitchen and spent the next three days avoiding him at all costs. Even going so far as to feign a cold.

Her only reprieves were her secret walks on the beach when she snuck out the window in the library. She needed the cold air, the exercise. The solitude.

But the walks kept getting longer, more frequent, and still she could not walk away from her thoughts, her jumbled feelings. Whether Danil was in her line of sight or not, she could not push his words from her mind. He had been here for almost two weeks now, and it felt like he'd been here forever. Like she wanted him to be.

She could tell his childhood had been more painful than hers. That he too was haunted by what-ifs. She was so much more privileged than he, she knew, and yet they seemed to understand each other.

Danil had spoken of *saving* her, because he saw through all the masks she put in place, or tried to.

And yet she did not need saving. Could not accept saving.

This was the circle her mind kept going in—and she could not stop it, because she had no answer. Only the whirl of thoughts and conflicting feelings.

She walked faster along the shore, her boots making squelching sounds in the wet sand. There was a place up here, far away from the castle, where she could hide. Where she could yell and scream and beat her fists against the rock and no one would ever know. No one could see and disapprove. Or send her away.

Where else is there to send you to, Elsebet?

I could save you from that which you do not want.

She squeezed her eyes shut for a few more steps, knowing the way by memory and not needing her sight. She tried to shove it all away, let the wind blow it out of her system. But she felt as she had in that first year here on the island.

Angry, wound tight, ready to blow. Which was why she was heading to her little secret place, which she'd discovered in her first year here. Because as angry as she'd been, then and now, it had never felt right to take her frustrations out on Nielson, Win or Inga. They loved her and cared for her, and she would not take the burden of her feelings out on them.

So she'd walk to the edge of the cove, climb into the cluster of rocks, and then let it all out any time the frustration overwhelmed her.

Less so lately, but it cropped up every once in a while. A tide that needed to rush in and out before it could settle. The past few days had pushed her to an edge and she needed to let it go.

Lest she explode.

Or make a giant mistake.

She was starting her walk a little late and knew she would not make it to her spot before dark tonight, but it was a clear evening. The sunset would light her way there, the moon would guide her back.

She was practically running now, her breaths coming quickly, and that felt good too. Like she had a million years of unspent energy inside of her that she needed to get out. She made it to the edge of the cove, where rocks and boulders spiraled up and stood shoulder to shoulder. She climbed the familiar footholds that wind and surf had eroded for her. Then she slid down one rock somewhat like a slide and landed on the sand in the middle of a tower of rocks.

No one could see her here, even from the tallest point of the castle. Here in this tiny, *tiny* space she was free to do as she pleased, hidden and muffled by strong, ancient rocks.

So she screamed. She stomped and shouted, and none of it was words or coherent. It was just release. She hit the edge of her hands, where she had the most padding on her palms, against the rock. Not as hard as she could, but hard enough to sting. She even kicked one of the rocks. It was no doubt the most foolish kind of outburst, but she always felt better afterward.

However, today none of the tightness in her chest dissipated, though she kept shouting and flailing about. If anything, she felt angrier. As she stood, practically panting and near tears, she still felt as twisted and confused and full of that boiling energy that threatened to lead her toward mistake.

I could save you from that which you do not want.

But could he save her from knowing she had betrayed everything she had always held dear?

Because she *wanted* to save Mathav, to please her father, to do her duty. She *wanted* to be good so she no longer had to be hidden away. So her father no longer hurt over what he hadn't been able to give his country.

She *wanted* Danil, even though that would ruin all the other things.

So there were no answers. Nothing truly to be saved from. Every choice gave her something she did not want. Something she could not live with.

"That was quite a display."

This time when she screamed, it was out of surprise. She whirled, to find Danil lounging on top of the flattest boulder, looking down at her. He was gilded in moonlight and her heart beat triple time, a strange mix of fear and desire making her feel oddly weightless.

And all those conflicting feelings that had felt barbed and twisted inside of her lifted. Because when he was here, it was clear which want loomed larger than all the others.

Him.

But no… He'd seen her… He'd seen *all that*. Panic shot through her. He wouldn't want anything to do with her now either.

"You shouldn't be out here in the dark alone." His voice had changed after three more days of rest. It sounded less a rasp and more a deep, steady thing. She half believed he could lull the ocean tempests into tranquility with it once his throat was fully healed.

He slid down the rock with the kind of grace she would never have expected of a man of his size or with his injuries.

And then he was in the circle of rocks with her, their bodies creating a kind of cocoon of warmth, while moonlight shone down on them as if to spotlight whatever they chose to do here.

For good or for ill.

She was not sure how long they stood, not speaking, the only sound around them the crashing of the surf very close. The only thing they did was breathe and stare at each other, just out of reach. Both held back by something.

"What bothers you, Elsebet?" he asked into the quiet.

Elsebet. There was something about how he said her name. His accent, perhaps. Or the deep richness of his voice. Something inside of her that was wrong and broken because it felt like a shameful *need* when he spoke her name.

To hear him say it, over and over again. Closer. With his lips on her. With his hands on her.

She swallowed. He had not run away. He had asked her what was wrong. But oh, she could not tell him. He'd likely sail out on the first ship he could.

"I should head back to the castle." She could not trust herself out here in her secret place alone with him. "Nielson will worry."

"No doubt he will. Once he learns you snuck out."

She found she couldn't be surprised that Danil knew. Danil seemed to know and understand everything about her. So she needed to escape.

But neither of them moved.

"Why have you not told them you can speak?" she asked, her voice strained even to her own ears. Because she'd been desperate to know for days but knew the answer would hurt.

But here in the rocks and sand she could not seem to do anything but seek out *hurt*.

"I wish to save my voice for when it's important."

She did not miss the meaning. That speaking to *her* specifically was important. Her heart lurched in her chest. That *she* was still important. Even after...screaming and crying?

She knew her *role* was important to her father. She knew Nielson, Win and Inga viewed her as important because of her title.

But no one thought it was important to speak to her. For who she was in this moment. Not a princess.

Just a woman. With feelings so big she needed to let them out.

And he did not express any dismay or disapproval at her ridiculous outburst. He acted as he always did.

"You have always seemed quite sweet and on an even keel. Is it because when you feel anything else you come here and take it out on the rocks?" He asked it so casually, when it spoke to the deeper parts of herself she always tried to keep hidden.

She looked around at the moonlight space. Too small for the two of them—though any space would feel too small for the two of them right now, she was sure.

She could lie, pretend he hadn't seen what he absolutely had. She could leave. But instead, she told him the truth. Well, part of the truth. "It doesn't seem right or fair to take it out on the rest of them."

For a moment something flickered in his expression. She had seen this before. His reaction to something she said, confusion but something deeper than that. A kind of yearning mixed with distrust.

She would have to know him better to understand this look, and she knew that was not in the cards. Couldn't be.

And still he did not turn her away as though she'd done something wrong.

He cocked his head. "Why not? They *are* your staff, and you *are* their princess, are you not?"

"But they have done nothing wrong. My frustrations are my own. Caused by…"

"Me?" he supplied, but not with any kind of apology. With a silky kind of promise.

"You could say that if you wish to be arrogant, but it isn't so much about you as it is… My feelings are my own, Danil." And he had seen too many of them.

But remained.

He moved closer and she, fool that she was, did not back away. She simply let him take more and more of her space.

Because you wish there to be no space.

He reached out, touched his rough finger to her cheek.

"You saying my name has haunted me for many nights now," he said, his voice getting raspier the more he used it.

As if he felt the same things she did. But was he as conflicted as she was? Did he have a duty awaiting him? He didn't act like it, but she also knew the kind of yearning caused by a duty that chafed and had seen it in his eyes when he'd looked at her art.

Had heard it in his voice when he'd pulled away from her up in her tower. There was *something* in his *I cannot*.

And he was here, touching her face, rather than leaving or telling her she was wrong for having her feelings. If anything, he'd almost validated them.

"Tell me," she said, sounding more fervent than the situation warranted. She reached out and took his hands because she needed answers. She so desperately needed someone to have an answer. "When we were up in my tower, and you said you could not, what did you mean? Exactly."

* * *

Danil had known Elsebet had this kind of passion in her—the kind that could make her yell and scream and pound walls. He'd seen glimpses of it—flashes in her eyes, the way she'd kissed him, her own frustration. But he had not realized the depth of it, he supposed. That she worked so hard to suppress it.

He had thought it new. Timid. But no. She kept it on a leash for the sake of those she loved.

It stirred many things inside of him, not the least of which was the heat in his bloodstream, which could not lead them anywhere good. Not here, where no one ever need know…

No one…

But Danil would know. And if he was never to see her again, perhaps he could have lived with that. He could have taken her in his arms, indulged in all that she was and all he could give her.

But he could not live with it and spend the rest of his life watching her be his brother's bride.

And she *would* be his brother's bride. It was Aras's right to have her.

Not Danil's.

"Danil…"

He could not tell her the reason. He could hardly explain she had been promised to his brother. It was clear she had no idea her father had ever made or broken any such promises. She was still locked up here, awaiting her fate. Hiding in these little rocks when she needed a good yell.

It struck him in this moment as decidedly unfair. But then, when did fairness have anything to do with how the world worked? His life had never been *fair*.

Even if he wished the world could give Elsebet better,

this was not how anything worked. "You have made it quite clear you have a duty," he said.

She frowned, as if she saw it for the lie it was. But she did not push him. She dropped his hands, turned away. "I need to get back." She began to climb up a rock, as if it was something she did often.

She no doubt did. Isolated herself here where she could scream and yell and curse the world...without hurting the feelings of anyone she cared about.

Had he ever known such selflessness?

This of course did not matter. How it affected him, awed him. Nothing about her mattered because there was only the mission.

He was only The Weapon. Loss would never touch him again, because there was nothing to lose when you were only a tool.

He needed her to *want* to come with him. So he followed behind her, struggling for the words that might get through to her. She was afraid, clearly. Though she was strong and brave in many respects, had built herself into her own woman on this little island with her surrogate family and her art, she was still sheltered. She might *imagine* what was beyond this island, her father's kingdom, but she had no actual knowledge.

Perhaps if he had a few more days, he might find a way to offer that knowledge to her.

Why? So she can go to Gintaras, become Aras's bride, and never see it?

Because Aras would not give her freedom or independence. It was not his way. Everyone in Aras's court had clear roles and strict rules. The women especially. His queen would be the most...

Isolated.

It pained Danil. That word. When Elsebet already felt it so much. When she clearly yearned to see something more.

Something irregular and unknown shifted inside of Danil. He had a debt to pay. He did not go back on his debts, and yet...

He did not wish to see Elsebet trade one prison for another. Even if life was, essentially, its own prison. It was what you did with the duties, responsibilities and debts you owed that mattered—not what those things *were*.

Elsebet would understand that. She had to.

But the sense of unease didn't go away, no matter how hard he tried to push it away. He might have considered that deeper, and it might have fully changed something inside of him, but he saw something...out along the water. Beyond the cove.

A flash of light.

Danil stopped following Elsebet and held himself still. So still he did not dare breathe. It could have been a trick of the eye—that was always possible out in the vast ocean. And it had only been a handful of days. Though the weather had been calm and clear here, that did not mean it had been so between here and Gintaras.

Had a ship truly arrived so quickly?

The light flashed once more. Clear this time. It was the signal.

So it was time to act. There was no more time to think. *To question.*

This was good, he thought to himself. *Insisted* in his own mind. Questions led him nowhere comfortable. Nowhere good.

His ship had come. And here was his moment. It was dark. Nielson would no doubt come looking for Elsebet before long, and when he didn't find either of them, he would sound an alarm.

It wouldn't be enough time, but Danil knew there may be no other moment like this one. She was *right* here. If he followed the narrow beach up and around, the ship wouldn't need to come much closer at all. The danger would be much mitigated if the ship didn't need to try and anchor.

Once he had control of his ship, and Elsebet on it, he could outrun whoever the King of Mathav might send after him. They would still not know *who* had taken her or how. Not right away.

It was now or never, so it had to be now.

Danil caught up with Elsebet, took her by the arm and turned her to face out toward the opening of that cove.

"Do you see that light?" he asked her, pointing. Surprised at how desperate his own voice sounded when he should be calm. Relieved. Ready.

Not panicked.

She looked up at him suspiciously, then out toward the moonlit waves. It took a few humming seconds, but then it flashed. It would not flash again for thirty minutes. This was the signal.

This was his moment. He turned to look at Elsebet and did not understand the way his heart hammered inside him. This was the plan, had always been the plan. He was finally completing his mission. It should feel like relief.

Not like walking along a highwire.

"The time has come, Elsebet. That is my ship. My crew has come to collect me." The weather was perfect. Calm and clear. He did not know who had been assigned the captain's task, but clearly it was someone skillful enough to get here quickly.

He took her hands in his and drew her to him. "Come with me."

She did not pull her hands away, no refusal came from her, and yet... She looked at him, still and silent, for too long. Thinking too much. Thinking would not lead to the decision he needed her to make.

But the words he needed seemed to dry up inside of him. Lies about how he could give her freedom and adventure. When he was only another jailor.

He needed to convince her and quickly. But he could not find the words.

What was *wrong* with him?

Her small hands in his, the moonlight in her hair and her eyes. His little siren, and he was just another cage.

The pressure in his chest built until it wasn't just a lack of words, it was the ability to speak at all.

Perhaps he was having some kind of delayed response to his head injury. An aneurysm.

She tugged her hands, but he could not seem to let himself release her.

"I cannot go with you, Danil," she whispered over the lap of waves that seemed to echo in his ears now.

"You want to," he managed, because he could see she did. She *yearned* to.

"Yes," she agreed, and he thought perhaps he'd won, but she shook her head. "But... I have a duty. To my country, to my kingdom. To my father. Wants have nothing to do with my choices, Danil. They cannot."

Something hot and angry brewed inside of him. That she could so easily refuse him for her duty when he was struggling to do his. That she could look so sad when she was making her own choice. That she could have made this simple thing so damn difficult.

That she, like everyone, would choose something else above him. But why wouldn't she? He was *The Weapon*. Nothing more.

I have a duty, Elsebet had said.

Well, so did he.

He dropped her hands, but before she could turn and make her escape back toward the castle, he swept her up in his arms.

For a moment there was no response as he strode up the rocky shore, Elsebet over his shoulder.

"What are you doing?" she demanded, her voice high and tight, her body rigid with shock.

"My duty," he said grimly. And began to walk toward the sea.

CHAPTER EIGHT

ELSEBET WAS QUITE certain Danil had lost his mind. Maybe he'd never had it in the first place. Maybe he'd lost it during the shipwreck. Maybe he'd always been a raving lunatic but knew how to hide it with helpfulness and seductive smiles.

Either way, he was striding along the lapping waves in the middle of the night, carrying her over his shoulder like she was a sack of flour. Not *into* the ocean exactly, but along the shore. Up toward where the beach got more and more narrow until there was only ocean and cliff wall.

Where that little light had flashed.

He was heading for a ship, *his* ship, while the stars shone above like artwork, and she was bumping against his shoulder like said sack.

It hadn't even occurred to her to fight him, because… what was happening? How did this make any sense when he'd been so terribly injured only a short time ago?

But he had a ship out there. She'd seen the light herself. He was… He was taking her against her will. Whether she wanted to go or not.

She did *not* want and was a little horrified she had to remind herself of that very fact as he walked purposefully along the beach.

"Danil…" She tried to think rationally over the beating panic. "You must let me go. I don't think you know what you're getting yourself into. Please. My father won't rest. He will come after me. I think you're confused. I think…" Surely he didn't understand her situation. He thought he was saving her, doing something right, perhaps.

He could not be more wrong, of course.

Though he seemed like a man on a mission who understood well enough. And he spoke of duty.

My duty.

His own duty?

And it occurred to her then, oh, far too late, that this was never about *her*—not in the sense she'd fancied it. It wasn't about him understanding her, wanting her, saving her.

This was about the same thing her entire life had been about. Her being the Princess of Mathav. A political pawn. A negotiation term and nothing else.

Those first few days, she'd been suspicious, hadn't she? Then she'd forgotten to be. Because he listened. He smiled. He'd kissed her back like she might be important. Like he might have some way of offering her freedom when she had always known there was no freedom to be had.

He'd looked at her with such *understanding* when she'd spoken of being a hellion. That little shake of his head, like he couldn't imagine it, had warmed her for days. His kiss. His offer to save her. Speaking of making bread with his grandmother or wondering what might have been different if he'd had a father. Everything he'd done since he'd arrived.

But his *duty* had nothing to do with saving her, nothing to do with *Elsebet*, and everything to do with her being the Princess of Mathav.

She began to struggle then, ashamed it had taken her so long to find the fight within her. She kicked and she punched his back, but it was of course no use. He was so much bigger than her. It didn't even matter that he was injured. He seemed impervious to pain.

"You cannot do this, Danil," she said, trying to sound determined and imperial like her father did when he was angry. It brought tears to her eyes that she only sounded desperate.

"You have left me no choice," he replied grimly, still *walking*. As if this was normal and right. As if she weighed nothing and he hadn't been stitched up and unable to speak only two weeks ago.

My duty.

You have left me no choice.

Choice. He dared speak to *her* of choice. "They will come after you. My father will not rest. This is not the course of action you want to take. I do not know who sent you or what you want…" She wanted to sob then. Because clearly this was about her position, when she'd thought for the first time in her life that something had been about *her*. Elsebet, the woman.

Not the princess-pawn.

He hadn't censured her for her outburst. He'd still wanted her. Or pretended to. It was *all* pretend.

Well, thank goodness she'd chosen her duty. She'd give herself credit for that if nothing else. Maybe she was pathetic, foolish. Maybe she had everything to be embarrassed about, everything to fear as he continued his walk along the sea.

But she hadn't chosen him. She had to hold on to that little sliver of pride. When push came to shove, when wants came against duty, she had chosen Mathav. Her father.

"This will end badly for you, Danil," she said. She did not know how she finally made herself sound strong in the moment, but she did. Even as the pain and betrayal of it washed through her.

He said nothing. He walked on. Splashing in the water as he walked around the cove. She saw no more flashing lights, but he seemed to know exactly where he was going.

"Why? Why are you doing this?" And she knew she did not sound demanding or imperial then. She sounded like a sad child. Perhaps she felt like one. Some part of her had trusted him, even knowing he was a stranger. She had felt something...undefinable. A connection she thought meant something.

She was a fool.

He continued on silently and no amount of fight dislodged his arm banded around her. No amount of struggle stopped his forward movement. He simply *kept going*. Until he was nearly waist-deep in the water. Until she could make out the outline of a small flotation device or raft bobbing ever closer in the bright moonlight.

"I'll... I'll...jump off," she said, trying to dislodge his grip on her. She had to fight. She had to do something aside from feeling so deeply betrayed. She could not let him put her on that ship.

He laughed then, a low rumble that somehow moved through her like heat even when she was so angry. Hurt beyond reason, and still her body reacted to him. How patently unfair.

"You can try, Princess," he said, his voice getting raspier, no doubt the exertion and the speaking working against his injuries.

Good, she thought to herself. He deserved every last one. And more. She would find a way to give him more.

Then and there she decided she would not simply fall apart. She would not let the pain and betrayal fell her.

She had been nothing but a pawn all her life. She had *let* herself be that, but now she was something else. Though she had often felt a prisoner under her father, she had also been in that prison somewhat voluntarily. She had taken it because it was a bit of a punishment she deserved for being so unruly. Because it had been partly her duty. Her legacy. Because if she did her duty, made her father proud, maybe he could look at her and not see her long-lost mother.

Regardless, she had not given in to Danil. Even when she'd desperately wanted to. Which meant she couldn't now. She could not be the person always accepting whatever *men* threw at her.

Now she had to be strong. Now she had to *fight*. When she'd never been taught how. When she'd never allowed herself any true rebellion.

She did not know how to fight yet, not as Danil got her on the raft, not as they were pulled toward a bigger ship. Not as she was lifted from raft to boat against her will.

But she would find out. Danil would not win.

She was the Princess of Mathav, and she would be no one's prisoner ever again.

Danil got Elsebet onto the boat, though it was a struggle. She had fought, and he supposed it was a bit perverse to be proud of her. Glad that she would try to fight rather than cry and take her fate easily.

She was a strong woman. This was good for her future. She would need to be with Aras. That thought felt as cold as the icy water had.

He climbed into the boat himself, trying not to let the physical toll on him show to the men who awaited him. But his injuries from the shipwreck were still not fully healed. He never would have been *breathless* at such exertion before.

He didn't let it show. Not because of Elsebet, though she

was clearly angry enough to use it against him, but because he was back on one of his ships. He was captain once more, and the two men who had helped them up were his crew.

Danil breathed a sigh of some relief. This was comfortable, familiar ground. His ship. Him in charge. The dark sea around him and navigating it.

He did not look at Elsebet but kept a good grip on her lest she try to see through her threat to jump off. But looking at her would take away this feeling of sturdy ground. So he nodded at the men. "I was not sure anyone would come," Danil said in his native tongue. He did not think Elsebet spoke it, but he wouldn't put it past her. Still, they'd speak it until he knew for sure. The less she knew the better.

Danil studied the two men who stood before him. Peet had often been on his crew through a variety of missions. He was a good sailor, with good instincts. He could be timid when faced with authority, and had never made the ranks of guard, but Danil always took him on seafaring missions for his proficiency with sailing.

Riks, on the other hand, was a member of King Aras's council. Not much of a sailor in any way, shape or form, so an interesting choice of second man. Especially since he looked a little worse for the wear, as if he'd spent most of the voyage sick.

"The King was quite adamant," Riks said stiffly.

"The Princess is a flight risk as of yet. She will be locked in the captain's quarters at all times, unless I, and I alone, accompany her. Can you handle getting us back to open sea while I get her settled, Peet?"

Peet nodded. "Yes, sir."

Danil kept his grasp on Elsebet's arm and began to pull her down the deck toward the stairs that would lead them down into the accommodation. She did not resist exactly, nor did she come easily. It indeed needed to be a *pull*.

Her chin was up, her eyes blazed with anger. He had to admit, he'd expected a little bit more weeping and wailing. Actually, he'd expected it to take longer for her to put together that he was not simply taking her because he wanted her, or because she wanted him. He'd thought he might get to Gintaras before she grew cynical enough to see the truth.

But she had put it together quite quickly. It had only taken him calling it a duty for her to realize she remained what she'd always been under her father's thumb. Simply a pawn.

It almost made him sad.

But he pushed that away. Perhaps it was not her fault that she had been put into such a position, but her father should not have broken his promise to Aras.

Danil made it to the captain's quarters. He was pleased to see neither Peet nor Riks had made the mistake of claiming these quarters for themselves. *He* was the captain of the ship. Always.

"This will be your room," he said to the Princess without looking directly at her. "Should you feel sick, there is a bathroom through there. You will sleep here, eat here, but if you behave, I just might let you above board for supervised walks." He knew it was too harsh. Honey attracted better than vinegar and all that.

But something he did not recognize held him in its grip and the only way he could see his way through it was to be cruel.

"So this is to be my dungeon?" she said, chin up and eyes hard. Nothing siren about them now. Just cold.

He refused to let the guilt take a hold. He looked around the room. The nice bed. The separate bathroom with a door. It smelled nice and clean. He sneered at her, compelled by all this anger inside of him. "If you think you can call this a dungeon, *Your Highness*, you have clearly never been in one."

"And you have?"

He said nothing to this question, meant to be impertinent when it was anything but. He thought his silence was terrifying enough, but he did not understand the way her expression changed. From fury and defiance to something sad. "Why would you have been in a dungeon, Danil?" she asked softly. Gently. Almost as if she'd reach out and touch his chest like she had in her art gallery.

Almost like she cared.

But her expression changed as she said his name. "Danil," she repeated. Then she laughed. Bitterly. "Is that even your name?"

"It is. I have no need to hide who I am, Princess. Not behind my art or in secret-rock hiding places."

Her eyes narrowed. Fury practically leaped from her, and again he felt that backward pride that she would have such fire in her.

"No one from nowhere?" she said, all scathing bitterness.

"I am Danil Laurentius, also known as *The Weapon*. Head of the Gintaras King's Guard and Navy. Your father promised you to our king, and so you will be delivered to him."

"If my father promised me to your king, I would be with him. This surely would not need to be so cloak-and-dagger."

"Your father broke his promise. And he should be grateful that my brother's only revenge is to take you by force. He could do worse."

Elsebet was silent for a few humming moments. Danil needed to take his leave, he knew he did. Lock her in here and take over as captain. Breathe the sea air and find his footing once more.

But he did not move.

"You'll deliver me to your king, and then what?" Elsebet asked, very, *very* quietly.

And when he spoke, his own voice sounded strangely quiet, oddly strangled. Not the rasp of his injuries, but something else. Something he could not acknowledge. "You shall be his bride. The Queen of Gintaras."

"Is that what you want, Danil?"

He looked at her then, because *want*? He wanted to laugh in her face, but he only spoke the truth. "Have you learned nothing, Elsebet? Our wants do not matter. There is only duty. And I am better at doing mine than you or your father are at doing yours." He wrenched open the door. "You will be locked in. There is an intercom should you need anything."

He did not slam the door behind him, though he wanted to. He simply pulled it closed, ensured it was locked, then strode away. Up to the captain's seat. Where he would guide his ship back to Gintaras.

Because he was *The Weapon*, and that was his mission, and any feelings swirling inside of him like their own dark tempest did not matter.

Ever.

CHAPTER NINE

SINCE SHE WAS ALONE, and it seemed unlikely anyone would return right away, Elsebet let herself cry. She did not *only* cry. She also planned. But the tears streamed down her cheeks as she planned.

Her heart felt bruised. And she wanted only anger and hatred, but… Oh, she knew better than to think him not answering her question about what he wanted might *mean* something. She would be a fool to believe *he* had also felt the connection between them that she had, or kissed her and spoken of saving her because he *wanted* to.

But her heart *had* nursed that notion, and apparently her heart was a fool.

What did it matter anyway? Regardless of what he wanted, he was taking her to his country, his king. Giving her away. Choosing his *duty*, just as she'd chosen hers.

But something eased inside of her. That this might be duty over want. Believing, no matter how her brain told her not to, that he didn't *want* to hand her over to his king. Maybe she hadn't been so *totally* fooled. Maybe there was some…side of him that felt some of the things she felt. She had seen yearning in his eyes. She had *felt* his response to her when she touched him, kissed him.

Surely such things couldn't be faked…could they?

She didn't know. So she cried nearly silently and she

searched the entire room. She didn't know exactly what she was looking for. A weapon? A way out? A telephone? *Something* that might give her a chance.

But the room was essentially empty aside from bedding and toiletries. There was a tiny circular window, but it was dark outside, so there was nothing to see.

There was a little desk connected to the wall and she looked through its contents, finding a few pens and pencils. She looked at the door.

When she'd been a little girl in the palace, she had often tried to learn how to pick locks. She'd never gotten very far. A chaperone always showed up before she could accomplish anything, and the palace locks were much different than anything on this ship.

But what did it lose to try? She had literally *nothing* to lose at this point.

So she knelt at the door with the pens and pencils gripped in her hand, studying the lock. It did not look as though it locked from the outside, but when she tried to turn the knob it didn't budge. So there had to be some sort of mechanism.

Maybe it was a pointless endeavor, but it gave her something to focus on. She took apart one pen, used the bits and pieces to poke at the lock.

She could not give up. She had to find a way out. *What then? You're on a ship.*

She could jump overboard, of course, but they'd likely sailed far away enough from shore that a swim home wouldn't be possible.

Would she rather die than be taken to a king, drown in the vast ocean?

She knew nothing about this king. Was it really so different than what her father had planned for her? Wasn't he also planning on delivering her to a stranger?

Except she liked to think her father would have given her information. Time to come to grips with the upcoming change in her life. Meet the man a few times, maybe even ask her opinion.

When has your father ever listened to your opinion? She pressed her forehead to the door, trying to stem the tide of tears. It didn't matter what her father would have done.

Danil was giving her *nothing*.

Because this was his duty.

Why can you not think of him as the villain in this story when it is nothing but clear?

She focused anew at poking the bits of pen and pencil into the lock mechanism wherever she could manage. Nothing changed. Nothing budged, but she thought she heard a faint *click*. Maybe she'd—

The door swung open and she stumbled back, fell on her bottom.

Danil stood there in the space he'd opened. He frowned down at her. "You should have rested," he said, looking down at her with some hint of—

No, she had to stop letting her heart think he might be looking at her in any specific way. She was his prisoner and he was her kidnapper. There were no feelings here.

If only.

"How do you know I did not?" she returned, trying to make her position on the floor look purposeful. She shook her hair back and looked around imperially. "Is there some sort of surveillance watching my every move in here?"

"There are bags under your eyes, Princess. And the fact you're still in wet clothes." He held out his hand, as if she should take it so he could help her to her feet. "You need to take those damp, dirty skirts off."

She did not take his hand, and she considered remaining

seated on the floor. She was a prisoner—why not lounge on the hard floor as part of the whole thing? But he was so *tall*, so intimidating as he loomed above her. She couldn't feel on *even* ground, but she had to claim some kind of power.

She got to her feet herself. Her skirts *were* wet, and she was uncomfortable, but it matched her gloomy mood. "And wear what? You did not leave me any dry clothes."

He moved toward the little built-in closet that she'd already snooped through but had only found empty. He opened the door, then stopped. He frowned a little, as if he had not expected to find it empty. But the frown was quickly replaced by something far more stoic. He closed the door, turned to face her. "Take them off and get under the covers," he said pointing to the bed.

Elsebet looked down at her skirts, then at the bed, then at the way he stood there, arms folded like he was just going to...watch.

Which sent a wave of heat through her. The idea of him watching her take off her clothes. Even if she left her undergarments on, he'd see more of her than he had before. She'd felt his hands on her, but only through fabric.

The idea of his bare hands on her bare skin...

You are fantasizing about the man who just kidnapped you against your will.

And yet she couldn't break his gaze, couldn't ice away the heat inside of her. Whatever this was, she did not seem to have any control over what it did to her body. And with her body *reacting*, her brain seemed to weaken. She couldn't hold on to those *rational* thoughts.

She was lost in the dark brown of his eyes, the memory of his mouth on hers. The size and heat of him when she pressed herself to him. The way he'd looked at her art, his heart thumping under her hand as he'd offered to save her.

A lie.

She struggled to care.

"You want me to take off my clothes?" she said, breathless.

He stood so still she could have mistaken him for a statue, if not for the heat in his eyes. "My king would not be very happy with me if I brought him a flu-ridden bride. You should get dry and warm."

My king. Bride. He was taking her to a stranger. When he'd held her and kissed her and walked with her. When he'd looked at her art with yearning and not been offended by her outburst in her hideout.

It twisted in her, dark and angry, but she was sad and hurt too. And for the first time in her life, she wanted to take her hurt out on somebody. On him. She *wanted* him to hurt the way she did. Feel as conflicted as she had from the moment she'd laid eyes on him.

She could not hurt him physically. Her only hope was that...he *did* yearn for her. After all, his voice sounded rough. Maybe it was his injuries. Who could say, but she thought she saw anguish in his gaze. She knew she *wanted* to see some there. And maybe it was a figment of her imagination that he might be struggling with the same thing she was.

Desire. Even with all this complication, all this betrayal. If he really *did* want her, if that anguish was real...couldn't she torture *him* with it? Couldn't she use it, the way he'd used hers to get her here?

My king, he'd said, as if she was only a prize to be doled out. Well, maybe that was all she would ever be. But if she was a prize for the King to win, that meant Danil was the loser. Maybe she could make him *feel* it.

He began to turn his back to her, some nod to privacy,

perhaps? But the anger in her boiled and she spoke, hoping to keep his attention.

"Will your king be happy with me?" she asked, innocently enough. But she reached back and pulled down the zipper of her dress. She held his gaze the entire time. "Do you think he'll find me attractive? Want to kiss me? Touch me?" Her voice faltered at *touch*, because she pictured Danil being the one to do these things.

But she did not stop.

"I have not been truly *touched*, as I'm sure you're aware if you're doing this for your king. Maybe everyone in the world is aware." A bitter thought for a bitter moment.

She had been told over and over again, in such vague terms it had taken her a long, long time to understand, that her virginity would be seen as an asset. If Danil was taking her to his king, Danil must know this about her.

Would it be appealing to *him*? It had certainly been talked about as if it was the be-all and end-all in royal weddings. No matter what she'd heard, she'd never been able to understand *why* her virginity mattered. Only that it *did,* to some.

The men who would want her, anyway.

She surveyed Danil now as she let the dress shimmy off her, until she was standing in her undershirt that skimmed her upper thighs, and the thick stockings that might have kept her warm if they weren't damp from the ocean.

Because *he* had dragged her through it. *He* had taken her against her will. She wished this would cool any of the things happening in her body, but no. Her body was its own riot of reaction. That throbbing, that wanting. Wrong and traitorous, yes, but it kept her going. Because if Danil was having these same reactions inside of him, if he wanted her and took her…

He would not be able to deliver her to his king. Not without something coming back on him. This would be revenge.

And adventure.

Because, though it shamed her to admit, it was nothing but true. Even when she saw him as the very devil, her body still reacted to him in such a way she did not think it would be a *physical* hardship, while it would certainly be an emotional one.

She had two choices. She could either go to his king untouched, allowing Danil to do his duty while she had *nothing* for herself, or she could have this thing she wanted, even if she shouldn't, and then be delivered to this king all the same.

Well, why not take what she wanted in this moment? Why not give herself *something* on the way to being yet another man's pawn?

She walked over to the bed, which put her closer to him. He stood *very* still. So still she knew it was a reaction. No one was ever that still when *nothing* was going on inside them.

Besides, his eyes never left her body.

She sat down, rolled the wet stockings off her legs, watching him through her eyelashes. His gaze followed the move of each stocking, roamed the exposed leg. Yes, he wanted her. And if she gave herself to him, she would have something she wanted *and* revenge.

Though her arms shook—a mix of fear and excitement—she lifted her shirt over her head and let it fall to the ground with her damp stockings. She was in nothing but her underwear, sitting on the edge of the bed. He had moved in that short time, but only a few inches.

Closer.

She couldn't help but think he wasn't aware that he'd done that, when it seemed like Danil *always* knew what he was doing.

But he wanted her. She could see the evidence of his own arousal, jutting against the fabric of his pants. His expression *had* changed. Gone fierce. On her. As if he was cataloging every inch of exposed skin.

He wanted to touch her. She had no doubts in this moment, hot and potent. Maybe she had no knowledge of men and women, of the world outside her little island and a palace in Mathav. But she knew Danil. And she could seduce him. She could ruin *his* plans.

The knowledge speared through her like power, twisting with the desire of her body.

She would find some of her own pleasure, because no matter how this had all gone disastrously wrong, no matter how she could never forgive him for what he'd done to her, she knew he would bring her pleasure.

And that was something no one would ever be able to take away from her. Not her father, not his king. It would be hers and hers alone.

Finally.

She stood and moved toward him, gratified when he moved, like he was about to take a step back and only at the last moment stopped himself. Wants fighting with duties. Pride fighting with desperation.

She felt her own war over both those things, but if she had to be kidnapped and taken away to some unknown king, and not even for her father and her duty, why shouldn't she have some pleasure before her life was over?

This wouldn't be for Danil. It wouldn't be for any dreams that he might have a change of heart if she shared her body with him. This was just for experience. For curiosity. For, at least this once, getting something *she* wanted. So she crossed to him.

"Your clothes are damp still, Danil. Perhaps *you* should take them off as well. And join me under the covers."

She reached out with the idea to help him, or run her hands over his chest, *something* to close this distance between them, but he took her by the wrists before she could. For a moment, she thought it was to stop her, push her away. But instead he drew her closer, tilting his head down.

She raised her mouth, certain his would touch hers. Certain he would kiss her like he had at the beach, dark and desperate. And oh, how she *yearned* for that. For the way sensation could obliterate all rational thought.

But he didn't kiss her. He lowered his mouth beyond her lips and to her ear. He spoke, the vibration of his voice against her ear making her shudder with need. Even as his words landed like blows.

"I see what you're planning, Princess, and while it's quite a cunning choice to try to rid yourself of your innocence, it would only end in your death." He dropped her hands, glared down at her. "So I would not recommend it."

Elsebet's eyes widened. Her hand came up before Danil had even gotten the rest of the words out, but she was clearly not used to striking people, because it was easy enough to catch her by the wrist and stop her palm from making contact with his cheek.

Though a blow might have done him some good. Heaven knew he deserved it.

He'd stopped her from slapping him because he was afraid if he let her make contact, it would snap this little bit of control he'd managed to maintain.

When control had never, ever been the issue. Control was who he was.

But she tested *everything*.

He wanted her. A want so all-encompassing he was sure he'd never survive it. Because he'd never wanted for anything this much. He was a practical man. He had always known wants were not for him. Even when his life had been small and full of love, they had been poor. In need.

He'd known.

He was *The Weapon*, even before that had been a nickname. He was not Danil Laurentius. He was a tool for everyone else. His mother's husband. His brother. It did not matter. He'd been made to be a tool.

This had always been a comfort to him as Aras's right hand. Always. But tonight it felt like a prison. With memories of cozy dinners with Elsebet and her little faux family. He hadn't been a tool or weapon among them. Just family. Just like the one he'd had as a boy.

And now he was a man with Elsebet nearly naked before him. Perfect in every way. And he knew she desired him. This was not *all* put-upon. But she wanted to give herself to him in this moment so his brother would not want her, or so he would be punished, or *something*. She wanted to share herself with him to *hurt* his plans.

"It would end in my death?" she replied, trying to laugh, but it just came out a kind of breathless sound that drew his gaze to her mouth. It mattered not that it had been nearly two weeks since he'd done it, he could relive every second of their kiss on the beach. Her taste, her warmth.

Sunlight in a dark storm, and oh, how this felt like a storm.

She is not yours. She is Aras's.

"My king was promised a virginal princess. He would not take kindly to finding you were not the innocent he wanted." For the purposes of heirs. For the purpose of having more people under his thumb.

Danil tried to forget these traitorous thoughts. She was nothing but a siren, putting lies into his brain. He served his brother, because his brother was king, and as such held all the power. All the wants.

This was right, or at the very least, the way of things.

And still he did not drop the wrist he held, did not leave, did not look away from the sweet swell of her breasts, rising and falling in heavy breaths.

But he was not kind. "If this is so offensive to you, I'm afraid you'll have to take that up with your father. Once you are able, of course."

"Does it matter?" she asked, and her eyes were full of so many emotions that twisted his heart, that reminded him of places he'd been. At the mercy of his mother's husband. An angry king—his biological father. Then dungeons. So tired of being twisted around by everyone else's plans that he didn't think anything he'd ever say or do or want would matter.

To anyone.

It matters to her.

He looked at her in the eyes, those dark, midnight blue eyes. The first time he'd seen her he thought they promised storms, and he had been right. She was nothing but a storm inside of him, no matter how small and placid she seemed.

Her breath came in pants, and he did not feel as though he had *any* power. Because her lips were pink and glossy. Her skin, as creamy as any delectable dessert. How he wanted to taste her. Everywhere.

Would she taste of the sea in every swell, every dip, in the sweetest places of her? The pain became so sharp he wondered if he'd survive it.

"You want me," she whispered.

There was no point lying. This was the simplest truth and

she knew. It was no question. It required no affirmation, but it was drawn out of him all the same. "Yes."

He would have to face his brother. He would have to face her as his *queen*. Already it seemed torture, and all he'd done was kiss her. Once.

But he could not deny that he wanted her. With every fiber of his being. He was so hard he ached. So drunk on the scent of her, the blue of her eyes and the yearning in them. He could not seem to uncurl his hand from her wrist. Soft like velvet, small and in need of protection.

She is not yours to protect.

But those siren eyes told another story.

"Danil. Your king would never have to know it was you."

His breathing became labored then, because the quiet whisper of that possibility was insidious. Aras would know.

How?

"Have you ever been allowed anything you wanted, Danil?" she asked him then, almost desperate. Her hand curled into a fist, but still she did not wrench it away. Still her eyes were wet. Still…she seemed to understand, even after he'd betrayed her.

Had he ever had anything he wanted? In his whole life? His ships, the comradery from his army of guards and sailors, but all these things had to be kept at a careful distance lest Aras see they meant too much and take them away.

To make you a better weapon…

"We recognize each other, because we are the same inside," Elsebet said, like she was so sure. Like she knew everything and he knew nothing. "Yearning for something. For freedom. You cannot offer me any, but you can give me this. Give me this."

She reached out and took his hand. He could not stop her. He could not seem to get his muscles to work, when he was the strongest man he knew. She pulled his arm and his hand went to her. She pressed his palm to her chest.

"Touch me."

It did not feel like a ploy, like an attempt to get out of having to marry Aras or some twisted desire to see him punished.

Her demand felt only like truth.

CHAPTER TEN

ELSEBET'S HEARTBEAT ECHOED in her ears like gunfire. His hand was hot, pressed to her skin. He had wars in his eyes, and she wanted to give him peace.

Even if he'd kidnapped her. Even if he'd hurt her. She saw herself in his inner conflict.

Wanting to do your duty.

And wanting what you *actually* wanted, no matter how opposing those two things were.

He did not pull his hand away. He spread his fingers wide, the rough skin of his fingers sending a cascade of sensation over her chest. Warmth spread after, lower.

His other hand still held her wrist, as if he was afraid she would turn away, when she was the one initiating this. Insisting on this. She'd forgotten all about punishing him, about hating him.

Her heart was too soft, no doubt, but she only wanted what they could make each other feel. If their duty lay on the other side, so be it, but first they had an entire ocean journey.

And she wanted him. Not punishment, not freedom.

Him.

Slowly, impossibly slowly, he tilted his head down closer and closer, until she could count each individual whisker. The stitches Nielson had put in there two weeks ago now. Fading bruises and healing scrapes.

He had risked his life to kidnap her for his king. She should hate him for this alone.

And yet she could not find any hate within her in this moment.

His nose practically touched hers, his eyes dark and ablaze. Their breath mingled, their breathing moved in time. Loud against the quiet of the room. They watched each other, as if they were still waiting for some reason to stop. Some reason to save themselves from this temptation, this want.

Every moment of her life that came before had been a series of not choosing her wants. Even out on that beach tonight, she had chosen duty. But duty had been taken away from her. So she let it go. She reached up on her toes and pressed her mouth to his, much as she had back on the beach that night.

There was a moment of tenderness. Just sweetness and warmth as he kissed her back with a kind of gentle care that made her eyes prickle with tears. And with that, her anger at him fully melted away until nothing was left.

Maybe she should not be so soft, but she could not help but think they were both prisoners in this strange life.

So why not take a moment to enjoy a bright spot?

His lips trailed down her neck. His mouth hot, stirring fires of need inside of her she did not know how to survive. He slid the straps of her bra off her shoulders, pressing kisses there as his hands slid over her rib cage, then tugged the bra down.

Cool air teased her, but only for a few seconds before it was replaced by his mouth, his open kisses, his tongue. The sensation of his mouth on her breast arrowed through her, a lightning strike. Electric and thrilling.

And he stayed there, right there, feasting on her as she

grew more and more incoherent, the only thought in her head *more*.

She didn't recognize the noises that came out of her mouth, didn't know what else to do but writhe and gasp under his attention. She wanted more, but she wanted this. She wanted, wanted, wanted.

His hands, so large, so rough, touched every part of her, until it felt as though he possessed her. Every inch of her was his. His, his, his.

He slid the underwear off her hips, and still he did not touch her where she throbbed. "Danil."

But he silenced her with his mouth on hers once more. A kiss as wild as any ocean storm. Him holding her so close she could feel the hard length of him pressed to her. His hands tangled into her hair, possessive and needy.

She would give him everything he needed if only he'd help her find that which her body pounded for.

"Please," she murmured against his mouth when she thought her legs might give out. When she thought she might simply swoon if she did not get *more*.

He pulled his mouth away, even drew her away by her shoulders, cold air sliding between them. She was naked. He was fully dressed. Elsebet blinked. She had never been fully drunk before, maybe a little tipsy on New Year champagne, but not *drunk*.

This felt like that must. Not just a little giggly and out of sorts, but fully unbalanced. And wonderful, in the moment. She tried to reach for him, to find anchor in him, to touch him in *any* of the ways he'd touched her.

But he stopped her, shook his head. "Sit."

Her breath caught at the command, at the look in his eyes. She did not think twice. She sat.

He crouched before her, spreading her legs wide. There

was some dim thought to modesty, but it never fully formed. He looked at her with such hunger, and she was nothing but a mass of hypersensitized cells that clamored for the release she had only read about or found for herself.

His finger traced up her inner thigh, and she watched its journey in utter fascination. The long, rough, blunt shape of his finger against the soft, pale skin of her thigh. Then tracing the seam of her, through the triangle of curls. His finger, touching the most intimate part of her.

She watched, fascinated. She watched, as a feeling so complex and threaded together with sensation swept through her. She did not have the words to express what was happening.

His finger tracing patterns, finding places that made her gasp, sigh, moan. She wanted to close her eyes, drop her head back, get lost, but as if sensing this, he looked up at her in that instant.

Their eyes locked, clashed, and she could not look away. She walked some highwire of this needy, sensual dance. She could not break his heavy gaze. Until he lowered his head as if...

And then there was no doubt. His tongue touched her, licked deep into her like she was a delectable treat. Devouring her. Chasing ribbons of feelings and desires and needs. Until she was shaking, begging, pulsing apart like something had *exploded* within her.

But he didn't stop. He nibbled his way out and then back in. His dark hair between her legs, his clever mouth, the sensations warring inside of her. Like an epic battle and she did not know who or what would come out on top, only that wreckage would be left behind and that would be all right.

More than.

There was no way of knowing. What it felt like to have

another person touch you as reverently as a beautiful piece of sea glass. The way a mouth could send her flying to places she'd never been. Waves of feeling, of pleasure. A storm, wild and beautiful. The kind she'd always dreamed of sailing into.

They had both chosen their duty, but they had not known. If they had known *this*, surely they would have chosen each other.

She was shattered, sated. Made new by him. She wanted to reach for him, but he…

He stood. Wound so tight, holding himself back. All for his duty. And because in this moment more than any of the others she understood how much this sacrifice meant to him, even if she didn't know why, she did not press.

"This must be enough," he ground out. Sounding as in pain as he had when he'd been washed ashore, broken and bloody.

"No. It is not enough."

"Elsebet, we cannot."

Cannot. So many cannots between them. But his anguish was too much for her. She understood. He could do this act because it was not irrevocable. In some archaic world, he had not taken her virginity here. She could still be "pure" for this king.

Maybe it should have hurt more than it did. But she understood the complicated, thorny tentacles of duty too well. He'd given her all he could.

So she must give him all she could. She pushed herself up, then slid off the bed and kneeled for him, though he made a move to stop her. But she would not let him.

"Elsebet," he ground out. Not refusal. Not even warning. She thought it was a plea—only even in the depths of his soul she did not think he knew what he asked for.

So she would show him.

"I have read about this," she told him. And truth be told, in books it had seemed rather strange, but faced with the powerful length of him, the way he had made feelings and sensation cascade throughout her body again and again, she wanted to give him the same.

She wanted to give him everything.

Danil knew he should stop this. It was already too far. Even if he did not tell Aras what had happened here, Danil would spend the rest of his life with Elsebet's taste on his tongue.

Knowing she was his brother's.

But she pulled the zipper down on his pants, freed him with her delicate hands. Soft and warm as she stroked him with a noise of appreciation.

There was no power in the world that could stop this. If there was, he did not have access to it. He wanted her too much, and if he could not have all…couldn't he have some?

She leaned forward, touched her tongue to him. So innocent, so eager. His perfect princess.

He forgot who he was. No longer *The Weapon*. Not bastard son of the old king. No, he was simply Danil.

And his beautiful Elsebet, with her small hands and clever mouth. Those beautiful eyes looking right up at him as she took him deep.

Her blond hair spread out over her shoulders, the sweet way she used her tongue, and the avid exploration as if every move was reverent. He had already been too close to the pounding release just from touching her, kissing her, tasting her.

And now she pushed him over that last edge so quickly, with a climax so powerful, he felt, for the first time in his entire life, weak-kneed and uncertain. More so than when he'd woken up bloody and bruised on a very cold beach.

But Elsebet only smiled up at him as she got to her feet. "Thank you," she said, putting her palm to his chest as she had so many times now. As if she liked to feel the *thud* of his heart beating.

When he'd forgotten he had one there in the first place. Purposefully. He knew what he'd done was wrong, but in this moment, his blood still pounding loudly in his ears, he could only cover her hand with his and watch as her smile grew wider. Beaming at him.

But a little shiver ran through her—not excitement, but the cool air taking the heat out of her cheeks. "You're cold," he murmured, nudging her back onto the bed and pulling the covers around her. He zipped up his pants, then picked up her discarded clothes and carefully laid them out across the desk and chair so they would dry by morning.

Morning. He would still not face Aras yet. There would be days more at sea. But that would not change the ending.

"Come. Sit," Elsebet ordered him. He should not, this he knew. Staying solved nothing.

Unfortunately at this juncture, neither did leaving. So he returned to the bed and took a seat next to her.

"What troubles you?" she asked, reaching out and brushing her fingers over his now disheveled hair. He would have to fix that before he returned to the captain's chair.

Which he should do. But he sat. *What troubles you?*

It was no use to tell her. This whole interlude was pointless. He should leave. But her hand slid over his shoulders, wrapping him in a hug that was somehow casual and intimate and all-encompassing at once.

He dared not look into her siren eyes or he would be lost

once more. So he stared at the empty built-ins where his clothes should have been. But they had been cleaned out.

Because they'd all thought him dead, no doubt. Someone had decided he no longer owned his fleet. No longer existed. And all he was should be erased.

Had anyone mourned?

It should not matter. It *did not* matter. He was *The* Weapon. Or had been until this moment, when he'd betrayed everything. And still he did not push Elsebet's arms off him, or move away from her. He sat. He stared. He spoke.

"I have betrayed the man I owe my life to."

"Why do you owe him your life?"

"He saved mine. I would be dead, many years ago, if he had not interceded."

Elsebet grew very quiet for a time. But her arms stayed around him. The soft warmth of everything she was. Sweet and kind, with a head full of dreams she had been too practical to believe in. When someone like her should have all the dreams reality allowed.

"So you've spent the years since...working for him? As payment?"

It was not so simple as that, but he did not know how to explain to her the complexities in their situation. That his mission was to turn her over not just to his king, but to his *brother*.

"I think... I understand this. It is like me going to my secret place to scream and yell. Knowing Nielson, Win and Inga did so much *for* me, I did not wish to burden them with my own feelings."

"I am not sure how this is the same."

"Not life and death, I grant you. But service born of gratitude."

"I suppose."

"This is different, though, Danil. It is about more than sparing your king's feelings. It is about the way I am being treated like I am property. My father is included in this. We can dress it up in duty, but at the end of the day, I cannot be simply *happy* to do my duty when it is against the things I want."

"I have no wants, Elsebet. It is not for me."

She shook her head. "You *do*. And you have a right to those. You aren't property any more than I am. We are *people*. Not inanimate objects with no feelings or needs of our own. And your king should not feel betrayed that he did not get the pretty little piece of property he wanted when there are plenty more out there."

He looked at her then. So beautiful and fierce. That kindness inside of her, those feelings did not make her weaker somehow. She seemed…strong. Stronger than any screaming threats he'd seen in his day.

He agreed that *she* should not be treated in such a way, but him? "I am *The Weapon*."

Her mouth turned downward in disapproval. "That is a foolish notion. You are a man." She placed her hand over his heart, where it beat and he wished it did not. He had so many wishes, and none of them mattered.

"I have never been one. Not until you came along. You have changed me, Elsebet, but I could not possibly be…" What did he wish for? A life where he could be hers? Where he could live as a humble sailor and soldier, with a wife to come home to.

When she was a *princess*. Who would marry a king or prince no matter if he delivered her to Aras or her family back on the island.

He had no rights to her, no matter what he wished. But… could he really just deliver her, against her will, to Aras now? Beyond what they had just shared of each other, he was not sure he could hand her over to his brother knowing how cruel and harsh Aras could be when angry.

"What is it you want, Elsebet?" he asked, not sure he'd ever be able to give it to her. But he could try. "To return to the island? Your father?"

She stared at him quietly, searching his face for something. He did not think she found it. "You would get in trouble, would you not?"

He thought of Aras. His brother. Danil had never once considered returning as a failure. Never wondered what might happen, because he didn't tolerate the possibility.

Now, for the first time, he considered.

Would his brother be forgiving? He had been the one to save Danil. The only one who'd ever seen him as anything *useful*. Not because of the blood that ran in his veins, but because of what he could *do*.

And still… Danil had seen Aras do many terrible things to those who failed him. Sometimes, his own blood relations. Their father included.

Danil had no fond feelings for the sadistic, former king, but he thought on it now. Would *he* have sentenced the man, his own father, to death if *he* were in charge?

"Danil?"

He shook his head. Surely his brother would not put him to death? Surely…

"I do not wish to see you in trouble," she said earnestly. "I do not wish to worry that you are harmed because of *me*."

"Whatever failures there are, they are mine."

She rolled her eyes at him. It should be incredibly insulting. She shook her head and gestured around the room. "You did not break any promises here. I am no expert on the technicalities, but I'm sure I will appear every bit the virgin. If it is what you wish, I will go to your king. Willingly."

He frowned at her, beyond confused. She had just said she didn't want to be property. She had been so mad he'd taken her, and now... Now she'd given herself to him, in a way. And she was willing to give herself to Aras? "Why? Why would you do such a thing?"

Her eyes tracked over his face, and he *felt* the warmth of her feelings. He did not understand how. But he could *feel* her care. "Because it would ease your pain," she said softly. Then she leaned forward and pressed a soft kiss to his brow. Like she was taking care of him once more.

"You will take me to your king. He will know nothing that happened here, but I will endeavor to talk him out of the marriage. Surely I can appeal to his heart."

Heart? Did Aras have one? Danil had always thought he meant *something* to his brother. Or why would he have been saved?

But after watching Elsebet and her staff... He did not think his brother had ever cared for him the way Elsebet's little family cared about each other. He did not think he himself had cared for Aras in such a way. Their relationship was duty. Missions to accomplish. Danil had left the idea of family behind when his grandparents had died and his mother had married a despicable man.

"This is what we'll do," Elsebet said, Princess to the last, as though she got to decide. Perhaps he should let her—it was likely she'd never really decided anything in her life. And if anyone could get through Aras, it would be Elsebet.

But he feared she would not. And she would be married to him and Queen of Gintaras before she even had a chance to argue.

He could not let her sacrifice herself so he wouldn't get into trouble. He would have to do something else.

But he didn't have to tell her that. So he nodded, and encouraged her to get some rest before he left and headed back to the captain's seat.

He would guide the ship back to Gintaras.

And he would take on his brother himself.

CHAPTER ELEVEN

ELSEBET SLEPT LIKE the dead. Exhausted, sated and determined—all conditions making it possible for her to sleep for hours and hours. When she woke, she was groggy and starving.

She stretched and looked around the room. There was nothing to eat here, but she could get dressed and see if Danil had kept her locked in here or not. Her clothes were draped over the chair and table.

Danil had carefully laid them out to dry last night. She wondered why the memory of such a simple act spread through her like warmth, like care. Particularly when the man had *kidnapped* her last night. And yet no amount of reminding herself of this fact changed how she felt.

Particularly knowing he felt he owed his king his life, but still…cared enough for her to risk something. It left a fluttering in her chest that threatened all sane, rational thinking.

She blew out a breath while considering what to do, but really there was nothing else to do but attempt to find food.

But before she could throw off the covers, the door eased open. Slowly at first, then Danil saw that she was awake and entered quickly.

He closed the door behind him. "You must get dressed," he said, nodding toward the clothes on the chair and desk.

She considered this. After last night, she thought she

might be able to tempt him again. But where would that lead? His guilt and self-condemnation. Even if she got something pleasurable out of it, it would only be momentary.

That had been enough last night, but today she felt differently. Getting something for herself was selfish, even if she'd wanted him to have his wants too. Because wants were not so easy, this she knew. She had been burdened by duty too.

He was risking something with her. A risk far larger than her own. Because whether she married his king, or the man her father chose, her future was the same. A political affiliation with a stranger, no love.

However, Danil risked punishment, perhaps even his life. And she... Oh, she had been so angry at him last night and it had melted away, like she was so simple that a soft touch and a kiss would change everything she knew to be true.

But it had. What he risked changed the tenor of everything. He was as conflicted as she. How could she hold him at fault for that? How could she be angry when he had his own debts and duties?

Ones that, if he did not fulfill, could claim his life. And she could not bear the thought of his life being taken away. So she would do whatever she could to ensure Danil did his duty, even if it went against hers.

Was this love? In some ways, she thought it was. Because she understood the things inside of him that felt like the things inside of her. But she also understood there were other things locked in Danil's mind and heart that she did not know or understand.

Could you love a person knowing they had secrets and mysteries? A whole past that she did not know, and might not ever?

Could she marry someone else thinking she might be in love with Danil?

If it saved him, the answer was yes. She would sacrifice for him, because... He had given her something no one else had. Even during a kidnap.

She slid out of bed but brought the blanket with her. Not so much out of modesty, but because she did not wish to tempt him in this moment. She wished to give him everything he needed.

She got dressed under the blanket, focusing on the clothes and not whether he watched her or not. Once she was finished, he nodded toward the door.

"Come," he said stiffly.

So she did. She followed him out the door, down the narrow corridor that gave the impression of three other rooms below deck. Then they went up the stairs and onto the deck. Last night had been dark and she'd been angry, so she had no idea what to expect, but it wasn't blinding brightness. She was surrounded by blues that melded together in waves that made her dizzy.

The boat itself wasn't *exceptionally* large, though it was a little bigger than the small royal cruiser that had taken her from Mathav to her island when she'd been thirteen.

Danil took her by the arm and led her forward. Right toward the edge of the ship where, if she looked over the railing, she could see the ship cruising through the ocean.

Nothing but ocean. Blue everywhere. Everywhere she looked. Water and sky. *"Oh."* It was...more amazing than she could have imagined. She had lived with the ocean every day of her life, but almost always from land. Not from the center of it. Not when there was nothing for the eye to see but water and sky. "Oh, Danil." She wanted to lean into him, but he kept inches between them, even with his arm still on her arm as if steadying her.

"The one behind us works for my brother," he said, speaking of the other man out on the deck. "I do not trust him."

Elsebet looked over at the man. He was watching them rather intently from the other side of the ship, but too far away to hear them speaking. She was more concerned with how Danil's brother fit into this. It was still hard to imagine Danil with family at all. He seemed like a mythical creature sprung from the sea, washed up on her beach. But he'd spoken of grandparents, of a missing father, a brother. Maybe his brother could help? "Who's your brother?"

His mouth firmed as if dealing with an unpleasant truth. "Aras. King of Gintaras."

Your future husband.

It had never occurred to her that this king might be... But that meant... "I don't understand. You're...a prince?"

"No. Aras is my half brother. Son of the old King and Queen. I am the previous king's bastard. The old king wanted me dead. Aras intervened." Danil spoke with no inflection, his dark eyes focused on the water.

Elsebet tried to keep up with this new information, but it made her feel...winded. This man had touched her intimately. She had... Suddenly marrying this *king* to keep Danil safe was more complicated. "I...would be your brother's wife?"

A muscle in his jaw ticked. He gave a sharp nod and did not meet her gaze. When he spoke, his voice was very quiet, almost impossible to hear over the swoosh of waves and wind. "If we move forward, you would be." He looked down at her then, gaze inscrutable. But he *looked* at her and that was something. "But this does not have to be the end result. There are...options."

She wanted to grab on to any and every option that wasn't marrying his *brother*, but she understood too well. If there hadn't been options *before* last night, why would there be any now? Unless they weren't *true* options. "Are any of them safe?"

He looked back out at the sea. "Quite safe."

"Safe for *you*?"

For a moment he was very quiet, and there was only the sound of the ocean. Such a strange stillness as everything rocked in the waves. "I am *The Weapon*, Elsebet."

"I do not like that nickname at *all*."

"It is apt. I may be the son of a king, but there is nothing royal or honorable about me. I have lived in dungeons. I have protected my brother with my own bare hands, not caring who I hurt in the process. I *am* a weapon for the crown of Gintaras, as befitting my station."

"Shouldn't your station be prince if you are the son of a king?"

"Bastard of the King."

Elsebet sighed heavily. "Honestly, royalty is forever complicating things."

For a moment, the briefest second, his mouth curved. He reminded her of the man he'd been at the dinners back at her castle. Never relaxed or *easy* exactly, no matter how he pretended, but someone who could amuse and be amused. Someone who could find joy in life, like when he'd teased her about doing chores. That simple but warm and caring life.

"On that we can agree." Then he sighed and the tiny smile was gone. "I will have to keep you locked in the room for the time being. I wanted to give you a moment of fresh air, of *this*. If the weather holds and all is well, we should be in Gintaras in two days. I will bring you out for walks around the deck as I am able, but you must act like someone put out by me. Peet will bring you your meals."

"What happens when we arrive in Gintaras?"

He was silent for long, stretched-out minutes that had Elsebet holding her breath. She knew there was much she didn't know about him, but she understood parts of him. She could all but see his brain working.

He considered what he'd done last night a betrayal to his brother, and yet, he cared for *her* in some way. He would not betray them both. He'd tried to betray her, and he had not been able to fully bring himself to do it. Perhaps last night he'd even attempted to betray his brother, or been tempted to, but he had not. Not fully.

He would find some way to make this right on both sides. How, she did not know, but she pondered what she would do if she was in a similar position. If she had to choose between hurting Danil and hurting her little family back on the island, which would she pick?

She would sacrifice herself first, for those she cared about, for those she owed.

"Fear not, Princess," he said, confidently. "I will handle everything."

But he did not smile, and she found all she could do was *fear*.

Not this king or her future, but what Danil would now do to save her from the fate he himself had assigned her to. And how little a say she would have in it.

Danil did not trust himself to be alone with Elsebet for long. Neither did he trust Riks's eagle eyes on him at all times. There was something predatory about the way his brother's staff member watched him with such *ferocity*. All would be reported back to Aras, and this would normally be quite fine.

But it felt...bigger. Was that Elsebet's influence? Something to do with Riks? He could not determine. So he stayed out of his own chambers where Elsebet was kept, only venturing there to take her out on a walk for fresh air. These moments he could not resist giving her.

Every single time she ascended the stairs and the ocean came into view, her breath caught, her eyes widened. Every *single* time, there'd be a moment at the top of the stairs where she was completely and utterly still, taking it all in. Then she'd let her breath out, a long, slow sigh. And she would smile broadly and brightly.

He had known in his bones that it would affect her this way. He could not say how. Just that the ocean always had the same effect on him. No matter what swirled dark and edgy inside of him, the vast, sparkling blue always settled him like nothing else ever did.

Except the blue of her eyes. Which was what he watched now, every time. No longer the vast ocean and sky, but the way she lit up. A yearning fulfilled.

He had given that to her and wanted so badly to fulfill every want. Forever.

Because he had seen her gaze at the entrance to her cove with yearning and he had known she would feel the awe and amazement he felt in the middle of the ocean.

But he could not let the moments linger. No doubt Riks had suspicions. This would not help Danil's cause. He had not figured out how to approach the problem of his brother and was running out of time, but the closer they got to Gintaras the more he knew he could not hand Elsebet over to Aras.

She might go willingly to save him—some miracle he still did not understand—but he could see, as if it had already happened, how easily his sharp-edged brother would damage her. He had been talking himself out of that from the beginning, but the more reality threatened, the less he could believe his own lies.

Danil could not allow her to be part of Aras's court of meanness and harsh punishments and cold isolation. A place where her soft, wonderful feelings would be punished—even worse than he believed they already had been by her father.

Danil needed a plan. Every walk along the ship's railing cemented this to him. Every moment of sailing the ship alongside Peet made him wonder how he would, for the first time in his life, refuse his duty.

"If the weather holds, we should be in Gintaras by the end of tomorrow," Peet said eagerly that afternoon, after Danil had left Elsebet back in her room following their walk. "Everyone will be eager to see you succeed."

Danil knew it was no success, but that nagging feeling he had that Riks was analyzing his every move kept him pretending all was well. "Was there any doubt?" he returned, offering Peet a smile.

But Riks clearly did not think this was amusing in any light. His pinched face got even grayer. "We thought you were dead. They even got rid of your things." He laughed to himself as if this was funny.

Neither Danil nor Peet joined in.

"Not to mention, when we learned of your survival the King did say to kill you if you didn't have her." Riks smirked, clearly irritated they did not find him amusing. "So I suppose there was *some* doubt."

Danil turned his gaze from the sea to Riks. He stared at the smaller man with a fierceness that must have been terrifying, because Riks—even with all his self-important posturing—shrank back.

Surely *kill* was an exaggeration, a figure of speech? Aras had *saved* him. Why would he turn around and...

But Riks, for all his cowering, did not relent. "It would have been right," he insisted in a voice that had gone up an octave. He was clearly scared of Danil's reaction. "The proper punishment for a failure of that magnitude. The King wants the Princess of Mathav, and so he shall have her."

Normally, Danil would have agreed with him. Aras was exacting. He had put men to death before for their failures, but...

Aras had *saved* Danil from death. They were brothers. Family. And family *cared*. It did not...punish failure with death.

He wanted to shake this thought away because it was foolish. They were not family in *that* sense. Danil was a bastard. Not as important. A tool to serve Aras, because of Aras's goodwill. Just as he had been a tool used by his mother's husband for his own gains. This was what he was *meant* for.

Any thoughts of care and family were just figments of his imagination. Some strange side effect of his injuries. Or...

Elsebet. For the first time in his life he had watched what a true family might look like. Or, worse, he'd been reminded. Although his childhood had been complicated, he *had* been a part of dinners like the ones Elsebet and her little family had, before his mother had married *that* man. Everyone helping, all shoved together in a table. His mother and grandparents sacrificing to make sure he had enough to eat.

He had set those memories aside. In a different part of his life, but Elsebet had reminded him, and worse, shown him it did not have to have anything to do with blood. She had treated her staff like family, and vice versa. She had gifted him her smiles, caring for him even after he'd betrayed her.

If he hadn't met her, he would agree with Riks's assessment. That he should be put to death for failure to serve the King. It would not feel it like a blow. Like betrayal.

Why wouldn't his failure be punishable by death? Simply because he was the King's bastard brother? Foolishness. He knew his place.

And yet... Even as he let the conversation go, he could not let the *feelings* combating inside of him go. This was not what family did. And ever since Aras had saved him from that dungeon, the King had insisted they were *family*. That Aras had looked out for him, so Danil needed to do the same.

This was brotherhood. The only kind Danil had ever known.

But he thought of small, beautiful Elsebet yelling at rocks so as not to make her staff feel bad about her being upset. He thought of all the ways Nielson had tried to protect her from the likes of *him*. Without ever hurting Elsebet in the process. *That* was care, brotherhood. *That* was looking out for one another.

No threats of violence, death or betrayal involved. And he wanted to believe it was different because she was a woman, a princess. He was a bastard, a servant.

But he could not fully believe it after enjoying the warmth of their dinner table.

After Riks went to bed for the night, Danil could still not let it go. He looked at the stars above and then asked the simple question of Peet. "Is it true?"

Peet did not meet Danil's gaze, nor did he pretend to not understand what Danil asked. He frowned at the moon. "Riks is the King's man. Not me. I am a member of *your* guard. *Your* crew."

Which only meant Danil was his direct boss, but they

both still served the King. And if Peet was on this ship and mission with Riks, he would have to know something of Aras's instructions. "But you would have received the orders to kill me, because we all know Riks could not kill me on his own. Even if he knew the right end of a gun."

Peet darted a glance at him then, but quickly looked away. "I knew you would not fail. You are *The Weapon*. But more than that, sir, you are our leader. The King may be in charge, but your sailors and your soldier guards follow you because *you* are…" Peet trailed off a little, almost as if he was embarrassed. "You made a crew and army out of us, sir. Many of us appreciate that above all else."

But it was not an answer. Certainly not the one Danil wanted. Even if it warmed him in these old, shut-up spaces. That he might have made a crew, an army. Those weren't families, but they were…close.

Danil studied the starry sky above him. He wanted Elsebet to see it before they got close enough to land where the city lights would diminish all the sky offered. The vastness of the night. The brightness of the stars. Like her little island but supercharged out here in the middle of nowhere. No monarchies or royals or lands to fight for.

Only the water. Only the sky.

For a moment that stole his very breath, he wished that this was all there was. His ship, this ocean and her. No countries, no brothers, no duty.

When his entire life had been dedicated to *duty* because that was simple. That was accomplishable. All else was complicated. All else twisted and tore at his heart until it was impossible to breathe.

But duty… Duty was simple. Or had been.

Now there was Elsebet and nothing was simple anymore. So no, there was more than just this ship and this ocean and her. And he had to be strong enough to put her first. To make certain she was safe above all else.

Death was on the table if he faced down his brother and refused to give him Elsebet. And no amount of feeling betrayed by that knowledge changed the fact.

He thought of Elsebet. His sweet little siren. Who had forgiven him for his betrayal. No punishment necessary. Because she understood him. Cared for *him*. The way she cared for all those she loved. His selfless princess.

He would face down death before he let her sacrifice herself for the likes of *him*. Or anyone for that matter.

His duty had changed, here in the open sea where he thought best and was most himself. His duty was to her and her alone.

And if he died doing it, it would be worth the pain.

CHAPTER TWELVE

ELSEBET WAS EXCELLENT at isolation, or so she'd thought. Being locked up in this little room on this ship was its own kind of torture now that she'd seen what was outside. The sea, the sky. Like everything she'd dreamed about, but real. *Freedom*.

And Danil, always by her side while she took it all in. She could forget everything out in the vastness of it all, but here in this tiny room, she had nothing to do but *think*.

She worried about home. Nielson, Win, Inga. They would be so upset over this. She even worried about her father to an extent, though it was hard not to put some blame on him for this predicament she found herself in.

Which wasn't fair, since she couldn't seem to blame Danil for anything. Because duty was complicated, and she knew this too well to hold on to her anger over his kidnapping her.

Danil was in a state of conflict, and she so wished she could help ease it. The idea of marrying his brother... It filled her with more than the sort of beat-down acceptance she'd learned to embrace when it came to her future political marriage. She *recoiled* at the notion of marrying his *brother*.

She would have to forget that this king was connected to Danil. Put Danil aside. Forever. A stranger would not matter, or so it seemed. But Danil's *brother*?

Elsebet would do anything to save Danil and yet she did not know how to wrap her mind around this eventuality.

The door eased open, in Danil's careful way. She had not expected him again today as she knew it was getting late and thus far all their walks on the deck had been during the day. But he did the same thing he always did. Stood by the door. Held out his hand and said, "Come."

And every time, she did. Crossed to him, took his hand, and let him lead her up to the top of the ship in utter silence. She knew part of this silence was due to the King's man he did not trust and so did not want Riks overhearing anything, but part of it was him. Even with his voice healed, he did not need to chatter on like she had always liked to do on their walks on the beach.

Until he'd brought her here. Because now she too held her tongue. Every word she did utter felt...weighted, dangerous, filled with portent. But she forgot all those negative feelings as he led her up the stairs and into the dark.

Dark but not dark, because the night was clear and sparkling. She had always loved looking up on the beach at night, but it was not like this. Even the ceiling windows in her art studio were not like this. The sky seemed to *pulse*. Those stars and moon that had seemed like fixed beings on solid land were more like their own entities now. Moving and swirling.

"Danil..."

He squeezed her hand. A silent sort of *I know it is amazing.* "I thought you should see it before we get any closer to land," he said quietly.

They were getting closer to Gintaras. Every day. Every hour. And then what? She had said she would marry his brother to save him from whatever punishment awaited him, but... The reality of that was a panic beating in her chest.

She could not let him see that. Luckily it was dark. But she could not quite keep the words or the yearning inside. "I wish we could just stay right here forever."

He pulled her closer, until she was leaning against his chest and his arms were around her. He rested his chin on the top of her head and for moments of silence aside from the lapping of waves against the boat and the faint hum of engine they stood like this, watching the stars pulse.

He did not say a word. While he was not a talker as she was, something was still odd. The way he held her, so gentle. The way he said nothing, just looked at the stars. It all felt…tense, even though it should be a wonderful moment of peace before so much happened.

But maybe that was it. Something would happen and soon and there would be no peace. But he had not done this—held her, watched the stars quietly with her—the entire time they'd been on his ship. It was as though something had changed, though she could not imagine what.

"Has something happened? You seem…" She searched for the right word. It wasn't the tenseness or the leashed darkness. These things were all part of him. Not even the grimness was different. But something lurked in the way he held her that was off.

It felt like goodbye.

But when he spoke it was not words of goodbye. It was a simple question.

"If you refused to do your duty, and your father could not simply force you to do it anyway, how do you think he would react?"

Elsebet was tempted to laugh such a question off since she had no power, but he seemed so very serious. So in need of a truthful answer. She considered it. "It is hard to say.

Any time I have pushed back at what he wanted me to do, he tends to just wave it away as though I don't know what I'm talking about. Assures me it is the right course of action. Sends me away so I don't burden him with my feelings on the matter. If I flat-out refused..."

Elsebet really tried to picture it. She had seen her father angry, but never raging. He didn't yell. Oh, maybe he'd raise his voice in frustration, but he did not lose his temper.

He was the King. He believed in moderating his emotions for his kingdom so that they could trust he would always make rational, careful decisions. Since there was one decision he had not been able to make when it came to more heirs.

Which was why he expected the same of her. Always. Or maybe she'd learned to expect it of herself. To ease some of his guilt.

But she thought more about Danil's question and said, "I suppose he would be very angry. There might be a punishment. I could certainly see him forcing me to marry the man he had chosen. Not out of anger, but out of the assumption that I did not know better."

And now a strange new world had opened up to her, after Danil had kidnapped her.

What did a world look like if she did not follow her father's instructions? She did not know. Because while she had often voiced *opinions*, she had never fully refused her father. She'd always let him sway her. Always been determined to do her duty. To *help* ease his pain.

Like the man holding her now. She twisted in his arms so she could better see his moonlit face. "Why do you ask, Danil?"

His expression was grave, and he did not meet her gaze.

He stared at the dark sea beyond the rail. "You have...people who care for you on your island. A family of sorts. Do you think your father cares for you?"

She did not understand why he asked these questions, in that dark rasp that she was beginning to assume was his voice and not the result of his injuries. They were speaking of serious things and still that rasp sent a shiver of want and memory through her.

His hands. His mouth.

Focus, Elsebet. Did she think her father cared for her? "Yes. As much as he can, I suppose. It's complicated. You see, he loved my mother very much. Never remarried. Never... I know he wished for a male heir, but he could never bring himself to...handle that." She sighed, wishing she did not have to cast back and think about her father. She could never view him as the villain, even when she wanted to.

But so also with Danil, so maybe she was simply too softhearted, too foolish to hate the people she should. Maybe this would forever be her downfall. Never getting what she wanted as she served those who could not see her.

But Danil did. He'd shown her the ocean. She *knew* he was thinking of a way not to deliver her to his brother. Finding a way to *keep* her, rather than send her away. They shared a connection, even if neither knew how to put it into words. And she'd rather be here, in Danil's strong arms, conflicted and hurting, than stuck in that tiny room, or even her island castle and *hate* everyone. She'd gone through that phase too, and it didn't change anything.

Bitterness was no match for love. It felt...smarter to harden her heart, but it didn't *feel* better. It didn't feel *right*. She was starting to accept she'd rather feel love and warmth than worry about *smartness*. No matter how that might disappoint her father.

Maybe she would regret this someday, but she would always remember the way the stars pulsed above and Danil's heart beat under her palm.

"I look like my mother. I think part of my isolation was for my protection, but Nielson believed part of it was that it hurt to look at me." And it had made sense. Lived within her.

She was a bad memory. Or a good one, depending on how you looked at it. But as a young girl it had made her all that much more determined to make her father proud, happy. So he might look at her and see... Elsebet. Not the mother she'd never known. So he might not worry so much about *protection,* rather see her as a person. His daughter. Someone to share the duties of the Kingdom with, to be part of his life.

But whenever she'd tried to be herself, whenever she'd hurt or been angry, he'd shut her away, sent her off. Everything she was and felt was more burden to her father than bounty.

She'd spent the past few years hoping that if she married whomever her father wanted to, if she did her duty as the King asked, he might finally be able to look at her like he had when she'd been a child. As her own person, important in his eyes, and not as the ghost of her mother.

Elsebet sighed and leaned deeper into the warmth of Danil. "So, yes, I think he cares, but I think... It is not the way you might wish for a father to care. Did your mother care for you?"

"Complicated," he said gruffly.

"Tell me."

And to her surprise, he did. "I was raised by my mother and grandparents. I did not know who my father was. This suited us all well enough, though we were poor and struggling. But after my grandmother died, my grandfather's health faltered. Mother spent much time caring for him, as did I. When he died, it was as if we were…adrift. Without them, we had no anchor."

He took a careful breath, his gaze on the ocean. "Not long after, mother married. I believe she was searching for that anchor. Things became more difficult after this marriage. She told the man truths that she'd never told me. The King was my father. Her husband was a lazy sort, and he leaned on me to do most of the work for the family. But knowing I was royalty? He saw this as a ticket to riches. Then, so did my mother."

He spoke very coldly as he continued with the story. As if none of it mattered, but the fact he shared it with her at all proved it did. From the way his mother was swayed by this man, to being marched into the castle, to being thrown in a dungeon.

"Aras stood up for me. Saved me from our father's death sentence. When he became king, I became his most trusted guard. I would go on missions. My mother begged to see me, but I refused. I could not bring myself to forgive her. For putting that man above my safety. His needs above my own. So I did not see her. Refused. I returned from a mission for Aras with news she had died. An accident."

She heard the grief and guilt, even if he didn't voice the words. He blamed his mother, had been hurt by her, but these things did not erase love.

She understood this on a deep, enduring level. And now that she had the full picture of him, she understood what had started these questions. "Are you afraid of your brother's reaction if you do not bring me to him?"

"According to Riks, if I did not have you, they were meant to kill me on the spot."

She sucked in a breath of shocked pain. *Kill* him? "I do not have siblings, but this is not the mark of family. Of love."

He was very quiet for a very long time. "Aras is the only one who has ever tried to protect me." His gaze turned to her then. "Until you."

That gaze, those words, shivered through her. *I will always protect you.* But she could not vow it out loud, because she now understood how much he risked even in this moment, because of Riks's prying eyes.

"I should go back to my room. You needn't accompany me."

But he held her still. "Elsebet."

She shook her head. "You should not risk yourself for me," she whispered fiercely. Because that was what he was doing by being out here with her. Telling her these things. Giving her a chance, a hope. Himself.

"What better thing would there be for me to risk myself for?" His hand swept over her hair, a gentle touch. Because for as large and rough as he was and could be, he had a well of gentleness inside of him he did not seem to know how to wield.

Except when it came to her.

"I had vowed I would never be in search of an anchor like my mother was, but you are my anchor, Elsebet. Vows or no." His mouth pressed to her temple. Her cheek. She should resist. Refuse. But his words were spoken roughly and with emotion. "Let me give you everything you want, Elsebet. My princess. My siren. Let me be yours."

It was that last sentence that swayed her. He did not wish her to be *his*—as was her only experience in the world. A belonging to be passed along. A pawn. A *thing*.

But no. He did not want to own her or possess her. He wished to *give himself.* To her. And this was all she wanted. Body. Soul.

And heart.

He kissed her there under the stars with the sounds of the ocean. Risk and Aras be damned. His entire life be damned.

For this was the one thing no one could turn against him. He had tried. Kidnapping her. Convinced he would deliver her to Aras.

And still she was here. Kissing him back with that warmth. Wanting to protect *him*, even after all he'd done to put her in danger's way.

It was painful, conflicting, but he could not deny her truth after having spent time on her little island. Violence was not what family did to one another. This was not love, or care.

Those things involved wanting to protect and giving the other person everything they desired. A complicated tight-rope.

Elsebet held on to him, but she pulled her mouth away. "Danil, if Riks sees…"

"Come." He moved her to the staircase and back down into the boat. Toward his quarters. Danil was quite certain Riks was fast asleep, eager to be back on solid land, but it did not matter. Danil found nothing at all mattered anymore except finding a way to keep Elsebet safe.

And his.

He ushered her back into his room as he always did. He usually left her at this point. No touch, no kiss, nothing that might give him away. Nothing that might change *everything*.

But everything *was* changed. He closed the door behind him and they stood staring at each other.

He cupped her perfect face in his hands. Stared into those midnight blue siren eyes. While something old swirled in him. Something he thought had died. Stronger than duty.

But he did not have the words for it. Not here.

She rose to her toes and pressed her mouth to his anyway. So he tried to pour his feelings, those storms into his kiss. They wrapped their arms around each other like anchors. Like they could survive the hurricanes that brewed within.

And without.

He knew they could not. Not together, but for this moment, he would have this together. He would be hers in all things. He slid his hands over her braid, her back, pulling down the zipper of her dress.

His body hardened, but he did not rush ahead. He lost himself in the scent of her, the silk of her skin. Carefully, intentionally, he rid her of all her clothes. Then his own. He shed his shirt, and she spread her fingers across the scarred skin of his chest before looking up at him. "This will not be like last time, Danil. I want all of you."

Their gazes met. He could refuse. It would give him some kind of plausible deniability when it came to Aras. A workaround when he faced down his powerful and dangerous brother.

But he did not want that. He did not want a loophole. He wanted his beautiful siren, and he would have her. Safe, whole, his. She would never suffer at the hands of another.

It would have to be goodbye. Maybe not forever. If he could get through to his brother, he would return to her. But he could not until he knew she would be safe, always, from Aras's wrath. If he could not protect her, her father would. And whatever happened to Danil himself would be a sacrifice he was willing to give her.

She had sacrificed for him. She had showed him what love truly was, or reminded him. Either way, she had awoken him from a long slumber. Breathed life into *The Weapon*.

She would be his for this, and he hers. And if it had to be enough, it would be.

So he kissed her, touched her, revered her. He tasted every inch of her, until she shook, begged, was so gloriously, desperately his, naked underneath him. He took her to the peak, again and again, his name forever on her lips.

Until it was time. "It might hurt. I promise, only for a moment, but I cannot promise away the pain."

Her gaze met his. Hazy with desire, yes, but calm. Certain. And knowing. "Nor can I." Because she spoke of more than physical pain. She spoke of everything to come. They could not promise it would not hurt.

But he could protect her.

And he could give her this.

Perhaps he had lost his handle on everything. Perhaps this was selfishness and wrong. Perhaps…

He did not care. He was changed. By her smile. By her kindness. She had saved him, in all the ways there were.

And if he went to Gintaras and died by his brother's hand, this moment would be worth it.

Entering her, his beautiful, perfect siren. One with all she was. Freedom. The ocean. *Love*. All he'd ever yearned for, right here in her.

She sighed his name as if she too had been waiting for this, just this. No matter the discomfort, she accepted him, moved with him, until he could see that pleasure on her face once more, feel the force of her climax against him, bringing on his own.

The release was the biggest storm that had ever battered

him. From somewhere so deep within he had not known it existed. She held on to him tightly as it raged through both of them, wrapped up together as they slowly, inch by inch, came back to reality.

She trailed her fingers down his back, and he nuzzled into her hair. He felt her heartbeat and for a moment simply basked in all that he had been given.

He knew he was destined to lose it, but that was okay. If she was safe forever, that was okay.

As if she could read his mind, she pulled away slightly. She sat up on her elbow, glaring down at him. "I will not forgive you if you let him hurt you."

She was so serious. Such a princess in this moment. This her royal decree.

"Then I will endeavor to survive, Your Highness." He smiled at her, a true smile that felt foreign on his lips. Only she had brought that smile out of him since he'd been a boy. He would cherish her forever for it.

"We will face Aras together. As a team. As a family," she said. Still ordering him about. Perhaps he should have been offended, but he liked the side of her that took charge.

Even if he could not allow it.

Family. A fairy-tale dream these days. She still believed, and he wanted to give her everything he believed.

He pulled her into the circle of his arms, brushed her hair off her face as she drifted into sleep. He waited in the dark, making his plan. To keep her safe. Always.

So, no. She would not be coming with him. They could not be a team in this.

Because he knew Aras. He would want to punish Danil, yes. Kill him, probably, for what he'd done, even if he delivered Elsebet. She was no longer the untouched princess promised.

But Danil would not turn her over. He could not. Because Aras would not leave it at punishing Danil. He would not let Elsebet go unscathed. So Danil had to make certain she was safe above all else.

It was his fault she was in this mess at all. He could not let her be hurt because of it.

So this would have to be his goodbye. Temporary, hopefully, but if it had to be permanent, so be it.

CHAPTER THIRTEEN

WHEN ELSEBET WOKE, he was gone. Something like dread crept into her chest. But that was silly. He had slipped out before morning in order to avoid being found out. He was likely off doing something important with the boat. They would not have much time left before they arrived in Gintaras.

She knew Danil did not plan on turning her over to his brother. But she had told him they were a team and she meant it. They would work together. She had spent her entire life being protected, and she could not stand the thought of him joining those ranks.

Surely he understood that. How important it was to stand together. To be equals. She was no pampered princess to be isolated away while *he* handled everything. He knew that.

Right?

She chewed her lip, wondering. He had not *disagreed* with her when she said they were a team, but he hadn't *confirmed* it either. He had not said, *Yes, Elsebet, we will confront Aras together.*

He'd said nothing.

Dread settled heavier and heavier, like an anchor on her chest.

She got dressed quickly and rushed to the stairway. As she breached the stairs, she saw land. Not far off. Shining buildings of a city. Unlike Mathav, the beaches looked quite welcoming and not rocky. Though the air was a brittle kind of cold she was used to. This was no tropical isle, that was certain.

Still, the only person she saw was the crew member who brought her meals. Peet was his name. He was doing something with ropes and… Elsebet watched as the shore seemed to get oddly…farther away.

She whirled to face Peet. "Where is Danil?" she demanded.

The man blinked at her. He had not spoken to her at all the entire time she'd been on the ship. He seemed to get tongue-tied and blushed a deep red. But she could tell he had a kind of hero worship toward Danil, so she did not worry about him.

She worried about Danil though. If he was not here, and they were moving *away* from shore. "Where is Danil? Answer me. *Now.*"

"He's gone ashore, miss. Ma'am. Lady," he babbled, tacking on all sorts of honorifics. None of them correct.

She could not possibly care less.

"And what are you doing? Why are *we* not ashore?"

"Erm, well. Ma'am. That is, Your Highness." He bobbed a strange little bow.

"What are you doing?" she repeated through clenched teeth, her hands curled into fists. She was rarely tempted into violence, but this man's nonanswers were getting her there.

"I have my orders, miss. That is, Princess."

Orders. *Orders.* "Your orders are to turn around. To take me to Gintaras."

"Miss." Peet shook his head, hat squashed in his hands. "Do you know how much trouble I'll be in?"

"From *who*?"

"Danil, of course. The captain. He's ordered me to take you to Mathav. You'll be safe there. He's only trying to protect you."

Mathav.

It was a knife to the heart. Not just trying to protect her but sending her away. As her father had done. Always little more than a piece of property to be shucked about. She swallowed against the hard lump that formed in her throat.

It hurt, but that hurt did not take away the *fear*. Not only was Danil treating her like a pawn to be shipped away, but he was putting himself in danger. Alone.

"And if *I* am safe there, where will Danil be safe?" Elsebet demanded of the man. "Because I do not think it is on Gintaras without me. If he goes to his brother without me, what happens to *him*?"

Peet blinked a few times, mouth open but no words coming out.

"He is your captain, is he not? Do you wish him to *die*?"

"King Aras is his brother. I can't imagine he'd put Danil to death. Not really. I know he threatened it, but sometimes a threat is just a threat. Especially from King Aras. He's a bit of a hothead. That's all. They're brothers."

Elsebet almost felt sorry for the man, who looked more like a boy the more he spoke. She had thought the same once. But she knew Danil did not overreact. If he thought his brother might harm him for failing, the King surely would.

"I wish I believed this to be true, but I have my doubts. He is sending me away to keep me safe because *he* will not be safe." She wanted to damn him for such a stupid decision, but he was not *here*.

He's shipping you off so he doesn't have to deal with your theatrics when you do not get what you want.

It was her father's voice, frustrated and dismissive. He'd sent her away.

"He's only trying to protect you," Nielson had said, patting her hand as she'd cried on the boat to the island.

But he hadn't been. He'd been protecting his own bruised heart. And it wasn't that he didn't love her, and it wasn't that Danil didn't love her, but they did not know how to let their walls down to *see* her.

And now Danil was sending her away. Without him. So *he* could handle everything, and *she* could go have her emotional outburst elsewhere.

No.

"We must put a stop to this, Peet. We must not let him sacrifice himself."

"B-but I don't think we should interfere," Peet said, trying to stand taller and puff out his chest. Poor boy trying to play at being a soldier. "He is *The Weapon*," Pete said, as if such a foolish nickname could make a man, flesh and blood, invincible.

"He is Danil Laurentius. He is a *man*, strong and good as that man may be." *Sending you off like a piece of sea glass.* She shoved that thought away for the time being. First, he had to survive, then she could be angry with him. "And from the sound of things, this King Aras is *not* good. If he was set to have Danil killed for failing to obtain me, how would he react if Danil tells him he has obtained me and then let me go? Not well, I would think. Turn the ship around and bring me to shore, Peet."

Peet's expression grew more and more unsure. "But... what can *you* do?"

Elsebet lifted her chin, fixed him with the harsh royal glare she had learned at her father's knee. "I am the Princess of Mathav. I will do what I must." *This* was her duty. And she would not let anyone take it from her.

Even Danil.

Danil was not nervous. He might not know what waited for him, but he knew that he was right. That Elsebet was safe.

These were the only two things that mattered. He felt that, all the way through the morning. Walking into the castle. Being asked to wait—naturally. Aras always liked to play his games.

Then, when he was summoned, it was not to Aras's office or parlor, but the grand hall. Where Aras's court was arranged like this was some grand event.

Or trial.

Danil walked slowly up the aisle, his gaze never wavering from his brother on the throne. Danil knew he still *looked* injured, and perhaps a few more days at sea would have returned more strength to him, but these thoughts were irrelevant.

He was here to set Elsebet free, and so she would be.

He had walked this road before, though always after a success that Aras had deemed not *quite* successful enough. Those times he had been filled with shame, the desire to do better for the man who had saved his life.

Danil felt no shame now. He felt like an entirely different person. And it was a strange feeling to walk the same path, face the same people, and see it from all new eyes, when he'd been certain, only a few weeks ago, that he was *The Weapon* and he would bring back his cargo.

But being shipwrecked, being taken in by Elsebet and her makeshift family, had changed everything he'd known. People were not cargo. They were not weapons.

And Aras was no family. He was no different than Danil's mother's husband. Out for himself. Out for power.

Meanwhile, somewhere on a strange little island, three people were no doubt worried sick about the woman they all loved. As they'd worry for a daughter, though she was a princess and they were her subjects.

Danil knew he did this for them, and the kindness they'd shown him, as much as he did this for Elsebet. Peet would not return her to them right now. It was too dangerous with Aras knowing where she was, and that small trio not strong enough to fight whomever Aras might send.

So Peet would take Elsebet to her father. Mathav might not have a strong army, but they would protect their princess.

And if he marries her off to some other king or prince in the meantime?

Danil could not concern himself with this. If she was alive, not married to his cruel brother, this was all that mattered. If he lived to tell the tale, he would stop whatever, save her in whatever way. If he did not, he had left Peet instructions.

"So. You have returned empty-handed."

Danil looked up at his brother, lounging in his throne, looking cold as ice, but Danil knew that was a lie.

He was enraged. "Where is my man?" Aras asked, his fingers dancing over the jewels in the scepter he held like some sort of dragon in love with his riches.

Maybe he was, and Danil was no prince, but he would save the Princess all the same.

"He will be returned to you," Danil replied, trying not to smile. Because he had dropped Riks off at Piyer, a small island used in the summer for swimming larks. In the winter, basically isolated and cold.

He would suffer for a few hours, and then Danil or Aras would send someone to fetch him. "When I see fit."

Aras eyed him, dark eyes that Danil had always seen as the same, but now they were cold. Detached. "You have gotten quite big for your britches, *brother*. A man who shipwrecks, nearly dies, and then returns without his cargo should not be quite so confident, I wouldn't think."

Yes, love will do that to you.

"Things have changed."

"I hope this is the head injury speaking." Aras glanced back at his court members, who laughed. On command.

So many things given to Aras on command. And how was Aras different from their father? Danil had always considered him good because, well, if the old king had survived, would Danil be alive? No.

But now he wondered. Was it simple enough to save someone, or did it require more to love? More, he thought. Much more. "How do you rule differently than your father, Aras?"

"I do not know what has come over you, *Weapon*, but this is not the topic at hand. Where is my princess, and how do you dare return to me without her?"

Danil moved up the stairs—where he was very much not allowed. He watched as Aras fidgeted in his chair, flicking a glance at the soldiers who lined the walls.

The soldiers did not meet Aras's furtive glances. They watched Danil. Because, as head of the King's Guard, Danil was in charge of them. Not the King.

An interesting realization. Reminding him of Peet's words. That his sailors and soldiers were loyal to *him*, because he'd brought them together. Made them a unit.

Something like a family.

Danil kept walking. Past the normal point where he would

stop and bow to his brother. Instead, he walked right up to the throne.

Aras's eyes widened. "Guards!"

But Danil held up a hand. A signal to *his* men, not to draw their weapons or move. But to stay put.

They stayed put.

"*I* am the head of the King's Guard, if you recall," Danil said, and this time he *did* smile. He was surprised, at first, to see the fear in the eyes of his brother and the court members, but in a strange way it all made sense.

They were weak. Ruling with manipulation and *weapons*, but not their own strength. Unless ordering people to the dungeons was power. When they did not have their weapons to do their bidding…they were just scared weaklings.

As a young man, Danil had thought commanding people was power. But now he knew. Power was in protecting those you loved. And those who had no power.

Aras had no love. And he had no true power.

"The Princess of Mathav is not yours to have, Aras. Now, you can accept this, or you can make it difficult. The choice is yours, but the result will not change."

Aras's eyes narrowed. He was clearly working on banking that fear, on figuring out a new tactic to put Danil under his thumb, but Danil would not go. He would not give in.

He was a changed man. And in that change, whatever power Aras had once held over him was gone. Splintered and lost, like his beloved ship.

"You think you have a say here, *Weapon*? You are mistaken. I will find her. Guards, arrest this man!" When no one made a move to do anything, Aras smashed his scepter against the ground. "*I* am your king."

There were some shared glances among the guards. Silent conversations among brothers not of blood but of missions. Of hard training. Of a common purpose. To serve and protect Gintaras.

Danil understood these men, had trained these men. They were conflicted because they had taken oaths. But those oaths had been to Gintaras.

Not a spoiled child of a king.

Danil turned his back on Aras—a great offense—and addressed the guards lined up, fidgeting, unsure what to do. "Men. Brothers. You have a choice here. You may in fact follow the King. If you think he is right. If you think Gintaras will succeed with his rule, I encourage you to protect him above all else. Arrest me, if you must."

"And if we don't?" Corbel, one of the veteran guards that Danil had always thought would be a good replacement for him should he ever perish in a mission, asked.

"Then you may follow me, my brothers."

"*I* am your brother."

Danil turned slowly to face Aras. "No. I thought you were, but you have only ever seen me as a tool. Your *weapon*. This is not a brotherhood, Aras."

"You have no choice! I am your king!" Aras stood, waving his scepter wildly at the guards. "If you do not arrest him, all of you will be in the dungeons!"

Danil felt foolish and a bit disgusted with himself for ever feeling swayed by this man. But that was what a crumb of light could do in years of darkness.

Elsebet, luckily, was no crumb. She was the entire sun, and she made him see this for what it really was.

Even Aras's court looked embarrassed.

"I resign as your weapon, Aras. I have no desire to be part of the King's Guard. I am leaving Gintaras." He looked at the guardsmen who lined the walls. "Whoever wishes to come with me may meet me in port by noon."

"I will have you killed!" Aras shouted.

Danil began walking away. He didn't even look at the man who'd claimed to be his brother but hadn't cared at all. "By whom and with what army, Aras?"

Danil left the castle and did not look back. He headed for the docks, where he had three more ships. He also had two ships in other ports, and he would need to collect those as well.

This was not over—Aras still had riches and allies. But without his guards it would take time to mass an offensive.

In the meantime, Elsebet would be safe with her father. And Danil... He was not worthy of any princess, but he could be her protector. Go to Mathav and dedicate his life to her. Ensure that she did not have to follow any of her father's proclamations.

Thanks to his siren, he was free, and he would spend the rest of his life ensuring that she was as well.

CHAPTER FOURTEEN

ELSEBET STOOD ON the deck of the ship, leaning against the railing, impatiently waiting for Peet to anchor the boat at the dock. It was a pretty morning in Gintaras, but her mood was black.

He's only trying to protect you.

How many times had she heard that in her life? And yes, she had been protected, but she had also never been seen in all that protecting. She had thought Danil was different.

He was not.

Once the boat was *finally* secure, Peet began to lower a ramp onto the dock. At a snail's pace. Elsebet waited, trying very hard not to tap her toe. She scowled at Peet, who was clearly taking his sweet time, as if that would change anything.

He'd brought her back to shore, hadn't he?

Once the ramp was firmly in place, she sailed past him and down it onto the dock. It was bustling with people and Elsebet did not know where she was going. This was not like the island or Mathav, where the castle was immediately visible from shore. How far would she need to go to reach it? How would she find it without help?

Oh, damn every man.

She turned back to Peet to ask him, but he was wringing his hands from the deck of the boat, looking out at the crowd. She heard something, a commotion of sorts, and turned toward it.

There he was. She was so angry at him and still her heart soared. Danil was unscathed. Whole and perfect. And she couldn't help but realize some of her anger had been in an attempt to blank away the fear that his brother would hurt him because of her.

But no. He was whole and here. She might have forgotten herself and run to him, but his expression was furious as he stormed toward them. "What the hell are you doing here?" he yelled.

But all that anger, the yelling, was directed at Peet up on the boat. As if she didn't even exist. And she was angry all over again.

She lifted her chin and tried to pin him with a hard gaze while he didn't even *look* at her. "I told Peet to turn around."

Danil turned angry eyes on her. "For what purpose? To throw yourself in the midst of danger?"

"You have. Why should I not?"

"Because I am a king's guard. Well versed in battle, pain and punishment. And you are a pampered princess who cannot follow simple instructions."

The words pierced deep, where she already felt soft and vulnerable. *Stay away, Elsebet, you are not wanted.*

"You have left me no instructions, Danil. You just *left.*" She would not let her eyes fill or her mouth waver at that, at the possibility that was what hurt most of all. Him sneaking away with no goodbye. Throwing her back to her father like she was an unwanted fish.

"We do not have time for this," he muttered, taking her by the arm and steering her back up the ramp onto the boat. "I have left my brother's employ. I have renounced my citizenship. Many of the King's guards are coming with me.

We will escort you back to Mathav. Any of my men who wish it may pledge allegiance to you or your father, helping Mathav's military weaknesses somewhat."

She pulled her arm out of his grasp at the top of the ramp. "Did it occur to you to ask what *I* wanted?"

He frowned down at her, clearly beyond confused. "I have taken care of everything. You will be protected and safe."

"Because I am incapable?"

"Elsebet."

"What if I wanted to go back to the island? What if I wanted to go away from *all* these places? Who are you to determine I am to be returned to my father?"

His eyebrows drew together, his mouth a firm, harsh line. "You are lucky it was I who kidnapped you. Not everyone would see the error of their ways. Not everyone would return you at all."

"Lucky?" She might have screamed it, that was how much of a slap it was. *Lucky.* As if any of this was *luck.*

"We will return to Mathav. I have taken care of Aras, but he may buy himself another army at some point. He will never forgive me for my betrayal, but worse, he will insist on breaking the toy he could not have. So, Elsebet, we will do as *I* say."

"Perhaps I can protect myself."

Danil laughed. *Laughed.* She curled her hands into fists. She did not use them on him, though it was *tempting.* Still, she whirled away from him. "Peet?"

"Yes, Miss Highness?"

"I would like you to take me back to my island. I will pay you handsomely. But Danil Laurentius is not allowed on this boat."

"But it's his boat, ma'am."

"I'll buy it."

Danil's voice was a growl. "No, you will not."

Elsebet shot him a hard look. "I'm not talking to you, Danil."

"You are talking about *my* boat, and Peet has no leave to sell it."

"Do you have a boat yourself, Peet? Or know someone who does?"

The poor man was the color of a tomato, fidgeting and uncomfortable as he looked from Danil to Elsebet. "Erm."

"Fine. You're of no use. I'll go find someone who *is* of use." She strode down the ramp toward the crowd, which was mostly paying them no attention except for a growing number of men with their uniforms and weapons, who must be soldiers. She didn't care. She would storm down the entire dock until she found someone who would sail her home. Not Mathav. *Home.*

And then, just as she had been back on a beach days ago, she was suddenly in Danil's arms. Bouncing against his shoulder as he carried her onto his boat. This time it wasn't shock that kept her from screaming or hitting him, it was the *crowd.* She could see *many* curious eyes on her now.

He shouted out orders to different soldiers. Some on this ship, some on that ship. All the while he carried her across the deck of the ship, directing Peet to cast out to sea once more.

When he finally set her on her feet, she was seething with rage. But instead of like the *last* time he'd manhandled her onto the boat, there was no stoic response. No guilt. There was only her own anger turned back at her.

"This was wrong of you, Elsebet. Did I not make it clear how dangerous my brother is?"

"And yet here you are unscathed, while I was meant to be shipped off. To what? Never see you again?"

Some shock worked through that fury on his face, but not enough. "I was going to follow you to Mathav, Elsebet. Once I knew my brother could not be a threat."

"And I was supposed to know this how?"

"Trust?"

"Trust? You are a kidnapper!"

Everything in his expression cooled. From heat to ice. And she shivered, her heart a painful ache in her chest.

"Perhaps by the time we arrive in Mathav, you will have calmed yourself and understand that I will always protect you, no matter how little you like it."

Calmed yourself. Because this was always it, was it not? She could not hold in all those swirling emotions and she had to be sent away. Until she was calm. Until she could be *used*.

Never was she meant to just be a *part* of someone's life. "Protect me?" she said, trying to be that *calm* everyone so desperately wanted. "By carrying me onto ships and taking me places against my will?"

"If your will is flawed."

All attempt at calm evaporated. She narrowed her eyes at him, moved forward with her finger pointed. She jabbed it into his chest but was met with only the hard wall of him. "When we arrive in Mathav, I will have you…" Her anger wilted. She had been about to say thrown in jail. But that was what his brother had done to him, and even in her anger she could not say it.

But she could see in his expression that he knew exactly what she'd meant to say, and it made her feel worse than she already did.

"You have wronged me. Twice," she said, willing the crack out of her voice.

"Yes, you punished me so the first time by inviting me into your bed."

It burned because it was true. She'd been mad at him for all of five minutes before he'd twisted her heart into knots.

Well, not this time. This time she was determined.

Except the whole part where she was desperately, irrevocably in love with him. With his honor.

He did not see her, did not value...who she was. This should make all that love evaporate.

But it didn't.

"You should have asked," she said, and she was calm, though tears leaked through. She would not sob, she would not create a dramatic scene again so he'd have even stronger reason to send her away.

But she couldn't help the crying part as she said the rest, holding his gaze. "You, of all people, should have treated me as a person instead of cargo. You have heard me speak of feeling as though I am nothing but a pawn, and yet you have chosen to make me one. Again and again."

He looked stricken, and that made her hurt. When she *wanted* him to be stricken. She wanted him to understand. And yet...she couldn't watch. It made her want to reach out and soothe.

So she turned away from him and went into the room. Her prison. She shut the door quietly behind her. Right in his face.

Danil brooded. The stars shone above, making his mood all the more foul. Because Elsebet was in her room. Refusing to speak with him.

He *should* take her to Mathav. It was foolish to give in to her wants. He needed to protect her.

Perhaps I can protect myself.

He hadn't ordered Peet to change course yet. They were still on course to make it to Mathav the next day.

But the island weighed on his mind. Elsebet's words weighed on his mind. The hurt look in her eyes. Those words, in an echo of surround sound.

You, of all people, should have treated me as a person instead of cargo. You have heard me speak of feeling as though I am nothing but a pawn, and yet you have chosen to make me one. Again and again.

A pawn. He of course did not see her as one, but he could not make an argument for his behavior. He had kidnapped her twice. And right now, if he didn't tell Peet to change course before midnight, he would take her where she did not wish to go.

You should have asked.

Danil sighed. He could not risk the sail into the cove. Not with her on the boat. Not with what had happened last time. But Peet could drop them off at the edge of the island again. That *would* be safer.

Giving her what she wanted was not smart, though. Her little staff could hardly protect her if—no, *when*—Aras found someone brave enough to sail there.

He was only trying to *save* her.

You should have asked.

Frustrated by these rotating thoughts, Danil forced himself into the captain's room, where Peet watched the instruments that led them toward Mathav.

Peet looked up. Surveyed him. "Change of plans?"

Hell. "Not just yet, but be ready. I…" He had always been honest with his staff, his soldiers. Straight with them, because that was how loyalty was built. But he didn't often let his *emotions* get in the way of that. It had always felt like a weakness. His men looked up to him to be *The Weapon*.

But he had hardly been that on this return voyage, and still here Peet was. With no promise of payment or return to his home. As though loyalty mattered more than what he'd made himself into.

And Elsebet made it seem like feelings, emotions, honesty and vulnerability...these things had power. "I should ask her what she wishes."

Peet took in this information, nodding thoughtfully. "She's a bit scary when she's in a lather."

Danil chuckled. Not the word he'd use, but he understood. She was beautiful when angry. Such a force. But she didn't wield it all the time. She used her smile. Her kindness. The way she saw people.

She had anger and fury in her, but she did not use it as a weapon unless pushed to the brink. As he'd done to her.

He should take her to her father and wash his hands of this failed experiment.

"She feels I have behaved wrongly. Going to speak to my brother, returning her to her father, without asking what she wanted." Danil still wasn't *fully* convinced, because of course he knew the right course of action.

But maybe what would make her happy wasn't so much his *doing* the thing she wanted as caring enough to ask? Having a discussion?

He thought of that evening at her kitchen table on the island. When they'd spoken of the cracked window high above, and Nielson's fear of heights. How Elsebet had said she would handle it. Because she *knew*.

And so Danil also *knew*. What he should do. How to protect her.

You should have asked.

He heaved out another sigh.

"It seems she's probably right," Peet offered. "The way my mother tells it, women usually are."

But she was *wrong*. To land on Gintaras. To want to go

back to her island unprotected. "How can she expect to protect herself when she has never once had to? Answer me that."

Peet took some time to consider this, staring thoughtfully out the darkened window. "Maybe you should teach her. Before they married, my sister taught her husband how to dance for some event he had, and he fell head over heels. Now she's about to have my *third* niece." Peet shook his head with some disapproval.

"It is not so simple with a princess and a bastard, Peet."

"You *are* a king's son. Even if not a queen's." Peet shrugged, as if the bastard part held no weight. "You have been the head of the King's Guard for quite some years and inspired such confidence and loyalty that they follow you. Away from their king and country, because they know. You are the noble one."

Danil was surprised at Peet's simple response. As if it was obvious to anyone with eyes that Danil was worthy. When…surely no one else would think that. Not the King of Mathav when it came to his daughter.

"It doesn't hurt to ask for permission," Peet continued. "I rather think you're a charming couple."

Again Danil wanted to laugh, but the sound caught in his throat. He could admit to himself, in the privacy of his own mind, that he loved Elsebet. Everything she was. And he knew he was strong, an impeccable soldier. He had much to offer many.

But not a *princess*. Any request to her father would no doubt end with refusal. "He will say no."

"You've fought your own brother for her. I do not know why you wouldn't fight her father too."

Danil looked at the man who had been with him on many a mission. Who was not a leader, but a good man. Always willing to do his *duty*. And in this moment, not afraid of the truth as he saw it.

"You are very wise, Peet."

Peet chuckled. "Name your firstborn after me as tribute, sir."

Firstborn. What a strange thought. Curling around him like dread...but not that, because it was lighter.

Hope, he realized. A feeling that seemed foreign now, but he had felt it once. It had died when his mother had married, when his childhood had changed, when he'd become a tool. And then *The Weapon*.

And now there was Elsebet, who had warmed him from the inside out. Melting those old protections until he felt as unsure as a boy. As unprotected as any newborn.

"I will keep course to Mathav for the time being, sir, but we can always change course. Whenever you're ready."

Danil nodded. "You are a good man, Peet."

Peet offered a little salute and Danil turned. Elsebet was not *right* about what she wanted to do, but she was not *wrong* about how he had handled it poorly.

And yet what future was there for them? A princess and a warrior? He could hardly promise one or ask for one. She cared too much for her father, her kingdom.

And he cared too much for her.

Perhaps the lesson was simple enough. Instead of just deciding...he needed to ask. Which went against *everything* he'd turned himself into as *The Weapon*. Do not ask. Do not worry. Act, do. Accomplish.

But he was no longer *The Weapon*.

CHAPTER FIFTEEN

ELSEBET LIKED TO think she'd calmed down. Found a rational, reasonable center. She had made an error. Thinking Danil, or *any* man, could see beyond their own noses—or other appendages—to see women as anything other than property to be hefted about.

That was fine. She would dedicate her life to a convent, perhaps. Learn how to pray away her feelings.

She sat on the bed, cross-legged, chin in her hands, and cursed herself for a fool.

Men or convent, neither choice really gave her comfort. Or solved what ached and swirled within her, an annoying, heavy conflict.

When a knock sounded on her door, her heart soared, even as that heavy conflict grew barbs and settled on her heart. Impossible situations with impossible answers.

Danil did not slip inside the room as he had these nights past. No. He waited. Because he hadn't locked her in this time. She had locked *herself* in. She scowled and got off the bed, opening the door.

He stood there, looking stiff and stoic, hands linked behind his back like some sort of soldier. And he was a soldier, there was no doubt about that.

"I would like to have a discussion," he said, and before

she could tell him he could stuff his wants, he gave a little bow. "What would you like?"

Oh, damn him for trying. It should make her happy, but it only made her mad. She whirled away from him. Because she didn't *know* what she wanted beyond *him*, and the past few days had made it painfully clear that there was no simple way to be together. Between his brother, her father, and royal kingdoms, things were complicated.

Add a few kidnappings into the mix and it went *beyond* complicated.

But before she could think of what to say, how to put it into words, Danil moved into the room, closing the door behind him, and continued on.

"I realize why you might want to return to the island, but it simply isn't safe. And in this case, safety must come before wants. *Both* of our wants."

He was not wrong. Now that she'd cooled off some, she understood that. He'd mismanaged dealing with her, but he was not acting *wrongly*. Just treating her as though she didn't matter.

So it wasn't the course of action she was angry with, it was the way he was dealing with it. And how this was the story of her life. Not *disagreeing* with everyone she loved. Simply wanting to be part of the decision-making of her own life.

She had thought he understood, but he didn't. She tried to find the words to explain that to him, but she didn't have them without coming apart at the seams. And wasn't that always the problem? When faced with a difficult feeling, a difficult situation…she hid. Closed herself away in a room or a cluster of rocks and yelled her frustrations to the ether.

She had learned long ago not to voice them to anyone, for they never mattered. A shout, a sob, any of those negative emotions had always gotten her sent away from her father.

"So you will take me to Mathav," she said, working very hard not to sound bitter. She was an adult. She was a *princess*. She should be able to handle all of this herself. She would *not* let him see everything that swirled inside of her. "And what happens then?" she said, coolly. Or tried to be cool anyway. "You return me to my father, and then what?"

His eyebrows were drawn together, his mouth a grim line. "I am asking what you want, not telling you what I will do."

What she *wanted* she could not have. That was always the story. Tears stung her eyes and she did not want to cry. Did not want to fall apart in front of him. Anyone. "I am trying to be reasonable and understand your plan. We go to Mathav. I am returned. Some of your soldiers join my father's army. Then what will you do?"

"What is it you want me to say, Elsebet? I am asking what you want and now you won't tell me?"

She stood there, silent and frustrated, because she wanted him to say he'd fight for *her*. Pledge himself to *her*. Be *hers*. Like he'd said the other night. But if she told him...

Father, I do not wish to be sent away. I want to be with you. To help you with the Kingdom.

No. She would not be pushed back there. She would not cry and feel like that little girl again. She'd cried then and what had it gotten her? Being sent off to the island to be alone. It had turned out better than being locked away in the castle, really, but it didn't make it any less lonely.

It didn't make her feel any less abandoned. "You only care for what *you* want," she shot at him instead.

He took her by the shoulders, all fierce, avenging soldier. But there was something else in his eyes. Something that tried to pierce the guard she was attempting to have over all the hard feelings in her heart.

"I am trying to *save* you," he growled. "Why can you not see this?"

Save you. Protect you.

Never was it *love you*.

"You want me to ask you what you want. You want me to come to you and *ask*, but you do not want a discussion. *You* do not want to ask *me*. You want to hide away in your rocks and have everyone else think that you are fine and well and above it all."

The lump in her throat kept growing.

"What is it you want if you do not want me to save you from those who would harm you?" Danil demanded.

"It will harm me to return to Mathav and not have *you*." She knew she should not have said this, and still, against all better knowing, she hoped. Hoped he would understand. Hoped he would say the words.

Instead, his face went blank. And cold. He dropped her shoulders and stepped back.

"I have already been one man's toy. I will not now be yours."

Those words were like a slap against the strange panic rising within her. A *toy*? "What does that mean?"

"Just because you are a *princess*, Elsebet, does not mean you can *have* me."

She found herself speechless. And hurt. Why did he think that? How had this turned out to be just what she wanted, and twisted wrong in so many ways?

He looked at her coolly now. Like a man uninterested. "Tell me plain. What is it you want, Elsebet?"

You. You. You. "I want to go home," she managed, her throat too tight. A desperate handle on the tears threatening.

He nodded sharply. "Then I will take you home."

* * *

Danil jerked the door open, a kind of painful hurt and anger twisting inside of him, but he could not force himself to walk out. Because something was not right. Something didn't add up. Like a mission missing a piece, or an army not properly motivated. The sense that he was *missing* something.

He looked back, expecting to see her icy or angry, standing there like a princess who was sending the commoner away.

Instead, her chin was at her chest, and one tear tracked down her cheek. His heart ached. He could not leave her. Even if he did not understand what this was, he could not walk away.

So he retraced his steps, took her face in his hands and tilted it up to face him. Her eyes stubbornly refused to meet his.

"Please go," she rasped. Like she was the one with trauma to her vocal cords.

He remembered, in clear detail, that night on the beach. Where she'd yelled and cried and kicked rocks. Thinking she was alone. Isolated. Not wanting anyone to see what she truly felt. And he thought he understood now, what all this was about.

She was afraid. That he did not feel the same? That her hard feelings would send him away? He was not certain of *what* caused her fear, but he knew it was there. Was sure of it.

He used his thumb to brush away the tear on her cheek. "Why do you hate for anyone to see you hurt?"

She kept her eyes resolutely downcast though he had tilted her chin up in his hands. "It is no one's fault if I hurt."

But he had hurt her. He might not understand it, but in

trying to save her, he had hurt her feelings. "Is it not? You treat me as if I have wronged you, but I do not understand how. You will have to tell me, Elsebet. I am in the dark."

She swallowed, but resolutely did not speak. The tears kept falling though, and he wiped each one away, his heart feeling bruised that she would have such anguish inside of her and be so unable to explain it.

"What are you so afraid of?" he asked, trying to work through things from her perspective. "That I would send you away?"

Her chin came up, and though the tears were there, that fierceness was in her as well. "You did! You are! You sent me away from Gintaras while you stayed behind. You are taking me back to my father." She pushed him away and he let her. "What was I meant to think?" she demanded, turning her back on him. "I know my emotions are too much. I know that I should not cry or yell. I know that begging never works."

He watched the stiff line of her back. "When I found you crying on the beach screaming and going on, what did I do?"

Her eyebrows drew together, as though she did not understand the question. But she answered it. "You kidnapped me for your brother."

It wasn't funny, but he found the odd urge to laugh. "No, I watched. I rather enjoyed the impressive show. And then I tried to convince you to come with me. When Peet made the signal, I remembered myself. My duty. But in the moment, nothing about your outburst changed what I wanted, how I felt."

She chewed on her bottom lip, clearly confused by this. "Is this about when your father sent you to the island?"

She looked away, but she answered him. Quietly. An attempt at stoicism that turned into more tears. "I only wanted to stay. I only wanted for him to let me help. I did not want to be sent away. Why must everyone always send me away?"

He could not hold himself apart, though maybe that would have been better. But he needed to touch her, hold her, press his words into her so she believed them. "I do not *wish* to send you away, Elsebet. I have changed the entire course of my life for having met you. For loving you. Nothing else but this giant force would have changed what I had been conditioned to believe."

She blinked once, her siren eyes wide and surprised. "You...love me?"

"I have loved very little in this life, but that small taste... It gives me no doubts now. I love you, Elsebet. I would do anything for you. Except allow you to be harmed by anyone. That is the only reason I sent you away. I needed to know my brother could not touch you. And perhaps..." He sighed. "Elsebet, you are a princess, and I am but a soldier. I may have some money, and a fleet of ships, an army at my disposal, but this does not make me royal. It does not give me what your father might want for his princess. It isn't *befitting* a princess."

She fully turned to face him now. Eyes bright, full of emotion. No, not just any emotion. *Love*. Because she was good at this. If it was a positive feeling, she showed it with no concern or attempt to hide. She could be the kindest, the sweetest, the most loving.

It was all those darker emotions that seemed to be a struggle. And as he had dealt with his stepfather's reaction to anger, he understood. The man had turned him into a tool. Had used his love for his mother against him. *Don't you want your mother to have a better life?*

So he'd gone along. Faced the King. Almost died. And learned that loving someone was a weapon. Being a tool was all that mattered.

Elsebet had begged her father to stay, to have what she wanted, and been sent away. She had learned that being upset got you punished, having wants were off-putting.

Once again, on the inside, they were the same. But they were quite different on the outside.

"Danil, I do not care who you have been. I do not care what my father wants for Mathav. I care that our love is big, important."

"*Our* love?" he asked, those last vestiges of an old ice around his heart fully melting.

Her mouth curved and she took his hands in her small ones. "I love you. Even if you did try to kidnap me. Twice."

"I did not *try*. I succeeded."

This made her laugh, which he knew was a little dark, but they were here and she… She loved him, the bastard son of a king who should have been killed.

"I am an unwanted bastard with blood on his hands." He held them up, as though she could see the blood there.

But she shook her head, pressed a kiss to each palm. "You are wanted here. You helped Win in the kitchen when you were injured. You looked at my art as though it mattered. And though you kidnapped me, though you served your brother, when faced with the right choices, you made them. You let yourself love." Her eyes tracked over his face, then she smiled that siren smile, full of secrets and power. "My father will understand. If he doesn't, we will fight until he does."

"I will fight for you, my love. If that is what you want. But you must not be afraid. To hurt in front of me. To trust me with all that you are. I want your tears and your anger and your hurt as much as your love and joy and kindness. I want all of you. Always."

Her eyes studied him, big and dark blue. Siren that she was, but his. He could see it in her eyes. They had given each other something they had been missing. Opened up new sides of each other.

She had brought him back to life, and now he was strong enough to be everything she needed.

"I love you, Danil. No matter what. I am yours and you are mine. This will be what we fight for."

"Forever, my siren."

EPILOGUE

AND IT WAS FOREVER. King Alfred of Mathav was skeptical, of course, but he had never seen his daughter quite so determined or sure as she was when they arrived on Mathav the next day.

They had been met by a hostile force that was both smaller and weaker than Danil's own. When they landed ashore, Elsebet demanded her father be summoned at once. Then she marched along, pulling Danil with her, up to the castle gates.

There were many people trailing them, asking pleading questions of Elsebet, demanding to know who Danil was.

Neither of them spoke or answered anything. They simply marched on until Elsebet burst into her father's office. He was already on his feet, angrily speaking to someone, until Elsebet entered.

His entire face changed. From a dark, ferocious anger to utter shock. Then he moved forward and pulled Elsebet into his arms. "My sweet. You're here. You're whole." He pulled her back, studied her face. "Are you unharmed?"

"Yes, Father. Thanks to Danil." She looked back at him.

But the King's expression hardened once more. "This is the man who kidnapped you." King Alfred tried to maneuver Elsebet behind him, as if he could form some kind of wall of protection. But Princess Elsebet Thore would not be maneuvered.

Ever again.

"This is the man who saved me, Father. And I wish to marry him. Soon."

King Alfred's mouth swung open in shock, and stayed there, as Elsebet relayed the events of the past few days.

Leaving out certain...parts.

Before she finished, King Alfred had needed to take a seat. Now he sat, looking up at his daughter, and the man who'd kidnapped her. And set her free.

He sighed heavily as Elsebet concluded her story with the same sentence. "I wish to marry him. Soon."

There was only a drawn-out silence for long minutes. But Elsebet did not move. Did not endeavor to beg her father or anything else. She stood, chin high, hand in Danil's. And waited.

"I have tried for the past year to find you a husband. One who could be an ally to Mathav. An asset. But also one who would treat you with fairness and kindness. And the very few times I began to consider someone, I could only think of your mother." King Alfred looked down at his hands, where he still wore his wedding ring. All these years later.

"I wanted to save you from the pain of loss." He looked up at Elsebet, and the pain of that loss was there on his face. "But it sounds as if I've caused you a different pain along the way, and for that I am sorry."

He got to his feet once more, crossed to Elsebet and cupped her face in his hands. "She would not have wanted a political marriage for you. And I do not wish to fail you any further." His gaze slid to Danil, cool and assessing. "I cannot immediately approve such a match, but we will discuss it."

"You will approve, Father." Elsebet smiled at him, then at Danil. "I'm sure of it."

And a few weeks later, King Alfred did, just as his daughter had predicted.

"Why did you ever make such an arrangement with my brother?" Danil asked him once, after King Alfred had given his permission, but before he and Elsebet married.

The King shook his head. "I never made such a deal. I listened to his proposal, but I refused. I knew he would never be kind enough to my jewel. All I wanted for her was a life without pain and loss. A safe life."

"Life is not safe."

"No. Even locked away on a tiny island that is supposedly incapable of being breached, you might find your daughter kidnapped." The King gave him a hard look, but Danil had come to know the King.

He had built walls to hide the hurt at losing his wife, and now that Danil loved, he understood. And so had Elsebet come to understand. The ways they had hurt each other had come from love and fear.

But when you learned to accept fear and love, you no longer needed to hide.

So Danil and Elsebet were married on the island of Mathav in the great castle of Elsebet's family, with all the royal fanfare of her station. They lived many of their days on a tiny nameless island, bringing four children into the world to be taken care of by Nielson, Win and Inga, and doted on by their grandfather when they visited Mathav for holidays or political meetings.

The oldest, a girl, they named Peeta, after Danil's best friend and strongest sailor, who soon worked his way up to be the King's personal sailor. While those soldiers loyal to

Danil built a strong army that protected Mathav from Aras's sad and disorganized attempts at revenge.

As years passed, laws were changed. And many years later, when Alfred passed away peacefully in his sleep as an old and beloved king, Elsebet was crowned Queen of Mathav, rather than attempt to find a royal man for her daughter to marry.

Mathav's army and her allies had grown thanks to Elsebet and Danil's efforts, and then their children's diplomatic initiatives. They were safe and whole and their family had become a dynasty. Not of riches, or armies, or lands. But of love. The kind that was not afraid of tears or fights or loss, but instead felt them all, along with hugs and joy and love.

When their eldest daughter insisted on marrying the son of a farmer, they gave their blessing, remembering that day many years ago now when King Alfred had given them his blessing.

Because of love.

Love, after all, was the only duty worth committing oneself to.

* * * * *

COMING SOON!

We really hope you enjoyed reading this book. If you're looking for more romance be sure to head to the shops when new books are available on

Thursday 23rd November

To see which titles are coming soon, please visit

millsandboon.co.uk/nextmonth

MILLS & BOON ®

Coming next month

A BILLION-DOLLAR HEIR FOR CHRISTMAS
Caitlin Crews

'What exactly are you trying to say to me?'

Tiago sighed, as if Lillie was being dense. And he hated himself for that, too, when she stiffened. 'This cannot be an affair, Lillie. No matter what happened between us in Spain. Do you not understand? I will have to marry you.'

Her eyes went wide. Her face paled, and not, his ego could not help but note, in the transformative joy a man in his position might have expected to see after a proposal. 'Marry me? Marry *you?* Are you mad? On the strength of one night?'

'On the strength of your pregnancy. Because the Villela heir must be legitimate.' He looked at her as if he had never seen her before and would never see her again, or maybe it was simply that he did not wish to say the thing he knew he must. But that was life, was it not? Forever forcing himself to do what was necessary, what was right. Never what he wanted. So he took a deep breath. 'We will marry. Quickly. And once that happens, I will never touch you again.'

Continue reading
A BILLION-DOLLAR HEIR FOR CHRISTMAS
Caitlin Crews

Available next month
www.millsandboon.co.uk

OUT NOW!

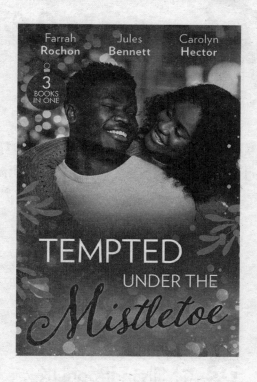

Farrah
Rochon

Jules
Bennett

Carolyn
Hector

3
BOOKS
IN ONE

TEMPTED
UNDER THE
Mistletoe

Available at
millsandboon.co.uk

MILLS & BOON

LET'S TALK

Romance

For exclusive extracts, competitions and special offers, find us online:

- **f** MillsandBoon
- **𝕏** @MillsandBoon
- **◎** @MillsandBoonUK
- **♪** @MillsandBoonUK

Get in touch on 01413 063 232